Paul fit the dis[...] stud. On the scr[...] still pictures of early manned space launches, then vast crowds of demonstrators.

"The space shuttle," said a recorded voice, "the last of the great bursts into space, was sold to private industry, and the bulk of that private industry was overseas. Whatever could be done to aid the American economy came too little and too late.

"Israel continued, out of necessity, to refine her technology. By the time of her final war, Israel had spread a broad political and economic base over the rest of the world." Impressive shots were shown of the early Israeli colonists boarding primitive shuttles, settling on the moon, and building the mass driver. Finally, the space city Hazera flashed on.

"It is with the Israelis that the UN places its final hope, within the 21st century, of successfully launching an interstellar probe. After two failures, the UN's space program has become a prime target for those expressing dissatisfaction with the UN's workings. The survival of the UN as a republic may well depend on *Svenglid*'s reaching her target star. We of the UN would like to thank Hazera for bringing together a starship of unbelievable design."

DIASPORAH

W. R. YATES

BAEN
science fiction
BOOKS

DIASPORAH

This is a work of fiction. All the characters and events portrayed in this book are fictional, and any resemblance to real people or incidents is purely coincidental.

A Baen Book

Baen Enterprises
8-10 W. 36th Street
New York, N.Y. 10018

First printing, August 1985

ISBN: 0-671-55974-5

Cover art by Alan Gutierrez

Printed in the United States of America

Distributed by
SIMON & SCHUSTER
MASS MERCHANDISE SALES COMPANY
1230 Avenue of the Americas
New York, N.Y. 10020

August 12, 1997   Somewhere in the Negev
Av 9, 5757   Tuesday
6:17 a.m., Jerusalem Time

The sign is in a gatepost of blue Elat tile. The road on which it stands branches off from one of the main highways which lead from Beer Sheba to Elat. It is narrow, but paved with gray asphalt. The sign reads:

המרכז החקלאי למחקר

הכניסה אסורה

Agricultural Research Center

Keep Out

المركز الزراعي للأبحاث

الدخول ممنوع

ממשלת ישראל

Government of Israel   حكومة اسرائيل

Zvi pulled up to the gate and rummaged for his wallet as the guard leaned out of the booth. Zvi handed him the card and pressed his hand against a plate of glass. The card and handprint both verified that he was, indeed, Zvi Sivan. The formalities over, Zvi pointed to the sign. "When are we going to take that thing down?" he asked. "I think that the only people who believe it anymore are the Israelis!"

"Be fair," laughed the guard. "There really is a research station here."

Zvi shrugged. The electronic gate began to swing open. *"Ad mahar,"* he called to the guard, driving through.

Zvi's comment was probably right. The inhabitants of New Persia had possessed spy satellites for nearly six years. Reports from the Mossaad, the Israeli intelligence service, had shown that they knew where the major Israeli missile bases were located.

Zvi parked the white '87 Mercedes in a space by the administration building. Opening the trunk, he pulled out a fitted tarpaulin and began stretching it over the vehicle. "How can white fade?" someone had once jokingly asked him. But it protected the finish against the sun. The heavily waxed surface was still as bright and shiny as it had been on the day he bought it.

With his hands on his hips, he surveyed the rows of maturing orange trees. It was somewhat odd to see so much green here. The shifting sand of the Negev still dusted the horizon with a reddish haze. If the experiments worked out right, the whole desert would bloom with purified water from the Mediterranean. Then the dust would cease to attack the eyes and block the nostrils.

But more Israeli *dinarim* had been spent on what lay below the ground than above. The blue of the irrigation canals and the green of the shrubbery concealed Israel's deadliest and most secret of weapons. Twenty feet beneath the canals, safe within their cradles, nestled *Yoshua*, surface-to-surface cruise missiles.

Nobody questioned the military look of things. The guard towers, the barbed wire, the electrified fencing had surrounded every major Israeli installation for nearly fifty years.

The high whine of a jeep engine made Zvi turn back toward the parking lot. He grinned. It was his new driver. The dark-skinned figure braked to a halt and Zvi got in next to him.

"Where to, *Adonai*?" the man asked.

"Installation *Yoshua*," answered Zvi. "You can drop that *'adonai'* business. We're very informal around here. I am Captain Zvi Sivan. You can just call me Zvi. And you?"

"Sergeant Major Ibrahim . . ." The other grinned. "Name's too long to say in one breath. As long as we're so informal here, just call me 'Ib'."

Zvi felt his flesh tingle. He looked again at the other's dark hair, skin, and eyes. "You're *Sephardic*?" he asked.

Ib's mouth twisted as though he were enjoying a private joke. "Arab," he answered. "And a Muslim. Don't worry, *haver shelli*. I'd be damned well checked out before I'd be here."

"I wasn't aware that Arabs worked at the *Yoshua* installation," said Zvi.

"My parents may have been Palestinians, but I am Israeli," answered the other. "My grandfather told me that my people used to die by the thousands from hunger, thirst, disease, and exposure. But that was before the Jews came. My parents considered him a traitor. They and the rest of my people cannot accept your strange ways. You are too alien to them and they don't wish to learn. The fact that my people no longer die is what made me go to the university. My father disowned me."

"I'm sorry," answered Zvi.

The other grimaced. "It is no matter," he answered. "My father would have me herding goats."

Zvi laughed and remembered his own father's failure to understand. "We are doubly friends," answered Zvi. "I, too, saw the world as it is. My family has been in this country since the time of the Spanish Inquisition. I am Sephardic and learned to adapt. Nothing is given to us, my friend. Whether it is a nation or a fine home, you must fight to gain it. And you must take care of it."

"I agree with your point, if not your metaphor," answered Ib.

"Then you are not Israeli," answered Zvi. His eyes twinkled at the other.

"I didn't say that I agreed with Israel's manner of coming into existence. Merely that I agreed with its existence."

"You are an intelligent man, Ib. How is it that you are only a sergeant major?"

"I was once with the Mossaad," said Ib quietly.

"I don't know what their pay scale is, but it is certainly higher than the air force. Why did you quit?"

"It was I who discovered how the Arabs and the Persians perfected the bomb," was the answer. "It is a painful thing."

"I'm sorry," Zvi answered.

How long it had remained an international secret, Zvi himself did not know. But once released it had made headlines around the world. By using political prisoners—Kurds and Sunni who refused to acknowledge his power—the successor of the Great Mamoud, the Imam of the Time's Caliph, The Twelfth Imam's Caliph had dispensed with the need for expensive shielding. Those who worked with the deadly radioactive materials lived only three weeks.

The memory made Zvi's blood run cold. He quickly changed the subject. "Did anything happen in the night?"

"One of the missiles, *Yoshua Heth*, is out of order.

Decay in the grain of one of the boosters. One of the *Kaleb* spy satellites was blinded by a laser."

"That happens all the time," put in Zvi. "They're probably trying to sneak somebody across the border. I always dislike the blind spot that leaves. At any rate, *Sharm el Sheik*'s already got another on the pad. It'll be in orbit before this shift is out. I wish we didn't have to clear it with Cairo. Things would go a lot faster."

"Here we are." Ib braked the jeep to a halt.

"Thanks," said Zvi. "I owe you a glass of tea sometime."

Ib grinned. "I think I would like that. See you later!"

"Salaam," responded Zvi in Arabic.

As the jeep whirred away, Zvi turned toward the small pump shed, brought a key out of his pocket, and inserted it into the lock on the door. There was nothing to show that the interior was any more than it was supposed to be. There was the whine of an electric pump in one corner, the drip of water on prestressed concrete and light tile, a nest of hoes, rakes, shovels leaning against one of the walls in the corner. Near the door, as though something were intended to hang there, was a nail. Turning back to the door, and being careful to stand on a tile of a slightly different color than the rest, Zvi gave the nail a twist. Almost immediately, the tile began to sink into the floor, and Zvi with it. Above Zvi's head, another tile closed. In the darkness, the concrete of the shaft whispered past. Finally, the ring of a chime announced his arrival. A double door slid open and Zvi found himself facing a small room. Next to the elevator, three men sat hunched over a backgammon board. A man behind a desk stood up. "You are late for the first time in three years, *Seren* Sivan. Shmuel will be angry."

"Trouble with the car," explained Zvi. "Tell Shmuel not to be too put out."

The man grinned. "There's a rumor going around that they're going to cut the shifts to an hour each. Knesset seems to think that we aren't keeping on our toes."

"It would cut the strain. But I think we can handle what we've got. If you will excuse me . . ."

Zvi inserted a card into a slot and again pressed his hand against the glass pane of a box before the door. He waved a greeting to the other men as the door slid open.

The door slid shut. The bickering of the men in the outer office was lost in silence. Compared even to the sunlight of early morning, the room was cool and dark.

Directly ahead of him was a map, a gigantic computer display. Flanking it were three television screens. One was adjusted to the ultra-violet radiation that was absorbed in the Earth's upper atmosphere—pictures from the orbiting *Kaleb* satellites. Theoretically, the UV image would show the radiation released by the explosion of an atomic bomb on the Earth's surface. In front of each division of three television screens sat two figures, each at a console.

One of the figures turned, her blonde hair glowing eerily in the green light. "Shalom, *putz*! You're late! We thought you'd gone to synagogue!"

"There's nothing about today in *The Commandments*," Zvi replied curtly.

P'nina smiled, and Shmuel threw back his head in laughter. If Zvi reddened, it was with embarrassment. Rage wasn't permitted in the *Slikkim*.

Shmuel rose from his chair. "Serves you right for being late, Zvi. I'll see you tomorrow. Shalom."

"Do you always have to give me a hard time?" he asked P'nina as the door slid closed behind Shmuel.

P'nina's name was Hebrew for pearl, and the whiteness of her teeth reflected it as she gave him another of her wicked smiles. "Couldn't resist," she answered. She reached into her purse, extracting a pomegran-

ate, two figs, and a banana. These she placed on the
table that formed a part of her console—then opened
a book as Zvi turned attentively to the screens. He
thought of reporting her, but was stopped by her
remark, "If anything happens, *putz* ... you're nervous enough to let me know about it."

He remembered the long-ago day of their first surprise inspection. Then, too, P'nina had been reading—
against regulations. But a thoughtful workman had
placed a chime, both in the outer office and in the
Slik itself. The arrival of the elevator was signaled in
both rooms. With a single movement, she whisked
the fruit into the drawer; the book followed. By the
time the inspecting general entered, the drawer was
closed and both of P'nina's feet were on the floor.

Zvi found her both amusing and repulsive. Time
after time he'd thought of reporting her for an acid
word that she had given him. These, and her nickname for him—a Yiddish obscenity—had really bothered him at first.

It had been two years before, at a Synagogue picnic on the beach at Caesarea. After the food had been
eaten, he and a group of Shul members had decided
to engage in a game of soccer. He kicked at the ball
with his bare feet and it glanced off to the side.
Spitting into the sand, he chased it beneath the arches
of the old Roman aqueduct. His eyes hadn't adjusted
to the shade within the mouldering arches and he
knocked a diminutive figure to the ground.

"Oh! Sorry!" he apologized as he took a slender
wrist into his hand. Pulling her to her feet, his eyes
swept over a blindingly beautiful figure in a two-piece
bathing suit. They came to rest in a pair of familiar
blue eyes.

"P'nina!" he exclaimed. "Shalom! Come over and
meet the group! There is plenty of tea and beer!
Drink with us! Some chicken may be left ..."

"Zvi, no! Please! I parked my car down near the
old fortress. I've been walking here ... swimming

and thinking. I saw you playing and stopped to watch. I *can't* spend any time with you out of the *Slik*. I'd love to come and play with you and your friends but someday, if anything goes wrong in the *Slik* ... I might have to kill you. I'm very fond of you, Zvi. More fond than I should be. For my sake—for the sake of our country—don't make your death under those circumstances impossible!"

Without warning, the slender arms went around his neck. The rapid kiss that she gave him was salted with a tear. She turned and ran.

It was with some confusion that he retrieved the ball and rejoined the group. He had only been, as with Ib, making an attempt to be friendly. Until that time, he hadn't understood that P'nina's rudeness had been a mask—as much for herself as for him.

He remembered the controversy that had broken out when it was revealed that two people of opposite sexes were locked together in a room beneath the ground. With women like P'nina, Israel had nothing to fear.

His thoughts were interrupted by P'nina's laughter. She was gazing into the book.

"Sholom Aleichem?" Zvi asked.

Disgust showed on P'nina's features. "Is he the only humorist that you know about?" she asked. "No, this is an American writer—Robert Benchley." She put down the book. "You have met Ibrahim?" she asked.

"You mean the Arab?" he asked. "*Ken*. Yes. He drove me in."

P'nina smiled. "Nothing to worry about," she said. "He used to work for the Mossaad."

"My father used to work for the Mossaad."

"Then maybe that's not such a recommendation," answered P'nina.

The barb was lost on Zvi, for in his imagination, the roar of his father's laughter filled the room. It had been just before midterms at *Technion*. His father worked hard with the others, but was frequently called away on "government business," sometimes for weeks or months at a time. Everyone on the *Moshav* had suspected his being an agent, but nobody asked.

Zvi had been studying aircraft mechanics at the time. He remembered the tattered blue cover of the book, the varnished feel of its yellowing pages, the smell of dust and paper. He remembered how that smell fought with the smell of newly turned earth breezing through the open kitchen window. And he remembered how his studies were interrupted by the hard plunk of a bottle on the table. He looked up at the yellow, red, white, and black label.

From there, he looked into the face of his father. It was a blurred silhouette against the glare of the kitchen bulb.

"Drink!" his father laughingly commanded. Vast arms swung wide. "Tomorrow, you return to Haifa! There was never such a Purim and you missed it! Your cousin! Ha! Ha! What a beautiful Esther she made. What a long flowing gown!" His father winked. "As long and flowing as a gown can be—on a 4-year-old!" He threw back his head in laughter.

Zvi looked at his book. "I won't be a farmer," he said.

"Who said that I was asking you to become one?" His father turned his back, folded his arms, and sat on the table. "Ah! But you missed such a harvest last year!" He clenched his fist and shook it. "You never saw such beautiful bananas! And so many oranges, grapes, lemons!" The glow went out of his eyes and he lowered his fist.

"Son," he said. "I'm not asking you to become a farmer. I'm merely asking you to be happy!"

"I am happy, Father."

"With books? I want you to dance, to drink, to sing, to play! To find yourself some nice girl! But continue to laugh! This is why God put us here!" His father sighed. "But how can I ask you to continue what you have not begun? Why, even soccer, you treat like an attack from Syria!"

It was the last time he had seen his father.

He had continued studying that night and returned to Haifa before his father's awakening.

An Islamic leader had been assassinated nearly a thousand kilometers away. Nations were disemboweled, absorbed. Jordan became a province, renamed New Palestine.

His father's dark skin, hair, and eyes blended perfectly with those of the Arabs streaming across Allenby Bridge.

His father had never come back.

Once again, P'nina's voice interrupted his thoughts. "Here's the blind spot," she said.

Zvi looked up. The three color television screens, which showed what was picked up by the orbiting *Kaleb* satellites, were filled with snow. His eyes returned to the readout screens and he noticed another change.

"We've got three launches from Tehran, P'nina."

She straightened in her seat. "Call *Slik Aleph*."

Zvi picked up the phone and hit the aleph on the punch board. "*Slik Aleph*? This is *Slik Gimmel*. We've got a reading of three launches from Tehran. Have you the same reading?"

"This is *Slik Aleph*, *Gimmel*. We have a copy."

"This is *Slik Yod Daleth*," broke in a voice from the speaker on their consoles. *Slikkim Heth* and *Yod* confirm your readouts. We've got trouble. Should we wake the Old Man?"

"*Ken*," whispered Zvi.

He and P'nina simultaneously pushed identical blue buttons on their consoles. A majority decision was shown by the button's answering glow.

Above, a siren sounded. A group of terrified farm workers ran for the administration building.

At another *Slik*, a member of the Palavir, the Israeli

air force, picked up a red phone. He didn't bother punching a number. In a modest Jerusalem home, a Knesset office, and a parked automobile, identical phones were already ringing.

After a pause. "I've got the Old Man," came a voice. "He's getting on the hotline to Mecca."

"Two more launches from Jidda." Zvi looked down at his readout screen.

"We've definitely got a critical situation here. Might they be attacking Turkey?"

"Aw, come on! Every Arab country they have taken was by invasion or work within! Why bother with a missile attack?"

"Let's see what the Old Man says."

"Negative on Turkish attack. The missiles, if they exist, are headed in our direction."

"Could it be Cyprus?" came a voice.

"Look at your map!"

"The Old Man says that Tehran denies any launches. They warn that any attack will be met by retaliation."

"Any attack will be met by retaliation!" cursed Zvi under his breath.

"Could those three from Tehran have been a mistake?"

"Just a second," said a voice. "I'll see if the Old Man can talk Mecca into calling the Tehran base."

"What about Jidda?" asked P'nina. *"Slik Seventeen?"*

"Possibly the launches from Tehran were sensed and the other two were sent as a panic response."

"They shouldn't have been," answered P'nina. "There was a full minute ... one minute exactly, between launches. They may not have the *Yoshua,* but their response time should be as effective as our own. Read your reports from the Mossaad!"

"Four more from Damam."

"The Old Man says that they deny any attack."

"Goddamnit!" cursed P'nina under her breath. "They haven't had time to call their base!"

"Tell the Old Man that we've got nine missiles

headed in our direction. If it's a mistake, they'd better find out pretty damn fast!"

"The Old Man says to go to condition yellow as soon as those missiles cut their thrust. If the targeting displays show military targets, activate!"

Zvi raised his brow. "The agricultural center's going to be awfully pissed if we activate under a false alarm."

"They'll be even more pissed if we take no action at all," answered P'nina. "Their families live here." She began punching the aleph button, trying to get through to the red phone.

"Tell our enemies about *Yoshua*, if you have to!" she said when the button finally illuminated itself.

Zvi began counting aloud and then silently to himself. "We have six from Isfahn," he said. "Still better than twelve hundred kilometers from our borders. If they think this is a surprise attack, they're insane! We couldn't be given more response time!"

"The Old Man's got them calling their bases. Maybe they're starting to listen."

P'nina breathed a sigh of relief and settled back in her chair. "That part of the battle's won," she said. "At least they believe in us enough to check with their bases and confirm whether or not a missile's been fired."

"Fourteen missiles with warheads of ten megatons or better. If there isn't something wrong with our equipment, do you really think that our country can take . . ."

Two targets illuminated the screen. Zvi half rose from his seat. "Masada!" he fairly screamed in perplexity.

"Sit down, *putz*!" cried P'nina. "It's an old ruin, nothing more!"

Nearly 2,000 years before, Herod had built a palace atop the butte of Masada. A butte rising nearly 440 meters above the Dead Sea. Less than a century later, it was used as a fortress by the Zealots, who held it against the Roman hordes for nearly three years. When, at last, an earthen embankment was slowly built to its edge, the Romans entered to find a hollow victory. Rather than be sold into Roman slavery, the Zealots had committed suicide—men, women, and children.

"Shezor?" said P'nina. "Not a military target ..." She swiveled in her seat and began punching keys. "A farming community in Northern Galilee," she said.

"And B'nai Naim," answered Zvi. "Another meaningless target and we've got four additional launches from Hamadan."

"Switch to primary backup computers," came a voice from the loudspeaker.

"At this point, that sounds like a good idea," said P'nina. She flipped a switch. "Readings haven't changed."

"A first reading on one of the Jidda targets," said Zvi. His forehead wrinkled. "Ziorah," he said.

"These aren't military targets, *putz*. They're total nonsense! Some of these targets are little more than post offices. And an old ruin!"

Another target silently illuminated itself.

Zvi's forehead wrinkled. "Could they be trying to confuse us? Definite reading of launches ... and definite targets ..."

"But they're destroying the things that *they* would need! Any occupying force is going to need food!"

"I don't think there will be an occupying force," Zvi said. "Remember the words of the Caliph: 'Our shrines are walked in sandaled feet. They must be purified so that this abomination cannot take place again'."

"And that's why the UN no longer patrols our demilitarized zones? That's why they got out?"

"Not officially, but probably."

P'nina straightened in her chair, looking at the readout screen. "Hebron!" she exclaimed. "A military target! Activate condition yellow and arm!"

Both of them activated yellow switches. They watched pilot lamps illuminate as machinery took over.

Twenty feet overhead, locks slammed shut in the irrigation ditches. Underground pumps moved the trapped water into hidden tanks. Seals broke and sections of ditch, formed of concrete and steel moved upward and over on powerful hydraulic jacks, uprooting orange and grapefruit trees.

"Five more launches from Tabriz."

P'nina's voice was swift and certain. The upper row of pilot lamps indicated that the portals were opened. "Arm!" she barked.

For the first time in close to three years, the enameled surfaces of the *Yoshua'im* gleamed in the early morning sun. Carriages moved upward, pointing noses toward the sky. The stubby wings began to unfold as soon as the *Yoshua'im* cleared the ground.

"The Old Man says that they've called their bases. They deny charges of launching an attack."

"My board reads a total of thirty launches. We shouldn't expect any strikes until six thirty five," put in Zvi.

"Yes sir," said a voice. "I'll patch you through."

"This is the minister of defense. I request that you switch to your remaining backup computers at one-minute intervals. I assume that you are already on primary backups for confirmation. Each of you is equipped with your own input system, so at this point, I would have to set the likelihood of a mistake at literally billions to one. Our condition is now yellow. If I don't see you again, die bravely, *Haverim Shelli*. Switch to secondary backups . . . Now!"

"Five from Mastura," said Zvi. "A definite pattern is showing itself. The launch areas are getting closer."

"And I suppose they sneaked in Hebron, Jaffa, and Haifa, thinking we wouldn't notice?" asked P'nina.

"You're forgetting that the *Yoshua'im* and our detection system are secrets that we've kept for three years. They know there's a missile base here, but they don't know what kind. All their bases are part of a single detection net. Things can go wrong on that. What the Persians and Arabs don't know is that our system, by its very nature, has a hundred backups with twenty separate systems of input. There is no mistake, *tsiporah katanah*. This is the Second Holocaust."

"After all this time," said P'nina. "They couldn't let their hatred die."

"Six from Mastura," corrected Zvi.

"Backup Gimmel," said a voice.

"No change," said P'nina. "It's in our hands now, *putz*. Do we fire?"

Zvi shook his head. "Not until the last minute, P'nina."

Her face paled. "It's this waiting," she said.

"Hey, *putz*? Could you call in a replacement? I'm going to be sick."

When he heard her words, Zvi swallowed the taste of his own bile. "No, P'nina. Use one of your drawers, if you have to. I want you here," he added truthfully. "With me."

A blush colored the paleness of her features.

Zvi turned back to the screen. "Five from Baghdad," he said.

With this, P'nina turned away from him and opened a drawer.

"Backup *Heth*," said an electronic voice.

"This is *Slik Mispar Aleph*. No change," said another distorted voice.

"*Slik Mispar Beth*. No change."

P'nina came up, wiping her mouth on a sleeve, a questioning look on her face.

Zvi answered her unspoken question. "Final confirmation. We're being told when to fire." He picked up the mike and added his voice to the electronically sobered hysteria of the rest. "*Slik Gimmel*. No change."

The laughter of Zvi's father again filled the room.

"There is nothing wrong with being a farmer!" the voice rang out. "If it weren't for farmers, what would we eat, eh?"

"Would I be happier as a farmer?" Zvi asked himself. "Would I be happier not knowing?"

"*Slik Mispar Yod Gimmel*. No change."

"*Slik Mispar Yod Daleth*. No change."

Something teased at his brain, a hazy memory from three years in the past. "The Turtle"—an affectionate name given a general with a beak of a nose which joined with his forehead.

"Fire!" came the order.

Automatically, he and P'nina pressed the red firing studs.

In 38 sealed chambers, far overhead, nitric acid poured over cores of powdered aluminum in a rubber matrix. Solid fuel boosters roared to life. At a 45-degree angle, all of the missiles, save one, soared upward.

Zvi pinched his nose. What was it that the turtle had told him? He remembered and frantically opened the top drawer of his console.

At 200 feet, the missiles leveled off. Robot control surfaces adjusted themselves. Jet engines caught the wind and fired into keening life. Although they had all been launched in the same general direction, they began to turn as winds caught aelerons and rudders.

Hatzav was the name of the aged general who had trained them. Half his face had been destroyed in the Lebonese War and he wore a partial mask of black satin. But his nickname, the turtle, came from his large beak of a nose.

Hatzav had pulled him aside during a preliminary inspection of the installation. "Zvi," he said in a dry whisper. "you are a bright boy, and very brave! I know that you are one we can trust with the responsibility you are given. It is not a usual thing that those in the *Slikkim* should know their targets. But should you ever—may the Master of the Universe make it not so—should you ever have to push that button, the target on this card should help you in your last moments. *Attah talmid tov*, Zvi. Shalom."

"Shalom," Zvi whispered back. He took the sealed envelope which the old man extended and put it into his pocket.

Zvi was pulled back to the present by another whisper.

"Oh, my God!" said P'nina.

The second screen illuminated itself, doubling the number of Persian and Arab missiles. These were launched from Israel's very borders.

The speed with which Zvi rummaged through the coffee- and tea-stained reports increased. At last, his hand grasped the yellowed envelope.

"Zvi," she said. "Number fifty-three."

Zvi saw that the target under number fifty-three was their own base.

"*Shalom*, Captain Sivan," said P'nina.

"*Shalom*," Zvi returned.

He held up the file card. "P'nina?" On the file card was written, in Hatzav's spidery Hebrew script: "Target: Mecca!"

The target couldn't have been Mecca itself. Israel's powerful religious party would not have allowed it. It was more likely the missile sites north of there. Zvi saw comprehension enter P'nina's face and the beginnings of a smile. The emotional satisfaction was the same as if the target were the holy mosque itself. The smile. Before the flesh was seared from his bones by a brilliant flash.

Thirty-five miles away, a young woman dived beneath a kitchen table, just in time to avoid being crushed by a collapsing concrete wall. Her name was Rachel Cohen. And it was no longer with Zvi, P'nina, Ibrahim, Hatzav, or Shmuel that the fight to survive would continue. It was through she, Rachel Cohen.

Chapter I

August 13, 2086   A mile above the Lunar Alps
Elul 3, 5846   Tuesday
12:30 p.m., Jerusalem Time

A star rose above the horizon and proceeded to the zenith of the velvet-black sky. There, it winked out.

Everyone knew the blue-white spark of the *Kappa*. With a height of only 16 meters and an empty mass of only 80 tons, she plied the lunar skies every three hours. Moving at half orbital velocity, the trip took an hour. With a half hour to load and unload, an hour was left for Toshiko's relaxation—if the owner of a craft which virtually flew itself could be said to be in need of relaxation.

Most of the *Kappa*'s bulk was taken up in tanks. Not tanks for fuel—they took up only a quarter of the *Kappa*'s total volume, for she was powered by atomic fusion. The larger tanks supposedly held water: an expensive and precious substance, away from the ice caves at the lunar poles.

Water was expensive and useful enough to be stolen. But the *Kappa* carried materials that were valuable even to those unthirsting.

Copyrights and patent applications bound for the UN offices on Earth. Stocks, bonds and other magnetically capped and coded negotiables stored in bundles between the *Kappa*'s upper and lower decks. The *Kappa* had once been fired upon from the darkness of a lunar shadow. But only once.

"The nail which projects shall be struck down." It was an ancient Japanese proverb which had lost its

18

meaning in the lunar outback. With the moon's colonization, the discipline of the Samurai, the eldritch concept of *wa*, rapidly melted. Here the individual, not the group, gained prestige and wealth, if not honor. Oftimes, like the nail mentioned above, at the cost of tearing another's vacuum suit.

The average lifespan of the pilots who had previously flown Toshiko's mission was three years.

She had been flying it for six.

Paul Greenberg wondered what had awakened him. While he was used to all types of assignments on Terra, he was new to the environments of low- and microgravity. He reached up, fumbling for a handhold, and raised himself from the support of five padded hooks: one at the crotch, one at each armpit, and one at either side of his head. It was amazing what could be comfortable in a little more than a sixth of a G. He hung there for a moment, finding his balance of mass, before allowing himself to float slowly to the floor.

It was amazing, the environments in which the UN expected him to operate. The Pacific floor had been bad enough. But at least you weighed *something* there while in the domes! Here it was a wonder that he hadn't spent more time being spacesick! It was easy for the Little Man to sit on his fanny and send people off—not only in disguise, but into environments in which they could barely function. And to top it off, into political situations where their discovery would mean death. Changes in environment, whether they involved the vacuum of space and zero gravity or the density of water and varying bouyancy, could not only cause death by explosive decompression, crushing, poisoning or drowning—it could make it goddamned impossible to get away when a human adversary was trying to stop you from doing your job! Particularly if that adversary had been raised in the alternate environment.

A rumor cropped up every few years within the UN secret service. As an agent got older, the more difficult and dangerous his assignments became. The rumor was that this was more than simple reliance upon experience. The UN had a bet going: that an agent would get himself killed before he lived long enough to retire and become a walking source of UN secrets.

It was true that Paul had been trained for this environment, after a fashion. But the UN thought that it would be more believable if he appeared not to be functioning well in space.

The UN was certainly willing to sacrifice far more than he in the name of realism.

The people who inhabited the moon—the Selenites—were understanding enough; they had to deal with tourists from Earth all the time. The inhabitants of the only American space city, Astropolis, were as well; they were partially in the business of training "Earthworms" in the use of their unusual environment.

But lately there had been rumors that the natural contempt of the Israeli space cities for Terran ignorance and clumsiness was extending toward the desire for political control. For one thing, the outbreak of an unusual plague and the quarantine that followed effectively cut off Hazera Ysroel's activities from UN view. It made it far too easy for the space city, if it had the mind, to get away with something. Under such conditions rumors could not be ignored. Particularly rumors which stated that Project Svenglid, one of the UN's own creations, was to be somehow used against the UN.

The UN had reason to be nervous. Since the small brush-fire nuclear wars late in the twentieth century and the panic responses of nations to them, the UN had been in complete control. This was because it had, through a combination of accident and design, obtained absolute control of nuclear weapons.

But a nuclear explosion in space amounted to little more than a hard burst of X-rays. And the job of pushing such a weapon out of Earth's gravity well was far more difficult than it might be for a space city to drop a large asteroid on the new UN General Headquarters in Geneva.

That's where Paul came in. Hazera Ysroel had for a number of decades been hard at work on a UN project named after a mythical spear once carried by Thor. Project Svenglid was a natural "in," and Paul—disguised as an electrical engineer—was ostensibly on his way to doublecheck the electrical controls to Svenglid's automated probes.

It was lucky that the use of RNA in learning had been rediscovered and at last perfected. With it, Paul could take a "crash course" in whatever form of expertise his "character" was to have. This time, he was an electrical engineer. And he had to be good enough to fool Yonah Goldstein, another engineer with whom the UN had arranged he live and work while in Hazera Ysroel. Due to the plague, the hotels had been closed for five years, along with everything else that dealt with the once thriving Hazera tourist industry. The monorails were closed. So, here he now was, bound for the almost-abandoned equatorial city Dos Telerl from the lunar spaceport of Selene, on board the vacuum equivalent of a helicopter.

Paul pulled open the opaque screen and squinted against the light which shone through a spiral staircase from a small kitchenette. He mopped his brow with the beta-cloth sleeve of his coverall. The interior of the *Kappa* was warm and humid, almost tainted with the smell of perfume, cooking, and incense. How as traditionally clean a people as the Japanese had found an environment without water for bathing, he didn't know. They must have revolted against it, but they hung on.

It was difficult for him to believe that all this originated with Toshiko. Like most Selenites, she was a heavy user of perfume. It followed her in a cloud wherever she went.

Paul breathed a sigh. One of the expensive premoistened towels with which these people bathed would feel good about now. The location of the bathroom was a problem. He looked around for a small room with a sign. There were two of them:

Almost predictable, he felt nature's call. Another dank sigh. He knew that one of the two tiny rooms had been the airlock through which he had entered.

He looked through the barred openings of the stairway. Toshiko wasn't in the kitchen. If she were in the control room, it probably meant some small emergency. It was best not to disturb her with his biological problems. So he carefully hopped the few steps to the large yellow door directly ahead of him. He halted when his sleep-rimmed eyes saw a porthole and a glowing green light. Few bathrooms had windows. Again he hopped, floating to the floor to face in the opposite direction. Silently he congratulated himself. This low lunar gravity was going to take some getting used to.

So, the other little room had to be a bath. Delicately, he moved in the slight, hopping gait that had been taught to him in the low-G tourist rooms of Astropolis. He goofed and his forehead collided with one of the steps of the spiral stair. He paused to rub his injury and cursed silently. But it was only a long step sideways, a step forward and back again which brought him into the small chamber. He was relieved to find the facilities bisexual and as he eliminated, looked about for the premoistened towel dispenser. There was only one and it dispensed large bath towels. He smiled to himself. The waste of the rich. Without bothering to zip up his suit liner, he stood and extracted one of the large foil-wrapped packets. The fact that Toshiko completely ignored the smaller hand and face towels had to be the Selenite version of using a thousand dollar bill to light a cigar. He took advantage of her extravagance and used it to bathe the entire upper portion of his body. He then pressed a button, whipping both the towel and the packet into a vacuum receptacle.

Suddenly, he realized what had awakened him. Quickly zipping up his suit liner, he ran out of the bathroom, nearly knocking over a small Shinto shrine. "Toshiko!" he cried in an angry voice. "You've switched off the fusion drive! What are we running on?"

It was true. The small ship no longer trembled on nuclear flame. The low rumble no longer filled the ship. The incessant roaring had vanished. In its place was a suspicious hiss.

At Paul's cry, Toshiko cursed in Japanese, turning down the volume of the cartoon she was watching. She rose from her seat and turned to face Paul, who was climbing through the hatch. "What are we running on?" he demanded again.

Toshiko shrugged. There was no reason for her to lie. "We in dangerous place," she answered. "Over Alps. Many shadows. Bad men hide. Try shoot down us. Bad men light see, when engine running."

Paul placed his hands on his hips. "So, you're using oxygen. Do you always break the law while watching cartoons, Toshiko?"

Oxygen composed some 40 percent of the lunar surface. It was enough of a waste product to be blasted about indiscriminately as a propellant or simply disposed of by letting off into the lunar vacuum. At the same time, oxygen was heavy enough for the lunar gravity to hold for several thousands of years, and the vacuum industries were getting upset. After all, if the moon suddenly gained an atmosphere, they would be out of business.

"*Do itashimashite.*" Toshiko presented her wrists for imaginary handcuffs. "I never go court; pay right people. Selenites like money, not law. UN bring in people like law, maybe things change. But UN must bring in much people like law. One people, two people not live long change thing!"

Paul sighed. He knew that she was right. There was no use in having laws that couldn't or wouldn't be enforced. He looked out the clear plastic of the dome. The Lunar Alps moved by like low dunes.

"Much pretty, no?"

Paul nodded absently. The Selenites had strange notions of beauty. The lunar landscape for him could be summed up in one word: *dull*!

"Soon we come to *Palus Putredinus*. Very pretty!"

" 'The Swamp of Decay'," his mind translated. Yes that ought to be interesting . . . if something was really decaying. Doubtful.

He turned back to the cartoon screen behind Toshiko's chair. On it a boy with a determined face unleashed a bolt of lightning from a stick. An animated witch dissolved into a ghoulish skeleton.

"My favorite!" the young woman said excitedly. "Witch in form of fish jump from water. Eat goat of boy. Boy go wizard. Learn magic . . ."

Paul dismissed the rest with a wave of his hand. "Let's skip the synopsis," he laughed.

Toshiko snapped off the screen angrily. "That two time you ruin life!"

He chuckled. "If you're talking about the fight I got you out of, beating up on a woman is frowned upon where I come from."

"I take care of self," she declared. "Fight dirty. Kick place lady no have. Use brass knuckle. Now, I must fight two time number of people. Two time number of fight! Bad enough when helped by Selenite. Earthman maybe little, but strong! Fight with Selenite not fair!"

Paul was more than a little surprised. He'd heard that the weakness brought on by being raised in lunar gravity had equalized the sexes, but . . . "Okay," he finally said. "I apologize."

"Apology accepted," Toshiko said. "How you . . . I . . . How you say? *Cho? Sabal?*"

Paul looked at her, perplexed for a moment. "Oh!" he finally said. "You mean stomach! Much better! Thank you for your concern, Toshiko!"

"You hungry, maybe?"

"Not really." The Selenites may have been pushovers in a fight, but Paul's illness hadn't been of help. Ninety-five out of a hundred got over spacesickness in a day. Paul belonged to the unlucky five. Without drugs, which Paul shunned (they still made one drowsy), everyone became spacesick. The balance of fluids in the middle ear was completely eliminated in microgravity. The three-day trip from Earth had been *hell*, and he didn't look forward to the three days ahead. Hazera Ysroel was some 63,000 kilometers *beyond* the moon!

"I fix you *tomagodofu*! Very good on bad . . . stomach. You have whole day of rest at *Dos Telerl*."

"Full day . . . I mean, a day's rest? I understood that we'd be leaving immediately!"

Toshiko smiled and shook her head. "Is Tuesday," she explained. "Jew launch *Parr*, ship, today, must put docking machinery in motion on Saturday. Is against Hazera law. Religious party in Second Israel powerful. Now, very powerful. No dock on *Shabbot*!"

On reaching the kitchen on the lower deck, Toshiko pulled out a foil packet, inserted a water gun, and pulled the trigger. Resealing the packet, she began squeeze-mixing the contents. She then emptied the packet into a bowl. Paul raised his eyebrows. It looked like custard. Toshiko placed the bowl in a chiller, pressed a button and extracted the dish at the sound of a chime. She then set it on the table with a cup of pear nectar as well as a cup of coffee that she had prepared from a sort of syrup. He took a bite—and Toshiko had been right. He was starving! He quickly wolfed down the Japanese pudding, the coffee and nectar.

He was still hungry on completing it, but felt considerably better. At least he would be eating like a gentleman when he got to Dos Telerl, not a survivor found on a raft at sea. He leaned back as Toshiko repoured his coffee. He had been worried about his ulcer kicking up on re-entering a gravity well. He hadn't been able to keep down solid food since leaving Astropolis, and he feared the inflow of gastric juices on regaining his appetite. But the *tomagodofu* would obviously do a good job of coating his stomach.

"You mentioned 'bad men' hiding in the shadows," he shouted above the engine's roar. "Have you ever been attacked?"

She nodded "Once," she answered. "Still like to shut off motor. Bad men forget, maybe."

"Forget what?" he asked. "The *Kappa*'s unarmed, isn't she?"

"I swing low," she answered. "Use rocket motor."

"Good God!" Paul exclaimed. "I can see why you haven't been bothered since!" For a moment, he pictured in his mind the suits vaporizing. Their internal pressure blowing them apart in the three-million-degree heat of the *Kappa*'s exhaust bell.

"I make sure one man live," continued Toshiko in innocence. "Toshiko see him run. No try catch. Tell others, no bother me."

For the first time since leaving Astropolis, Paul laughed. She wasn't merely tough, but smart as well. His laughter was greeted with a smile.

He felt the rocking motion of the *Kappa* cease. It was replaced by a new force which he recognized as centrifugal. A slight pull toward the outer wall. The *Kappa* was turning, balanced on its nuclear flame. "What's happening," he shouted.

"Much trouble in last three or four years," she answered. "Other cities want metal on moon. Very bad. *Kappa* carry coded plate, change every trip. *Kappa* point plate at radars, Dos Telerl. Robot guns no shoot."

"Robot guns!"

"Situation very bad!" she answered.

The *Kappa* was hovering now, slowly turning the tubular airlock door toward a similar, but larger tube which projected from beneath the lunar surface. Paul knew that the *Kappa* was turning. He could feel a slight centrifugal pressure toward the wall. There was a clatter and a long, drawn-out ringing sound, like that of a chime.

The *Kappa* moved downward at a forty-five-degree angle. The tubes slid together, like the parts of a spyglass. The larger tube, projecting from the ground, pushed back the ladder which permitted ingress to the *Kappa* from the ground.

Around the *Kappa*'s tubular airlock, ring-shaped, rubbery seals blew outward, creating a seal within the larger ground lock's tube. Paul heard the unmistakable, growing hiss of pressurization.

The *Kappa* had landed.

Chapter II

August 13, 2086   Port Weizmann, Dos Telerl
Elul 3, 5846   Tuesday
12:30 p.m., Jerusalem Time

Emerging from the *Kappa* was uncomfortable for someone raised in Earth's gravity.

You began by leaving its double airlock. The outer lock was a tube, sloping downward at a 30-degree angle. Then you moved along a chain "monkey bar" eighteen meters above the lunar plain, and finally down the widely spaced rungs of a ladder which led down one of the landing legs.

A recess in the lock at Dos Telerl received arriving visitors. Paul emerged from the wall of one of Port Weizmann's abandoned passenger tunnels. He nearly fell, trying to balance his existent mass in .18 Gs. The tile-lined tunnel echoed eerily at even the lightness of Toshiko's slippered arrival. The tunnel was fully fifty meters across. Broad walkways, connected by bridges, ran on both sides of a magnetic double track. The track obviously was meant to be bustling with unloading goods and visitors: businessmen bound for appointments in Selene, Astropolis and Amsterdam. The newsstand across the way was obviously meant to be filled with tourists buying newsdiscs, art prints, and last-minute souvenirs. But now there was the plague. Though the full-length glass of the newsstand's front was so clean as to be invisible, it was markedly empty.

A little train silently approached. Obviously, it was intended for at least 120 people. A door to the driverless vehicle opened. The way to the passenger compartment was blocked by two small gates. In the space that might have been occupied by a driver, the image of a girl appeared. It was obviously a recording—her clothes, makeup, and hairstyle were five years out of date. "*Shalom*," she smiled. "Welcome to Dos Telerl. This is Security Check Number One. Please place all metal objects on the belt to the side of the gate. These items may be retrieved after passing through the inner gate. Please move along so that we may make room for the people behind you. We regret any inconvenience that this may cause."

Paul stopped for a moment and looked this way and that with his mouth open. He could see no way of contacting the people at the terminal and there was something that they ought to know. Finally, he shrugged and placed his wallet, a few UN francs, and a penlight-stylus combination onto the belt. The belt whisked them into a long box and the outer gate opened. He stepped through the first gate and was greeted by the immediate dropping of two quartz doors, which fell flush with the floor within the two gates. A man trap—and the sliding doors were probably proof against everything from lasers to shrapnel.

Paul ran a hand through brown, curly hair. "Dr. Greenberg!" cried a loud, masculine voice behind him. The image of the girl was replaced by that of a lithe, middle-aged man. A pair of dark brows scowled above a neatly trimmed goatee. "It is obvious that you have considerable quantities of metal on your person. Please remove them and place them on the belt." The two doors of the man trap slid upward. "The joints and valves of your suit liner have already been taken into account," continued the little man sternly.

"I'm afraid that I can't put it on the belt," Paul answered. "My left arm and eye are artificial. I've had the arm surgically attached to the bone."

The man's brow lifted. "Oh? An amateur athlete,

then?" Ninety percent of what could be done by a normal, healthy arm could be accomplished by a prosthetic merely attached to the stump. The remaining 10 percent could only be done with direct attachment to the bone, which was considerably more expensive. Only athletes or spacers, who tended to swing about on bars and tethers like chimpanzees, would consider paying the additional cost. It was a logical enough conclusion.

Paul thought quickly. "No," he answered. "The arm was attached in a way that I could avoid preferential treatment. If you'll check my personality file, you'll find that I'm a goat for self-reliance. I had to pay considerable money to have knowledge of the injury lifted from the UN memory banks. I hate being treated like a cripple when I can function perfectly well." His voice held the carefully controlled anger that might follow a secret's uncovering.

The projection folded its arms and looked at an unseen figure to the side. After a pause: "May we ask how you lost your eye and your arm?"

Paul sighed as though extremely irritated. "An air crash," he lied. While truth drugs were cheap and easy to obtain, some of the UN's enemies found sadism more pleasurable. An air crash had been placed in the false files to cover such a discovery. He hadn't expected it so soon.

"You'll forgive our caution, Dr. Greenberg. Who made your eye and your arm? We'll adjust our equipment to consider it."

Paul gave them the answer that had been fed to him on Earth.

"Thank you, Dr. Greenberg. You can come through, now."

The projection turned to face them as he and Toshiko found a seat in the front row. "Toshiko! laughed the figure. How are you?" The projection leaned forward without waiting for a reply. "Have you got it?"

She reached into a pocket of her jacket and produced a transparent object the size of a poker chip. "Right here," she answered, holding it up.

"Excellent!" came the reply. "Oh, forgive me, Dr. Greenberg!" the projection said, turning suddenly toward Paul. "I forgot to introduce myself. I am Dr. Yonah Goldstein. Tell me, Dr. Greenberg. Do you like ships?"

Paul's brows shot up as the bus rounded a curve and entered an abandoned reception area.

"I'll see you again in the restaurant," said the image of Goldstein. *"Shalom."*

Paul looked around the abandoned terminal. "Restaurant?"

Toshiko laughed. "Restaurant close," she answered. "I like cook. Bring food in luggage. Make food for passenger in restaurant. Last time you have pork teriyaki plenty long time."

Paul laughed as Toshiko raised a bow. "I forget," she said in concern. "Is passenger-*san* keep kosher?"

"No," Paul answered. "I'm Jewish by birth, not practice."

They departed the train and walked through the immense terminal. The fact that Port Weizmann had been abandoned for five years gave it an eerie feel. They descended a frozen escalator into what was obviously a baggage claim. A single small case was waiting for them. "You get luggage on other side," she explained.

It was obvious which sections of lunar architecture had been designed on Earth. For the benefit of tourists, the escalator looked exactly like those on Earth. Steps three- and four-feet high can be disconcerting to someone raised in a "normal" G well.

The feeling of eeriness passed through Paul again as they went by what had been a hotel lobby. It seemed to go on forever—and not a soul in sight.

"Here restaurant," said Toshiko.

Paul did a double take. It was obvious that not all

of Dos Telerl had been designed for tourists. A good deal of the furniture in Selene had been designed to *look* comfortable, right down to heavily padded armchairs—actually, totally meaningless at .18 Gs. In the *Kappa*, he and Toshiko had seated themselves on low stools, in keeping with Toshiko's love of tradition. Here, the chairs were merely T-shaped bars extending upward and outward over the floor. A third bar grew from the wall, providing back support. Following Toshiko's lead, he seated himself in a booth that contained a large wall screen. Toshiko leaned over him and flipped a switch, and the wall screen lit with the image of Goldstein. Toshiko gave the screen a pleasant wave and walked toward the kitchen.

Paul returned Goldstein's laugh with a smile. The pleasure on Yonah's face vanished. "I hate to spoil your meal, Dr. Greenberg, but I'm afraid that I'm required to repeat our warnings before you enter the city. We have come up with a virucide; however, it only renders the victim a carrier. The disease is not caused by a virus, but a viroid. I'm not a medical doctor, so I can't begin to explain it. Apparently, a viroid is something like a super-conductor—a simple polymer without even a jacket of protein. The molecular bond is extremely powerful in this creature, and while we can make the body immune, we cannot destroy the viroid without killing the host."

Paul leaned back on the metal bar; it was surprisingly comfortable.

"We can give you none of the serum on entering," Dr. Goldstein continued. "We have every reason to believe that we have confined the organism to three of the Byuttim, as well as our Knesset. However, of the two dozen UN engineers that have been sent to us, I must point out that four have died. Three were in unfortunate accidents. But this is to be expected among people who aren't used to the conditions of space. The fourth, however, died of the disease . . ."

Yeah, thought Paul. *I'll bet.*

". . . During the course of which he infected Byutt Asher," continued Dr. Goldstein. "As I have said, we can give you none of the serum. It is useless if the disease has already been contracted, and the organism is small enough to be nearly impossible to detect.

"We've created some computer models and found that we can expect 97 percent of the population to be wiped out, should it ever get loose on Earth. Terra is our biggest customer. Therefore, it may be one life—your life—against the many."

"Well," asked Paul. "If you have a serum and know how to make it, why haven't you given the formula to the UN?"

"We have," came the answer. "Unfortunately, it's far too expensive and difficult to make. And like many pharmaceuticals, it can only be made in microgravity—an environment that can be hard to duplicate on Earth. Besides, think of producing it for ten billion people. The disease has an incubation period of only 20 days. Even with all of Terra's resources, do you really think that you could produce enough of a drug, using rare biological substances, for ten billion people? *Nu!*"

"Have you sent the formula of the drug to the other cities?"

Dr. Goldstein grimaced and muttered to himself in Hebrew. "The other cities can take care of themselves," he finally said. "Besides," he began cautiously, "we think that it may have begun in another city. Unfortunately, we haven't sufficient evidence to press charges."

"Are you saying that it could be a deliberate act of biological warfare?"

"It's possible," continued Goldstein. A hand covered his eyes. "If you please, Dr. Greenberg. I lost my dear wife in the plague." The hand dropped and Goldstein smiled. "Let's talk shop," he said.

Paul leaned back and half closed his eyes. The first question was the inevitable one.

"Why must Svenglid be completed so quickly?" Goldstein asked.

"I can answer that question and intend to," Greenberg said. "However, I have been instructed to reveal that information only to the Prime Minister."

"Rachel Cohen? I . . . I'm not certain that this can be arranged, Dr. Greenberg."

"Svenglid is your largest current project, is it not?"

Dr. Goldstein straightened. "Of course it is, Dr. Greenberg. Without the faith that the UN has placed in us, Hazera would have gone broke with the coming of the plague."

"Then you are aware of Svenglid's importance to us. Two of the other cities have failed in building probes. Pure science projects are extremely expensive, Dr. Goldstein. It is lucky that all three projects were started simultaneously. Even then, it is touch-and-go all the way. If this fails, we can expect a wait of at least 50 years before trying such an ambitious project again."

Dr. Goldstein leaned back and smiled. "I think that would break the hearts of half the people at work on Svenglid. I know a few old geezers who are going to stay alive just to see the results!"

Greenberg laughed. "Well, with the speed we're giving it," he said, "that won't be such a challenge. It's easier to wait five years than 50."

"Hoo ha!" exclaimed the other. "You can say that again!" I am sometimes surprised by my own enthusiasm. Everyone on the project wishes to go themselves!

"Of course, we are grateful to you, Dr. Greenberg. Our wealth in volatiles has increased tremendously simply from the leftovers."

"The factory ships?"

"*Ken!* The *Kalnitim!* You are neglecting your meal, Dr. Greenberg."

Paul looked down at the steaming plate that Toshiko

had set before him, took a piece of meat, and raised it toward his mouth.

"Is that pork, Toshiko?" asked Goldstein.

"Mmm-hmmm," affirmed Paul, still chewing. "And quite good, too," he added.

Toshiko smiled.

"Then you do not keep kosher?"

Paul shook his head. "I'm a Jew by birth, not practice." He smiled to himself as he raised some rice to his lips, looking for the doctor's reaction, but Goldstein had already turned to Toshiko.

"I hope that you won't let the others know that you've been using their cookware to prepare pork, Toshiko. Dos Telerl has become quite a Chassidic community, and you may have to buy them new cookware."

Toshiko gave an "I-can-afford-it" shrug as Paul wolfed down more food.

Dr. Goldstein leaned back. "Svenglid," he said in a stage whisper. His voice wandered off into Hebrew. Finally, he looked up. "It is difficult for me to believe," he said, "that after twenty long years, the project is almost completed."

Greenberg smiled. "Sort of anticlimactic?" he asked.

Goldstein grimaced. "It probably won't be when we launch it!" he exclaimed. "I can't imagine the equivalent of twenty bombs—like the one that destroyed Haifa—going off per second, as anticlimactic! Now it's just a matter of a little more fuel. Just a little more fuel!"

"And probably a little more credit," answered Paul.

Dr. Goldstein's face became a question mark.

"Your projects, other than Svenglid, have been a little too ambitious. Some of the terrestrial companies are starting to complain that you're exceeding your credit ratings."

Goldstein's eyes twinkled. "The *goyim* have always banked on Jews and now they're losing faith?"

He was answered with a chuckle from Paul.

"I'm afraid that you'll have to take that up with some of the Knesset's members. As I asked you before, Dr. Greenberg. Do you like ships?"

"I can't say that I really do," answered Paul. He automatically assumed that Goldstein meant space ships. Most Terrans knew spacecraft by the misnomer of plane.

"I'm one of the five percent who are prone to space sickness," finished Paul. "And I don't like drugs."

Goldstein clucked and waved a hand. "No! No!" he declared. "I mean— Put the disc on the screen, Toshiko."

Toshiko again brought out the poker chip object from her pocket and placed it in a slot at the bottom of the screen. Almost immediately, Goldstein's face was replaced by the blueprint for a 19th century, four-masted sailing vessel with triangular sails.

Greenberg laughed.

At the other end of the circuit, Goldstein stripped away the exterior planking via the computer. The bare ribs of the ship rotated 360° horizontally, then vertically. Twice the image rolled over on the screen. By the time his image returned to the screen, the ship's design was already recorded on one of Goldstein's own chips. Toshiko's chip fell into a slot beneath the intake. "These are beautiful, Toshiko! Just beautiful!" Goldstein paused. "Have you ever seen the ocean, Dr. Greenberg?"

Paul nodded. "Of course," he answered.

Goldstein smiled and chuckled to himself. " 'Of course'," he repeated. " 'Of course'. I keep forgetting how common such sights must be to a Terran. The ocean—water stretching in every direction for as far as the eye can see! To me, such an extraordinary experience! But to you!" Goldstein raised his shoulders in an accepting shrug. The ship's image flashed back onto the screen. "Slave ship," mused Dr. Goldstein. "Nasty business, that! But they were so beautiful!

"Well, as Toshiko must have told you, we've got a full day with little to fill it. The city is within walking distance of *Surveyor VI* if you'd like to look over a piece of history, Dr. Greenberg. You can suit up and stroll over there with me as soon as you come through, if you like."

In many ways the virus was more frightening than the dangers of the space environment. Death from it would be slow and painful, should it come. Paul considered such a death in an abstract sort of way. One had to be a bit suicidal in this job, but he did have to admit to himself that death through explosive decompression or an old-fashioned bullet in the head would be more desirable.

There might be a 20-day quarantine for exiting from the inhabited section of the city, but entry was deceptively simple. It was through an airlock, much like those used for going from a pressurized environment to hard vacuum. There was the smell of disinfectant. He was certain that the pressure in the rooms directly outside the airlock was higher than those within—a guard against the virus escaping on random currents of air. But the only purpose that disinfectant could possibly serve was psychological. Goldstein was waiting for him on the other side.

The glass of the window overlooking the switchyard was almost a dozen centimeters in thickness. Goldstein pointed. "There's our ship." An object that looked like two mailing tubes, one longer and pushed inside the other, moved out of a distant airlock and glided down one of the many slots cut into the heavy fiberglass coverings of the yard. Beneath the slots were the ship's two accelerators—four superconducting magnets mounted on trucks, much like the wheels of a boxcar. The ship's 200-meter length literally floated on the track's magnetic fields. Beneath the yard, other magnets changed polarity, pushing the ship forward.

Goldstein smiled at Greenberg. "Welcome to *'Ham-'silat-Barzel Tranquilatis'—'The Tranquility Railroad.'* You can see why we call it that, Dr. Greenberg."

Paul nodded. Except for the harshness of the sunlight and the intense lunar shadows, he might have been looking through the window at a terrestrial switchyard. There was even a roundhouse, with a turntable housed in a convenient crater. But this railroad led to the sky itself. By the time the manned *Parrim* and the unmanned *Parot* reached the end of the 800-kilometer track, they would be moving at better than 2,400 meters per second—lunar escape velocity. From there on, the track and ground would fall away.

Goldstein began to walk away from the window. "Come," he said. "We'd best be going. I daresay the ship has already reached the loading dock.

"I think you'll find takeoff from Dos Telerl quite comfortable, Dr. Greenberg. From here, our acceleration will be only a little over a third of a terrestrial G."

"Wasn't the first mass driver built right here?"

"Yes, it was," Goldstein said. "I know that an acceleration of a third of a G strikes many as extremely low."

They boarded an escalator, headed away from the viewing chamber.

"And," continued Goldstein, "it's a long and complicated story." As he stepped off the escalator, Goldstein looked over his shoulder. Greenberg followed his brisk step down the corridor. "Did you know that Hazera was supposed to have first been built at L5?"

"No, I didn't."

"I am preparing you, Dr. Greenberg."

"For what?"

"You are a representative of the UN. *Lo*?"

"Yes."

"Well, as I've said, Hazera was originally supposed

to have been built at L5. Everyone was understandably upset by the destruction of the Second Israel.
However, it is interesting how quickly one's sorrow
can fade when one discovers that they've given away
something that was to their economic advantage. So,
after having given us L5, the UN took it away again."

They boarded another escalator, leading beneath
the lunar surface.

"So," continued Goldstein. "They gave us L2 with
all its difficult station-keeping requirements. Fortunately, politicians are not scientists. They did not
know that L2 was the ideal site for a mass catcher."

They stepped off the escalator and began walking
down a long tunnel.

"And," he went on, "the UN General Assembly did
not know that the lunar nearside was the ideal spot
to build an accelerator. We *begged* for mining rights
to the lunar farside. The haggling was over in a
single morning, and no experts were present in the
conference room. It may be difficult for us to understand, now, but reason told the UN politicians that,
to reach a point above the lunar farside, you had to
launch *from* the lunar farside. As it was, we were
awarded mining rights to any point within a 2,000-
kilometer circle, with its center at the exact center of
the moon as you see it from Earth—right where we're
standing! As it is, any point exactly 800 kilometers
from this spot is perfect for launching to L2."

"I'll bet they were angry when they found out!"
remarked Greenberg.

Goldstein chuckled to himself. "They certainly were!
In fact, it prompted the passing of two laws within a
matter of weeks! Both of which, by the way, have
now been repealed."

"And they were?" asked Greenberg.

"One of them stated that mining had to begin within
a five-kilometer radius of the geometric center of all
mining grants. The second law said that launching

facilities had to be built within a five-kilometer radius of all mining operations."

"So you built a mass driver 800 kilometers long."

Goldstein shrugged. "Length wasn't specified," he said.

"And so, what are you preparing me for?"

"Well, the UN still isn't very popular around here, and the crew of the *Harpo Martz* . . ."

"*Harpo Marx?*"

"*Ken*. The crew of the *Harpo Marx* is being rotated home after three weeks on the lunar surface. They're apt to be in pretty high spirits, so you're in for a rough time, I'm afraid. Don't let them get to you."

By the time, they were walking down another corridor. Ahead, it expanded into a small waiting room. "Here we are," said Goldstein. "I daresay they've already loaded our luggage. Our captain should be coming through that door any time.

"If I had known you were prone to space sickness, I would have seen about pulling out one of our old passenger ships. They were large enough to produce gravity by rotation, and they were designed for that purpose. These are far too small, but at least they give you a feeling of up and down. They have a floor and ceiling. With the magnetic slippers, I'm sure you'll find that chronic space sickness is psychosomatic."

The door to the loading dock slid open. A large, portly man entered. "*Boker Tov*, Yonah!" he bellowed, followed by an inquiry in Hebrew. Goldstein made a noncommittal response and motioned to Greenberg. Paul was certain that he was being introduced.

"And, Dr. Greenberg," Goldstein tacked on. "This is Captain Brezinski. He'll be acting as our captain on the trip to Hazera."

Greenberg felt his hand squeezed by a meaty fist. Brezinski said the one word in his vocabulary that he knew Paul was sure to understand. "*Shalom.*"

Paul noted that the man's skin, above an immense

growth of beard, held the puffiness that he'd come to
associate with people who spent a great deal of time
in zero G. The side curls, he noted, had been rolled
around a finger and held in place with a hairpin.
He'd wondered how the Chassidim handled side curls
without gravity. The man's great beak of a nose held
several broken veins. Had he encountered explosive
decompression in his life? Greenberg wondered.

The conversation between Goldstein and Brezinski
continued in animated fashion as they walked up the
narrow tunnel leading to the ship. The tunnel was
designed to expand like a telescope—the walls and
ceiling were accordion-pleated. Ahead was the narrow door to the interior of the *Parr*.

Brezinski led the way into the airlock. The outer
door closed rapidly enough behind Greenberg to make
him jump. He hit his head on a padded ceiling and
Brezinski broke into laughter. Goldstein scolded him
sharply and got a slap on the back in response. The
captain then led them into a narrow corridor. Paul
assumed that it ran the length of the cylindrical
command section, which he had seen earlier. The
way was blocked by a double door that held a beautiful color mural of terrestrial trees. It slid open as
they approached. Another could be seen about 10
meters farther on. Greenberg noted a rubbery seal
about them—airtight. He paused for a second to feel
the thin line of silicate plastic. Goldstein turned
around. "Decompression door," he affirmed. "Merely
a safety device. There are three of them." He pointed
to the first two of six sliding doors that lined the
hallway. "These are restrooms," he said. "I'm afraid
that we don't have better facilities aboard a freighter."

As though perfectly timed, there was the "whoosh"
of a vacuum flush toilet and the loud click of a
premoistened towel dispenser. "Since you don't read
Hebrew, I'll let you know that the one on the left is
the ladies' room; the one on the right is the men's
room." A light above the door on the left changed

from red to green and the door slid open. A slender blonde woman stepped out to mutter a hasty, embarrassed "*Shalom.*" She went to one of the doors farther down, pushed a button, and entered as it slid open.

Goldstein's eyes twinkled. "I'll introduce you to the rest of the crew later on," he said. They continued down the hall to the second pair of doors. Goldstein pointed to the left. "This is your cabin, Dr. Greenberg. Outside of not having a private bath, I think you'll find it comfortable." They entered. "We don't want you to think that there's any danger, Dr. Greenberg, but I've been asked to show you some of the safety equipment. You should know how to handle it in case of an emergency. Assuming decompression, the door to your cabin will automatically close. It's airtight. Your suit locker is over here." He walked to a large box in the corner of the room. "In case the ship is damaged in this room, the box itself can provide life support. Although your window is attached with explosive bolts, we must ask that you stay within the ship unless a battery-powered, overhead strobe begins to flash. In such a case, put on your suit, float above the desk and as near the window as you can. The bolts are set off by this covered button. The suit is equipped with a homing beacon, so you can expect to be picked up in a couple of hours." Goldstein smiled.

"Now for some of the conveniences," he said. "Across the way, by the window, is a writing desk." Goldstein walked over and flipped up the top, folding it back. "Underneath is a computer terminal. Your readout screen folds out from this partition here. The bed is on the other side. Elastic sheets will hold you in. Storage is both under and over the bed.

"Oh, yes! If you want hard copy, it comes out of this slot beneath the readout screen."

Greenberg looked out the window. Atop the 50-meter

wall on which the mass driver was mounted, another slot paralleled their own.

"What's that slot over there?"

For a moment, Goldstein showed distraction. "Oh," he said. "That's for the ships coming in."

"You mean these ships land the same way they take off?"

"Attitude jets and the computers line up the ships with the landing slot. It's perfectly safe.

"You can store your shoes in this compartment below the desk. I'd suggest that you get into these magnetic slippers now, so you won't forget." Goldstein walked over to the rear wall and flipped a switch recessed into its padded surface. A section of padding folded itself into the semblance of a reclining chair, tipped on edge. "A chime will sound 60 seconds before takeoff, and again at 30 seconds. If you stand directly in front of the chair, the acceleration will waft you gently into it. There's a similar chair on the opposite wall for deceleration. A vacuum mask is here at the side, in case you feel ill once we enter free fall.

"I'd guess we'd better get ready. I'll be back to check on you in about fifteen minutes. *Shalom*."

"*Shalom*," answered Paul, as he donned his slippers. The moon's gravity was low; bouncing on one foot, he lost his balance and thudded softly against the metallic floor. While he was there, he took the opportunity to put on the other slipper. With a single push of his hand, he was again on his feet. The first chime sounded and he gently sidestepped toward the acceleration couch. The slight fold against which his knees would bend was a little above them. Well, a third of a G was small enough to give him some time in which to nestle. The chime sounded a second time. He placed his hands against the padded rest and found himself bracing for a much higher acceleration than actually came, for the landscape began rushing past before he felt himself gently pushed into the couch. It was as though the room slowly tilted. He had to turn his face away from the window in order to avoid panicking. Unlike the ships he had previously taken, this couch did not have the multitude of straps and harnesses. There was nothing to assure him that, should he suddenly stop, he would not be thrown into the padding of the far wall. The Jews must have felt that such bits of reassurance were meaningless. The launch ramp, he had been told, was well guarded and under constant repair. They seemed pretty sure of themselves.

But once in space, the ship seemed to have been designed by a paranoiac. Paul had heard that the methods of guarding the "railroad" were constantly in legal trouble. The mine fields and robot guns had been responsible for the deaths of six men—four had had their suits torn on barbed wire, so deadly that it had to be strung by robots. Yet each time one of these murders had been brought before the UN subcommittees, the Jews calmly pointed to the continuous warnings. Broadcast in French, German, Japanese, Hebrew, and English, they filled the suit phones of anyone who approached within 30 yards of an array antenna. The antennae ran in a continuous loop all around the launch ramp, at a distance of 20 kilometers. The upkeep on all of this must have been astronomical, yet it was continued, even now, during the economically debilitating plague.

The massive cut through the highlands that separated *Sinus Media* from *Mar Tranquilatis* passed in a sharp blur.

It was obvious that the Jews were not afraid of nature, but of other men. Paul shook his head. It was a racial paranoia from which he had been divorced all his life.

His final instructions had been received in Astropolis, a city in Near Earth Orbit, the construction of which had begun in the last century.

A door slid open before him. "Come in, Greenberg."

"The name is 'Green'," corrected Paul

The Little Man, sitting behind a desk, raised his brow. "Yes," he said. "Your grandfather dropped the last syllable. Nevertheless, Green*berg* is the name. And it's one that we can make use of on this assignment. Would you like a drink?"

Paul shook his head.

"Your name is Green*berg*," repeated the Little Man. "You don't think we'd overlook something like that, do you?" The Little Man poured a drink for himself. He studied the amber liquid in the glass.

Something about that last sentence unnerved Paul. It had been spoken calmly, yet it was the sort of sentence that would have carried emphasis on "that" in a disced thriller.

"Have you ever been in a synagogue?"

"No." Paul eyed the Little Man coldly.

"Did you ever receive any Hebrew training?"

"No."

"Do you know any Hebrew?"

"Yes."

"How much?"

"*Shalom*," answered Paul.

The Little Man's jowls shook with laughter. The laughter broke off into a hacking cough. "Excellent!" he cried. "Excellent! I'll tell you why you have been called for this assignment. It concerns Hazera and Svenglid. I'm sure that you've heard the rumors. We think that the Jews either plan to use Svenglid against the UN or that UN funds for Svenglid are being diverted for something else which will in turn be used against the UN. We've always been a bit peevish about the space cities and Hazera has been out of our view, so to speak."

"And you need a Jew to check it out for you."

"Precisely! Mind you, the UN Space Agency has about twenty people at work in Hazera on Svenglid at all times, all of them on different aspects of

Svenglid, so you probably won't be meeting any of
them. And all of them are very well paid for going
through the quarantine zone. As a result of the expense we could only have one agent there at any one
time. We've lost five people up there, over the past
year. All of them were agents. It might not mean
anything. After all, a good deal of their time was
spent in hard vacuum and microgravity, without any
training for such. But, on the other hand, it could
mean that one or more of them were caught, executed; and that they're on to us . . ."

"And you're afraid that a Jew who goes to synagogue . . . a Jew who can understand Hebrew, might
agree with whatever's going on?"

"Exactly! Your intelligence has always amazed me,
Mr. Green! Er . . . Greenberg."

Paul sighed. "And you believe a Jew will put them
off guard. You're certain that those who died were
killed. Killed because they were caught snooping."

"Will you take it, Green?"

Paul pursed his lips for a moment and then nodded.

"We were hoping that you would. Your career has
already been changed in the data banks."

"What am I supposed to be now?"

"An electrical engineer."

"More RNA?"

"I'm afraid so. We'll be giving you a doctorate.
There will be some problems, I'm afraid. For one
thing, the hotels in Hazera do not possess the proper
computer connections and electrical codes that such
an engineer is apt to need. A good deal of Svenglid is
classified. Therefore, assuming that you *were* an electrical engineer, it would be best if you were staying
with someone else who was working on the project—
one who had a computer with the proper encoding.
So you can't work out of a hotel this time—you'll
have to work out of a private home. It's apt to make
things more difficult . . ."

*   *   *

The *Parr* reached the end of the launch ramp and was thrown into space. Paul reached for the vacuum mask.

Afterwards, he cautiously brought the magnetically soled slippers against the metallic floor. There was a knock, and the door to his cabin swished open.

"Are you all right, Dr. Greenberg?"

"Fine!" Paul answered. He stood upright in his slippers, swaying softly, and looked around. Yes. The floor was definitely a floor, the ceiling definitely a ceiling, and the walls definitely walls. He smiled. "Say!" he said. "This is all right!"

Goldstein grinned. "Walk around a bit until you get used to it. I'll meet you in the relax room. It's down the hall, through the second pair of doors on the right." Goldstein popped back out again, and Paul did as he was instructed. The cabin was quite luxurious. He walked over to the window and looked into the void. The stars stood still. He flipped a switch for the computer. An electronic voice from the speaker probably said, "May I be of assistance?" or, "May I help you?", but it said it in Hebrew. Paul sighed. Well, that wasn't going to be very much help.

Carefully, he walked about in his slippers. He still had to walk carefully when, at last, he padded to the door and pushed a button at its side. The door opened. In the hallway, a young man was standing on the ceiling. He was thin and blonde and his head was level with Paul's knees. The young man looked up/down at him and grinned. The scraggly young beard floated in a cloud, and the sidecurls, without a hairpin, stuck out at a crazy angle. *"Ma hadash?"* he said.

All of a sudden, Paul's world tilted crazily. The floor was no longer a floor, the ceiling no longer a ceiling. He was falling headlong inside an elongated box. Instantly, he turned and tried to run back into the room. His earthly muscles were too strong, pushing him free of one slipper, clear of the floor. He found himself kicking free, hovering near the ceiling, and then, still kicking, he once more found the vacuum mask.

Paul grimaced as he reentered the hallway. The young man was gone and the corridor empty. Examining the floor, he noted that the blue paint had been worn off by countless footsteps. He looked up to see that the paint on the ceiling had not. Yonah had been right. He was apt to be in for a rough time.

Chapter III

Allon ben Isaac rode the little car through the long straightness of the abandoned tunnel. He was grateful for the hardness of the floor. He hadn't been sure that it would hold against the heaviness of the trailer that he pulled. Even the pneumatic tires probably couldn't have held against the shocks that a bump would have caused. Cautiously, he scouted ahead for any rock fragments which might have fallen from the ceiling. Most of them were large enough to steer around, but the two-way, double-trough design of the tunnel didn't leave much room for maneuvering.

There was a stone too large to go around. As he got out of the vehicle, he was momentarily grateful for the poverty of his family during his childhood. The poorer residents of Hazera's blocky skyscraper of a living space—called Byutt Nephtali—lived either in the "upper" floors, close to rotating Hazera's center, or like his own family, in the lower floors near the outer edge of the great rotating wheel. Housing was cheaper there, because the closer to Hazera's hub one went the lighter the centrifugal force, which was used in place of gravity. Earth normal, One G, was in effect at Byutt Naphtali's center. Throughout the gigantic structure, gravity varied by only about a fifth of a G. Yet it was amazing, the difference in strength that could result in growing up on the bottom as against the top floors. Allon doubted if an *upstairsnik* could have lifted the stone. It was a large piece of slag. He carefully hoisted it over the lip of the trough and onto the roadway for repair crews headed in the opposite direction.

Rounding a corner, he cursed to himself. Ahead of him was the turnoff to one of the coolant pumps. Part of the space was already occupied by one of the cars designed for use in these tunnels, its wheels stretched out at an angle, riding the curving walls of the trough like a train rode a track. In this part of the coil section! He'd checked and double-checked—the chances of meeting someone here during the day had to be thousands to one. At this time of night, he'd guessed that it had to be millions to one.

Something must have gone wrong with one of the pumps. *Now*, of all times! He checked the airlock lights on the little compartment of the pump shed. The light was throwing out a ruby glow; the airlock was cycled. That meant that the breakdown had to do with the pump's electrical system. The volatile coolant within the tubes could not be exposed to the air, and the pump itself had to be repaired in vacuum.

The vacuum and the softness of the fiberglass tires had prevented his approach from being noticed. He raised his hand to the front of his helmet in perplexity. He'd been working for the industrial interests of Nouveau Paris for close to 10 years. He guessed that this made him a traitor. Now a new crime would be added to that of industrial espionage—murder—when the repairman emerged from the pressurized chamber.

Allon's name had been David . . .

"Deuteronomy," said his father, seating himself. "Chapter Nineteen."

Young David ben Isaac stood in front of his father, his heart quickening. His stomach jumped. Why ask him to repeat something that he had learned months ago?

"The priests, the Levites and all the tribe," began young David in a shaking voice. *"Shall have no part*

*or inheritance with Israel; they shall eat the offering of
the Lord made by fire . . ."*

"Chapter Five!" commanded his father. "Verse
Thirteen!"

"Six days shalt thou labor, and do all thy work . . ."

"Go on!" his father said.

*"But the seventh day is the Sabbath of the Lord thy
God: in it thou shalt not do any work, thou nor thy son
. . . nor thy daughter . . ."* His father rose from his
seat. Young David was shaking now.

"Nor . . . thy daughter," continued David, beginning to sob. His father was taking a fiberglass rod
from its rack on the window.

"Perhaps," shouted the ominous figure, "if you spent
more time with your studies and less with your games,
the lessons would be learned!"

"I know it, *Av shelli!"* cried young David. "I know
it!"

"They say that some boys were playing baseball in
the park. They told me that you were among them!
How many times have I told you, David, that your
time is not to be wasted! Do you believe yourself to
be a *goy* that you can so waste your time? Are you an
apikorsim, that you can play games instead of study?"

"Our teacher says that it's good to play!" cried out
young David. "There were all kinds of games at the
Hebrew University in New York!"

"And look what became of them!" said his father.
"Lower your pants!

"I said, lower your pants!"

The fiberglass rod was raised above his father's
head.

The rod was held to the heavy plate glass of the
window by two epoxied eyes. Its shadow fell across
young David's bed when the sun reflected from the
overhead mirror of morning. Its pencil-thin shape
was thrown against the curtains by the streetlamps
at night. His entire childhood was spent in its shadow.

"Yacob," a friend had said. "You mustn't beat the boy this way. Someone will report you to the authorities! You expect too much from little David. Children grow according to their standards, not your own!"

Years later, his father confronted him about his name.

"Nu?" his father said. "Now, you change your name? And to that of a tree? And so you commit the same heresy that our ancestors did in the Second Israel. Forsake the names of our fathers for those of nature! *'Allon.'* What is an oak? It is strong, yes. It is hard. But can it walk? Can it think or talk? Does a tree study *Torah*? Does a tree discourse on the *Talmud*? So! You would no longer be a Jew. I loved David. I spit on Allon!"

"And Allon spits on you," returned Allon. He did so for emphasis. It was strange how small his father had become over the years. Allon now towered over a weak old man, cowering in a corner. "You never loved David. You saw him only as one who could achieve all those things that you were too weak or stupid to achieve yourself!" He turned away from the old man. "I've accepted a post with Magen Metals, Ltd.," he said, walking into his bedroom. He threw a lightweight suitcase on his bed. "I'm leaving now! You won't see me again." He pulled down several beta-cloth suits from hangers and threw them into the suitcase.

"David!" shouted his father's voice behind him. "Come back. Your father is sorry! David! Please!"

He booked passage to Dos Telerl and wondered at his feelings at the hotel. Still in Hazera, sitting on a bed, he picked up a copy of the *Tenach* that lay on a table, leafed through it, and thought.

Now, such ideas no longer bothered him. That was 12 long years ago. His beard was long again. The side curls once again hung down the sides of his face. He sat in the synagogue each Saturday. The habits that had been shoveled into his brain were difficult to erase. At first, he had cut off his side curls, played games or read novels on Shabbat, but this had made him uneasy, so he had gone back to his religion—for two reasons.

From the retorts, rock hammers, and pressurized tractors of his early days, he rose in the company. Within two years, he was in charge of one of the geological teams, and then transferred into the sales division. The change from maps and mascons to Israeli pounds and UN francs had been difficult, but not insurmountable. Or maybe it had. He'd found himself stuck in the same job, unable to advance.

"Monsieur," yelled Pierre into his ear. The raucous music would have drowned out his voice even a meter away. "You have brought us a great deal! For zis, we are truly grateful!"

Allon grimaced. "Then why have you arranged to meet here?" he asked, waving a hand at the crowd of dancing, naked figures.

"Ahhh, yes," replied the Frenchman. "Delightful!"

Allon blushed.

"Because in loudness and crowds zere is privacy."

"I beg your pardon?"

Pierre held out his hand. In it were a pair of what appeared to be earplugs. Allon shrugged and put them in. The noise diminished. "Ze plugs contain a computer which sorts out ze sound," explained Pierre, in a voice that came from the plugs. Allon smiled to himself.

"These are the tools of a spy," Allon said. "I know what it is that you are asking. The answer is no." He rose from his seat.

"Do you wish to continue to live on ze moon, *Monsieur* ben Isaac? Do you physically wish to reach a point where you can no longer visit ze lower levels of ze city which gave you birth?"

"We have gyms on the moon," answered Allon.

Pierre grinned. "And you visit zem?" he said. "How often?"

Allon grimaced.

"Your bones and muscles weaken every day zat you spend here. Do you think you could still win in a fight against a Terran? We offer you money, *Monsieur*. Money to move to a fine flat. And we have ze ways of covering your gains."

Allon walked from the table and stopped in mid-stride, before jerking the devices from his ears and grinding them beneath his foot.

Back at the table, Pierre Nachon twisted the jewel at the top of a ring. "He paused on the way out," he whispered into it, in French. "I think that he is taking the bait."

"Allon!" cried Yigal at the private company hearing. "You must tell them! By the name! Tell him! For God's sake! I was with you all the time at Selene! You know that!"

"Even if he did," said the vice president, "he could not account for the several hundred thousand pounds which have so mysteriously appeared in your bank account."

"How could you possibly know about that?" Yigal looked about, flustered and reddening. "I mean—even if so much money did appear in my bank account, there is no legal way that the company could know about it."

The vice president poured some water from a carafe, stood up, and walked over to a window. As Hazera slowly turned, the stars swung by. He sipped silently for a while. Finally: "You can, of course, sue Magen Metals for just cause and invasion of privacy. You are a rich man. In any case, it is doubtful that you could take on the resources of this company. And in any case, we cannot offer you a letter of recommendation. Since the coming of the plague, our sales have dropped 90 percent. We have had to lay off thousands of employees. Only three things are keeping Magen Metals solvent. One is the financial support of the government, but the supply in the treasury is rapidly dwindling. The others are those industrial processes on which Magen owns a UN patent, and those industrial processes that are the secrets of Magen Metals. Even these are only used on robot vessels, outward bound, never to return. In the past six years, we have lost three of these secrets. This has caused the laying off—has deeply affected the lives of—some 1,800 of our employees. They have been given enough severance pay to support them for three months, if they're prudent. From there on, they are wards of the State. The lower and upper levels of the Byuttim are already crammed with people who are out of work. I hope that the money in your account is enough to keep you from being among them. So, in order to avoid unnecessary legal entanglements, we are asking for your resignation, *Mar* Karp."

"Whatever is in my bank account, it is not enough! And I don't know how it got there! I swear it!" said Yigal. "No amount would be enough. Enough for me to . . ."

He looked up imploringly at Allon. "You were with me the entire time. You know that I have done nothing! Nothing!"

"Messages can be passed in many ways," returned Allon. "A microdot can be the period at the end of a sentence. If you left a hard copy somewhere, would I notice? Did you get some message in the wrapper of a candy that you bought? Would I know it?" There were still no feelings; Allon wondered at this. Although Allon was quiet, taciturn, Yigal had sought him out and spoken to him as a friend. There should have been something, but there wasn't, and Allon was betraying the first friend he'd had since boyhood— making suggestions to the vice president that he knew were untrue. "I'm sorry, Yigal," Allon finished. "If there were some proof, I could come to your aid. The fact of the matter is, I just don't know. I cannot attest to what I cannot know."

Pierre kept his hands in his pockets as Allon extended one of his own. "You have been to ze city!" Pierre said. "You went to Hazera!"

"The plague has been confined to two houses," answered Allon. "There is no danger."

"So you say! Still, you can see our reasons for caution. Not only are we cutting off personal commerce with you at Selene, but we must cut off personal contact altogether. The monorails to Dos Telerl and Akkiba are already closed. I take it zat since you have a second career in ceramics, that your house is near ze surface?"

"How else could I run a kiln?"

"Heated by ze sun?"

"*Ken.*"

"You are moving, *Monsieur* ben Isaac. To ze southwestern corner of Dos Telerl. She is a livable section of ze city, *non*? We have a big order for you. Zere, you will build a kiln to fire a gigantic vase. In ze motif of, uh, classical Greece. For zis your *Kaisarian*, uh, benefactor will pay you 20,000 UN francs. That's 5,000 Israeli pounds. But ze lunar night chills your ceramics too rapidly, *non*? Ze kiln will be chilled by ze passage of gas through ze kiln itself. Also, in ze outer wall will be zis . . ."

Nachon inserted a disc into the small table viewer. The screen showed a square microwave antenna built into the side of the kiln. "It is only natural zat the components of ze antenna cannot be expected to function until ze latter half of ze night. With all zat heat, who's going to notice a few microwaves?" He sighed. "It would be so handy just to use radio. But, unfortunately zat would be— How do you say it in Hebrew, *Monsieur*? Public? Yes, public!

"So. You will receive our private instructions

through zis receiver via maser from the Japanese sector.

"We can, of course, arrange our legal transactions and ze sale of your ceramics via radio. A perfect cover, *non*? We will give you ze exact coordinates and directions for building ze face of ze wall."

Allon lay on the bed with an arm across his eyes. In the lunar gravity, the chihuahua had grown to four times its terrestrial size, so it was heavy enough for him to notice when it landed on the bed. Allon laughed as the dog licked his face.

"Shalom, Rav-Tura'i!" he said. "My! Aren't we the bold one today." He sat up, scooting himself against a wall, as the dog settled itself affectionately in his lap. The dog whined at Allon's uncertainty. His house was built beneath an overhanging ledge of stone; it was one of the most expensive in this section of Dos Telerl. The surface of the moon was right outside a window of double plate glass with lead shutters. Even so, only the sun reflecting from the lunar plain could be seen. The house was so built that the slow passage of the sun across the sky was invisible. From his bedroom, he could look directly outward, onto the lunar surface.

Allon could see the top of his majestic kiln. The dog followed him as he rose from his bed and walked into the workroom. He took the latest sculpture on which he had been working, and placed his eye next to the surface of a miniature, crude wooden table. A tiny scroll was unfurled upon it. An ancient rabbi leaned on the two rollers with horny hands; the eyes squinted through tiny, wire-rimmed glasses as he read. Across the table, another rabbi stood, this one younger than the first. A finger pointed toward a passage of the *Torah*; his other hand was raised in a gesticulation of insight. A third looked on with interest, clutching a pewter tumbler of wine in his hand. The scene was reproduced with photographic realism. Where was it? Obviously eastern Europe. The figures were those of *Chassidim*. The time could have been any where from the 18th century to the 20th. The old rabbi might have been the Bal Shem Tov himself, disgusted at the idea of one of his brethren reading more into the *Torah* than actually existed.

"I wonder what Monsieur Nachon would say if he saw one of these," Allon said to *Rav-Tura'i*. The animal whined in response.

Allon opened a plastic bag and threw a minute amount of clay onto a potter's wheel. After flicking the wheel into a spin, he fit his fingers into the guiding framework of a pair of waldos.

As gears and levers deformed the rubbery silicate plastic of the tiny artificial hands, he pressed them into the clay. His hands and their extensions worked smoothly and efficiently. He backed off; the clay had been transformed into a tiny urn. He turned off the wheel and, with one of the waldos, bent down an upper edge. The urn was now a pitcher, but it needed a handle.

"You know what I am, *Rav-Tura'i*? I'm a schizophrenic. I have to be. The trouble is—" He paused, took another wad of clay and attacked it with a rolling pin. "—I don't feel anthing!" He stopped, waiting for a wave of grief to sweep through him. It didn't. With a knife, he cut a long strip out of the flattened clay. "I should, you know. I really should. There are other companies I could sell secrets to. The ones operating the mines at Mar Tranquilatis. They'd pay just as well as those of Nouveau Paris. Why did I pick someone not of my people?" He began to flatten the edges of what was to be the pitcher's handle. "Why did they have to pick me?" He raised up, examining his work.

"One of the bosses called me into his office today. He was concerned about my success in the world of fine art. He asked if there was any danger of my leaving the company. I told him that my ceramics had always been a hobby, would always remain a hobby. That the company held more rewards than money. And you know something else, *Rav-Tura'i*? He believed me!" Allon carefully nudged the flattened strip of clay off the ceramic top of the table, and threw the knife down. "Are there men who think that way, *Rav Tura'i*?" Are there men who get as much pleasure out of closing a business deal as I do out of finishing a piece of sculpture? There must be! Otherwise, would someone as high in the firm as that believe me?

"Look at my rabbim, *Rav-Tura'i*! The stuff that the Parisians and DeGaulians buy is, by comparison, junk! 'Self-sculpture'! What a fraud! A group of puzzle pieces that one takes apart and puts together! They call such junk art! Like that big vase! Like all the other blasphemous, enormous pieces that people put on order!" He took some powdered clay and put it into a cup, then carried it to a waste water tap and began mixing slip. He whipped the stirring stick angrily. "All so some *narkoman* can take my exquisite little people apart and put them together in obscene ways!"

"Nachon says that I am a potter and nothing more! Ha! He says that realism is no longer a part of the arts! The only realism that sells anymore is pornography! So! Every time I took a business trip to Selene, Pierre would make sure I'd have to wander into a bar filled with filthy, naked Japanese! Selene! Where every woman is a *zonah*! Where they sell drugs as they sell wine!"

He bent the handle into shape and gently held it up against the pitcher, pressing it into the side. With a brush, he began using the slip as a glue, cementing it firmly to the side of the pitcher—a feat not possible in Earth's deep gravity well. Again, loading the brush, he gently began cementing the tiny pitcher to the top of the miniature table. "If I feel anything, *Rav-Tura'i*—if it is only anger—then I want out! Out!"

* * *

The sun completed its two-week journey across the sky. Another week extended the evening into midnight. Allon was watching 3V when the call sounded. Carefully, he balanced the communications center's switch between the "on" and the "off" position; a contact was made with a unit built separately from the Israeli-owned network.

"Your holograms at ze art show in Selene were a huge success, Monsieur."

"Drop the sarcasm" interrupted Allon. "I've been waiting for you to make contact. I've got an important message for you, Monsieur Nachon. I'm getting out!"

"Oh, I don't think so, Monsieur Ben Isaac. You see, it concerns that process for meteorite shielding zat you sold us." Nachon clucked his tongue. "Of course, you know zat ze real problem is not meteors, Monsieur. In fact, one could only expect a hit zat would cause real damage, say, once every 10,000 years? So! What we are really talking about is ze tiny bits of stone zat are launched from ze mass drivers. You and I both know zat with sufficient speed, a pea-sized rock can do ze damage of zeveral tons of TNT. We have found zat if ze stone is ze right shape and mass ..." Again, Nachon clucked his tongue. "Our leader, ze general, is *very* pleased! We can put *Svenglid* itself months behind? Of course, we must be discreet! The UN will look into it if we are too ..."

"I get your point!" Allon bit back. "If I stop now, you'll see that my government has me shot! With martial law in effect, nothing will stop them. What is it that you want?"

"Just one small favor, Monsieur. Zen we will be happy to let you go."

"Then it must be something big. What is it?"

"Sabotage, Monsieur."

Allon was silent for a long time. Stealing secrets was a passive activity—it fit with his personality. Sabotage was more active—and incriminating.

"Will anybody be hurt?"

"Possibly." There was a pause. "You will do it?"

"If I'm to be free of you, I'll have to."

"Ahhh," replied Nachon. "Ze kind of traitor zat ze general appreciates! One who will stop at nothing! I often wonder what a man like you feels, Monsieur."

Allon answered truthfully. "Not a thing," he said.

Another pause. "Tell me, Monsieur. How is it zat ore is transported to Hazera?"

"Mass driver. You know that."

"You have manned vehicles operated by your own company, *non*?"

"You mean the *Parrim*," answered Allon.

"*Oui*," said Nachon. "Ze ore is melted down and zome separation takes place on ze moon. *Non*?"

"It's melted and separated into usable ores here," said Allon. "Anthracite, ilmenite, and other compounds are poured into specially shaped ingots, loaded on the *Parrim* and *Parot*, and shot down the mass driver."

"Just so," replied Nachon. "One of zese ores has an appearance like black glass. You have a large kiln. I am certain zat you could make a hollow facsimile."

"They'd see right through it," answered Allon. "Those things mass at better than a ton!"

"It will be weighted, Monsieur. With a block of lead balanced at its center. Lead wool, so zat it won't shift around too much.

"Chilling metal or ore in a vacuum is always a problem, zo a series of coolants must carry ze heat outward through ze lunar soil. Zere is one such coolant zat is ideal! It has a low melting point and a high flash point. It is a magnificent conductor. It can carry heat for many kilometers. Alas! Zey cannot use it on Earth. For if it were to meet with an oxygen atmosphere—" Mentally, Allon could see Nachon make an exaggerated shrug. "Ha!" finished Nachon.

"You're talking about the intermediate magnesium coils."

"But of course!"

Immediately, Allon could see the plan. Through a bit of economic and political fumbling, Magen Metals had lost the use of a mass catcher at L2. All incoming material had to be unloaded at Hazera. Nobody would suspect a bomb the size of a desk and weighing better than a ton—it would most certainly be overlooked. The metal processing plants were in the same orbit as Hazera, but separate from it. The heat of melting and refining required that the workers wear 'hot suits' in temperatures of six and seven hundred degrees. During the refining process, oxygen was bubbled out of the ore. Eventually, it was blasted off into space as part of the factory's station-keeping requirements, or leeched carefully in all directions. Still, the oxygen levels inside the factories had been known to make substances as volatile as iron burn.

The ball mills consisted of huge cylinders rotating in micro G. Inside were huge spheres of almost indestructable ceramic crystal. Banging into the sides, crashing into one another, they were used to smash the great ingots into manageable powder.

A hard-pressed block of magnesium wool, sealed against the air by a glass covering, would enter the ball mill only to be smashed into blue-white incandescence. The destruction would be enormous! Magnesium under those conditions would burn so rapidly it would explode. Coolant coils, leading to the factory's great radiating fins, would melt. Pumps would be welded shut or vaporize entirely. The rest of the huge structure could not withstand, or contain, the heat.

So Allon found himself waiting outside of one of the pump rooms that pushed the molten magnesium through the cooling coils. The airlock leading to the little room had been cycled, which meant that the problem with the pump had to be electrical. No one in his right mind would expose molten magnesium to breathable air. Allon could not afford to be found here—there would be far too many questions to answer. Without giving a thought to the morality of his actions, Allon picked up a jagged piece of slag, and placed his helmet against the coolness of the refrigerated, pressurized room. The gurgle of coolant boiling echoed through the lining of his helmet. For long moments, he waited. At last there was a click and the sound of air being pumped back into holding tanks. The red light above the airlock changed to green and the door opened. As the man emerged, Allon grabbed him from behind. It took three blows against the man's face plate before the glass was finally broken. The gold leaf, so thin as to be transparent, no longer protected the man's face against the harsh infrared radiation of the surrounding walls. But it didn't matter. The repairman was already dead from explosive decompression.

Chapter IV

The bed in Greenberg's room may have been padded, but it didn't have to be. It was equipped with elastic sheets, which he found himself clutching once the slippers were off. The snap of an elastic sleeve sent his shirt sailing toward the center of the room. He decided to leave it. He knew he'd find it plastered against the suction of a nearby ventilation grill in the morning.

They breakfasted on eggs, olives, and perch in sour cream, with freeze-dried pineapple as a sort of dessert. Paul found the combination different, but was already missing bacon. The large readout screen was showing an entertainment in Hebrew. One of the crew members had been nice enough to program Gollum, the on-board computer, for English subtitles.

Paul wasn't sure that he liked all this sour cream. Sooner or later, it was sure to affect his digestion.

Dr. Goldstein walked up behind him in the mess and tapped him lightly on the shoulder. "As soon as you finish your breakfast, there's something that we'd like to show you."

When Paul had finished and placed his utensils in the cleanser, Goldstein motioned him toward the door.

"It is unfortunate," he said as they entered the narrow hallway, "that you didn't come at the time of the full moon, as you see it from Earth. Then you

64

would have seen a sight! But no matter. I'll show you a projection of our new moon later on.

"Our biggest expanse of clear glass is in the control room. I've asked the captain's permission to let us enter. Straight ahead there."

Goldstein led him through an additional set of double doors. The control room was quite large by most of the standards of space flight. Goldstein and Greenberg were separated from the main control center by a low railing. The center was divided into two sections by the cylindrical hump of a great bar magnet—protection against solar storms. Facing the huge window were two seats. One held the captain/pilot, Brezinski. The other was occupied by Orah Zamaroni.

Dr. Goldstein spoke a word and Greenberg found himself hanging on for dear life as the ship spun around. Paul nearly toppled over the railing and into the forward glass.

The captain and Orah doubled up in laughter, as Goldstein spoke sharply in Hebrew.

"Yeah!" barked Greenberg. "Whatever he said goes double for me! I could have put my foot through that glass!" He was tired of being picked upon. "Are you people crazy?"

The impressive view of the lunar farside was blinded by his anger. "I might have hit one of the controls," he continued.

Goldstein spoke, translating Paul's statement.

Brezinski placed one foot against the now-closed panel, did a shuffling sidestep that bounded him from a side wall to the ceiling and landed him against the rear bulkhead, where he squatted, looking down on the two men like a leering gargoyle. He almost laughed again at Paul's startlement, but the Hebrew tones were low and menacing.

"He says that the ship was programmed to turn after a 30-second pause. By the time the ship made the turn, the panels were covered."

Brezinski's hands went to his hips. "You want to make something of it?" said his expression.

Paul heaved a sigh of anger and disgust, whirled about, and pressed the switch that opened the door. Storming from the room seemed to be strictly a terrestrial habit—one did not "storm" in zero G. He moved too fast and found his feet leaving the floor. He was drifting, rather than storming. His ears burned as laughter exploded behind him.

"Dr. Greenberg. Dr. Greenberg!" shouted Goldstein with some distress.

Paul felt Goldstein's hands helping him to the floor. "Please, Dr. Greenberg. I must apologize! Captain Brezinski has never behaved this way before. I'll be certain to see that Magen Metals has him suspended, at the very least!

"Come!" Goldstein continued. "Let us go into the mess. There is some sacramental wine there. Have a drink with me—it will settle your nerves."

"What about putting my foot through the glass? You didn't translate that possibility, did you?"

"Glass is cheap here and the mass driver is designed for launching great weight. Therefore, the glass is too thick for that to be a possibility. I'm sorry, I—"

"Didn't want me to appear more of an 'earthworm' than I already am?"

"They don't realize that some people weren't raised in this environment. They know no other."

"That was an action of more than harmless amusement. I could have been hurt in there! That was outright animosity! My superiors will certainly hear of this, Dr. Goldstein."

He was silenced by a wave of Goldstein's hand. "Come," he said, stepping toward the mess. "Have you ever had a cat, Dr. Greenberg?"

Paul shook his head.

"Part of the animal's appeal is its independence. But a cat is *not* independent, and the animal knows it. There follows a grudging acceptance. We used to have a cat when I was a boy," Goldstein laughed. "When she was angry with us, she would literally stomp about the house. It was very funny. Thud, thud, thud, across the carpet. Perhaps I'm being anthropomorphic, but I used to think that the cat was making fun of the way we move. I don't know, but Jews are like that cat. We are dependent on people of other faiths for our survival, and we resent that dependence. The rest of the world has been a cruel and sadistic master. I don't need to back that up—history speaks for itself. Isolated as we are, coupled with our awareness of history, and the fact that we're experiencing a great many troubles with roots in anti-Semitism, we do tend to distrust outsiders. A good deal of our industry has been destroyed. We expect to be engaged only in information services unless the plague is conquered. And a Jew can have no friends, because he cannot tell who his friends are—especially now." Goldstein handed him a drinking tube. "Do you understand?"

Paul wrinkled his forehead. "I think so," he said. "Your wine's too sweet to get drunk on."

Goldstein slapped him on the shoulder. "Then as two Jews, we are two friends." he stated. "I agree with you that the wine is too sweet." His face became stern for a moment. "Most of your problems stem from some silly rumors going around that Svenglid is not just a space probe—that some great secret surrounds it. There is political loyalty to Hazera and every man views a UNi as a spy."

Paul's forehead wrinkled in thought. *Then the rumors aren't just going on back home*, he thought. *And I am a spy*.

"You must call me Yonah," interrupted Goldstein.

"And I'm Paul," returned Greenberg.

"I take it that your parents weren't good Jews, either."

"How is that?"

"It is not often that one meets a Jew named Paul," Goldstein answered.

He left Greenberg to puzzle that out.

Although they did not return to the control room, Paul did manage to see a projection of the moon's farside that had been taken in its darkest splendor. He had been told that the lighting was natural and that no false colors had been added. It was beautiful! *Oomi Mi*, the gigantic radio telescope, was a flashing pentagonal jewel that filled Mare Moscoviense. Goldstein pointed out a tiny flashing green light which marked *Unterirdische Mondstation I*, a neutrino research laboratory 10 kilometers beneath the lunar surface. The lunar cities that flecked the darkness were clearly visible from Earth, but the terrestrial atmosphere dimmed their splendor.

As he got into bed that night, Paul thought of the courage with which the Hazera'i were facing the plague. The Little Man had warned him that it had become a new pornography—it wasn't to be talked about unless that conversation was absolutely necessary. The fact that Hazera was still a-building, 12 sections which would eventually grow into a torus, helped confine the plague to two, then three of those sections. In the remaining nine "houses," life went on as best it could. The plague was mentioned as little as possible. The symptoms—the running sores, the dizziness, the nausea, the convulsions, the coma, and death—were not mentioned at all.

The atmosphere aboard the *Harpo Martz* began to lighten considerably as the week neared its end. Even the Hebrew-speaking crew began to lighten in their animosity.

"What gives?" asked Paul of Yonah, as Orah sang out a happy *shalom*.

"Tonight is *Shabbat* eve," explained Yonah. "It is traditional to have one who does not celebrate *Shabbat* over for dinner. So, tonight and tomorrow, you are looked on no longer as an enemy, but a guest."

"I see," said Paul, still bitter. "The token *goy*."

The next day, for the first time in his life, he found himself in *Shul*. None of the entertainment appliances in his room were functioning. Gollum would not carry on a conversation, and indeed would do nothing but the most elementary problems. He had slipped back a century. For a moment, he unfolded the dator from his pocket, unrolled the screen, and thought. Then he folded up the tiny machine and walked down the hallway to the rec room/synagogue. There was a short break for lunch. Like the dinner the night before, it had been prepared by hand and was now kept warm in heated tile boxes. Goldstein was kind enough to translate for him, since all of the service was conducted in Hebrew. As Paul began to get bored and the novelty to end, the day and the Sabbath was over.

Chapter V

Paul was awakened by a chiming in his room. It took him a moment to place himself. "Time to get up, Dr. Greenberg," said Goldstein's voice through a grill above his head. "*Harpo Martz* is docking in 45 minutes." A tray opened from beneath the writing desk and Paul gulped hot coffee from an insulated tube.

"Have we cleared for a conversation with Professor Cohen?" asked Paul, dressing in midair.

"*Ken*. The docking bay is only a short distance from the Knesset. The Knesset, of course, was infected about three years ago, so you can't see her personally. We've arranged for a television linkup, however. Maximum security, as you've asked."

"Fish for breakfast, again?"

Goldstein could be heard chuckling. "We've arranged for some coffee, juice, toast, and cream cheese. You'll have to be quick."

"I'll meet you in the dining hall," returned Paul, already struggling into the magnetic slippers. He shaved and quickly exited.

Ms. Israel smiled warmly as he entered. "*Boker tov*," she said.

"Uh, *boker tov*," he returned uncertainly.

"Good morning," said Goldstein. "I've had *Hazera* transmit those circuit diagrams that you requested.

70

You can check them out while you eat. There are a total of 6,000 fail-safe codes to prevent discharge of the erosion cloud, before Svenglid is up to full speed."

Paul smiled and shook his head in near disbelief.

With a gentle rocking motion, the *Parr* docked on its attitude jets. The rest of the people rose slowly from the table to gather bags and effects. Paul had already packed, so he rushed back to his room to gaze out of the huge window.

There was nothing to see but the stars. These were blanked out slowly by the insertion of the *Parr*'s command module into a narrow docking sleeve. It was as though a curtain had been slowly drawn across the stars. There was only blackness. Paul sighed.

"KE-WHUP!"

Four electromagnetic deadbolts popped out of the command module's side, locking it into position. Two innertube-shaped seals, circling the *Parr* in front and behind the deadbolts, inflated.

"WHUSHHH!"

"Nothing to see from here," said Goldstein's voice through the open doorway.

There was a growing hiss as the docking bay-turned-airlock was pressurized.

"Come across the way," he continued.

Paul and Yonah entered a vacant room. Half of the cylindrical airlock, into which the *Parr*'s command module had been inserted, began to rotate, a long doorway sliding upward and across into its appointed slot.

The enormous spherical room easily enclosed a cubic kilometer. Airlock-docking bays for the *Parrim* projected inward, giving the loading area the appearance of a harbor mine turned inside out. Connecting these was a spider's web of thin rails leading to four beams. Down these, nets rushed to an exit port. Tiny figures were busy unloading a *Parr* nearby. The rails must have been connected some way—probably ra-

dio and computer—for when one of these was moved,
three others followed it. Three of the four rails were
telescoping guides, down which ran belts of hooks.
The hooks were carrying huge ingots toward the rushing nets at the center. There, the ingots were caught,
vanishing through a large circular doorway. The fourth
rail was a guide, fitting through a hole in the ingot's
center. As such, it was much sturdier than the other
three.

The scene changed as the command module slowly
spun on its great hinges, rotating away from the
cargo bay. When they were looking directly across
the great chamber, the command module stopped.
The *Parr*'s airlock door now connected with another.

A workman drifted slowly by outside, giving them
a friendly wave. They waved back.

"We'd better get going," said Dr. Goldstein. "You've
spent the past three days in zero G. Do you think you
might be ill if you were to drift around for a while?"

Paul thought for a moment and then shook his
head.

Captain Brezinski glared at them as they approached
the airlock. Goldstein explained their delay in Hebrew,
but the captain's gaze didn't change. He shook Paul's
hand.

"*Tsar li,*" Brezinski began, continuing in Hebrew.

"He says that he would like to apologize for some
of the things that happened during the trip," translated Yonah.

"I can see by that look on his face that he really
means it," Paul answered sarcastically.

Goldstein turned from them both to chuckle in uncertainty. Brezinski added more.

"He hopes that the trip was otherwise a pleasant
one and he wishes you a peaceful and happy stay in
Hazera."

"Be certain to thank the captain," said Paul. Then,
in his politest tones, Paul added several additional
rude comments.

The captain smiled and nodded politely.

Goldstein grimaced and refused to translate.

Brezinski headed in the direction of the control room for an unstated purpose; Paul and Yonah stepped into the airlock. "Put your luggage in that box, there," Yonah pointed. "Hang on to your overnight bag. I would imagine that you'll be wanting to freshen up before meeting the prime minister." He looked at his watch. "We still have a couple of hours yet. Perhaps you'd like to take a dip in the hub pool—unless you're prone to motion sickness. I'd imagine that and spacesickness are the same thing, aren't they?

"*Ken*. The hub pool is in the shape of a ring and is rotating rather rapidly to keep the water in place. Your magnetic slippers go into that box over there. You'll be able to pick up your suitcases at my place. I'm having them sent on ahead."

Paul noticed that two armed guards were floating outside the airlock, waiting for them. He sucked in a breath and saw that Yonah failed to take heed of them.

"Put the strap around your wrist," Yonah said.

"Huh?" The guards had momentarily startled Paul.

"On your overnight case! Put the strap around your wrist!"

"Oh."

"You okay?"

"Yeah," returned Paul. "I'm fine. Who are these two clowns?"

"You did ask for top security until your meeting with Professor Cohen, did you not?"

The two men floated on either side of them, moving an arm or leg occasionally in the flapping semi-swim of micro gravity. Paul knew enough not to talk to either of them, assuming that they did speak English. He noticed that Yonah chose to do likewise. Paul remembered his training as a bodyguard for UN bigwigs. You weren't to know the subject that you were protecting. It was more than acting as a humorless robot. It was the best way to remain on the alert. Just who his enemies might be, Paul didn't know. There was the possibility that the codes had been broken—that the maser sent ahead to Hazera might have attracted other ears. Paul bit his lower lip. Yonah had obviously dealt with hardline security people before. They were to be perfect subjects for protection. The two could not be distracted from their job, and Paul knew that they would do their best to discourage any friendly conversation.

Yonah grasped a handle near the door and drifted out of the airlock. The four of them were in a narrow, gently curving corridor. One of the security people grasped a strap and hung on, waiting for Paul and Yonah to reach him. He released the strap when Paul caught up.

The guard hung there, looking over his shoulder, while Yonah explained the intricacies of what could only be called a micro G escalator, which formed one wall of the chamber. He pointed to a series of rungs, moving slowly.

"It's a little tricky, but not too difficult. Grab one of the rungs. Centrifugal force is quite light here, so you'll have to look 'down' to see when your feet come in contact with the lower rung. Brace yourself against it with your hands."

During the pause that followed, the security man gave them a demonstration, and Goldstein followed, launching himself toward the ladder. Paul found the maneuver quite easy. The other guard followed close behind.

"What was this about a pool?" Paul finally asked.

"Oh, yes. The hub pool. Well, it's the only place in Hazera where you can spring off the high dive and still hit the water while going straight 'up'. We use centrifugal force for gravity, of course, and in order to put a pool in the hub, we had to shape it like a doughnut. We've got the longest diving board in the known universe."

While Paul couldn't see Yonah's face, the voice held a hint of a smile. "The pool used to connect with the hotel 'below' it. But we found that newcomers had a hard time figuring out where they'd be coming down—from the diving board, that is."

Paul looked ahead of them to a door which was slowly approaching. "Grab one of the handholds next to the door," Goldstein instructed. "Be ready for a somersault. Otherwise, your inertia will twist you around and you might have to let go."

Paul smiled to himself. It amused him to see as distinguished a man as Goldstein—a man of late middle age—swinging about like an acrobat. But he followed Goldstein's example and was soon floating beside him. The forward guard twisted a handle and the doors slid open. Paul guessed it was some sort of an airlock. When the guard who was following had entered, Goldstein twisted another handle and the door closed behind him. Paul found himself drifting back in the direction from which they had just come. Then he realized that it was not himself but the room that was moving. They must have been crossing an intervening space of hard vacuum. It was obvious that they were moving to a torus which was in motion around the stationary docking sphere. Six thousand years of engineering had still failed to produce a seal between rotating surfaces. Paul heard the clank, whirr, and hiss of locks and inflation seals. The room tilted and moved into a slot recessed into the wall of the torus. A door on the opposite side of the car opened. Upon drifting out into the hallway, Paul found that there was enough centrifugal "gravity" to keep him kicking away the floor.

"The pool is through here," Goldstein pointed. "It doubles as a *mikveh*, now. Some of the more Orthodox among us like to purify themselves after coming up from the moon. Nudism is a natural for the Japanese in a shirt-sleeve environment, if you spend most of your time in a space suit. Unfortunately, a good many of the Selenite women are desirable, even if you're dealing with 3V. Nudism for us is forbidden by Rabbinic Law, so it's hard to get used to."

"Sort of a sacred cold shower," observed Dr. Greenberg.

The two guards' magnetic shoes came in contact with the metallic surface of the floor. Greenberg looked at them jealously.

Goldstein was laughing at Paul's observation. "Exactly," he said. "The washing away of unclean thoughts."

"But a diving board?"

"The Chassidim started it after the coming of the plague. The *mikveh* is a swimming pool just as *matzoh* is good with hard-boiled eggs. *Matzoh* is *not* just for Passover."

"Then I can really swim?"

"Of course."

Paul enjoyed the water and the centrifugal gravity, even though Goldstein sobered him by standing waist deep in the water for a long moment of prayer. "I told you that I tried to be a good Jew," he explained after dunking himself.

Paul ate lunch, the first he'd had since entering the *Parr*. He then took a short walk to a room in the empty hotel. One of the guards checked ahead of him and then returned to take a station with the other, outside the door.

Paul was awakened by Goldstein ringing at the door. He found that he had just time to shower, shave, and dress for the meeting with Prime Minister Cohen. The elevator that they boarded took them down several floors. The gravity was one G "normal" when it stopped. An opening door was flanked by two more armed guards. Predictably, those guards who were already with them preceded them into the hallway. The guards who had met them at the door took up stations, marching behind.

"You appreciate the security?" asked Goldstein.

Paul was somewhat flustered and a little embarrassed. "Yes," he said.

"The additional guards were mostly necessary for the laying out of your video connection. We had to make sure that there was no way it could be tapped. The computer is opened for your disc, and we've arranged to have a cap placed on any information that the disc contains."

Paul nodded. They walked through a carefully guarded door. A "cap" consisted of a coded pair of mathematical functions: an encoder and a decoder. Each of them was based on a prime factor of a large number. Even a century after its development, there was no easy way to find just what that cap was. Paul guessed that the Hazera caps were like those used by the UN. The ones at the UN would require 15 million years to work out, on the fastest computers.

He smiled. The Israelis had a lot of practice at security. He wondered what other secrets those caps might be hiding.

One of the guards motioned to a door in a long hallway. Two more armed guards stood on either side of it. Like the first two, they both checked his ID card. This was passed through a slot that, on a readout screen, translated its printed surface into Hebrew. One of them looked at the screen and then nodded to the other. The double doors hissed open.

"I'll wait outside," said Goldstein.

Paul found himself in a room little larger than a closet. He sat in the single chair, rolled up his sleeve, and pressed what appeared to be a freckle on his artificial arm. The syntheflesh folded away, leaving the bare mechanism by which the arm operated. As he reached for a data disc, concealed in a small compartment, the opposite wall began to clarify.

He quickly set the disc on the console, resealed the "wound," and pulled down his sleeve as the three-dimensional image of Professor Cohen solidified. Her eyebrows shot up.

Instantly, Paul's senses tingled. His voice was being checked with some sort of lie-detecting device. The best method of acting is to become the part you are playing, so Paul filled his body with the sort of strain one might feel in meeting the matriarch of Hazera. With luck, it might cover any lies that the device was capable of detecting. Paul flushed his face with embarrassment as he quickly buttoned his sleeve.

"I'm dreadfully sorry, Madam Prime Minister!" he exclaimed.

The cobweb of wrinkles that made up her face deepened into a smile. "That's quite all right," she said. "I've seen artificial arms before—but with so many compartments! And a gun! Goodness!"

Paul's blush deepened. "Terribly sorry!" he blurted. "I have, of course, several reasons for coming to Hazera. My meeting with you is top secret. If any of the other cities knew that I was carrying top secret information concerning Svenglid, my superiors feared that there might be trouble."

Rachel Cohen nodded. "Indeed, there would have been," she answered. "There's no need to apologize for carrying a weapon. Besides, we knew you were carrying it when you entered."

Paul smiled in mock relief. "How much else do you know about what I carry?"

"Quite a bit," Rachel answered. "But nothing for which someone in your position would not have a use. The telescopic eye is a tremendous device for examining something the size of Svenglid. The pneumatic solenoid that you've placed in your space helmet is a means for controlling the eye's power of magnification."

Paul bit his lower lip. He had expected her to have intelligence sources, but how much else did they know?

"So," continued the prime minister. "What causes

a young gentleman like yourself to disturb a lonely old woman?"

"I would like, first of all, to thank you for the tremendous improvements that your people have made in Svenglid's design. The amount of fuel that must be consumed in getting her up to speed is one thing. But to add the fuel to slow her down!"

Professor Cohen waved a hand, clucking her tongue. "It was really nothing! After all, the carbonacious asteroids are too dangerous to mine on that scale. Therefore, we had to develop disposable scoops to harvest the Jovian atmosphere. The fuel itself is not expensive, but developing the technology to obtain it was. Once the ships were in production, and deuterium was being obtained, the additional fuel to slow Svenglid was cheap. The prospectors in the asteroid belt are understandably jealous of our new technologies—we'll never have to buy water, carbon, or nitrogen again—and jealousy breeds violence. Originally, we planned to build Svenglid around Callisto. However, the *Yas'arot*—our scoopships—had to be built with too many defense mechanisms for us to trust placing a manned station so near the prospectors. Even with all the sophisticated devices with which the *Yas'arot* have been equipped, they still have a failure rate that is close to 20 percent. You can bet that it would be closer to 2 percent if they weren't being deliberately destroyed. Besides, a good deal of the materials that would go to waste at Callisto we can use here.

"Our fail-safes and the sophistication of Svenglid's circuitry design were merely a matter of waiting until the engines, fuel tanks, and support assemblies were built. By then, designing a computer of human intelligence was child's play. Of the three interstellar probes, we are certain that Svenglid will be the one to succeed! Placing it in orbit around Proxima Centauri and then having it proceed to Alpha A and B has its advantages. I daresay that Svenglid will be broadcasting back information a thousand years from now.

"Now let's see that disc that you found so embarrassing to conceal within your arm."

Paul fit the disc into its slot and pressed a stud. Although marked in Hebrew, it was in the usual position for "play."

His guess was right. A large piece of paper or plastic appeared to unroll between them. On it was a picture of one of the early astronauts on the moon. The poster was made to look like the front page of a 20th century newspaper. The headline over the picture was as meaningless to Paul as it would have been over a picture of Columbus on San Salvadore. It read: "So What?"

Rachel Cohen leaned back in her chair. Her eyes carried the twinkle of a smile.

"This is a reproduction," said a recorded voice, "of a mass-produced art form popular during the late 1960s and early 1970s, designed to be attached to the walls of a home or office for short periods of time. Many carried political or social commentary.

"The early efforts of NASA moved ahead sporadically. Because the benefits of a space program reached the public slowly, their origins were often unrecognized. Many believed the space programs to be worthless. Indeed, worse, for it was a widely held belief that the money spent on space programs could alleviate poverty, feed the hungry, and solve a vast number of social ills—social ills that turned out to have far more complex solutions. Solutions so complex, in fact, that the application of mere currency now seems ludicrous."

"Yes," muttered Rachel Cohen. "I remember."

On the screen between them flashed still pictures of early manned space launches, then vast crowds of demonstrators.

"But this feeling was counterbalanced by a feeling that the United States government was too huge, too expensive—that it was bleeding both itself and its citizens on nonessentials. The space shuttle, the last of its great bursts into space, was sold to private industry, and the bulk of that private industry was overseas. Whatever could be done to aid the American economy came too little and too late. The American Republic ended in military coup and the revolution that followed.

"Israel continued, out of necessity, to refine her technology. Dependent upon it for survival, refining and improving it became a fact of life." The prime minister became solemn as scenes of actual combat footage were shown. "For Israel had, by the time of her final war, spread a broad political and economic base over the rest of the world. It was time to begin again." Impressive shots were shown of the early Israeli colonists boarding primitive shuttles, settling on the moon, and building the mass driver. Finally, Hazera in its present form flashed on.

"Buttering up the employee?" asked Rachel.

Paul blushed.

"It is with the Israelis that the UN places its final hope, within the 21st century, of successfully launching an interstellar probe. After two failures, the public mind is again turning against continuing our expanse of pure knowledge. History has shown that any nation that becomes dissatisfied with itself ceases to move. Eventually, stagnation and decay set in. The government and basic culture is now, however, worldwide and, being an international republic, we cannot risk following the examples of the United States, Rome, and the Weimar Republic.

"The UN's space program has become a prime target for those expressing dissatisfaction with the UN's workings. Like the NASA of the 20th century, money expended on interstellar exploration is being considered waste—a waste of money and a waste of time that could be better used in solving our social ills.

"Fortunately, decreases in the expense of technology have met with the budget cuts that followed the failures of the two previous probes. Perhaps Hazera has been wondering why so many useful and beneficial space projects have been abandoned in favor of Svenglid, and why Svenglid must fly so near lightspeed, despite the enormous consumption of fuel required.

"On May 2, 2079, a panel of experts on historical psychology was assembled under the auspices of the International Space Program Director. The results of the panel show that Svenglid must show results and show them within 12 years—if additional probes are to be built and launched before the latter half of the 22nd century.

"Computer models show that public opinion is riding with Svenglid. The continued survival of the UN as a republic may well depend on Svenglid's reaching her target star.

"As for the economic and social benefits for Hazera, there is no doubt in the panel's mind that the success of Svenglid will bring about no less than five authorizations for interstellar probes. The contract will, of course, be awarded to that city which has built the only previous successful probe. Your city—Hazera. The UN need not stress this economic importance to a city already under great economic and social stress. Five additional probes will employ millions of Hazera's citizens who are now expensive wards of the state. They will also provide equipment and money for the eventual conquest of Hazera's epidemiological problem.

"So, we of the UN would like to thank Hazera for bringing together a starship of unbelievable design, at well under cost. Our best wishes and *mazel tov*.

"This recording is self-erasing and cannot be replayed."

"Well!" said Professor Cohen. "I can see why this is

top secret. I know how the public feels about having itself manipulated. If this got out—"

Paul nodded.

"*Nu!*" said the prime minister. "So, now I know why you ordered the ship as you did, and why we had to step up production on the *Yas'arot*. I know how much time it took to finish Svenglid. Now, I know the reasons!

"Okay, Dr. Greenberg," she sighed. "I would like to repeat our request to the UN concerning official protection."

Greenberg raised a brow. "I'm afraid," he said, "that the UN anticipated this request. Should the subject be raised again, I have been told to remind you of the demands being made by the terrestrial population to increase the fleets in orbit around Earth. While we are concerned for all of the orbital cities, the UN must first look after its own interests. We are aware of our image as something of a thorn in the space cities' sides. It would be a simple matter for one of them to casually drop a 200-ton asteroid on Geneva. Those ships are to divert that asteroid and punish those responsible. Surely you must be aware of the problems of enforcement. A call for help from Hazera couldn't be answered for several days. From Near Lunar Orbit, the time factor would scarcely be better.

"We are aware of the difficult station-keeping requirements of L2. Even Hazera's somewhat more stable halo orbit is no guarantee that it might not fall into the moon. However, even assuming that Hazera should lose its equilibrium, by the time we could add emergency jets the necessary thrust would do nothing but break your city to pieces."

"That the city might lose equilibrium is the least of our problems," interrupted the prime minister. "What we are principally worried about is sabotage by other cities—principally, particles of stone accelerated to high velocity."

Paul laughed. "Small stuff," he said. "One can anticipate that sort of thing and guard against it."

"We're assuming that the plague was artificially induced," said the prime minister. "One can scarcely call that small stuff."

"Unless you can prove that the plague is artificial, it would be best to leave that out of the conversation," Paul warned. "Yes, I'll have to agree that enforcement is a problem. Let's suppose a rock were thrown at Hazera. Assuming that the UN fleet were in orbit around the moon, they *could* plot the path of the stone back to its source, and they would have the jurisdiction to punish the offenders. However, a fleet in Near Lunar Orbit presupposes a good deal. Such a fleet would be composed of pilots and technicians from Terra, if we want loyalty to the UN, and such a fleet presupposes that there be a city for exercise. There are no graduating levels of G force on Terra. There are only two things that we could do about that. One would be to enlarge one of the cities in Near Earth Orbit. That would be cheapest. But given a reasonable tour of duty, that means that our technicians could spend up to four months just getting themselves in shape to go home. The other is cost-prohibitive. That would be to build a city in Near Lunar Orbit—and this would not only mean exercise rooms, but recreation centers, fueling and docking facilities, repair and maintenance centers." Paul shook his head. "The list is endless, and Hazera is in no economic position to pay for all this!"

"We could provide fuel," put in Professor Cohen hopefully.

"Yes," said Paul. "Possibly tainted with your virus. Your materials processing systems would have closed down a long time ago if it weren't for Svenglid. *That* should be your main concern. Neither you nor the UN can afford to rob Peter to pay Paul. Svenglid cost trillions of UN francs, but it was paid over a 25-year period. We can't afford the additional trillion or so francs that it would take to build such installations—especially for what is surely a temporary problem."

Rachel leaned back in her chair and folded her arms. "Then perhaps," she said, "the problem can be attacked from another, less expensive angle. Susan Gold's disc, *Ha'Texi*, is a best-seller. I understand that a dramatization is planned. Surely the likelihood of something like that recurring . . ."

"Excuse me?" said Paul.

"Tsli'kha," answered Rachel, making another meaningless sound. "What I meant to say was, *The Texan.*"

"Oh, yes!" replied Paul. "The novel!"

"Perhaps the facts that the novel has brought out will bring about relaxation of the Texas Willie ruling."

Paul shook his head.

Texas Willie had been one of the early "characters" of asteroidal mining. Although he had been raised in New Jersey, he identified strongly with the prospectors of the 19th century—even going so far as to have his disk-shaped ship decorated with a Frederick Remington painting. The interior was as spacious and comfortable as that of a good many asteroidal mining ships, and like the others, it was heavily armed and armored. There, on his trips sunward, he entertained French women that he'd pick up for high prices at L-5. Moving into near earth orbit, after his sales to the tiny French and West German cities, he demanded cases of bourbon and "gen-yu-wine" Idaho vodka. The walls of his ship's spinning interior were decked with ancient rifles and pistols. The walls themselves were made with the look and feel of stucco and unplaned wood. When one leaned against the wall, Texas Willie would always jokingly ask them to "watch out fer splinters."

But Texas Willie was not that unusual. The trip out to the asteroid belt took a little better than a year—a time of boredom. Few had the psychology to stand such periods of loneliness. And those who did developed "tastes." Usually, a certain form or branch of literature, art, or music would take a miner's fancy. By the time a find had been made, that fancy had developed into a mania. If they were lucky, the mania would be wide in scope. If they were not so fortunate, they would find themselves suddenly in the depths of space with their mania complete. And for some obscure psychological reason, their minds had frozen into their interest. An emotion much like grief prevented them from searching for another. With every line memorized, every note, every brush stroke, some would spin about, firing their engines for a return voyage. But by the time they reached a point where an engine burn would put them safely in orbit around Terra, they were too insane to make that burn. They never returned.

Western fandom was a "safe" mania, and widespread. The broad base of literature, dramatization, and song insured a long life of study, and a good market for 20-franc discs—the 21st century equivalent of the pulp magazine.

Robot probes to the asteroid belt were cheap. And robot probes to the asteroid belt might have lasted if it hadn't been for a single, dangerous mineral—Lawrencite.

Lawrencite's crystalline structure often hid deep in the gigantic masses of nickel iron, invisible to the standard infrared spectrometers. When this iron chloride was heated, exposed to oxygen or water, it created havoc. Superheated chlorine had been known to digest metallic parts in minutes. Under the right conditions, it had been known to explode! Therefore, it was far more effective to buy from human prospectors who would laser the asteroids into thin sections, checking for the deadly material.

Once an IR reflection spectrometer told of nickel-iron, the prospector would immediately slice up the asteroid. If the IR spectrometer still showed no chlorine, then attitude jets would slow the sections in their orbit. Gathered into a wire and fiberglass "birdcage," they were sent in a long ellipse toward Earth.

Texas Willie had been a practical joker. It was often said that he conspired with his computer to fire an attitude jet when a "groundhog" guest was aboard. The resulting jolt could be enough to knock a visitor off his feet. "Musta been one of them damn meteors!" he would explain to a distraught planetbounder.

No doubt the disaster was another practical joke, but this one had gone sour. The load had been sent toward Earth. Texas Willie knew that it would not actually hit—the chances were a million to one. Earth shifted unpredictably through the slight interactions of other planets' gravitational and magnetic fields, the intensity of the solar wind, and the slight relativistic pause that Earth made at perigee.

In compliance with the requests of most cities, Willie registered the asteroid as stony iron—nickel-iron was the most valuable and therefore the most heavily taxed. While stone was used extensively in ceramics and glass, stony asteroids outnumbered the nickel-iron by 500 to one. Without telling Terra, Willie cobbled together an attitude jet with radar and a small computer. Why he hadn't realized that Terra would act in its own defense, nobody knew. The act occurred at a time of political crises, a time when the governments of Earth realized that they had given the UN enough power to usurp their own. Willie's asteroid became a show of power to the people of Terra by the UN. The small chance that it might hit the planet was blown out of proportion by the press. As it was, Terra launched a missile aimed at Willie's "birdcage."

After the destruction of New York and Moscow, the UN had to show that it was a protector and not only a destroyer. However, the missile had been built to destroy a *stony iron* asteroid. They hadn't counted on Willie's registering it as any more than what it really was. Instead of the explosion breaking up the asteroid into pieces small enough to burn harmlessly in Earth's atmosphere, chunks of nickel iron swept across central India. Fortunately, only 43 people were killed. It was enough. If it hadn't been for the launch of the missile, the "birdcage" would have swung past Terra in a hyperbola that would have brought it to the French cities of L-5. The onboard computer and attitude jet-radar unit would have made sure of that. But the radar-computer-attitude jet package had been destroyed in the explosion. "Willie hunting" became a major sport of the cities for the next 15 years.

It was the French who finally caught up with him. The coup on board Paris Nouveau had taken place and Villeneuve had taken over as dictator—a power that still held. Coldly, cruelly, they locked Willie outside his own ship, transmitting images of Willie's death agony as his oxygen supply slowly leaked into space.

Susan Gold's book, *The Texan*, some 25 years after the events actually transpired, reopened the case. While she sympathized with the UN, she painted an extremely ugly picture of Villeneuve. The book was unheard of at L-5.

In answer to Rachel Cohen's request, Paul slowly shook his head. Each city was now allowed to bring in only one asteroid at a time, and each asteroid or asteroidal fragment could mass no more than a thousand tons, so the orbital companies had grown until the growth had reached its legal limit. Attempts were made to bypass the laws by building additional tiny cities, but these attempts were quickly quashed. A large UN fleet had been placed in Near Earth Orbit to watch and guard against violators.

"No, I'm afraid that the Willie ruling still stands. We are, after all, altering natural orbits in the direction of the Earth-Moon system. All Susan has set in the minds of the public is that it *was* a terrible accident on the part of the UN. The public is still aware that asteroidal mining increases the chances of the disaster reccurring."

Rachel folded her arms. "The Germans don't concern us," she said. "They are working on developing a means of bringing factories directly to the asteroid belt and shipping the finished products back. Needless to say, they are meeting with considerable opposition from independent prospectors, but the prospectors are about as organized as the pirates of the 17th century. Technology should eventually stomp such independents. The only reason that we lost 20 percent of the *Yas'arot* to them is because it is cheaper to lose them than pay for additional protective devices.

"It would quiet us if the French cities were following the German; however, they are *not!* Every industry has to grow, and the Willie ruling prevents this, unless industry is moved to the asteroid belts!

"Within 30 years, the production of the French cities will have fallen drastically behind. They will be economically dead within a century.

"Our only conclusion is that they have their eyes on lunar mining—and that means taking our mass catcher at L-2."

"But the only way that they could do that—" began Paul.

"Is to destroy Hazera," finished Rachel Cohen.

Paul's mind reeled. The woman was serious, and obviously quite mad! Reason was taught in schools all over the world. In space—in the French cities themselves—the basic morality on which every religion was based was mutually agreed upon and taught! Murder, theft, and vice still continued, but not on the scale the prime minister was talking about—not the carefully organized murder of 5 million men, women, and children whose only crime was to exist!

"It happened in the last century," mocked a voice within his mind. "The bombing of New York," continued another. "Hitler was before the control of the UN," he answered the first voice. "The bombing of

New York was necessary," he told the second. As in any frontier society, there were squabbles among the cities. There were claim jumpers. There was sabotage. There were any of a hundred things that people did when money was involved, and control was impossible. But the destruction of an entire city was too noticeable to be blamed on error or nature. It was true that Paris Nouveau had tried to finance a short-lived flap of Neo-Nazism, but even with that imprint on human consciousness, it was doubtful that the UN would sanction—or worse, reward—such a crime.

Paul looked hard at the image of Rachel Cohen. She noticed his intense study of her and a slight smile touched her lips.

It was obvious to Paul that, as in all dictators, the fear of being assassinated, of losing her power, had overcome her reason. Isolated with her people, 63,000 kilometers beyond the moon, she had fallen into the deepest pits of paranoia. It was an old story. Like her, the people about her would be paranoid as well. It was a dangerous situation, one that he would certainly carry back to his employers.

Professor Cohen began absently pulling together discs on a desk before her. "You must forgive my blurting out such accusations," she said. "At least, before we have sufficient proof. Evidence is being gathered, however. We expect to present it to the UN in just a few years. *Oy!* But it is hard for such an old woman as myself to hold such responsibility. I understand that some of my own people already view me as a dictator. *Nu!* But the circumstances of the plague forced me to declare martial law. You *do* understand, don't you, Dr. Greenberg?"

Paul nodded absently. Could she have seen what he was thinking?

"I thank you for solving some of the mystery for us, Dr. Greenberg. I will pass the word on to a select few of the *Svenglid* team. I'm certain that they can be trusted.

"Oh! If you want to know more about Texas Willie, I'd suggest you speak with Susan Gold—Shoshanna Goldstein—Yonah's daughter."

Rachel laughed as Paul's face registered surprise. "Perhaps I'll have a chance to see you again. Let me assure you that we shall try our utmost to finish Svenglid by the stated date."

The three-dimensional image of Rachel Cohen faded from view.

A hundred meters away, she swiveled in her chair toward the lens set in the wall. Although she knew it was anthropomorphism, she occasionally thought she could see a twinkle in the cold glass of the computer's protective eye.

"Well, Gollum," she said. "I know that, with the cap on it, you can't remember the contents of Dr. Greenberg's disc. However, I'm not going to bother punching in the cap just now. If my judgments of the past are correct, you can remember your reactions to that disc."

"Yes," said a soft, feminine voice from the air. "Dr. Greenberg's disc struck me as quite reasonable."

Rachel sighed. "I know that you have other information concerning Svenglid beneath a cap. My question is this: Which is the most obvious solution to Hazera's protection—Svenglid as defined by the UN, or the *Ra*?"

"The answer should be no mystery," returned the computer. "Look at the screen. There given are the times and dates of the four attacks that have been made against Hazera since the beginning of the month of Elul. Do you see a pattern?"

"There are only four attacks," returned Rachel. "It would be difficult to find any pattern in so small a sample."

"Then let me print out the times and dates of the attacks for the month of Av."

"They look totally random to me," answered Rachel.

"That is just it," returned the computer. "They are and they are not. However, random chance would show that Hazera might expect a meteor collision once every 10,000 years. Yet as you can see, there was such a near collision 12 times last month alone. In the year 5843, we had some 20 attempts on Hazera, the combined total of which would result in 10 percent damages. Last year, the number of attempts was 6,836. The total estimated damage, had all been successful, was 44,277.926 percent. By the end of this year, the total number of successes will be nine."

"There have been eight, so far, this year," added Rachel.

"Now," continued Gollum. "If we check over the number of attempts that have been made since 5813, we find that this number has been increasing by 20 percent per year. By the same token, the total amount of estimated damage has increased by 30 percent. Last year, there were four attempts which would have destroyed Hazera completely. Next year, the integer for the number of attempts will be 9,844. The total estimated damage will be some 57,561.304 percent. Our espionage at L-5 tells us that when the number of attempts to destroy Hazera surpasses 10,000, it will no longer be cost effective to increase the number of attempts. What would you do if you were in the place of Nouveau Paris?"

"Increase the amount of damage that could be caused by 10,000 attempts," answered Rachel.

"Exactly," answered Gollum. "Hazera will not survive the five years it will take Svenglid to reach Alpha Centauri."

"Our chances?" asked Rachel. She looked at the screen and nodded to herself.

Chapter VI

August 20, 2086   Hub; Hazera Ysroel
Elul 10, 5846   Tuesday
10:40 a.m., Jerusalem Time

    Paul spent the rest of the day examining what he could of Svenglid through a telescope. Most of it was in the shadow of a great metallic disk. This was necessary to keep the great masses of deuterium in a frozen state—a difficult proposition this close to the sun.

    The disk itself was close to 15 kilometers in diameter. Svenglid's 30-kilometer length was protected, edge on, from the sun's rays. A series of similar disks ran Svenglid's length. Together with Faraday cages, reflecters, superconductors, and refrigeration equipment, they kept the ice at 3.1 degrees above absolute zero—as close to the three degrees of the surrounding vacuum as 21st century technology could achieve. Paul knew that if he could have seen into the elaborately designed series of shadows, there would have been 28 spheres of pale blue ice. Arranged in fours, they ran the length of Svenglid, each a kilometer in diameter.

    But the real technology of Svenglid lay in its structure and support. Once in motion, it would be held together by energy as much as by matter.

    The molecules of copper slide over one another so that it bends and fatigues easily. Tin is the same. Mix them, and the molecules interlock like the pieces of a puzzle, making a metal that is both hard and brittle. Now, imagine a metallurgy without gravity—the ability to combine metals that would float apart in a gravity well while still molten—and, along with that, the technology to design the crystalline structure of the metal itself!

Add to this the ability to produce gigogausses of magnetic energy, and you might solve the problems of constructing a skyscraper 30 kilometers high. But Svenglid was more than that. When its engines fired, flooding the moon itself with their brilliance, Svenglid would be accelerating at six Gs. The supports were for a building—no, a fuel tank—180 kilometers high! For two months, the engines would fire. Lasers would bounce back from mirrors, the absolute straightness of their beams balancing the ship perfectly. Flywheels would spin, turning it past chunks of matter that lay in its path. UV lasers on its nose would ionize dust and gas ahead. Its great superconducting magnets would pull in the resulting plasma, cycling it into its reaction chambers to mist with already abundant fuel.

When it reached a speed that approached that of light itself, the engines would cut off. Half of Svenglid's fuel would be gone, burned away, with half its tanks and support members thrown in to provide additional reaction mass.

Ahead of Svenglid, a cloud of metallic dust would blossom, the speed and grittiness of which would erode away small objects which lay in its path. They could include objects the size of Ceres—and larger. This, too, would be cycled down Svenglid's magnetic throat, and into her flickering engines, providing only enough thrust to counteract the drag of Svenglid's magnetic fields through the interstellar medium. Due to light aberration, all objects would appear to be ahead of the ship. Three telescopes, with a wide range of wavelength detection, would lock onto three forward stars. To those on Terra, the telescopes, through relativity, would appear locked in that position for four years, keeping Svenglid on course, but it would be only a few months to Svenglid. At the end of that four years, or few months, the magnetic fields would cease to feed its engines, acting only as a brake.

Then a device, a being the news discs had dubbed "I, Svenglid," would fire its engines, for from the time Svenglid had reached speed, it would have begun to disassemble itself. The large exhaust bell, no longer needed for acceleration, would move forward. Svenglid's magnetic fields were large, but not large enough to protect it through a normal rocket's turn for deceleration. Such a maneuver would break a structure the size of Svenglid into pieces. So, meticulously, parts would break away and climb the long relativistic hill toward the bow. The aft would become the prow, the prow become the aft. At a given second, two months before reaching its orbit around Proxima Centauri, the engines would again fire. Six Gs of deceleration would strain its now 15-kilometer length. Finally, when she was only seven kilometers long, the engines would sputter out. Svenglid would be in orbit around a star better than four light years' distance from the Earth. The exhaust bell would shed its radioactive lining. From that point onward, it would serve as a gigantic radio telescope, masering back pictures and data, receiving messages and commands across the vast expanse of void. But first, it would seek out the extraordinary, the beautiful, and the unusual—those things that fascinate the common man, enabling ships smaller, more practical, and slower than Svenglid to be built—timed to reach their target stars after a more reasonable and sedate 50 to 100 years.

Paul looked away from the telescope.

"That's probably as close to the speed of light as we're ever going to get," said Goldstein. "Ever. I wish I could tell—I wish you could tell me—why . . . *Ach!* So many questions! Why, consuming fully two percent of our world tax monies, Svenglid has deliberately tried to keep such a low profile! There are some terrestrial investors who can't understand why our materials processing companies are still solvent!"

"I don't know why Svenglid is keeping such a low profile," Paul answered.

"You don't?"

Paul shook his head. "The disc was played only for the prime minister," he said, choosing an acceptable lie.

Yonah's eyes narrowed uncertainly. "Then you're just a *schlemiel*, like me?"

Paul felt Yonah, in uncertainty, opening up to him. He smiled to himself.

Yonah placed his hands behind his back, fairly bursting with information that he wished to discuss. Greenberg followed him up the curving hallway.

"I ran some figures without Gollum," said Yonah finally. "You know that the best way to decide if a computer is at the core of something is to run the figures through another computer. Well, this is something that happens 80 percent of the time. Not 83.682, not 87.349, but 80 percent exactly! If you get solid percentages in multiples of five or ten, then you can bet that a computer is at the core of what appears to be pure chance. Some programmers can be awfully sloppy!"

"What sort of figures are you talking about?" asked Greenberg.

"Transmissions to Earth," answered Goldstein. "When Svenglid is mentioned, there is a burst of static that can last for five minutes or more."

"I would imagine that this happens quite a bit anyway," said Greenberg. "After all, the message does have to bounce to the far side of a very busy moon."

"Solar storms?" asked Goldstein. "Fusion engines firing? Masered messages?" He shook his head. "I've checked all of them. Svenglid is the touchstone. The word that causes the—I have to say it—jamming. Jamming beyond computer clarification, or so Gollum would have us believe. We've triangulated its course. It's one of the dishes at *Oomi Mi.*"

"The radio telescope?" asked Greenberg. "Really? Who is 'we'?"

"Myself and some friends of mine," answered Yonah evasively. Paul knew that Yonah didn't trust him completely. He was letting Paul know that there was more to Svenglid, and he was letting Paul know that he knew it!

"Really," repeated Greenberg. "That is interesting!" He had to admire Goldstein as an intelligent man. The UN was, of course, counting on Paul's silence concerning Svenglid. Silence generated rumors and rumors were healthy for space projects, as they usually came from enthusiasts. The rest of the population didn't care. They weren't interested unless returns were in the immediate future. But spiking their way into these positive rumors were some negative whispers, as well. If Yonah was willing to investigate these rumors concerning the UN's cloak of secrecy, there was the possibility that he had investigated some rumors concerning Svenglid's alleged use by Hazera. He might be as valuable an ally as the Hazera underground, the Materet!

Goldstein looked at his watch. "Well, I suppose that we've done all we can at the hub. You've seen our industrial processes; you should have access to the rest from my place. If there's anything that you'd like to double check, I'd suggest that you wait until it's worth a trip back up to the hub. Make notes of items, come back at the end of your stay, and double check then. To be perfectly frank, I'm quite anxious to be back with my family."

"Oh, yes! Of course, Yonah! You must forgive me!"

"That's quite all right. Svenglid is a sight! Grab your bag and I'll meet you in the hotel lobby. Right now, I've got to give my daughter a call."

Paul did as he was instructed. It was a trip via the airlock cages, from the rapidly spinning Knesset tour-

ist area, through the stationary industrial and customs section, to the slowly spinning section to which
the long arms of the Byuttim were attached. This
was another section that showed nearly the same
signs as the tourist section. Byutt Sebulon, one of the
dozen houses spinning at the end of Hazera's arms,
had been mostly an executive house—a 30-story structure that contained the parks, offices and apartments,
shops and theaters, of the near-elite. Therefore, most
of the zero G workers were absent from the terminal
to the large elevator. Even if this had connected to
another house, most of the workers would have been
absent. Materials manufactured at Hazera were kept
from Earth and most of the other cities because of
the virus. Only on such deep-space projects as Svenglid
was materials processing continued. These would sail
out between the star spaces, never to be seen again.

"You might as well sit down, please," said a man
behind the counter. "The next elevator is 15 minutes
late already." While the man had a thick Hebrew
accent, it was obvious that he had been placed here
solely for Paul's benefit.

Goldstein raised his shoulders in mock frustration
and motioned toward a row of seats. Paul sat and
began reviewing some circuit diagrams.

"Is there still some English translation in stock,
Danny?" asked Yonah.

The man behind the counter grimaced. "Every best-
seller of the past five years," he returned.

Paul saw an additional means of gaining Goldstein's
confidence when he turned to him, saying; "If you
want to buy some books for pleasure, I'd suggest that
you buy them here. English books are rare downstairs."

"Have you got a disc of *The Texan?*" he asked.

Goldstein beamed. "You liked that?" he asked.

"Thought it was great!" answered Paul. "I've been
examining the circuits that you've designed. I was
certain that such genius had to run in the family!"

A grin spread even further across Yonah's face.

"Are you going to show Dr. Greenberg your little ship?" asked Danny.

Goldstein blushed.

"Most people build little spaceships around here," Danny explained. "Goldstein builds little sailships."

"Solar sails?"

"No! Wind sails! And he uses circuitry that he developed to make them move."

"Move?"

"He should open museum," put in Danny. "You must see! Little man walk deck, raise and lower sail!"

"Never mind!" said Goldstein, as embarrassed as a child caught playing with toys designed for one younger than himself.

"Yes," said Paul, ignoring his discomfiture. "I noticed that he seemed greatly interested in ships and the sea."

"Have you seen sea?"

"I was raised in it," returned Greenberg. His childhood had not been changed in the computer records.

"In it?"

"*Ken,*" he said, remembering the Hebrew for 'yes'. "My grandfather was a pump mechanic for a thermal gradient power station. We had a house right off the coast of California. He refused to move after he retired."

"I have seen pictures of the underwater," put in Danny. "I cannot blame him. It is very beautiful!"

"Not everyone has anemonae in place of flowers for the garden," smiled Paul. His memory was flooded with the view out a heavy plate of plastic—the front window. A dolphin swam by to wink at him—its name was George. His grandfather had him help at the power plant, and George lived in a large cage on the surface. There, he would quickly exhale, take a gulp of air through the top of his head, and sink to the bottom of the cage. The cage was not to keep George in. Although sharks had been cleared out of the area, ancestral memories had been hard to erase. Even though the dolphins never deigned to learn English, a sort of primitive human-dolphin economy had developed. George paid for the security of his cage, and the raw fish, with the work he did at the plant. George had been killed in the earthquake of 2061. Paul had been saddened by the loss, but he was content with the morality of George's death.

He had learned to operate the complex programs which enabled dolphins to communicate with humans. From his conversations with George, he learned what George knew of the power plant, and of the bubbling liquids in the tubes—how they turned on the city's lights and opened the door to his cage with a coded squeak. He knew that the liquids inside the tubes were good.

"What if the liquids in the tubes got out?"

George picked up the stylus and punched 20 or so colored studs of geometric shape outside the window.

"Cold water in tubes good," answered George. "Outside tubes, bad. Make George sick. Kill George."

While dolphins hadn't the intelligence that had once been thought, they had the precociousness of a 12-year-old. George knew that his work was important; he knew that his work was dangerous, as well. George knew . . .

"Have you seen sailing ships?" asked Goldstein.

"What? Oh, yes! The *Uhura* used to sail by regularly."

"That's a fine ship," said Goldstein. "I haven't built any 21st century sailing ships. I'm very fond of the 16th century, however. Very colorful—brilliant wood-carving, gold and painted sails."

"I'm anxious to see your models," said Paul.

Paul realized that he had been letting the discs, brought out of storage, click between his fingers without even looking at them. He set a couple of them aside at random and pulled out the distinctive blue

UN credit card. "Put it on the account under research materials," he winked.

Danny grinned, ran the discs through a slot, and inserted a card. His fingers ran rapidly over the keys when the inevitable question, in Hebrew, appeared on the screen.

Paul had clipped *The Texan* into his dator, unrolled the screen, and began on the prologue when a chime announced the arrival of the elevator.

"*Shalom*, Dr. Greenberg!" called Danny. "Enjoy your stay!"

"*Shalom*," Greenberg called back.

The elevator was large. Fully 20 padded seats were arranged in a cone facing outward. They were the only occupants.

"Get near the top, so that you can see everything."

Paul shrugged. "It's an elevator," he said. "How can anyone possibly see anything?"

His question was answered when the twin doors closed. The patterns of the wall began to move upward, behind clear glass. There were, apparently, two additional levels in the system of the hub. The elevator stopped at both of them, despite the fact that there were no additional passengers.

"I don't know why they don't expand operation of this elevator into Gollum's consciousness," explained Goldstein. "Right now, it's handled like our heartbeat or our breathing, so it works automatically, providing services that are no longer needed. Gollum's consciousness is now expanded to the point where he could be aware of what services are . . ."

Then both caught their breath as the elevator exploded outward into sunlight. Expanding, all around them, was the glory of Hazera. It was obvious that they were traveling down the outward edge of an enormous waste heat radiator. Brilliantly colored glass caught the sunlight. Hazera was a maze of complex patterns and shadows that changed with the elevator's slow movement. Five of the Byuttim were visi-

ble, marching up a curving floor of black velvet. You
had to be inside Hazera to appreciate it. You had to
feel the heartbeat of its pumping systems, feel the
cool breath of its respiration, hear the thoughts of its
computer mind. But most of all, you had to see it!
Curving away in all directions, like a mighty wheel,
rolling across a terrain of hard vacuum, slung on
curving beams between the radiators and away from
their expanding heat were structures of every kind!
Greenberg knew that contained within them were
farms, fisheries, warehouses, factories, storage tanks—
industrial structures of every kind! Singing free of
Hazera itself, buzzing around it like thousands of
fireflies, were the glowing smelters.

Yet the necessities of balancing mass had added an
odd symmetry to what might have been ugliness.
The thing was more awesome than he had imagined.
"Jesus!" he whispered.

Goldstein heard him. "Believe me, Dr. Greenberg,"
he said dryly in a Yiddish accent that was more than
his own, "Jesus had nothing to do with this."

Paul chuckled in appreciation, but his mind drifted
backward in time. George. Why had he been thinking
of George all this time?

"You have been to school?" asked the dolphin.

Paul tapped the keys outside the dolphin's cage.
The panel inside lit with a 'yes'.

"What did you learn?"

Slowly, with much difficulty, Paul tried to tell him
of the huge, interstellar craft that the UN was ready-
ing for launch. Paul didn't realize the can of worms
that he was opening.

Outside of the astronomy that the dolphin knew
instinctively—outside of the astronomy that his people used in navigation—the dolphin knew nothing.
Occasionally, the dolphin became excited, an emotion it expressed by swimming out of the cage and
away, to arc a few times out of the water, to swim in
mad circles around the complex of cages and under-

water apartments. A few times, Paul had to surface and pull the oxygen mask away from his face to laugh.

"Are men!" declared the dolphin on the keyboard. "Are men in sky!"

He had some difficulty explaining the concept of weightlessness.

"Is water!" said the dolphin. "Is water in sky! Is as Mother say!" Here the dolphin gave the shattering shriek that symbolized the Cetacean deity. "Live in sky with men!"

"No," Paul tried to tap out. "Is no water in sky, is . . ."

But the dolphin had already bolted out the cage door. Again, Paul surfaced to laugh.

When the dolphin finally swam back, the inevitable question occurred. "Please, Paul," George tapped out. "Take George to water-sky. George bring back stars in mouth. Give stars to Sylvia. Give stars to Donna."

Paul looked nervously over to Sylvia's cage. She was taking a nap. Donna was probably working at the plant. Her cage was empty. The two female dolphins were not following the conversation. Paul was thankful for that. Most of the dolphins in the surrounding cages were at work or out playing. George always swam home to meet Paul after school.

"Stars be fun to play with," added the dolphin, hopefully.

"I can't take you to San-Diego-in-sky," punched out Paul. His eyes were already misting with tears. He was blushing when he realized what he had done. 'San-Diego-in-sky' was the closest word to 'city' in the limited vocabulary of the dolphin. "I can't take you to San-Diego-in-sky," repeated Paul. "I'm just a little kid!"

The dolphin gave a sighing whistle of disappointment into the surrounding water and sank to the bottom of his cage.

"Look, George," punched out Paul. "Don't tell this to the other dolphins. It's a secret, okay?"

"George not tell other dolphins," affirmed George. "Is secret. Is secret. George', Paul' secret."

"Yes," Paul returned. "Secret! Talk to Grandpa about it. Okay, George?"

"Okay!" the dolphin said excitedly. "George talk to Dave about it. George talk about it, Paul' Gramps."

Paul popped up through the lower entranceway. Pulling himself out of the circular tank-like structure, he hung his scuba gear on the wall and punched a switch on the blower, turning himself in the warm wind of dry air. "Boy!" he muttered to himself. "Grampa's going to kill me when he finds out!"

With himself reasonably dry, he stepped up the rough textured stairs and onto the living room carpet. He then rushed to his room to change out of his still-wet trunks and take a fresh-water shower.

By the time he was dressed and at his studies, Grampa was already back from the mainland.

Paul seated himself nonchalantly at his desk when he heard the rustle of plastic shopping bags in the kitchen.

"Oh!" his grandmother said. "What a beautiful day!"

"I don't see why you go all the way to the mainland just to buy groceries! The cost of the boat trip is more money than the trip saves you!"

"But it's such a lovely ride!" his grandmother declared. "Besides, if you spent more time on the surface or used a little lotion, you wouldn't get so sunburned!"

"More toys?" came his grandfather's voice. "We're already going to have to train George so that he can move to a bigger cage!"

"Speaking of George," said his grandmother.

Paul could picture her in his mind, looking out of the kitchen, across the living room, and through the great, plastic pane. Beyond it was George.

"He seems pretty excited about something," observed his grandfather. There was a quiet thudding as he ran across the carpet. Paul put his hands over his eyes. "Here it comes!" he told himself.

One moment passed, then two. All that could be heard was the quiet tick-tick of his grandfather's fingers on the communicator keys, and the long pauses in between while the dolphin responded.

Finally: "What?!"

Paul bit his lower lip.

"Paul!"

Paul rose reluctantly from his seat.

"What is it?" asked his grandmother.

"George wants to take a vacation," his grandfather answered.

"I don't think there's anything wrong with that," his grandmother responded. "Personnel has given him several days off—"

"In Astropolis?" his grandfather asked.

"Oh," said his grandmother. "Oh, dear!"

Hesitantly, Paul entered the living room. The dolphin was gone.

"Did you tell that dolphin about the space cities?" asked his grandfather.

"Y-y-yessir."

"I ought to paddle you within an inch of your life! Forget about the dolphin! Do you know how much it would cost to lift a tank of sea water into orbit?"

"No, sir."

"Plenty!" Grandpa answered.

"I didn't mean to," pleaded Paul. "When I got home from school, George asked me what I had learned, so I told him about Project Osirus. George didn't understand and started asking questions. I just answered them! I didn't know that he'd want to go!"

Grandpa sank back in his chair and chuckled to himself. He nodded and chuckled again. "I know," he answered. "I know. I'm afraid that I was a little hard on George, son. You know that we weren't designed to live out in the sea, don't you?"

"Yessir."

"And you know that there's a lot that we have to know in order to stay alive out here. You have to know how much air you have left in your tanks. You have to know how deep you can swim. And you have to know how long to stop, and where, before you surface. You're a smart boy! They thought I was going to kill you when I got you that scuba gear! You were only eight years old. Do you remember that?"

Paul nodded.

"And you didn't come down with the bends the first time?"

Paul shook his head.

"I knew you were a smart boy!" Grandpa said. "But, you see, space is a lot like water. There are certain things that you have to know just to stay alive! Dolphins are smart, Paul, but they aren't as smart as people. They live in the sea because that's where they're supposed to live. Why, George couldn't swim in space, even if we made a suit for him."

Paul giggled at the picture of a dolphin space suit.

"You can understand, can't you?"

"Sure, Grandpa. Like I said. I didn't know that he'd want to go."

Grandpa tousled his hair. "I'm sure you didn't," he said. "I'm sure that you didn't. Well, hopefully, this will all blow over by tomorrow morning. It'll be forgotten soon enough."

But it wasn't forgotten, for when Paul got off the school boat the next day, Grandma met him at the pier.

"It's George, Paul," she said. "I got a call from your grandfather at work. George didn't show up today. When he called George, the dolphin said that he was sick. I think it's this space thing. Sometimes Grandpa can show a lack of tact. Why don't you get into your diving gear and go talk to George. See if you can make him understand."

So young Paul Green went to see the dolphin. When he first saw George, he thought he was asleep. The tail swished only occasionally, bringing George's breathing hole above the surface. In fact, he was sure he was asleep, until the dolphin, on seeing him, turned away.

Paul swam over to the keyboard and tapped out a 'hello'.

But the dolphin was too busy pouting to look at the colored patterns on the screen. Paul pressed a bar, clearing the screen, and held his breath. Did talking to the dolphin merit the importance of—

He activated the emergency strobe, after punching out, "Easy, boy. It's only me."

The dolphin whipped about; Paul held the cage door closed. George looked over at the message screen and angrily punched out with his nose, "Shame on you, Paul! I thought that there was something wrong."

"I had to talk to you," Paul answered.

"What about?"

"I came to tell you that I was sorry about telling you about San-Diego-in-Sky," Paul answered.

"George no mad at Paul. George not mad at Paul' Grampa. George just sad. Want be left alone."

"You know how much it would cost?" asked Paul.

"If cost reason, George pay for himself. Move to smaller cage. George sell toys. Not eat so much fish."

Paul laughed beneath his mask and shook his head. "It would take more than that," he answered. "Cost of trip to San-Diego-in-Sky would take many migrations of cage rent."

"How many?"

"Fifty," Paul answered. "Maybe a hundred."

The dolphin floated in his cage, astounded.

"Then George wait," the dolphin finally answered. "Bring back stars for Sylvia. Bring back stars for Donna."

"If you bring back stars," punched out Paul, "you change sky. How do wild dolphins find their way? Besides, by the time George saves enough to go to water-sky, George be in water-sky anyway."

The dolphin floated for a moment, thinking.

"Paul right," he answered. "George wait until die. Get free trip!"

A burst of bubbles came from beneath Paul's mask. He had never heard the cetaceans speak of their religion so matter-of-factly. He swam into the dolphin's cage and gently stroked the dolphin's smooth side, then reached up and grabbed a plastic ring from the surface.

"George play?" Paul punched out on the dolphin's own communications panel.

"George play!" the dolphin returned.

Death came suddenly to George a year later—2062. An earthquake occurred that broke the seals around the thermal gradient turbines. The poisonous solution that fed them exploded into the water. Many dolphins and humans, seriously burned, plunged to the surface only to gasp heavily poisoned air.

Grandfather had been lucky. The seals held about the control center. Through the heavy plastic of a window, Grandpa had watched George die. "It was quick," he assured Paul. "It was quick."

The legal battles lasted for years afterwards, only adding to the anguish of the plant's operators. With some readjustments, the minor power plants continued to operate.

Now, years later, Paul looked outward at the wonders that George had hoped to find. "Do you see it, too, George?" he asked silently. "Are you here with the men and your deity?"

His eyes misted. And while he refrained from weeping, he realized that this was as close as he had come to crying in a very long while. The last time had been in the agony of losing his arm and half his face, but that had been a different kind of pain.

"Hey! Asher! Come here, you little *putz!*"

Asher Goldstein was on his way across from school. He'd slipped through the central park of the Byutt's Level 17. Isaiah's voice rang out behind him.

"Hey, *putz!* Got any money?"

Asher cursed beneath his breath. For weeks, he had been saving part of his lunch tokens in the lining of his jacket for a miniature of a patrol ship. He didn't have enough for it yet, but he'd crossed the park to gaze at it in the window of the little shop. Now, four older boys were chasing him.

Two of them caught him. In the lining of his jacket there was the click of plastic tokens crashing together.

"Why don't you leave me alone, Izzy?" demanded Asher.

" 'Cause you're such a *putz!*" the older boy answered.

Asher began thrashing, trying to kick Izzy in the shins. The others held him fast.

Izzy laughed and backed away, then swung for a punch in the stomach. As Asher doubled over, he felt hands going through his pockets.

"Hey!" cried a boy. "There's a hole in this pocket!"

"Maybe the plastics we heard are in the lining of his jacket."

"Yeah!" said another. "I betcha that's where he's been hiding all the money that he's been saving. Little wimp like him ought to eat more!"

"What ya wanna do with him, Izzy?"

The boy studied him for a moment, tucking his thumbs beneath his belt. Like many school bullies, he was overweight. His dishwater-blonde hair stuck out at angles like a burr.

Suddenly, his green eyes widened. "Hey!" he said. "You remember that field trip that we took to the hub last week?"

"Ken."

"Y'member how, when we were on the elevator, Asher wouldn't look over the edge?"

"Ken."

"Let's put him in the high end maintenance tube!"

"Yeah!" answered another. "They still haven't got the lock fixed! I don't even think they know it's broken!"

Now Asher really began to struggle. "No!" he begged. "Don't do that! Please! Don't do that!"

His pleading, of course, only egged the others on.

They began to drag him toward the waterfall at the high end of the school's level.

All the levels of Hazera were canted at about 20 degrees. This served two purposes. For one, it made the entire community appear to be sitting on a low hill. With so many of its workers spending much of their time on the moon or in zero G, the slope provided exercise for muscle tone. For another, each community was lighted by the sun from a mirror, which had to be canted to light the interior, so the floor of each level served as a reflecting surface for the level below it. The series of waterfalls served to cool and humidify each level. The water flowed down an artificial mountain from the level above, down a flowing stream that ran the length of the park, and into a grating at the lower end. The water was then pumped back up between the floor and the ceiling mirror, to fall down another artificial mountain.

Within the mountain was the upper level maintenance tube. Arranged at four points around each deck, they ran the height of the Byuttim. Through the tubes, men had access to problems with the air and water pumps, electrical, and light conduits—problems that Gollum, with his thousands of robots, was unable to solve.

Each level had a vertical series of 10 catwalks within the high end maintenance tube. Each catwalk was made of heavy sheets of tough, scratchproof, clearest optical glass, kept so clean and polished by Gollum that one might have been standing on nothing at all. Even the railings and stairways were formed of nothingness. Everything, with the possible exception of the maintenance robots, had to remain transparent for visibility.

Asher was dragged through the dense fern and brush, across a bridge, over a reflecting pond, and around a high, rocky stand of artificial mountain. He tried to scream for help, but one of the larger boys jammed a hand over his mouth. He bit it.

"Ow! Goddamn!" the boy cried.

"Stuff one of his sleeves down his throat if he's going to holler!" spat back still another. Asher's jacket had been removed to shake out the tokens. Part of it was balled up and stuffed into his mouth. They moved off the main path and up one of semi-flagstone, nearly invisible in the low ferns. A few seconds later, a thick stand of pine hid them from anyone who might chance along the path.

True to the boys' words, the door swung open at a touch. Asher was pushed in and onto the transparent floor.

"Look down!" commanded one of the boys.

Asher turned back toward the door and froze. In the pit of his stomach, he felt the spaces yawning out beneath him.

"Yeah, Asher! Look down!"

Each Byutt was composed of some 30 levels; each level was 50 meters in height. With his father a successful electrical engineer, and his sister quite wealthy from her writing, Asher lived near the Byutt's center. The school he attended was three levels above his own. Nine hundred meters, nearly a kilometer, stretched out beneath him.

"Hey, Asher! Look down!"

Unable to withstand the other's continued taunts, Asher did as he was told. The transparent floors beneath him could not have been absolutely clear.

Twenty levels below they took on a filmy translucence, but 20 levels beneath him was not enough. Asher's head began to spin. He felt the bile rise in his throat. Drunkenly, he stumbled.

"Careful, *putz!*" came a taunt. "Don't fall over the rail."

At the mention of falling, Asher desperately ran at the open door.

Izzy caught him, and pushed him back over the abyss. Asher landed face down on the hard, cold floor. His eyes were squeezed shut, holding back his tears of terror.

A robot climbed up the side, its TV camera eye rotating slowly about its center.

"Oh, no!" moaned one of the boys. "Gollum!"

Asher lifted his spinning head to look through the crystal railing. There was the black, gleaming eye of Gollum.

"Asher!" said an electronic voice. "What—?"

But Asher didn't stay to hear the rest. He bolted to his feet. The rest of the boys had already run through the door, which was left open. He ran toward it, across the tilting, transparent floor. He didn't know if the computer had seen the others, but he had not only been seen, but recognized! His feet slipping on the smooth surface, he ran for the door.

His eyes spotted the other boys hurtling off through the underbrush. As he burst out onto the pathway, he saw the last of them disappear into the greenery. He felt his face burning with rage and shame. Revenge became his only thought. Reaching down, he picked up a decorative quartz-white stone and he hurled it after his tormentors. His actions were met by the tinkle of breaking glass. He paled, and a hollow feeling formed in the pit of his stomach.

Asher followed the others into the shrubbery—not for revenge this time, but to see what he had done. From the greenery, he burst into an open plaza. There was a picnic table off to one side, a few park benches, and a pit constructed for barbecues. But in the center was a cylindrical 'guide'.

It held four holographic computer maps of the level, each facing in a different direction. One of these holograms was fuzzed by the smashing of a projector.

In dumbfounded shock, Asher surveyed the damage that his stone had just caused. Then, a strong hand gripped his shoulder. "Whether that was intentional or not," said a masculine voice, "you shouldn't be throwing stones, Asher Goldstein."

Asher looked over at the large hand, and the sleeve of blue beta cloth. It was the uniform of a *shōtair*—the uniform of the Hazera police.

Chapter VII

Shoshanna Goldstein got out of bed. Walking to the mirror, she tossed blonde hair over her shoulder.

"You're beautiful!" said a voice behind her.

Turning toward Abraham, she covered herself with a towel. "All this and brains too," she teased.

"You'd better not have brains," he said. "With beauty alone, a woman is just beautiful. When you add brains, she becomes dangerous."

Shoshanna answered with a low, throaty, and purposely evil chuckle.

Abe rose to kiss her beneath an ear. She giggled.

"Let's have a look at the readout screen and see how the latest is coming," he said.

Shoshanna glanced at the wall clock. "Oh, no!" she said. "It's nearly eleven forty-five! Poppa told me that he'd be arriving at noon!" She began changing the sheets.

" *'We are born in slime'*," quoted Abe.

"Don't go quoting the *Talmud* at me!" exclaimed Shoshanna. "My father doesn't disapprove of sex! It's you he doesn't like. Get dressed and out of here! I'll finish up."

She had just placed the sheets in the cleanser when the vid-phone chimed.

"That's probably Poppa now," she said, putting on a bathrobe. But the face that formed in the air above the vid wasn't that of her father. It was the familiar

114

face of one of the school counselors. "Oh, no!" she moaned, sinking down on the couch. "What has Asher done *now?*"

"A *shōtair* brought Asher into my office. He was caught throwing stones. That doesn't fit in with any of his psychoprofiles," admitted the counselor. "He was definitely provoked into it. By what or by whom, he isn't saying."

"Was anything damaged?" she asked.

"Ken," nodded the counselor. "Some property of Byutt Sebulon. Asher broke a map projector in one of the cylindrical directories."

"Oh, Asher!" Shoshanna said under her breath. "When Svenglid is finished, your Poppa will be out of a job! And whether or not we can save this apartment depends on how my new book sells. Why must you add more expenses?"

"What was the map's value?" she finally asked aloud.

The floating face of the counselor looked off to one side, and asked a question out of range of the microphone.

"The *shōtair* says that he doesn't know," returned the counselor.

"Asher's been saving for something," she said. "Ask the *shōtair* if that can be used as a down payment. Asher will pay the rest out of his allowance—including interest!"

The counselor looked off-screen and chuckled. "Asher wants to know what 'interest' is," he said.

"Put him on!" she demanded.

Her heart fluttered when she saw his tear-streaked face, but she remained firm, banishing the surge of internal warmth. "Who were you throwing stones at, Asher?"

"Nobody. What's interest?" he asked quickly.

Shoshanna grimaced. "Interest is the money that we pay for the privilege of the time it takes to pay it."

"*Mah?*"

"It's more money, Asher!"

"Awww! Sis!"

The counselor's face returned to the screen. "The *shōtair* just called Byutt Central. They'll accept the terms of your agreement."

Shoshanna closed her eyes and sighed. "How much?" she asked.

"Twenty pounds."

"Twenty pounds!" exclaimed Shoshanna.

"Yes. Some computer equipment was damaged, as well."

"Oh, Asher!" A pause. "Put him back on," she finally said. "Well, Asher. There goes your *Rochel.*"

Did his tears increase? "Yes, Sis," he said simply.

"*I* know, Asher. And your counselors know that you threw that stone at someone. We want an answer when you get home."

"I'll try."

"You'll do better than try, young man! I expect your Poppa to be home any minute!"

The child blanched. "See y'tonight."

"Yeah!"

Shoshanna tapped the "off" switch as Abe emerged from the bedroom.

"Trouble with little brother, eh?"

"Yes. And you'd better be on your way out of here. Poppa's going to be here at any moment!"

He kissed her. "It's been a lovely seven days," he exclaimed.

"I'll see you tonight," she said.

"At Solomon's Grill?"

"*Ken,*" she answered. "Around eighteen?"

"Eighteen it is! *Ad ha'erev!*"

"*Ad ha'erev!*"

The elevator gave a good view of the levels through which it passed. Each was about a kilometer in length and half a kilometer wide. A pleasant park, with an

artificial mountain, waterfall, hills, and a meander-
ing stream with bridges, ran the length of each center. At the end of the park, corrugated by chevron
shielding, was the sun. Visible from the upper internal stories, the greatest part of the external walls
was hidden by high apartment and shopping centers. With a ceiling 50 meters in height, there was a
definite feeling of being outdoors. The sunlight, reflecting from a mirror overhead, added to the effect.

Being a moderately wealthy man, Yonah lived reasonably near the Byutt's center. Level 14. Paul was
quite surprised by the appearance of Level 15. The
central park was missing. Half the sun was cut off by
a huge wall and a massive oaken "gate." The buildings were of stone and heavily roofed with steep,
shingled "wood."

"Part of our history," Yonah explained. "Most of
our history is not pleasant, so they've made it into an
amusement park—rides, fun and games. But through
it, our children learn something of our history.

"This particular park is a crude representation of
the ghettos of eastern Europe. The sunward side is
the museum; the other, the amusement park. You
can't teach young children without a sugar coating,
I'm afraid."

"Is there such a park in each Byutt?"

"Not really. There are only ten which are placed so
far in our past as to be considered 'fun'. The other
two are entirely museums to our Holocausts."

"Each taking up an entire level?"

"*Ken*. Here we are."

As they talked, another deck had sprung upward.
Each had been slightly different. A look of pleasure
crossed Yonah's face. It was obvious that he was
home.

"We live right over there." Yonah pointed just as
the elevator slid through the roof of a station. The
station itself was nearly empty, but since entering
the Byutt, there had been enough of a hubbub to

resemble normality more closely. With Knesset sealed off by quarantine, the only people who traveled outside the Byuttim were those workers who unloaded lunar ore and expensive products from Earth. Commerce within the Byuttim themselves was common. Though most of the people refrained from using the large central elevator, the three that flanked each of its sides were extremely busy. They seemed to work via air pressure. Paul wondered if there were holding niches where certain elevators would pause while others passed. Certainly, the multiplicity of them argued for more than one per shaft.

On leaving the station, they walked through the sweet, green, constantly flowering scent of the park. Paul enjoyed the walk immensely. While the park was flanked by more standard slidewalks and a computerized overhead delivery system, the exercise, after four days in zero G, was welcome.

"Just a fraction more than a standard Earth G," explained Yonah. "I purposely chose that for muscle tone and to raise a healthy family."

"Your daughter's a writer," began Paul.

"*Ken.* Shoshanna's been quite successful, too. But a writer's life is a perilous one, at best. We probably could have lived for quite a while on what her first successful book brought us. Unfortunately, she invested it in our local industry." Yonah laughed. "She put most of it into materials processing. Of course, the plague hit and it all went down the tubes."

"I'm sorry to hear that," answered Paul.

"She can always write another book," returned Yonah. "She's been researching one about the formation of the Second Israel."

"Sounds interesting."

"Our house is right over there," said Yonah, turning. Paul followed. The little path led pleasantly over a rushing stream, via a small arched bridge. Paul plucked at the wooden railing, experimentally. Fiberglass. But the trees were real enough.

"The Jews of the last century painted themselves as being too cerebral," Yonah sighed. "They were, I guess. There are so few Yiddish words that describe nature. But I think that we've done a fairly good job of keeping things pleasant here, don't you think?"

Paul nodded. "What about our luggage?" he asked.

"It's being delivered by Gollum." Yonah pointed to the overhead delivery system. Running above the doorways was a large chute. "He makes personal deliveries, and always in the best of order."

"Not bad," Paul admitted.

They crossed the little pathway that ran beneath the hissing overhead track. Yonah walked to a doorway and punched a few keys. A red light blinked on above the panel. "Press your thumb against the glass pane. We might as well program the house to let you in and out."

Paul did as he was instructed. The machine beeped almost immediately. "That takes care of that," answered Yonah. "You're an official member of the family now."

Paul chuckled as Yonah touched his fingers to his lips, then reached over to touch a mezuzah. The door opened. "A good way to enforce religion," Yonah observed casually. "The thumb plate is the lock and the mezuzah is the opening switch."

Paul was halfway through the door when something hissed to a stop on the track overhead. A small T-shaped bar, projecting from a slot beneath, came to a rapid stop. Paul looked up over his shoulder.

"Our luggage," Yonah explained.

"How does that thing work?" Paul asked, jerking a thumb in the track's direction.

"Shoshanna!" called Goldstein.

"Just a moment," answered a voice in Hebrew.

"Excuse me for interrupting," apologized Goldstein. He walked over to a bar. "Would you like a drink?"

"Please."

Yonah settled on the couch, handing Paul an iced glass. "Arak," he said. "Sort of saki with a kick.

"The delivery system works much the same as our lunar launch ramp. Trays are magnetically floated and move above the track itself. A counterweight, suspended from the bottom, serves to equalize acceleration. Small boys have been known to grab the counterweight and go for a ride. There was an act in Knesset to replace the counterweights with something less dangerous and tempting. That was before the plague. Since then, our city workers seem to have been engaged in busywork."

"What sort of busy—?" Paul stopped. A tall, blonde woman had just entered the room. She was rendered all the more striking by the gossamer garments that covered her and the complexity of her hairdo.

"I'd like you to meet my daughter, Dr. Greenberg. Shoshanna, this is Dr. Paul Greenberg. Dr. Greenberg, this is my daughter, Shoshanna."

"Formalities come later," she said, embracing Yonah about the neck. "How was your trip? Pleased to meet you, Dr. Greenberg. Don't you stand when a lady enters the room?" She took his hand.

Paul laughed. "Dreadfully sorry," he said. "But on Terra, we abandoned that practice over a century ago."

She nodded. "Only among the Orthodox," she said, "are women treated as respected chattel!"

"Shoshanna!" protested Yonah. "I'm sorry, Dr. Greenberg, but my daughter is trying to get another women's movement started among the Orthodox here. So far, it hasn't gained too much momentum."

"Motherhood can scarcely be one's sole purpose in an environment such as this, Poppa. We've come so far in some ways and have slipped so far back in others! We can, here, hold the same jobs as men—at the same pay—except the rabbinate! I want to change that."

"Dr. Greenberg is not a practicing Jew."

"Oh." Shoshanna rose to get herself a drink. She passed over the Arak and picked a bottle of white wine. "Karl seems to be speaking in the direction of women in the rabbinate. Poppa, did you read his article in *The Forward*?"

"No," he answered. "I was too busy reviewing circuit diagrams on the way up. Some of the people on the *Harpo Martz* disced its broadcast. I heard them talking about it."

"But we are being rude to our guest," Shoshanna said, "talking *b'angli, ken*. But of things that don't concern him. He must be tired after his journey. You must both be. Would you like to freshen up, Doctor?"

"After the drink, thank you." He wasn't sure that he liked the aftertaste, but it was strong, bracing. "Who is Karl?"

"A *Talmudist*," answered Yonah. "Although his views are unorthodox, even the Chassidim enjoy reading him. Some say he is as great as Rashi."

Shoshanna raised a brow. "Really!" she exclaimed. "I've never heard that kind of praise!"

The name "Rashi" was meaningless and even a little amusing to Paul. "Tell me more of this Karl," he said.

"There isn't much to tell," Yonah answered. "He's a man who, quite cleverly, writes very liberal ideas in a manner that the conservative can accept. Needless to say, this is a very dangerous thing. One must walk a very narrow boundary line and can never tell when this boundary line has been overstepped, so Karl is a pseudonym. I can see reasons for caution. Not many others can."

"The destruction of the Second Israel brought about a return to the more extreme forms of Orthodoxy. The Chassidim believed that the Second Israel should not have existed before the coming of the Messiah," added Shoshanna. "They viewed the Second Israel as a sacrilege."

Yonah sipped his Arak and nodded. "With the Second Israel's destruction, the Jews had to ask why. In extreme Orthodoxy, they found their answer—one that held the emotional appeal that they needed."

"The Second Israel was founded and built by Jews, largely from the concentration camps—Jews who had already been through the First Holocaust. Unfortunately, the reasons for the First Holocaust were even vaguer than those for the Second," said Shoshanna.

"Therefore," continued Yonah, "to those who survived, there were no reasons. To most of them, God was truly dead."

Both stopped talking, staring off into a painful silence. Paul decided that it was time to terminate the conversation.

"If you don't mind," he said, "I think that I'd better take a shower and have a nap. It's been a long trip up from Terra, and I think that Yonah and I will have to get used to being in a normal G field."

"Right upstairs," directed Yonah, following him. He pressed a mezuzah at the side of one of the doors, which slid open to reveal a hallway leading into a bedroom. The hall connected to a private bath via a walk-in closet. Yonah stepped back onto the balcony. "The shower is on your left. I'll pick up your suitcases."

"You'd better let me help you," said Paul, following him.

"I can't see why you brought your own space suit," said Yonah.

Paul remembered that the artificial eye had been found out and couldn't see any harm in elaborating. "I lost an eye," he explained, "at the same time I lost my arm. This eye doubles as a telescope and microscope. You know how important these can be in our line of work. The helmet has a device that can be used to alter the eye's purpose and to focus it."

"Couldn't that be controlled internally?" asked Yonah.

"Possibly," answered Paul. He helped Yonah with the cases. "But after buying a custom arm, I had only so much money. To control such a thing through the central nervous system costs four times as much, so I selected a magnetic switch instead."

Yonah nodded appreciatively. "You can hang your clothes up in this closet. The bedroom is straight ahead. *Shalom*, Dr. Greenberg, and pleasant dreams."

Paul walked into the bedroom. A terminal was built into the top of a desk, which emerged from the side of a dresser. The red light above Gollum's camera-eye was out, but that didn't mean anything. Paul took off his jumpsuit and casually tossed it over the dresser-desk-console. Unless the camera was equipped with infrared, it couldn't see what he was doing. Paul then reached for his pocket dator, unfolding it. IR sensing may have been able to see that he was unfolding a dator, but even computer enhancement couldn't have seen what keys he was punching.

His forehead wrinkled. The dator showed no detection equipment whatsoever! Odd in a dictatorial society. The computer terminal was completely dead!

Paul took out his combination light and writing pen, and tapped the top of the dresser thoughtfully. He was certain that if anything *were* going on, he as a representative of the UN, was suspect. This meant that the Hazerim considered him "innocent until proven guilty." Unheard of in a political entity under martial law. Odd. Very odd.

He pressed another key on the dator which set a green square to blink in the upper right-hand corner of the dator screen. It would tell him if any detection devices were turned on—the green square would change to red.

With the push of a few more keys, the dator showed a diagram of the room. He looked across it. Beyond the bed and wall was the hard vacuum of interplanetary space.

Paul switched off the dator and finished undressing. If he were to take a shower, he'd better take it now. The absence of the sound of rushing water might alert those downstairs that all was not as it seemed.

"Poppa," said Shoshanna, after Paul had gone upstairs. "Asher is in trouble."

"Oy!" And Yonah had been thinking of taking a nap himself! "What did Asher do?"

"He broke a holo projector in one of the civic maps."

"What? Oh! Oh, yes! You mean one of those big conduits that they have sticking up out of the ground."

"He'll be paying for it out of his allowance, and I think we can find some odd jobs for him around the house."

"Ken."

She sighed. "Poppa, I'm worried about this. Asher didn't break that projector on purpose! He was throwing a rock at someone who made him angry! I know it! But who it was, and why he threw that rock—he won't say!"

Yonah looked down, nodding.

"And this means that he won't be able to buy that little space ship. It's the first thing that he's wanted enough to save for. Did I do the right thing by making him pay for that projector, Poppa?"

"There are more important things than model space ships, Shoshanna."

"Like model sailing ships?" she asked.

Yonah chuckled. "You are such a good mother," he said. "I'm sure that you could get a license. Why don't you apply?"

"We can't *'be fruitful and multiply'* right now," she said. "And so long as that's the case, I've got more important things to do."

"At least get married, Shoshanna. You're 27 years old!"

She pushed a tongue into her cheek. "There is always Abe," she answered, knowing that this would end the conversation.

"That steel puddler! You know that he will be out of a job when Svenglid is finished! How will he support you?"

She laughed. "You'll be out of a job, too," she pointed out. "That's why I won't be getting married, Poppa. We only have 90,000 pounds left from *Ha'Texi*, and about 20,000 left from *Ha'Hatti*. That's 110,000 pounds. You and Asher need that as well as I. Your daughter is capable of supporting herself! And you!"

Her eyes filled with tears. "Oh, Poppa! Can't you be realistic? Your daughter is capable of supporting herself. She's certainly capable of supporting a husband!

"Perhaps the Jewish analysis of the Second Destruction is right! Perhaps the First Holocaust was a tempering process for God's chosen. Perhaps the Second Holocaust came because God's people abandoned him! Maybe it *is* wise to return to our old beliefs and ways—but not all of them, Poppa! The man doesn't *have* to be the breadwinner! His word in the home doesn't *have* to be final! Does not the *Talmud* state: *'Woman was not created from a man's head that she should be above him. Nor was she created from his feet to be below him. She was created from his rib so that she might be beside him'*?"

"It isn't that!" interrupted Yonah. "You can be the breadwinner if you so wish it, daughter. It's just Abe's strong work ethic, and his dangerous work. He won't abandon it until Svenglid is finished! Even if you make a thousand times what he does, he won't purposely abandon his work. It's part of him, and even though it will be over in a few months, the chance that you'll be hurt—the chance that he might be killed or crippled—I don't want you going through that, Shoshanna. However small the chance, I don't want to see you suffer as I did when your mother died. I know it's unreasonable, but . . ."

"My *books* are my children, Poppa. And they are the only children that I want to have! Marriage, for me, is the sanction to love and be loved to the exclusion of all others. It's not a selfish thing! It's the way love was meant to be!" She paused. "But I love you, Poppa," she added quietly. "And I respect you. I won't marry without your consent. That's important to me. But I can't marry someone that I don't love. I won't marry someone that I don't . . ."

"And you love Abraham," said her father.

"Yes, Poppa."

"I don't know, Shoshanna. Your Poppa must think."

Paul emerged from the shower and dried himself with puffs of warm, scented air. Still naked, he walked to the center of the bedroom, picked up the dator, and cautiously walked to the door. Again, he opened the dator's screen and punched out the two caps.

Once again, the screen lighted with the map of the room. Paul bit his lower lip. The green square still blinked in the upper right-hand corner. He paused for a moment, before setting the dator on the dresser and slipping into his shorts. The map would be five years out of date by now. He could see by the wall vent that an air conduit was probably in the same location. If any rewiring had been done, the sensors in the drill bit would take care of it. His pen was a combination light and writing pen. Along with the light for computer screens, the pen contained the three basic colors, plus black and white ink. They could be mixed into any shade. However, disguised in its complexity was a third purpose. When the pocket clip was rotated 180 degrees, then snapped outward, the pen became a miniature drill. The bit was a bundle of optical fibers and organic conductors about the size of a human hair. Chains of pizoelectric molecules straightened it into rigidity. Down one of the optical fibers fired the tight beam of a laser, which turned anything ahead of it into plasma. The outer jacket of the bit was cooled with an internal drop of liquid helium. So long as it held a temperature below that of liquid nitrogen, the jacket would be a superconductor. The natural repulsion of superconductors to electromagnetic charges was used to pull plasma away from the drill's tip. The jacket was threaded like the bits of the 20th century. And the entire unit rotated, pulling plasma out of the recently created hole, preventing the vaporizing material from blocking the beam's cutting edge.

Keeping his eye on the dator's square of blinking light, Paul again checked the door. Securing the lock, he listened. Only muffled voices could be heard downstairs. Again, keeping his eye on the dator, he silently lifted the bed, pulling it away from the wall. Within seconds, a small marking on the pen's clip glowed green, showing that the drilling was completed. He pulled the pen away and heaved a sigh of relief. A red glow would have shown that the drill approached an electrical or optical lead, and the exterior walls of a city were always a maze of circuitry, once inside the meteorite shielding. When he pulled the pen away, the bit remained in the wall. Disconnected from the laser, it would be an optical and electrical connection between his dator and an outside communications device. It would be nightfall before he could suit up and place the microwave dish for external communication.

Quietly, he lifted the bed and put it back in place. Then, he collapsed upon it and was soon asleep.

"Excuse me, Dr. Greenberg," said a woman's voice, "but I was told to wake you in time for dinner."

Paul jerked from his sleep, but relaxed when he saw the red glow beneath his jump suit. The voice was coming from the computer's vox box. He whipped the jump suit away from the computer's camera eye and dropped it down a laundry chute.

"Good evening, Gollum," he said.

"Good evening," returned the emotionless vox box.

"I've been wanting to talk to you," Paul said.

"Really? What about?"

"During the Shabbos service on the *Harpo Martz*," Paul said, "you were saying something on the screen. What was it?"

"Like any good Jew, I was participating in the service."

"But you're a computer!" Paul answered.

"And I am a sentient, rational being, capable of making my own decisions," the voice said. "By that definition, I have a soul."

"Oh," Paul answered. He walked downstairs shaking his head, wondering what Jewish heaven would be like when all those robots gathered above. This *was* interesting! Long ago, the Vatican had determined that any sins that were committed by a computer were the fault of the programmer. That decision extended itself to cover *all* computers—even those as sophisticated as Svenglid, UNEC, and presumably Gollum. Until this time, Paul had automatically assumed that the computers were content with that decision. The thought that a computer would declare itself to have a soul and, as such, take responsibility for its actions, was incredible! Well, this was a different religion. As such, it would hold different moral beliefs.

He continued down the stairs.

"Hello, Paul," said Dr. Goldstein. "How was the nap?"

"Quite good," declared Paul. "I feel quite a bit better."

"You look somewhat confused, Dr. Greenberg. Is something the matter?"

"Your computer told me that it's a Jew."

Goldstein laughed.

"Are all of your computers Jewish?"

"It depends on how sophisticated they are," explained Shoshanna, bringing a covered tray from the kitchen. "Sooner or later, the computer runs up against the concepts of morality, and since our concepts are codified the *Talmud*, we insert a memory of it. From that point on, all of our computers have behaved in a perfectly moral fashion.

"Sometimes, when working on a complex problem, the logic can be a little obtuse, but the computer always has a rational explanation—in terms of the *Talmud.*"

"And you trust them?"

Again Yonah and Shoshanna laughed.

"We all trust computers. Our society has become so big, so complex, that we have to. Gollum controls our breathing mix, delivers our food, stores our reading and entertainment, cooks our food. Surely Terra is the same way. Unless you want to fly a spaceship by the seat of your pants, it's the way it's got to be!"

A small figure entered the room. "Ah!" said Yonah. "Asher! Come in! Asher, this is Dr. Greenberg. Dr. Greenberg, this is my son, Asher." Goldstein gripped the boy's shoulder. "Dr. Greenberg is here all the way from Earth. He came to check and correct any mistakes that Poppa may have made on Svenglid."

"Then you know English, Asher?"

"English, Yiddish, Aramaic, Japanese, German, French, and a little Ladino," Shoshanna answered proudly.

"My goodness!" exclaimed Paul. "You're quite an accomplished young man!"

The boy shrugged. "German's fairly easy, if you know Yiddish," he answered. "Could I go up to my room, Poppa? I'm not hungry!"

"Asher! I'll have none of that sort of talk!" commanded Goldstein. "Now, come to the table and eat with the rest of us!"

"Yes, Poppa."

"If the boy isn't hungry—" Paul began.

"*Ach!*" responded Goldstein. "The boy just doesn't want to eat enough! It's as though he wants to die of malnutrition!"

"And he had a little trouble in school today," put in Shoshanna. "He's all right."

"I'll eat ice cream!" said Asher hopefully.

"You'll have roast goat with the rest of us and be happy," answered Yonah.

"Goat?" Paul asked, startled.

"It's kosher," smiled Goldstein. "Do you want we should lift a cow into orbit? We can do fertilized eggs now, it's true—but goat's become traditional."

"Then what they say is true? That you eat the flesh of once-living animals?"

"Does a beef vat have cloven hooves or chew its cud? Come, come! That isn't kosher. I told you that we keep a kosher house. Besides, you want that we should wait for the meat to drop over from natural causes?"

Again Paul swallowed. He had eaten meat-from-the-hoof in *yurts* on the Gobi desert and in wattle huts of the South American Indian, but he hadn't expected to find animals still being slaughtered within a technologically advanced culture. Cloned meat had come in because it was more economical. It produced larger quantities at less cost and with absolutely no waste. Once large-scale meat production began in the cloning vat, human morality had changed. A vat of muscle tissue contained no morally bothersome brain and nervous system.

When cloned meat's price dropped below that of meat on the hoof, and people's gorges settled from the idea of eating meat grown by culture, "animal rights" reached full acceptance. And it was animal rights that were used as a major part of Neo-Nazi propaganda. Until this time, entering a culture in which he had purposely not been trained to function, he had assumed that this was another part of the lie. It was obvious that he had touched a sore spot—he had angered Yonah.

The others smiled as Shoshanna lifted the cover from a curiously rounded portion of meat.

Yonah pulled Paul's eyes away by standing. Apparently the meal was to begin with more than a simple grace. It was to be a religious service. Along with everyone else, Paul tore open a small foil packet. Inside was a premoistened towelette. As everyone washed their hands, Yonah spoke. *"Barukh atah adonai Eloheinu . . ."*

Shoshanna translated. They all touched a switch and the towelette vanished into a vacuum slot built into the side of the table. The prayer continued.

Paul gulped at his wine. He was here to do a job, and that job depended on gaining the trust of those around him. The UN had been remiss in not telling him *something* of the culture into which he was going. It was one hell of a way to make a first impression on the rest of the family.

"There you go, Dr. Greenberg," said Yonah handing him a plate.

Paul accepted it with a smile. Gingerly, he tasted the meat. It was coarser, firmer, and more solid than cloned meat. He didn't know whether or not goat had ever been cloned. The meat had a pleasant, gamey quality. Venison, and a lot of other cloned meat, had similar flavor.

Then it struck him: the lack of sleep, the constant sunlight, the shifting time zones and gravity, the lack of food brought on by spacesickness, and the flood of gastric juices combined with the present social tension to produce a sharp burning deep within him. It came on so strongly as to distort his features.

"Could I have a glass of milk, please?" he asked softly.

Shoshanna threw a spoon at the table. "Enough!" she cried. "First, he criticizes us for eating the sort of meat that people have eaten for millions of years! Now he wants that we should buy three sets of dishes—one for meat, one for dairy, and one for *treyf*!"

Paul's ears burned. What had he done now?

"Shoshanna!" scolded Yonah.

She had risen from the table and now stood with her back to them.

Yonah's gaze fell on Greenberg and softened. "You are in pain, Dr. Greenberg," said Goldstein. "What is wrong?"

"Duodenitis," Paul said. "A sort of ulcer."

"Shoshanna!" commanded Goldstein. "Get Dr. Greenberg a glass of milk!"

"Tell me, Dr. Greenberg," he said, "what do you know of our dietary laws?"

"I know that you don't eat pork," Paul answered.

Shoshanna returned from the kitchen, and broke into an embarrassed giggle when she heard his answer. "Please forgive me, Dr. Greenberg," she said. "I suppose it was the meat thing that upset me. As a writer, I have been fighting the anti-Semitism that has been generated by the Neo-Nazi party. It can be difficult if your morality conflicts with that of the rest of the world. Cloned meat is the only thing—the only part of our religion—that seems in total conflict with the rest of the Earth-Moon system. It can be defended, but it is difficult when the other side is so prejudiced."

Goldstein swung his arms toward her. "My great, knowledgeable daughter," he said. "She doesn't know that a *goyische* Jew might not be familiar with his own customs!"

"I'm afraid that it's I who should apologize. I haven't been feeling well since I got here, and I let it show. I've been extremely rude."

Goldstein placed an understanding hand upon his shoulder. "It's quite all right, Paul. We understand, and you are forgiven. Would you like some more milk?"

Paul nodded. Shoshanna took the glass and left the table.

"I thought ulcers could be treated by freezing," said Goldstein.

"Not duodenitis," answered Paul. "It's an ulcer in the small intestine. It's extremely difficult to reach."

Again, Paul grimaced. "Of course, it can be treated

by laser cauterization. I've scheduled an appointment on Terra."

Three years before, Paul had been called into the UN's psychoanalytic labs in Chicago.

"What's this all about?" he asked a faceless intercom grill.

"Voice pattern identification completed," said the emotionless voice. "Come in and be seated, Agent Green."

The double doors swept open, revealing a small waiting room.

Paul bit his lower lip. What was all the mystery about?

Somewhat warily, he opened his dator and tried to catch up on some news.

A chime announced the opening of the doors to an inner office.

A tall, angular man stood in the doorway. He looked as though he had aged prematurely. "Come in, Mr. Green," he said.

"What's this all about?" asked Paul. "Why did I have to take an extra day off my vacation to come here?"

"You can leave your cape in the waiting room," the man said, ignoring his question. "Nobody's going to steal it."

Paul did as he was told and followed him into a small, comfortable room.

"Sit down, Mr. Green," the nameless man said, "and roll up your sleeve."

In perplexity, Paul did so.

The man opened a drawer, pulling out a hypodermic gun, then pressed the barrel against Paul's naked arm. There was a chug, a surge of pressure, and a kiss of moisture. Absently, Paul rubbed what remained of the drug away from the bruise.

Paul's reflexes were tested and found negative. Then the doctor leaned back against an ever-present console and crossed his arms.

"We've just gotten back your medical reports. They show duodenitis—an ulcer in the upper tract of the small intestine. That's why they brought you before psychological—it's a sign of sentimentality. Are you getting sentimental, Mr. Green?"

The voice was hard, acid.

"No, I—" Paul began.

"Because if you are," continued the doctor, "the UN can't use you, Mr. Green!"

The doctor reached behind him and snapped a switch. The standard white roomlights vanished, replaced by a somber, bothersome mixture of green and blue. The air was filled with a heavy, syrupy music—just the sort he didn't like. It was too slow to be catchy, and too complex to be restful.

Paul opened his mouth in protest, but words wouldn't come. He tried to get out of his chair, but the muscles wouldn't respond. Paralysis? No, something different. Something more complex. Something sucked away his anger, his need for action, and drew him toward a yawning pit of despair.

The doctor walked around the console and flipped a switch. A display of red tell-tales were showing Paul's breath, pulse, skin, and digestive chemistry. Their ruddy, sulphurous light cast itself upward over the doctor's face, like the light of hellfire on the face of a demon.

"Have you forgotten *her*, Mr. Green?"

"Who?" began the response, but it was answered before he spoke. Behind the doctor, a curtain was being drawn aside. Behind it was a standard 2D screen. A forgotten face smiled warmly from the screen. Blue-black hair fell down honey-colored cheeks; dark brown eyes glistened with desire. She tossed the hair over her bare shoulder with a long-fingered hand.

She looked exactly as she had 15 years before—the first and only woman that Paul had truly loved. The only woman that he'd desired, but never had.

Goddamn the doctor and his drug! Goddamn the

artificially induced despair! The drug *created* depression! If he had a knife, Paul knew that he would be slashing at his own wrists. If he could have found the strength, the desire to move, he'd be trying to dash out his own brains on the sharp plastic corner of the doctor's console. Only one thing made him want to live—that face! That honey-colored ray on the screen! He felt all will sap slowly from him. He felt his self-esteem flow away. He felt himself falling out of the chair and onto his knees, his arms raised toward the screen. Involuntarily, her name escaped from deep within him. It burbling from his lips in a cry of want, depression, and despair. "Kathy!" he sobbed. "Kathy!"

The doctor laughed—a laugh that carried mockery, disdain, and disgust. "No wonder you sickened her," he said.

"Don't!" sobbed Paul. "Please!"

"July 17th, 2068," continued the doctor. A photostat of a piece of parchment appeared on the screen. "Remember this?"

Another sob escaped Paul's lips. He blushed. "Where did you get that?" he demanded.

"A poem!" said the doctor, ignoring his question. "Isn't that sweet? And on parchment, too! Must have cost you a bundle!"

"Stop it!" demanded Paul.

"You talk of love," continued the doctor, "but that's not what you really wanted, was it?"

The image of Katherine returned to the screen. She was as he'd never seen her. Her pupils expanded into warm pools; he felt that he could dive into them and sink forever. Her lips were parted and glistening with moisture. She was as he'd never seen her; open, warm, and filled with sexual desire. Her head tilted back, and the camera followed her fall onto a satin-sheeted bed.

Paul felt his soul wrinkle inward like a collapsing balloon. He watched with revulsion and desire.

In half his mind, he knew that it was a computer

construct. But the other half wasn't sure. He was certain that they'd never tell him.

"Where did you get that?" he fairly screamed.

"You know the vid screens on the doors of the restroom stalls?"

"Stop it!"

"Slip in half a franc—"

"That's a lie!"

"Is it . . . Yid?"

Paul felt strong hands picking him up off the floor and leading him toward the door. "I don't know what that drug was that you gave me," Paul said under his breath. "But I'd better not find you when it wears off!"

He felt a foot meet his backside. "You won't find me, Green," assured the doctor. Paul collapsed on the carpet of the waiting room.

The doctor flicked a switch on the console. A television monitor showed the hunched, weeping figure in the outer office. He pushed another button, twisted another knob. "The treatment is completed," he said. "If he's not out of here in another two hours, I'll send for the ambulance. If he does recover, he should be good for another couple of years."

Paul didn't remember the incident. What happened from the time he entered that room until the time he emerged was no longer a part of his memory, only an angular, sardonic face—a face that he would crush with his bare hands, should he ever again see it.

He lay in bed and held his burning abdomen. It would be some time before the soothing milk reached so low in his digestive tract.

A chime sounded.

"Come in."

"More milk, Dr. Greenberg," said Yonah, bringing in a tray. "I've arranged an appointment for you tomorrow. We'll have that burn closed by tomorrow afternoon."

"You don't have to do that."

"We have medical facilities here," Goldstein said.

"I think that the milk is starting to take effect. I'm more tired now than I am in pain."

Goldstein placed a hand on Paul's shoulder. "We've got a lot of work to do. We can't have something as simple as that standing in our way."

Goldstein rose and left the room.

Chapter VIII

August 21, 2086   Home of Yonah Goldstein
Elul 11, 5846   Wednesday
2:30 a.m., Jerusalem Time

Paul suddenly found himself wide awake and staring at the darkened ceiling. Carefully, he reached up and pulled away a bit of plastiflesh—an artificial sleep inducer, the passage of a slight current through the brain. Without the twists and tugs, the emotional responses, and the sorting of information in dreams, it provided a full night's rest in just a few hours.

It was a discovery made by Russians in the latter part of the 20th century. Since sleep without dreams would eventually lead to madness, the public had promptly forgotten it. But since it took two or three nights to produce the first symptoms, it bought a spy valuable time—time when those around him were asleep.

Paul pulled out the dator; it still flashed green. He opened his arm, stripping back the synthetic flesh. From this he extracted the pistol and got dressed, tucking the gun into his belt, then adjusted his artificial eye to see in infrared.

"Two kinds of people live in Byutt Sebulon," the Little Man had said. "The rich and the unemployed. It means nothing. The unemployed are everywhere. Mostly in the Byuttim's lower levels. Our intelligence tells us that the lowest level is a detention center. Under most circumstances, the wealthy would not tolerate such a situation. However, the circumstances are extraordinary. The increase in unemployment has naturally brought about an increase in the crime rate. Sections are sealed off without special authorization. That authorization comes in the form of a credit card. We sent a UN credit card through our last agent to the leader of the underground. He reported that it worked. Gollum is not programmed to record small business transactions on a conscious level, so we're safe, as far as that's concerned.

"However, quite understandably, there is a high demand for credit cards in the lower levels.

"We've arranged for you to meet with a leader of the underground in an airlock section of the 28th level—a dangerous part of town, so to speak."

Silently, Paul tiptoed downstairs and out of the house. Cautiously, he moved through the park. A credit card was good only so long as its theft was unreported, or the money in the account held out. Assuming Jewish criminals were as moral as those on Terra, it was doubtful that the victims of such robberies survived.

Paul reached the elevator terminal. It was empty. Here he would be safe from such criminals—the stores were wealthy enough to contain voiceprint identifiers as well as those that identified the user by fingerprint.

A chime sounded and an elevator arrived. Paul pressed his card into the slot and pushed his index finger against the small glass pane. The elevator was totally empty. He pressed the button for the 28th level and took a seat.

The elevator stopped, and Paul stepped into a surprisingly well-lighted terminal. It was surprising because it already had the look of decay. A bracket on the wall was minus a camera; blows from a ball-peen hammer showed where another camera had been installed within the safety of a wall. Its lens had finally been smashed. Another silent lens had been blinded with a wad of chewing gum. Graffiti in unreadable Hebrew marred the porcelain and tile around him. Paul was grateful for the vandalism. He might have been discovered, had the monitoring and security equipment survived.

Like most 21st-century governments, Hazera provided housing, clothes, oxygen, food, and water, but there was nothing more, and the quality of goods freely given was poor. Presumably, as the ratio of unemployed rose, the quality of the leftovers and seconds would fall still more.

Paul could see evidence of this. The buildings were in need of paint. Glass was broken. A heavy stain covered most of the front window—some corrosive acid? Paul walked toward the heavy, sliding-glass door. He saw a slot in the side—it could only be opened by giving a credit card and a fingerprint. What if the machinery here were not programmed to contact Terra for voice-print identification? Did the underground know the security at the terminal? They made their way about the city via its air, water, and sewage conduits. Since the Goldsteins seemed to feel reasonably safe, probably more was needed than a credit card and a fingerprint. If such vandalism had occurred inside the terminal, what might the people be like outside? Paul sucked in his breath. Yonah said that the elevator systems were handled outside Gollum's consciousness, and unless security systems now and then required killing someone, they were enormously stupid. He inserted his standard UN credit card and a recording asked a question in Hebrew. Sweat trickled down Paul's face. The question was repeated. Unless he responded, Gollum might be contacted. "Paul Greenberg," he said. "UN Deep Space Projects Council, Electrical Engineer."

For long seconds he waited. He gave himself a chance of one in 25.

Stupidly, the security device did as it was programmed. Bypassing Gollum, it masered to a nearby satellite, which bounced the message around the Moon

and to Earth. The long transit time ended only after
the inquiries had been bounced back and forth to
eliminate distortions caused by static. The security
device was not programmed for artificial clarification and, having the intelligence of a dragonfly, by-
passed its problem by redoubling inquiries and
answers. It then lay the recordings one atop another.
When it did this, the message was complete.

So Paul waited, composing a story of how he was
unable to sleep and had decided to go exploring.
Should he receive an inquiry from Gollum, he doubted
that he would be believed. To Paul, the story sounded
impossibly weak.

But the computer confirmed the voiceprint and
that his budget was enough to make theft and vandalism an unlikely motive.

The door hissed open and then closed behind him.
Other, nonmechanical eyes had watched from the
shadows. The credit card would be a valuable item
and, though the eyes' possessors had no way of bypassing the voiceprint machine, they could still reach
some of the higher levels. The card could make *some*
purchases—some shops and stores were still open on
levels 25 and 26. The climb up the chimney of an air
conduit was tortuous, but it would well be worth
their while.

Paul remembered the Little Man's briefing on this
meeting, and his caution about going through the
park. He couldn't see that it applied. The grass was
dust, the trees and bushes stripped of vegetation. It
made an eerie hiding place. Still, he mindfully followed the face of the terminal toward the edge of the
enormous Byutt. This end of the level was the center
for distribution. The stores were not stripped of windows and contents like those farther down, but both
the windows and doors were protected by steel shutters. He looked nervously at the piles of trash and at
the darkened doorways. He was wondering if, even in
dodging the park, he were avoiding hazard. Here,

with four out of five street lamps out, there were
plenty of hiding places. Paul thought he heard something scrape behind him. There! A man had quickly
pulled into a doorway.

A metal food tin rattled. There could be no mistake. There *would* be trouble. He wondered how many
of them were there.

Paul looked back over his shoulder. Two silhou-
ettes stood against the light of a street lamp.

"Hey! *Razey!*" said a voice in a stage whisper. Paul
turned back again to confront a grinning, sweat-
streaked face. It belonged to little more than a boy.
The others stepped out of the shadows behind. Hungry wolves always hunt in packs. The first crouched
down, the long blade of a homemade knife in his
hand.

"*Yesh lekha keseph?*" the boy asked. "*Ten li hakeseph,
shellkha.*" A thin chuckle erupted from his throat.
"*Bevkhasha, Adonai,*" he added.

The others laughed appreciatively.

Paul, not getting the joke, looked back over his
shoulder. The other two had become three and were
approaching at a slow walk. One held up something
in his hand, kneading it between his fingers. It was a
small bit of plastiflesh that would harden in the air.
Paul knew that it was for taking a cast of his fingerprint. Adequately soiled with body oils, it was enough
to fool a checking computer. Paul knew that the pred-
ators intended to take the casting from his corpse.

In a stir of realization, Paul wondered how he was
going to get out of this. Spacer guns were fired with
compressed air; the bullets traveled at just under the
speed of sound. The bark of his own gunpowder would
wake the entire level, and they would know he was
from Earth.

"*Ten li hakeseph!*" This time, the stage whisper
carried the sharp bark of command.

Paul refused to answer. He knew no Hebrew, and if

he answered, word of his presence might get back to Gollum and Prime Minister Cohen.

The boy was barely three meters away from him when Paul heard an approaching hiss. It took a moment for the sound to register, then he remembered the conversation with Yonah about the computerized delivery system, and about the magnetically supported trays of goods counterbalanced by weight in the shape of an inverted "T". He turned. The overhead counterweight was approaching at about 30 kilometers per hour. If it would support the weight of a refrigerator and compensate for the weight of a child, it would compensate for his own. He leaped up, letting his artificial arm absorb most of the impact. Simultaneously, the metal ball-and-socket joint of his elbow twisted around at an unnatural angle, allowing him to see where he was going. The inhuman strength of his arm, the strength of pulleys and nuclear-powered cable, countered the backward swing of inertia. He swung his body forward, raising his legs against inertia, using a nuclear-powered shoulder joint. A swift kick caught the knife-boy under the chin. A simultaneous kick caught the man to his right. The third turned, stunned for a moment, as Paul whistled past.

Damn! Paul should have known better than to trust in a delivery system when all stores along both sides of the level had been closed for ages! The delivery was to a public distribution point on this side of the building. The counterweight stopped barely 200 meters from where he had first grabbed it. He went sprawling onto the filthy tile of the walkway. Soft, padding footsteps were following.

He got up and began to run. Hazera spun at better than 240 meters per second. Centrifugal force made gravitation at the Goldsteins' level about Earth-normal. But the farther 'down', the farther away from Hazera's center one went, the higher the gravity. Gravity here was increased by only about one tenth of a G, but it was the equivalent of carrying a knapsack of 18 pounds—not much, but enough to slow him down. The people who were following him had probably grown up in this environment; their muscles were more accustomed to the strain that was put upon them. Also, though Paul hated to admit it, they were younger than he. Unless he could cut down that alleyway to reinforcements, it would be a short race.

Paul spun around the corner and cursed to himself. He was already beginning to lose breath. The alleyway was just ahead. They were close behind. He plunged into the alley's blackness. Nothing lay ahead but the blue, dirty triangular light of an airlock window. He turned back. The alley was narrow—barely wide enough for two men to walk abreast. As the group of six spun to a halt outside and started, double file, up the alleyway, Paul turned over a trash barrel and rolled it toward them. The clatter would wake up half the level, but by the time people emerged from their homes, he would be safely through the airlock door. Some of the group scattered, but the second man that he had kicked had lost two of his upper teeth and suffered a broken nose. Blinded to the fact that he might be caught, he was seeking revenge. With the nimbleness of a lumberjack, he rolled the trash can beneath his feet and kept on coming. Quickly, Paul's fingers found the airlock's greasy opening switch. The door slid into the wall, but before he could turn to find the closing button, a heavy weight fell across his shoulders, knocking him to the floor. Paul rose to his knees. It was evident that the man did not have a weapon. If he had, Paul's throat would have been slit by now. Against both his weight and the boy's, he struggled to his feet. He arched his back, as though reacting to the choking of the boy's arm. Then with a swift motion, Paul reached up and behind, grabbing the boy's collar at the nape of the neck. With a backward kick, the attacker's feet were brought out from under him. A twist brought him forward and over Paul's shoulder to crash against the floor. Paul pulled out his pistol, hoping with its threat to force the other out of the airlock. The fellow ignored it and rushed for him. The pistol went off. There was a thin hissing and a light breeze. A klaxon horn was sounding; the light within the airlock had changed from blue to a flashing red. The other's face went pale. He rushed to the spaceward side of the room and placed his hand over an inch patch of darkness that had appeared in the outward wall. Still holding his hand over the hole, he turned a terrified face toward Paul. It was as though he were looking at a madman.

"Dr. Greenberg!" The voice came with urgency from behind him. Paul turned. The narrow door led to a hallway and a frantically motioning figure. The door was closing like the shell of a clam. In order to seal off the leak, one rubber-edged door was rolling down from the ceiling; another was ascending from the floor. Paul dived between them.

"That was very foolish, Dr. Greenberg! Come on. Let's go!" Six strong, youthful figures had joined the first. They lifted him to his feet and hurried him down the hallway. The flashing red light and klaxon horn vanished with the closing of the double door.

The figures led him through a maze of passageways and rooms that held the outer and intermediate airlocks. Finally, they stopped in a hall and ran toward a sealed door. One of the figures stepped toward a small board of keys and began pushing them.

"A combination lock," explained the slender, blue-eyed, bearded young man who appeared to be their leader. "Seventeen separate digits. If the *downstairsnikim* ever break that combination, there's going to be hell to pay!"

The door slid open on a tiny room. No—not a room, but a platform! Two escaladders, one going up and the other going down, stood at its edge.

"A maintenance shaft," explained the curly-haired young man. "The benevolence of our government has provided jobs by allowing human beings to make repairs via the airlock sections. Step aboard. We're going up."

The young man's voice carried sarcasm when he spoke of the government's 'benevolence'. Paul knew that this *was* benevolence. A benevolence that Hazera could ill afford.

"Let me see your gun!" barked the young man.

Paul handed it down to him. The other looked it over for a moment, opened a chamber, and growled in disgust. He barked a command to one of those below him in Hebrew. In a single motion, above a dizzying height, one of them leaped from the upward-bound escaladder to the one going down. The leader laughed as Paul closed his eyes against vertigo and clung tighter. The leader handed up his gun. "That was incredibly foolish, Dr. Greenberg."

"In my view, anyone who attacks someone with a gun barehanded is a fool," spat Greenberg. "I never draw a gun unless I intend to use it."

"A spacer who draws a gun in as thin-skinned an area as an emergency exit lock is a fool!" said the man. "And if the safety is off, he is a madman!"

"Lead bullets! They'll find traces on the tear. The leak has been confined to that chamber, so I'm banking on its taking the repair crews an hour or more to arrive. I've sent one of our men to suit up, go outside, and scrape off the edges. Spacers use glass bullets, Dr. Greenberg—fired with compressed oxygen. It is unlikely that glass bullets will puncture the side of a thin-skinned space craft and they're fired at a low velocity. They'll penetrate flesh, but not metal. You're already suspect just by being from the UN. Let's hope that you haven't given yourself away completely.

"Step off at the next level."

Paul did as he was told. Again, he was led through a maze of rooms and passageways.

"What about that fellow back in the airlock?" Paul asked.

"A pair of popped eardrums, and some frostbite where's he's sealing the hole. He'll probably come up with some story concerning being attacked. That's an emergency airlock leading directly outside. It's possible that a glass bullet could penetrate that wall if it were fired at very close range. He'll be all right, if you're worried about him."

"Not really," Paul answered.

The other smirked. Paul blushed a bit at his seeming amateurish. His rescue hadn't been quite as miraculous as it might seem. He and the Materet had an appointment in that lock. It was just lucky for him that the underground were punctual.

A door slid open before them. Inside was what had once been a machine shop. The long benches were now mostly empty. In one corner were four small tables covered with portable computer and communications equipment. Pocket projectors threw up images of Hazera, its various levels and substations.

"Do you think you could find this place again?"

"Are you kidding?"

The young man laughed. "I am known as *K'khol Sheva*."

"Is that a name?"

"No, Dr. Greenberg. It is a color and number. If one of us is captured it prevents them from identifying the others. We even refrain from recruiting new members of unusual appearance. We don't follow your actions in that emergency airlock. We try not to draw attention.

"We'll install your communications device if we have time. However, the reason for this meeting is to give you some information of great importance to the UN.

"Midsha Ah Shuai'm Asher?"

Another man punched out a code on one of the pocket projectors. An image was thrown on the wall.

"That's not Svenglid!"

"No, it isn't. It's supposed to be a solar furnace. Our government says that it's purely commercial. Rather ridiculous, wouldn't you say, considering that the only use to which we can put our metals is into the construction of permanently outward-bound robot probes? That thing is some 15 kilometers in diameter!"

"That's not quite so unusual," observed Paul. "Such heat could ionize and allow for new metallic combinations. Maybe—"

"Perhaps, but it is far too large for the production of heat alone, unless it were for the processing of extremely large quantities. However, our findings show that it is not a furnace at all." Again he spoke in Hebrew.

A video disc was slipped into the projector. *"Tsebah Sha'im Asher* took this with a black suit, Dr. Greenberg. Have you a black suit?"

"It's lining my regular suit," returned Paul. I know how to use it."

K'khol nodded. "Good. I don't want you getting roasted out there."

The projection showed a slow drift toward the bowl-shaped structure that Paul had seen in schematic. "There! Do you see that ring at the back of it, like a bead choker?" K'khol stopped the projection, and a portion of the image's backside grew until the quality became grainy. Paul looked closer. They looked familiar, but he still couldn't place what they were.

"Mitsu Mark 18 fusion generators," reminded K'khol Sheva.

"Aren't those the ones that the Japanese are making for the Germans?"

"For use in the asteroid belts," affirmed K'khol. "Sunlight's rather weak out there, so each one produces enough power to run a fair-sized city, several moderate-sized factories, and enough firepower to punch a hole through Phobos. And that's all we know definitely. Actual possible output has never been reported, but a monster Mark 18 was allegedly designed for use as Svenglid's engine."

"What use could this be?" asked Paul.

"We did a preliminary scan of the plasma rod at its center, before it was installed," returned K'khol. "It's phony. Camouflage. Like the cardboard tanks that Rommel—may he burn in hell—used in North Africa. It's our guess that it's used to cover something else. Tell me, Dr. Greenberg. What does the entire structure remind you of?"

Paul crossed his arms and raised a brow. "A salad bowl," he said. "If it were made from wire netting, I'd say that it might be a microwave . . ."

"Do you remember, about 25 years ago?"

"I doubt it. I was only ten years old."

K'khol snickered. "I wasn't even born," he said. "We found reference to something called *Project de Sauvon*. It was designed by one of the French colonies, before their new and radical government took over. It might have saved the UN billions of francs in space probes. Basically, it's a radar dish, one that would make dependable mapping of Uranus' and Neptune's moons possible. The UN turned down the proposal. Do you know why, Dr. Greenberg?"

Paul shook his head, although the implications were already raising the hairs at the back of his neck.

"Because, in order to generate and send a radar beam of that power," continued K'khol, "you must produce not only a research device, but a weapon.

"Most reflectors of light are also good for microwaves," said K'khol. "The adjustable panels can be used to vary the intensity of the beam, and to vary the point of focus."

"Who do you believe they are going to use this weapon against?" asked Paul.

"Who is powerful enough to justify the building of such a weapon, Dr. Greenberg?"

Paul's eyes glinted like gunmetal. He felt his fists

tighten and his skin pale in suppressed rage. "Earth!" he finally spat out.

K'khol nodded. "Why? We don't know. Magen Metals is in charge of production, but from everyone involved we hear nothing but glowing reports of how it will end all our problems and feed everyone. None of the diagrams are anything like the ones we see here—at least, close up.

"We're taking our suppositions from history, Dr. Greenberg. This isn't the first time that the building of an engine of war has been used in an attempt to pull a country or a political entity out of depression. And it isn't the first time that the masses have starved to build an engine of war. The plague is a perfect cover. As long as the viroid is active, nobody is coming here unless they absolutely have to. No one who knows anything can leave, and transmission of information through normal means is carefully monitored. *Nobody* can go out of the city! The plague struck so long ago that no one outside even thinks of Hazera, or takes it seriously.

"The plague caused the institution of martial law—instant dictatorship—and with a dictator whose brain is so old it's dried up! She's quite mad, Dr. Greenberg. The plague has prevented espionage, so what is really going on has been covered up. Even the populace doesn't know—the plague keeps everyone inside. Unauthorized personnel are not allowed outside the city, unless it's to scale the city's walls for repairs. The government has provided for its own protection. What we are told is that French ships would kill anyone who ventured outside unarmed. The use of private space craft is prohibited."

"How do you get around?" asked Paul.

"The black suits," answered K'khol. "Jump off, and centrifugal force will take you anywhere you want to go. Course corrections can be handled by standard suit jets—you just fall past what you want to look at. This halo orbit isn't empty, Dr. Greenberg.

It's filled with factories, abandoned commercial and private craft—just plain debris. The radar protection systems, to a certain point, just assume that you're a bit of flotsam. If you suddenly change direction, the computers assume that you've bumped into something that they can't see. They're designed to attack anything that masses about that of a one-man ship, or is going fast enough to do damage.

"Around *Svenglid* and *Ra*, however, there is an impassable barrier. Nothing gets close."

"What about getting back?" asked Paul.

K'khol laughed. "More flotsam," he answered. "The end of private space craft allowed us plenty of floating command centers—and factories."

This time, K'khol himself popped the video disc out of the pocket projector and inserted another.

"A lot of flotsam," he said, "is composed of old machine and satellite parts. Mechanical and electrical equipment of every shape and size occupy this orbit. Here's something that can't be told from any other—"

The object appeared to consist of a jumble of welded hand straps, fuel tanks, and attitude jets.

"It's spinning," explained K'khol. "Grab a handhold and its centrifugal force will take you in any direction that you want to go. The attitude jets help it maintain position, and the fact that much of this old stuff is still working allows us to install a homing beacon—solar cells."

"Pretty ingenious," said Greenberg.

"You'll be using it," returned K'khol.

"Okay. Assuming that the *Ra* project is what you say it is, what do you propose we do about it?"

The other looked perplexed. "It won't be easy," he said. "Around the perimeter are some 360 swivel-mounted lasers, one for each degree of circumference. Supplementing these are six charged-beam accelerators . . ."

"Jesus!" Paul leaned back and folded his arms.

"Okay," he said. "What do you propose we do about it?"

"Direct attack! And as soon as possible."

"Obviously, that's going to be a problem. Hazera is a good day and a half from NEO, and it sounds like it would take the UN's entire fleet to knock the thing out."

"Then use it."

Paul shook his head. "It would leave Terra unprotected," he said. "I'll report it. What will they do about it? Well, that's up to the Security Council."

"You might add that we can create a diversion," added K'khol. "Possibly a smoke bomb in front of a solar mirror." He chuckled. "We've done it before. They have a devil of a time clearing it away."

Unfortunately, Paul hadn't had time to place his communications antenna beyond the wall of the bedroom. He barely managed to make it back in time to 'wake' with the rest of the family. However, he did make arrangements to meet with K'Khol that afternoon, on the basis of what was probably a long shot.

Yonah waved a fork at Paul during breakfast. "We're going to the hospital," he said matter-of-factly.

Paul shook his head. "I'm really quite all right."

Yonah lifted a brow. "You're all right now, it is true. But what happens if it kicks up again while you're here? You will be wasting the UN's time, your time, and my own. I won't have it! We are going to the hospital!"

Paul grimaced. He was due to make his first report tonight. The receiver at *Oomi Mi* would probably remain open for several days, or until a report arrived on Paul's death or capture. Still, he always prided himself on his punctuality, and his request to Yonah for a break would probably be suspicious to him if they didn't spend the morning at work.

The treatment was brief. It consisted of a sonic scan and a zap with a penetrating laser. His internal wound was sealed shut. Paul was sorry to lose this internal gauge of sentimentality. The UN would be even sorrier. Here, it had struck Paul as a good part of the character he was portraying—something that had appeared on Terra and he hadn't bothered to have fixed. When one suffered from something for years, one tended to forget how easily it could be repaired. Paul's lack of sleep was causing him to make some dreadful social and logistical errors. His ignorance of Jewish custom had been aggravated by plain rudeness. A family with whom he was supposed to gain trust, may have been turned against him. May have grown more suspicious—Might be watching him more closely than he would have liked.

"*Nu!*" said Goldstein. "You feel much better now. We're ready to get some work done. Yes?"

A chill went down Paul's spine. A break from work after a morning in the hospital would increase suspicion. However, he would have to risk it. Using the electronic sleep inducer that night would make him even more irrational. He had to get some natural rest. And that meant that he would have to get away from the Goldsteins, out of the city, to get the maser transceiver installed. He grimaced and shook his head. "I've got four days of total time set aside for R and R. I believe I saw an amusement park as we were coming down."

Paul's nervousness increased as Yonah gestured with both his hands. "*Ach!*" he cried. "First he was sick. Now, he wants to play!"

Paul steeled himself. "Gnu," he responded, not sure what the word meant. "They were working me hard on Terra," he quickly explained. "Getting me ready to understand Svenglid and its purposes. After the trip, I think I deserve a break before we begin."

Yonah pondered this. "So, we will visit the Ghetto," he finally said.

* * *

At one time, everyone had thought that television would eliminate the natural need that people felt to get out and away. When most office work was done from the home via computer, every major city suddenly blossomed with an amusement park. Shopping was done from the home, via television, for most things. School could have been done from the home, but that was one idea that busy mothers quickly voted down. The security of familiar surroundings no longer held the fascination that it was supposed to have had. People needed surroundings with simulated dangers. On Terra, nearly the only wars practiced were against imaginary East and American Indians, Nazis, and Napoleonic soldiers. All of this was done inside huge, warehouse-like structures that covered many hectares. Each resembled, in great detail, the countryside that it was built to represent. Thus, an African veldt was actually hot, dry and dusty. An Amazon jungle was actually hot, steamy, and filled with gigantic but harmless insects.

As Paul had hoped, the Ghetto was crowded. His trick was one that he had successfully used in similar situations. A carnival, a fair, or a Mardi Gras had several times come in handy, allowing him to get "lost" and thus shake a companion in an acceptable fashion. The ruse could last up to several hours without arousing suspicion.

The effect of the Ghetto was stupendous! Ancient wooden structures towered over them. The streets were narrow and paved with cobblestone. The overall effect was one of incredible oppression. A massive wooden gate stood, locked at one end of the tiny city. Paul and Yonah were both properly costumed in peaked hats and dark robes with yellow badges.

As they worked their way through the crowded streets, Paul asked, "But what sort of adventure is this! Where's the excitement?"

"I'm looking for something, Dr. Greenberg. Ah!

There it is!" He led Paul into an overhanging doorway and out of the crowds. "The people of these times were brilliant and far more lettered than the Christians around them. Oh, many Jews knew mathematics, how to read, and so on! But other than that, they were very superstitious. They knew the *Torah*, the *Talmud*—but also something called the *Kabbalah*. There was nothing that they could do about the oppression, the offal in the streets, or the misery of their surroundings. They were often totally defenseless against the deadly excitement of Christian purges. But their main adventure was in their collective minds. Here, Dr. Greenberg, your adversary is the supernatural!"

During the course of the next hour, Paul and Yonah narrowly escaped disaster after disaster (an old woman had gazed on them with the evil eye). They were attacked by a creature of grayish clay, which Yonah said was the basis for the Frankenstein monster. A dybbuk, in a very realistic manner, attempted to steal Paul's body. Demons attacked them. Paul, in short, had a wonderful time!

Finally, while Yonah was buying bagels from a passing vendor, Paul managed to lose himself.

"You took your time," said K'khol.

"I had some trouble finding you."

"This level *is* confusing," answered K'khol, studying the narrow, winding alleyways. "The crowd probably made it worse. The Sharon dry-freezing people are having a celebration of some sort today. The rich have fun, while the poor must suffer. Come!"

K'khol led him down a narrow, winding alley, then disappeared into a wet, slickened side street. Amidst all the shingles, the clapboard, and the gray stone, the airlock door looked out of place.

K'Khol stepped to it and pressed a switch. The door slid open, and they stepped inside. "This is the same sort of room that you punched a hole in with your bullet," explained K'khol. "It's for emergency egress only. The maintenance people's suits are in those lockers. That door leads to the outside. The one we want is about two hundred meters down that hall." While he was saying this, he was burning the paint from a wall with a pocket laser. Two bright strips of metal showed. K'khol connected them with a strip of metallic tape. "That will short out the alarm system," he said. "We should be able to get at those suits now."

With two blasts, the bolts on the locker doors were sheared in half. Paul removed his belt and ripped a seam in the back. The tiny microwave dish was concealed inside it. The dish itself was made of foil, filled with pockets. The pockets were filled with a light pressure that would collapse it in the normal pressure around it. When placed in a vacuum, it would expand into a rigid dish. It was here that Paul would say goodbye to his pen, for as well as being a drill and a light-ink pen, it was the dish's receiver and masering device.

Paul took off his costume and began putting on the suit. There was something distasteful about wearing another person's suit. He could already smell the sweat and urine of the suit's owner. Carrying the dish and maser in his hand, with his helmet beneath the other arm, he followed K'khol down a long hallway.

"Blast doors." K'khol motioned with his hand. "Garages for private space craft. The outer doors to the garages opened downward as the craft fired their engines. The engines used to push the ships away from the city before they fell to the next level. Vertically, there's an open space between the garages of about ten meters. We should have a place to stand on. You say that your room is on the second floor?"

Paul nodded.

"Good," answered K'khol. "That means that your hookup will be at the back of one of the depressions. Of course, the UN planned it that way."

Paul nodded once again. "There won't be any danger of the structure blocking the maser's path?"

K'khol shook his head. "The slot is long," he said. "It opens to about 45 degrees of sky. The city always faces the sun, of course. Your transceiver on the moon should be in sight for the next couple of weeks. I take it that your maser is programmed to send and receive information in millisecond bursts?"

"It's best for security," Paul answered.

"I wish we could afford that kind of stuff. Here we are."

K'khol began punching out a code on the tiny keyboard of his watch. He noticed Paul observing him closely.

"It's made by Shahar L'phi Ha'zman," he explained. "Sort of a combination wristwatch and dator. It has somewhat limited use as a dator—the small size of the screen, you know—but it can be programmed to carry the sequences of every combination lock in the city. The information can be erased with the touch of a button. Simple, practical, and almost foolproof. Our equipment may be crude, but it's better to have with you if you're caught."

Paul found himself agreeing.

On the tiny screen, the code appeared. It was, in turn, punched out on the lock. The door slid open on a room about the size of a small, walk-in closet. They put on their helmets.

"Can you read me?" asked K'khol.

Paul gave him the thumbs up sign.

"Can you read me!" repeated K'khol.

"Yes!" Paul shouted back. "I can read you!"

"Good," said K'khol, with some disgust. "The reason that I demanded verbal response was to make certain that both suit phones were working. Ready?"

"Ready."

K'khol pressed a switch and the air was drawn from the room. Paul wasn't sure what he expected on the outside. He found himself standing on an iron grillwork. A thin railing separated them from the void. The sight of the stars spinning beneath probably did not give him as much vertigo as the perspective of the building. It might not have been so bad, if somewhere there *were* a bottom. The stars only served to tell him that if he fell from here, he would fall forever.

"Are you all right?"

"Yes," answered Paul into the suit mike. "Just give me a little time to get used to it."

He could feel K'khol grinning beneath his helmet. Here, he was a Terran—an outsider. He remembered the captain's derisive and dangerous actions aboard the *Harpo Martz*. The Americans aboard the space city of Astropolis even had an environmental slur from the old Buck Rogers comic strip. They called Terrans earth worms. He knew that, if the underground were not actively seeking the UN's aid, K'khol's actions would have been just as derisive—and dangerous.

Paul pulled heavily from his oxygen mask. "Okay," he said. "I'm ready. Let's go."

K'khol stepped over the abyss and onto a tube-encaged ladder. When only his head and chest were above the metal grill, he turned toward Paul.

"You coming?" he said.

Paul approached.

The garages, the ship locks must have been two stories high. It was easily 30 meters to the next level. Paul followed K'khol onto the metal grillwork. Although the gravity only varied a fifth of a G from the Byutt's top to its bottom, Paul was sure that he could feel it growing stronger as he descended. He breathed a sigh of relief as he stepped off the ladder and onto the more 'solid' floor of the grill. He felt even happier when they stepped off the grill and onto the roof of a garage.

K'khol pointed. "Your relay unit should be sticking out of the wall somewhere over there. Paul snapped the buckle off his belt. Its fabric was already fading and crumbling in the vacuum and direct sunlight. It didn't matter. He had a spare. A pair of rollers on the back of the buckle helped the belt slide through for locking. Now they served as wheels, as they traced a path along the wall. A green light blinked on at the side of the buckle as it detected the faint outgassing from the room within. Paul took his hand away as the buckle aligned itself and 'plugged in' to the tiny bundle of optical fibers leading from inside. The buckle then cemented itself to the wall and Paul attached the microwave dish and pen transceiver.

He backed away. "The message concerning *Ra* will be sent tonight."

"Are you going to help us sabotage it?"

Paul sighed. "I don't see how one person could help you. Can anything get near it?"

"No," K'khol said. "We lost three men and five robot spies trying. Those lasers are going to hit you no matter what your mass or rate of speed."

"What about Svenglid?"

"It's not so heavily guarded—at least, not the engine portion."

"How do the workers get through to these structures?"

"Their buses carry a beacon. Apparently, there's a machine aboard the bus and another on the structures themselves. These machines seem to generate a radio wavelength at random. And they both appear to make the same decision at the same time. The buses generate a flash of radio waves and the machines respond to let them through. Those that do not generate these wavelengths are destroyed by laser."

"Have there been any accidents?"

"Not to my knowledge."

"Has the government made any excuses for these overly protective actions?"

"They don't have to. Hazera has been sealed. No one is allowed outside without authorization. This is supposed to prevent the spread of our infection. As though sport flyers couldn't confine themselves to a certain sphere! One of the things that the government says is that most workers come from Byutt Yudah and Byutt Simeon. Our telescopes have taken photographs of the projects and there are some workers there with azure sleeves on their suits. Azure is the ID for Byutt Levi!"

"Isn't that the Byutt that's supposed to be dead? Wiped out?"

"That's right. Completely wiped out by the plague."

"And you don't think it has been?"

"Obviously not!"

"That Byutt may have been reoccupied. It has been five years."

"Why? Would overpopulation force Byutt Yudah and Byutt Simeon into Levi? There would be too much work to do, too much cleaning up. There are too many other things for us to do. Obviously, Levi has not been reoccupied. I want you to take note of two things, Dr. Greenberg. Oh, the plague is real enough. It was one of our own people who infected Yudah, an unfortunate occurrence, for reasons which I will now state. In ancient times, the tribe of Levi was a tribe of holy men—a tribe of priests in the temple. In modern times, there has been a strange irony. You see, all three of those Byuttim were atheist. Jews have an encyclopedia of rules called the *Talmud*. A religious Jew is motivated to obey those rules. An atheist is not. Therefore, the best place to recruit workers for projects disobedient to the *Talmud* are the atheist Byuttim. It so happens that the Byutt that we ourselves infected provided 500,000 new workers for these blasphemies.

"For a time, we were able to stay in contact with members on Byutt Yudah via maser. However, contact was cut off within two weeks.

"Some interesting things were occurring at the time, however. People were being called into the offices of their companies and given injections. What occurred after that, they themselves weren't sure. There seems to have been a time of questioning, mostly concerning our patriotism, our loyalty, our religious views, and our identity as a part of the Jewish culture."

"Truth drugs," said Paul. He could almost see K'khol nodding with his helmet.

"Truth drugs, yes," came the answer. "But truth drugs far in advance of anything that has come before. Ordinary truth drugs can be fought with hypnosis and conditioning. Their last messages involved inexplicable disappearances of underground leaders. The rest were losing their jobs and being sent to 'new quarters' in the upper and lower levels. Members in Byutt Yudah were unable to find one another. Otherwise, contact would have been renewed."

"The leaders?"

"Probably executed or in detention. There's one other thing, Dr. Greenberg."

"What's that?"

"They're going to notice that the suit lockers have been broken into. They'll be looking for something suspicious." K'khol pulled something that looked like a small panel from behind the space suit's utility belt, and unfolded it into a perfect replica of one of the many conduit boxes that studded the sides of the Byuttim. It was placed over the microwave dish.

"Your information concerning *Ra* will be sent tonight," said Paul.

"We already have a video disc prepared for your transmission."

Chapter IX

Prime Minister Tetsu rose from the cushions of his office as the doors slid open.

Tetsu bowed formally to Andreikimov as he entered. "*Ohayo gozaimasu,*" he said.

"*Ohayo gozaimasu,*" Andreikimov returned.

The prime minister motioned toward the windows. "It is a fine morning, my friend," he said.

Andreikimov winced inside himself. It was amazing, the number of ancient customs that refused to die, or worse, were reborn in space. What would follow would inevitably be several minutes of mutual compliments, empty conversation, and joking. All of this must be done before they got around to the business at hand.

"In space," answered Andreikimov, "when one wishes a fine morning, all one must do is open the shutters."

Tetsu chuckled. "By 'fine morning,' I meant that outside of the ragged edges of age, the feeling is fine. The tea is warm and sweet in the mouth, and the cushions are soft. Come. Be seated. Would you like some tea?"

"Hai. Dozo arigato," said Andreikimov.

Tetsu poured the tea into an additional tiny cup. "You interrupt my Sabbath," he said.

"Sunday is the Christian Sabbath," answered Andreikimov. "I thought you were Shinto."

"At my age," said the prime minister "one must take every day of rest that one can."

Andreikimov laughed appreciatively and added, "Then, perhaps the prime minister would be interested in the Moslem Fast of Ramadan. I understand that it lasts for 30 days."

Tetsu returned his chuckle. "The rest I could use," he agreed. "But I fear that the fasting would be too much for me." He looked down at Andreikimov's diplomatic pouch. "If the noble UN representative will forgive me, this is a primitive way of doing business. And armed guards at the door!" The prime minister placed his hands upon his breast. "Surely, you have not come to arrest me!"

Andreikimov, once more, returned laughter. Was Prime Minister Tetsu finally opening shop for business? Andreikimov decided against it. "The tea is good," he affirmed.

"Yes," said Tetsu. "It is jasmine and rose hip, with a little ginger. A fine combination.

"You will forgive my rashness," he continued, "but my curiosity has overcome me. Can it be that the documents that you bring are actually on paper?" This he added before Andreikimov could laugh at the joke about paper, "And why must you come directly from Terra? Why the armed guards and the special transport?"

So! The Prime Minister was opening his shop for business! "We are interested in the city, Hazera Ysroel," answered Andreikimov. "It concerns a company in this city and the purchase of a dozen of your Mitsu Mark 18 fusion generators."

"*Ah so!*" returned Tetsu, raising a finger. "I remember! A tremendous boost to our economy from a most unfortunate city!"

"Didn't you think there was something strange in that?" asked Andreikimov. "After all, Hazera is close enough to the sun to get all the power it needs. What could they possibly need with a generator that operated so efficiently by fusion?"

"The Israelis buy many strange things, Dr. Andreikimov. They work on many classified projects. There are, I understand, factories in orbit about Jupiter to manufacture materials and fuel for *Project Svenglid*. Such fusion devices could be of use on any of the dozen or so cometary probes they are building. Or, however unlikely, it may have something to do with their activities on Mercury."

"Mercury!" exclaimed Andreikimov.

"Yes," Tetsu affirmed. "Perhaps the UN has failed to observe the *Yas'or*. As is shown in the earlier diagrams, one part of the craft dips down into the Jovian clouds. And as in the early diagrams, another section stays in orbit. However, two additional sections have been added. These use Jupiter's gravity to slow into an ellipse toward the sun. These sections fall into an orbit around Mercury. One continues to Mercury's surface. But I thought you had observed all this."

"Our computers are supposed to point out to us those craft which are headed in the direction of Earth. We'll check our computer files to see if what you say is true. There are far too many space craft for us to personally observe."

Tetsu smiled. "This is a mystery which has largely been cleared to us. We had purchase orders for vast quantities of lead and graphite—shielding for *Svenglid*. Surely you are aware that the interstellar dust and gas would be striking the delicate electronics as radiation. At the speeds it is supposed to attain—"

Andreikimov waved a hand. He didn't need to be lectured on elementary physics. "Yes! Yes!"

"Well," the prime minister continued. "Hazera cancelled their orders to us. They said that they had found abundant supplies of it elsewhere. Of the elements that formed the planets, the lighter were pushed outward by the solar wind. What more natural location for lead and gold than the inner solar system?

What more natural place for heavy metals than Mercury?"

Andreikimov felt a chill run up his spine. When he said that they only kept conscious tabs on craft bound for Earth, he had meant the Earth-Moon system. They would have noticed ships approaching Hazera from Mercury. It didn't make sense that they would use the fuel necessary for a trip to Jupiter, only to use its gravity to fall toward the sun. If no ships loaded with heavy metals were traveling to Hazera, then they must be rejoining with the *Yas'or* somewhere beyond the orbit of Mars. Something clandestine was going on here—something that they didn't want the UN to know. And the heavy metals included those that were radioactive—uranium, which could easily be processed into plutonium, the stuff of atomic bombs. The world had had enough of these. If *Project Ra* were a device for taking over the UN, such bombs would undoubtedly be used on Geneva, Chicago, Astropolis, or the orbital fleet, effectively eliminating any chance of retaliation or attack.

"We found your 12 Mark 18s," Andreikimov finally said. He undid the lock on the diplomatic pouch and opened it into a disc viewer of considerable size. As the huge screen lit up, the prime minister registered surprise.

"The structure looks like *Ra*," he observed.

"Then why the fusion generators?" asked the UN representative.

"On a power plant for solar energy," continued Tetsu. "That is a mystery."

Andreikimov nodded. "It is until you remember *Project de Sauvon*."

"Ah, yes," said the prime minister. "A radar telescope, as I recall."

"And/or a weapon," said Andreikimov. "That's why it was never built. That's something *else* you will recall."

Tetsu gazed out the window in shock. "Prime Minister Cohen is a dear friend," he said. "I cannot believe—"

"*Think*, man!" demanded Andreikimov. "Think! Does it really make sense that she would send ships to Jupiter only to have them fall into Mercury? It has to be a coverup! Why all the secrecy? Why are they trying to tell us that *Ra* is a solar furnace?"

"I do not know," said Tetsu. "I am only certain that Ms. Cohen's intentions—"

"Ms. Cohen's intentions are beside the point, Mr. Prime Minister! The face of the matter is that by manufacturing such a device, Hazera Ysroel has broken the law! It is the duty of the UN to destroy it! We have come to ask Atarishi Tokyo for help!"

Prime Minister Tetsu was visibly shaken. "Help you?" he asked quietly. "I am dreadfully sorry, Dr. Andreikimov. That is something that I cannot do."

"The UN doesn't know much," said Andreikimov. "But we do know enough about the Mark 18 to know it's no more a fusion generator than I am a radish. How does it operate?"

"You will have to ask the company, Dr. Andreikimov."

"How many Mark 18s have you in stock?"

"Again, you will have to ask the company."

"You have 287."

The prime minister bowed his head. "It is a shame that the company manufactured for the extent of the patent. They have now retooled."

Andreikimov studied him carefully for a moment. The Mark 18 was clearly a new power source. The only patents upon it were unconnected with the way in which it worked. An industrial secret because, like the cotton gin, it could be easily copied—too easily copied. When he left the prime minister's office, the company would be contacted immediately, and the machinery for manufacturing it would be destroyed. He shrugged. It didn't matter. "What about the problems of converting the Mark 18s to rocket engines?"

Tetsu bowed his head again. "You tell me," he said.

"As I recall the engine for *Svenglid*, it is a simple matter of cutting a hole in the containment vessel and removing a magnetic pressor," answered Andreikimov.

"So many questions that bear their own answers," observed the prime minister. His eyes twinkled. "Surely, you are not testing my loyalty." He paused. "I take it that the Mark 18s will be confiscated."

"With your cooperation, we would have paid a fair price."

"Just so. Tell me, Dr. Andreikimov. How many— What was the polite term of the 20th century? Ah, yes! 'Devices.' How many 'nuclear devices' has the UN taken the liberty of planting in my cities?"

"One bomb for each city sounds sufficient."

"How terribly negligent of the UN. One might be found. One might fail to go off. We are, then, under martial law. All contact with the outside universe shall be through your subordinates via computer constructs. Won't you have another cup of tea, Dr. Andreikimov?"

Paul leaned back from the computer terminal and rubbed the bridge of his nose.

"Perhaps we have been working too long, Dr. Greenberg."

Paul nodded and asked the computer for the time. It was nearly noon.

"Are you hungry?"

Paul checked himself and shook his head. "I could use a drink, though."

"Arak?"

Paul nodded. He was beginning to like the stuff. While he was here as a spy, the RNA conditioning had given him enough knowledge of, and fascination for, electronics to really do two jobs at once. He was capable of filling his official presence by double-checking a large number of circuits for faulty design and efficiency. He sighed. In a few weeks, this fascination would be gone. It was a fascination borrowed and cloned from the brain of some great, though unnamed, electrical engineer. Like a flatworm fed the parts of a trained worm like itself, he picked up the subject rapidly. By now, he actually could have a doctorate on the subject. But the interest that had brought him the knowledge would fade; so would that knowledge that he had gained. Yonah was right. They had been working too long. Paul rose from his seat, placed his hand against his lower back, and stretched. Normally, the 'adult' hobby of playing with toys disgusted him. But Yonah's toys were different. Yonah's toys were electrical. "I have been here a week," Paul said, "and I have yet to see your fabulous ship models."

Yonah smiled. "Our friend Daniel has a big mouth," he said. "I'm afraid that my pride got the better of me. Danny knows very little of electronics, although he is good at electrochemistry. When he was fired by the company, I suggested him for the elevator terminal. You see, I knew you were coming and Shoshanna and I taught him English. I showed him my ships because I knew he wouldn't recognize the circuitry involved."

Paul laughed. "In other words, you used classified company circuitry on your sailing ship models." Paul found himself roaring. "I'm sorry, Yonah. There's just something that struck me funny about using the most advanced technology we have in representations of our oldest means of getting around."

"Then you won't turn me in?"

"As long as you don't put them on display, I don't see any reason why I should."

Yonah breathed a sigh. "Then come into my workshop, Dr. Greenberg." They walked out of Yonah's office and into the living room. He paused at the liquor cabinet to load two glasses with ice, then poured them each an Arak. He motioned with his hand. "On through the kitchen and across the patio." The door opened, showing a small patio separated from the street by a ceramic wall. The Goldsteins had their own tree, a picnic table, and a small shed. The latter was separated from the house and abutted the building next door.

Yonah pressed a thumb against the lock. "Only my dearest friends have seen what is in this building," he said.

The door swung open. There was a carving there, in the shape of a mermaid figurehead. But the outstretched arms held up the screen of an electron microscope.

"I like everything in here to have a nautical flavor," explained Yonah. A row of three windows, made from color television screens, backed the long workbench. Paul smiled to himself. The windows were four paned and imitated the windows of 19th-century New England. Beyond the windows, waves crashed against an artificial beach. They were partially opened and the curtains waved in a synthetic breeze. Paul smiled to himself. The colors were wrong and the scent of the ocean was so strong as to be overpowering.

"Is it exactly like Earth?" asked Yonah excitedly.

Paul knew people who were as great perfectionists as Yonah. He decided to answer truthfully and risk hurting Yonah's feelings. The others had been angry when they found that he had lied.

"Not exactly," answered Paul.

"Oh?" Yonah asked. "How strange. The fellow that I had program the pictures was an expert in fluid mechanics."

"No! No!" answered Paul. "The waves are fine! The whole effect is wonderful. But the ocean is grey only under a cloudy sky. Under a blue sky, the ocean is always green or blue. Also, the scent is too strong."

"The scent can be easily taken care of, but I'm

going to have to reprogram the pictures. That's going to take a bit of doing."

Yonah looked at the pictures and frowned. Already his dissatisfaction was growing. With one hand, he turned down the scent.

"Your ships?" Paul finally asked.

"Oh!" Yonah exclaimed. "I'm sorry."

He walked to one of the many cabinets and opened it. The model was small. From the size of the tiny figures moving about on deck, Paul guessed its scale as about one to 200. Like most of the models that Paul had seen in the nautical museums of Earth, it was contained in a glass case with two different weights of oil. The heaviest oil was tinted to represent the sea. A tiny pump kept the oil in motion as the ship floated upon it, tethered in place by wire stretched from underneath.

The lighter oil, into which the model was fully immersed, slowed the motions of the heavier, making scale waves and foam.

Behind the model, a CRT showed the cloudy scenes of a thunderstorm. An occasional lightning flash was provided by a hidden strobe.

"Most impressive!" admired Paul. "I don't think I've ever seen such tiny figures in motion."

"Our new microcircuitry," explained Yonah. "When it's turned on, a dozen dramas are enacted on deck."

"Incredible!"

"Yes," answered Goldstein. "But it is a fairly standard display. Everyone builds a model of the *Cutty Sark*." He placed the case back in the cabinet. "Here's one of my more unusual models."

The background was a lake—no, a fjord! The surface was smooth and glassy, and the oars stroked through it easily. Tall stands of cool pine drifted past against a brilliant blue sky. The tall dragon-prow snarled fiercely. Paul found himself looking more closely. The muscles of the tiny Vikings actually bulged with the effort of moving the great oars. One had an eye covered with a leather patch. Another grinned through rotted teeth. One was doubled over in back of the ship, evidently suffering from a stomach wound. In spite of the ministrations of a Viking shaman or witch doctor, he was evidently not long for this world. Paul leaned back from the tiny work. He had always thought that the Vikings had believed it an honor to die on the battlefield. Therefore, he had always assumed that the wounded would be killed. He shrugged. Perhaps the wound had been only superficial and had become infected on the way back from a raid. He found himself chuckling. The miniature scene was designed to bring about just such a train of thought. At the same time, the ship itself was so well researched and constructed that he felt he was viewing an actual part of history. "You're an artist!" he exclaimed.

Yonah smiled. "It takes many—I hate to sound like an egomaniac, Dr. Greenberg, but 'skills' is the only word that comes to my mind in English. It takes many skills to make an electronic model. It's still unacknowledged as an art form. I've tried to analyze the difference between modelers and artists. Evidently, an artist is given more free rein and uses only one skill. Perhaps perfected to the ultimate, but still now as diverse as that of the electronic modeler. It seems strange that the artist has more prestige."

"Nonsense!" interrupted Paul. "Model ships have been acknowledged as works of art for a very long time!"

Moses raised the two tablets of stone over his head in anger. Allon had used the face of a cliff to back and frame the figure, a detail that the artist who painted the original had neglected. Allon always pictured Moses as standing on a ledge rather than a pinnacle.

Today was the day that the bomb would be arriving. He'd called the company and said he was sick.

He couldn't deny being nervous or upset, yet it was far from a case of conscience. The nervousness rose from the expectation. Would the bomb work? Would anyone be killed? Was there some trace of evidence that would link him to it? He didn't believe that there was. He had covered his tracks at the magnesium pump with plastic explosive. The vial of liquid within the explosive had broken via a radio pulse. Within the underground pumping station, holding tanks had been ruptured, mixing oxygen with the explosive magnesium. Though he had murdered a man, it was looked upon as an accident rather than a case of deliberate sabotage.

The glass casing that Allon had made for the bomb had been carefully monitored by the kiln computer, enabling an enormous wedge of glass to be chilled in a matter of hours, instead of months. Minute sonic pulses had measured the various rates of expansion and contraction over its surface. Flaring radiation had been used to monitor and adjust its chilling.

Years before, Allon had bought a machine to spin high-temperature metals into fine wire to duplicate realistic hair and beards. He clucked his tongue. It had been a stupid idea. Still, it enabled him to spin the molten magnesium into a fine wool—a wool which, in vacuum, would end any questions concerning the different expansion and contraction rates of glass, magnesium, and lead. There was no way a sudden change in temperature could rupture the glass from inside. A lead wool had been packed at the bomb's geometric center. A heavy glass lid was placed on in a vacuum and sealed by laser. The same laser smoothed out the seams to that they wouldn't show.

An influx of neutral nitrogen passed through the kiln, carrying the heat into several thousand hectares of lunar surface. It was amazing how much lunar surface area it took to cool ceramics. In total, the coils of Dos Telerl extended several miles underground and expanded to fill the entire Israeli sector. At one time, an infrared scan of the lunar nearside would have shown the entire disk to be glowing dully. Of course, those days were past. It would have been much easier to smuggle a bomb aboard the *Parrim*, when metal was being processed for delivery to Earth. Now that Terra was legally cut off for delivery of metal and ceramic products, most of the cooling coils were shut down. It had made it far easier for him to buy the "real estate" that he needed to cool the gigantic kiln. But delivery to Hazera via the *Parrim* was almost a thing of the past. The demand for metal was about equal to the changeover in personnel. In the past, the bomb could have easily been slipped among the thousands of ingots. Now, one of the ingots would have to be removed and hidden. The bomb was large enough to make a noticeable difference in the pile, and thus draw suspicion.

The fact that the 'open air' warehouse was manned by a single shift made it easier. The ingots were hard to walk off with and so valueless, in themselves, that security was nonexistent. There wasn't even the bother of a standard 10-meter wire-mesh fence.

The fellow at the RV rental service knew Allon well. Allon tended to spot his vacation about the year. He spent his time sightseeing about the lunar surface. The RVs were little homes unto themselves. Large windows of transparent glass spotted their exterior and lead shutters automatically folded shut in the event of a solar storm.

Allon drove the vehicle to his home and loaded the ingot into the large storage hold. He then took his dog to the kennel and, linking airlocks as usual, loaded the RV with supplies. A collapsed lava tube passed the city to the north, which headed in a southwesterly direction. Allon had seen this as a means of going north, then heading south out of the range of the ever-present radar. He rode down to the tube's bottom via the vehicle's tanklike treads. It was a

paved road, well traveled. He passed an abandoned
hotel in the valley's southern face. A sign, its lettering browned by sunlight, directed the way to the old
American spacecraft, *Surveyor VI*. He finally turned
up the paved road that led to the mining complex.
There, he found a vast depot. The huge vehicles were
dark and, in the lunar vacuum, silent.

Allon used the manual override to close the lead
shutters, making the RV nearly indistinguishable from
the trucks, which hauled heavy equipment for the
repair of mining machinery.

The RV passed under the monorail that brought
the ore to be melted and settled in the great ingot
molds. The upper portions of these castings, mostly
common glass, were sheared off and broken up into
glistening piles of slag.

Allon continued north on the paved road. Here, all
pretense of preserving the moon's natural grandeur
had been abandoned. With only the vacuum to pol-
lute, industry gloriously did so. Lunar beauty did
not exist in the eyes of the Terrans. Most of the tourists had been Jews from Earth, on their way to see
what other Jews were doing. Preservation of the surface was carried out strictly for the Moon's inhabitants. Allon even remembered a Terran telling him
that the slag piles were the most beautiful thing he
had seen.

Allon looked at his watch. Although the sun had
already cleared the lunar horizon, Allon's 24-hour
clock registered nearly 1500. The area was deserted.
Cautiously, Allon drove the great tracked vehicle onto
the many hectares of storage area. Most of it was
empty. Near the shipping depot, however, was a small
pile of ingots. The great traveling crane was conve-
niently near. He linked airlocks with it and his employee's card got him aboard. For a second, he glanced
over the tiny keyboard. Magen Metals hadn't managed to change it since he transferred to the sales
department. It was obvious that even Magen could

not afford to modernize. He returned to the RV and opened the great hatch to the storage compartment. Reentering the crane, he programmed its several spiderlike robots to select an ingot and bring it to the crane's loading platform. The robots scampered easily to the top of the ingot pile. Once there, they pulled out one of the great quarter-disks and set it on the platform of the crane. Allon lowered the ingot to the ground. More robots unloaded the crane and scampered to the RV. There, they pulled out the ingot-shaped bomb and ran with it back to the crane. Once this was loaded onto the crane's bed, Allon raised the platform back to the top of the pile. The robots quietly replaced the ingot with the bomb.

Within three minutes, it was over. While Allon had done his best to disguise the RV as a maintenance truck, the move had proved unnecessary. In all this time of traveling, he hadn't seen a moving thing that had a soul.

On his way back, Allon realized the grossness of his error! The great, glassy, metal ingots were formed in settling tanks. How stupid of him to so carefully equalize mass! Allon had worked carefully to balance the three materials of which the bomb was composed. Yet he had balanced the mass throughout its entire structure! A real ingot wouldn't be like that. The heavier material would sink to the bottom of the casting tank. In ore that was so crudely and partially refined, the displacement wouldn't be noticed on the moon. But it would be noticed in the microgravity of space. The way it floated, the way it tumbled, the way it moved, would be totally different from an ordinary ingot.

The thought sent a chill through Allon. He had to pull the RV over to the side of the road and take several breaths of pure oxygen. It put the problem in proper perspective.

Even if the bomb did gain attention, there was no way that it could be linked to him. The government would first believe that the ingot had somehow been physically hauled in from the Japanese sector. They would check the carefully guarded perimeter. They would look for the telltale tread-marks of the vehicle that hauled it in.

But there would be only the treadmarks of an RV, from a paved road at the bottom of a collapsed lava tube. The tracks joined the road 200 meters from the ingot storage depot. It might or might not have had something to do with the placement of the bomb.

Security at the perimeter would be tightened. Guards would be placed around what had once been thought to be a harmless industrial sector. The fact that Allon had a kiln that might have produced the ingot was purely circumstantial. There were at least a hundred wealthy sculptors in Dos Telerl who had kilns of comparable size. And though at work, he was considered somewhat strange, it was a common enough trait among artists.

No, Allon's real fear was what might happen should the attempt fail. He wasn't sure whether the French cities would accept such a failure. Of course, Nouveau Paris could not point its finger. However, with some difficulty, it could manufacture evidence against him.

Taking another breath of pure oxygen, Allon climbed into a clear glass dome at the top of the tractor. He ordered a plum brandy from the machine's central computer and leaned back in the dome's single adjustable chair. Earth, as always, was directly overhead. The sky was clear, he noted, above Australia, Southeast Asia, the Philippines, and New Guinea. He studied the vast brown desert of Australia and thought. Quietly, he sipped the fiery brandy and felt the strain flow from his limbs. Slowly, he drifted off into sleep.

Paul looked up from his dator at the program that Asher was watching on Tri-D. It was a children's sit-com that had been recorded for Asher around midnight, and seemed to revolve around a fairy or gnome—some such fanciful creature. No, Paul decided. The creature was a tiny, fumbling angel. Although the fictional children were aware of the angel, their parents were not. But this angel was a 'he' —something that Paul hadn't seen outside of classical paintings and literature.

Although the dialogue was in Hebrew, Paul found the plot easy to follow. It was the old and still-funny story of the too-perfect hair restorer.

It began with the angel studying his bald pate in the mirror. He apparently had seen an ad on his supernatural dator.

Paul found himself roaring with laughter as, one by one, the family mistook the concoction for perfume, after-shave lotion, and deodorant.

The characters were painstakingly built up into 3-dimensional image by the computer. They were then animated, as actors supplied the voices. Like many children's sit-coms, the legacy of the cartoon was apparent in that the images were not totally realistic, but seemed to be caricatures made up as though from animated clay. Computer vox boxes were available, but actors and writers still had unions. Advertisers paid a flat fee for the inclusion of their commercials, but these commercials were computer sorted and sent only to those homes that could afford the products advertised. Gollum deliberated for fully two billionths of a second before including this commercial. To pour a little salt on Asher's wounds might reinforce his lesson.

The view on the screen changed to a blue globe surrounded by laurel leaves. The UN anthem, *Our World*, swelled in the background. In Hebrew, the announcer said: "The United Nations is our friend and protector, but the great fleet of the UN is over 467,000 kilometers away!" Here, the scene switched to a view of the UN police fleet in Near Earth Orbit. "It will take a day and a half for them to get here.

A lot can happen in that time. So, while the UN is coming, *The Hawk* is fighting!" Here the scene switched to a view of a hawk in a steep dive. This gradually faded to a view somewhere in the city, of a huge hangar. A space craft stood in a launching bay, pointed downward.

Paul sat up in his seat. Bristling with guns, rockets, and lasers, it was obviously a combat craft.

"Now, you, too, can join the *Pal-Halala*." Here the same ship, in the form of a toy, swept through the air. "Powered by compressed air, this exquisite model can be yours! You control its climbs, its descents, the blasts of its rockets and lasers!" A boy was shown with a radio control box. "Guided by sonic radar, as well as by radio, the model is completely safe for everyone! Its onboard computer prevents accident or injury! Should any system fail, the model will simply refuse to operate. And extra chips are available for mere prutot."

The scene changed back to the hangar. Centrifugal force pushed the ship downward and out the bottom of one of the city's Byuttim. Once free of the city, its engines fired to life. The ship swooped toward the camera. Dramatically, its lasers flashed. "While the UN is coming, *HaRochel* is fighting!" A fleet of the ships sped toward the camera above a lunar landscape. "*HaRochel*!"

Paul sat back. "That looks like quite a toy," he said. He glanced over at Asher. A tear was streaming down his cheek.

Paul made a mental note to purchase the miniature. It might help him heal over the wounds that he had inflicted on his first night here. More importantly, it might give him some additional material on Hazera's defenses. Every spy could easily recall the plastic submarine that had given away U.S. Navy secrets during the last century.

It was obvious that the Goldsteins would not buy

Asher the toy and it was beyond Asher's means to buy it for himself. It was also obvious that Asher wanted the toy badly. Some sort of punishment? Paul would have to risk it. If anything, it would bring him more tightly into the Goldstein circle, even if Asher's punishment and the reason for it were revealed. It would bring him into a 'family problem'. For what it was worth, Paul would photograph the model and send the pictures to the base on the moon.

The past week had yielded little fruit after the truth concerning *Ra*. While the family had been in shul the day before, Paul had again made contact with the underground.

He had questioned K'Khol on Goldstein's references to busywork on the city.

K'khol had wrinkled his nose. "While so much needs to be done, the bureaucracy has had the people doing, as you say, busywork."

"There might be some additional pieces of the puzzle here," Paul had mused.

"Isn't *Ra* enough for you? Have you received orders to inspect the city itself?"

"The city's defenses? I certainly have!"

"These have nothing to do with defenses."

"Let me look at them anyway."

"We'll have to go outside."

"I've got a suit."

"The sides of the Byuttim that face one another are carefully guarded," said K'khol. "You'll have to look at the absurdities from here."

Fully suited, they stood on an outside balcony, looking downward. The balcony stood between two great cylindrical structures. K'khol had already told Paul that these were the great spacecraft launching bays that he would see on the Tri-D commercial the following day. This high up, the structures possessed no windows or doors, and no locks or guards. Paul had then wondered what kind of spacecraft the building contained. There was no ingress, so it was impossible to tell.

K'khol pointed downward. "That's probably the most blatant piece of busywork," he said. Paul's eyes followed the long, curving, cylindrical structure that led from Byutt to Byutt.

"What is it?" Paul asked.

"It would be impractical to have to transfer people and materials from one Byutt to another only through the hub. You might call it an enclosed railway."

"Why do you call this busywork?" Paul asked. "It seems practical enough to me."

"About four years ago, each unit of exterior tubing was shortened and raised. They used to go through Level 18. Now they go through Level 15."

"What was the government's stated purpose?"

"None was given. There were rumors that it was to protect against vandalism."

Paul nodded. One could protect against vandalism for centuries on what raising the entire system must have cost.

"Level 15," Paul mused. "Isn't that the amusement park level?"

"Yes," answered K'khol.

Paul followed the rail tube down, leaning out over the railing so that he could see where it connected with Byutt Sebulon. He pointed. "What are those?" he asked.

K'khol leaned over the rail with him. Four short cylinders surrounded the rail tube, pointing toward it like the petals of a grotesque flower.

"Shock absorbers," K'khol finally answered. "You know that Hazera is in an unstable LaGrange Point. The rail tube blocks off our view of it from here, but there are attitude jets beneath it. There must be thousands of such packets all over the city. I don't think that we'd be able to stand on our feet if it weren't for such attitude jet shock absorber packages."

Paul stood and clung to the rail, thinking. He felt

not a tremor. "It works unusually well," he said at last.

He could almost see K'khol nodding once again. "Gollum controls it all," he answered. "You never feel anything." He pointed at two strings of what looked like beads. They went through the lower corners of the Byuttim, leading from one to another. "Those are water tanks," K'khol said. "They control Hazera's movement along its plane of rotation." He pointed upward. "When someone crosses a living room up there, Gollum compensates by pumping water from one tank to another down there."

"Then Gollum has a complete record of our movements?" Paul asked apprehensively.

K'khol disclaimed Paul's question with a wave of his hand. "We're always checking on Gollum," he said. "Privacy is still in effect. Otherwise, the government *would* be overthrown. As one of his duties, Gollum simply keeps Hazera from wobbling. That's all. It's as unconscious to him as breathing, pumping blood, or digestion. Gollum doesn't even know that we're here. This being Shabbat, I would guess that most of his energies are being devoted to prayer."

Paul laughed.

"What's so funny?"

"The image of a computer praying," Paul answered. "I want to come out here again."

"Why?"

"I don't know if I told you, but some people are still crude enough to resort to torture instead of drugs. I lost an eye."

"I'm sorry."

"That's okay. It was easily enough replaced with a prosthetic—one with magnification. Those aren't hydraulic shock absorbers—they're pistons hooked into bell cranks. Not that unusual, assuming that Gollum occasionally has to move the city along its axis of rotation. Such could be used to counterbalance acceleration. Still, there are some extremely large and

separate pumps. Next time we come out, let's bring
some binoculars or a telescope. I want to look at
those units a little more closely."

"Did you see something that you don't understand?"

"One of the hydraulic pumps has some lettering on
it," explained Paul. "Evidently surplus of some sort—
and quite old."

"How could you tell?"

"The letters were in the Roman alphabet," Paul
explained. "The design seems familiar. If those are
pivots for tilting the Byuttim, why did they move
them up three stories?"

"It would displace mass evenly on both sides,"
K'khol mused. "It might minimize the power necessary to tilt the Byuttim and hold them at an angle."

"Then why not build it that way in the first place?"
Paul asked. "And why the phony story about protecting the railroads? Why not just tell the truth?" Paul
shook his head. "Since our best postulations don't fit
the facts, it's obvious that the puzzle has yet to be
solved. It proves, to coin a phrase, 'there's more here
than meets the eye'."

K'khol chuckled. "C'mon. Let's go inside."

Paul was awakened from his thoughts by an inquiry from Yonah. He discovered that he'd been staring off into space and thinking of what had occurred
the day before.

"Paul?"

He jumped.

"What were you thinking about?"

"Nothing. Just daydreaming."

"I got to thinking that it was a shame that you
didn't go out to dinner with us last night. You might
have, had you gone to shul. I'm sorry. I didn't think."

"Shoshanna put me in charge of the refrigerator
before you left," Paul smiled."I did all right."

"I've been thinking that you ought to have a taste
of our nightlife while you're here."

"Isn't Sunday night against the rules?"

"Most people around here do their work through computer. Things may get hectic around deadline time, but most people are responsible enough to get their work done when they please." He turned to Shoshanna who had just entered the room. "Have you got anything planned tonight?" he asked.

She shook her head. "Just *Hasarig*," she answered.

"Great!" answered Yonah. "Why don't you take Paul along?"

A short while later, Paul stepped out with Shoshanna and inhaled the night air. Green with growing things, the city possessed the constant scent of spring. The shutters on the sunward side of the Byutt were almost closed. The exterior of the house was filled with artificial twilight. Streetlights illuminated the park across the street as well as the tiled walkways.

"Shoshanna?" he asked.

She walked grimly beside him.

"Have you a beau?"

She smiled, almost laughing. She had long seen a familiar hunger in his eyes as he looked at her. If she hadn't an emotional commitment to Abe, she might be willing to fill it. Paul was a rather bland figure, the sort which is always part of the crowd, never the face that you singled out at a concert or a soccer match. He was still attractive. And there was a virginal, new look to that hunger. She knew that he was a man in his thirties, and had to have had experience with other women. But it was as though somehow she were different and he himself had yet to realize it. She was tempted . . . very tempted. But there *was* Abe, and it was her relationship with him that mattered. It meant too much and wasn't worth throwing away. "I have a friend," she finally said.

"Haven't seen him," Paul remarked.

Her smile widened as she reinforced her message

with a shock. "Poppa doesn't approve," she said. "But Abe's a good . . . grok."

Paul started. The word came from a novel of the 20th century. It meant, then, to know and understand completely. In the 21st century, it also meant the practice of lovemaking—as an artform. It wasn't the sort of thing he expected from someone so concerned with religion. "You do that?!" he exclaimed.

"Of course." She looked at him. "When we moved into space, things were different. So different that the Sanhedrin was reinstituted to interpret our religion in terms of the new reality. At that time—around 2020—Hazera was much smaller. In fact, it was only the structure enclosed by what is now the hub. Population control was an obvious necessity. But how to go about it within the already prescribed bounds of our religion was another problem. Our First Commandment is *'Be fruitful and multiply.'* But now it was a commandment that had to be carried out with control and wisdom. It worked. Our numbers are now six million. So we are growing.

"However, the fight for population control was a long one. Long before we came into space, many of the rabbinate on Earth were concerned because the Jewish population seemed to be dropping. In fact, it was only the percentages that were dropping, not the actual number.

"Out in space, the problems were doubled and tripled—far more obvious than on Earth."

"Food," said Paul. "Oxygen. Water."

"Yes, and food that would be doubly expensive if we were to follow our ancient dietary laws. After the Second Israel's destruction, what had once been a minor sect became a swelling multitude. If we were to survive here, the beliefs of the Chassidim would have to change—particularly their beliefs concerning reproduction. It took years.

"Seven separate Sanhedrinim had to be established and, concerning matters of survival, they all had to

agree. These Sanhedrinim had some advantages that
the previous Sanhedrinim had not. Among them were
panels of experts outside the field of religion, and the
computer, Gollum.

"The first question was whether or not we could
trust in God to provide for an unlimited number of
people. It may seem silly to you, but it was a question that took nearly nine full months of delibera-
tion. The answer was; 'If God could give us minds
that could consider the limitations of the worlds we
were creating, then we must keep within those limitations'. Our historical studies proved the proverb
'God helps those who help themselves.'

"The second question took years. 'Was chastity
enough to control population growth?' Alarmingly,
historical studies showed that it was not. The morality of Victorian England was an outgrowth of the
writings of Thomas Malthus. Psychologists and phys-
iologists were called in. Dr. David Whittier, a Ph.D.
from Cambridge, was the man who really rubbed the
Orthodox nose in reality. Absolutely brilliant in per-
suasion, he touched our sore spot. He argued that
suppression of sex was an error, simply because sex
would express itself in other ways. That among those
expressions was the sadism that led to such things as
witch burnings and pogroms. Artificial birth control
had long been available, but ignored by most Orthodox Jews. However, everyone on Terra was using it,
and mankind was in no danger of disappearing."

"Then you practice what was once called free love?"

She laughed. "Of course not! There are certain acts
that are totally forbidden by the Commandments!
Homosexuality is not officially recognized in any but
the most liberal or atheist Byuttim. Incest is not
practiced at all—or frowned on if it is. The only thing
that the *Torah* seems to be vague on is premarital
sex—except with the ancient priests and so on.

"And hedonistic sex is practiced. Does that shock
you?"

"It certainly surprises me. I expected something approaching fundamentalist Christian morality."

She shook her head. "Physical reality won't allow it. This was one of the most difficult decisions that we ever faced. You must remember that some 15 million Jews were deliberately murdered in the 20th century, and for no other reason than they were Jews. The belief that there is safety in numbers is a hard one to break through. But with Israel as a nation state, driven off-planet, physical realities had to be dealt with.

"There are, of course, certain obligations that go along with this form of morality. For one thing, we believe that it is immoral to make love with someone for whom we feel nothing."

She looked at him. "And I don't," she said.

Paul felt himself blushing.

She giggled. "You and I are tentatively classified as 'friends.' Okay?"

"Okay," Paul smiled.

"Soloman's Grill is two levels up," she added.

"How do you feel about the Sanhedrinim?"

She inserted a credit card for one of the smaller elevators. "Well, something had to be done," she said. "At the end of the last century, Judaism was breaking up into dozens of different branches. There must have been 20 by the time the Rabbinical courts were re-established. Naming the organization the Sanhedrin was a brilliant touch. It rallied the Jews from all over the world! It must have been thrilling to be alive then. In spite of ..." she choked. "The Second Holocaust."

The elevator arrived. It was already filled with gaily dressed evening-goers. They boarded.

"One of the most obvious effects of the Sanhedrin was the final, solid foundation of the synagogue. The High *Zaddick* carries the same air of mystique about him as the Pope, and is equally sought after and acknowledged. Prized for his logic and wit, even the Pope has sought him out!"

"Do you believe that the results of the Rabbinical courts have been good?"

She shook her head. "One of the purposes of the re-establishment was to pull Judaism together. For some reason, our brand of Orthodoxy was bound up with the Chassidim, and the Chassidim now outnumber us. They hold most of the seats of our Sanhedrin. And since the coming of the plague, they've been having a gay old time!"

"What are their beliefs like? I only know their costume."

She wrinkled her nose. "A cult of visions and miracles," she said. "Totally divorced from reality, as far as I'm concerned. They've been known to study the *Kabbalah*—excuse me—Jewish magic. They seriously believe in possession, demons, the evil eye, werewolves . . . For this reason, they've got a movement going to close our amusement park on Level 15."

"You've got to be kidding!"

She shook her head. "Oh, there are rationalists among them," she said. "Doctors, physicists, mathematicians. If they can't prove such things exist, they rationalize how they could. For them, the physical explanation for a miracle doesn't keep it from being a miracle. 'God can do whatever he wants'—those kinds of arguments.

"They're good people, I suppose. They love God. And they enjoy their religion. That's more than can be said for those who make a martyrdom of their beliefs. And they stick together. None of the Chassidim are starving, which is more than can be said for people in this Byutt. They share with one another.

"Some of their beliefs are hard to understand. But you must remember that we have been physically isolated from most of humanity for 80 years. The plague has made that isolation final. Thousands of the Chassid have been put out of work, and this gives them more time for study, more time to pull themselves inward. And if you do that enough, physical reality has less and less meaning.

"The thing that scares me is that Chassidism is spreading. It seems to be blotting out our own brand of Orthodoxy. This entire Byutt used to be made up of Orthodox Jews who were not Chassidic, but certain things are catching on. If you look around you, you'll notice that about four in ten of the men are wearing yarmulkes, in spite of the fact that they aren't in shul or performing any religious duties."

By this time, they had stepped off the elevator and onto the bright deck of flashing lights and into the hubbub of conversation and music. The entire level was given over to nightclubs, restaurants, and theaters. A grouping of Japanese lanterns glowed gaily over the park. People seated at tables chatted beneath a kaleidoscopic projection playing over the waterfall. This was supplemented by an illuminated, constantly changing fountain.

"It looks like another amusement park," Paul observed.

Shoshanna laughed. "Not exactly. Each individual club has its own proprieter. It's not all part of a corporation, like Level 15. There's Sivchat Sha'ar Salome—over there."

"Just what does that name mean?" Paul asked.

" 'Solomon's Grill',"Shoshanna answered.

"That doesn't sound very religious," Paul commented.

Shoshanna folded her arms. "Solomon is the name of the owner," she replied.

Once again, Paul found himself blushing.

She laughed. "It's a hangout for Byutt Sebulon's—how would you say it—'Literati!' I hate to use that word! It sounds so uppity!"

Paul followed her, darting between sidewalk tables and into a doorway.

She moved so rapidly that Paul had a hard time keeping up with her.

"Our table!" Shoshanna declared, waving a hand. A number of people rose at her approach. Shoshanna kissed a tall man with curly brown hair.

"This is my beau, Abe," she smiled. Paul felt his hand gripped strongly. "Abe, I'd like you to meet Dr. Greenberg. Dr. Greenberg has been staying with us for over a week. He's such a workaholic that this is the first time we've had him out." Having made her speech in English, she translated it into Hebrew. "He's working on *Svenglid*," she explained.

"Shoshanna!" declared a little man with a pot belly and a balding head. It was obvious that he was having a difficult time containing himself.

"Morris!" Shoshanna scolded in Hebrew. "Whatever you've got to say can wait until I've finished introducing my guest. Don't be so rude!"

The little man was silenced, but continued to open and close his mouth like a fish out of water.

Shoshanna politely passed over him, going counterclockwise around the table. "This is my literary rival, Orah Rosenberg.

"Orah, *ze* Dr. Greenberg." Orah rose to shake his hand.

"You'll have to forgive Orah, Dr. Greenberg. She doesn't speak English. It's a little sad, really. The translators have massacred her books. At least I can do my own translating."

"Shoshanna!"

"Not now, Morris!"

"This is Professor Weinberg. He's teaching history at Hazera University. He's been a great deal of help on the book I'm working on. He's a specialist on the 20th century Israel."

A smile played about Weinberg's lips as he rose to take Greenberg's hand. "I'm very pleased to meet you, Dr. Greenberg. *Shalom*!"

"*Shalom*," returned Paul.

Shoshanna raised a brow. "And finally, we come to this rude gentleman. Last, but certainly not least, this is my agent, Morris Buber."

"*Shalom*." Buber gave Paul's hand a perfunctory shake, then blurted out something in Hebrew.

"Yes," answered Shoshanna. "My novel should be finished by next week."

The babbling continued while Shoshanna went white and silently sank into her seat.

"What did he say?" Paul asked.

"He says that if I can get the novel finished by next Tuesday, it will be put up for auction on Terra. A large group of international publishers are interested in it, and they're willing to start the bidding at 500,000 francs—sight unseen!"

Abe laughed, giving her a hug and a peck on the cheek.

Buber spoke once again.

"He says that I'm scheduled to be on Isaac ben Isaac's show a week from Thursday."

Chapter X

Security Head Ingrid Magnusson rose from her chair and banged a gavel, silencing the muttered conversation. She moved a hand through blonde-turning-silver hair. At one time, she might have been mistaken for a model or actress, instead of a military strategist. Out of college, however, she quickly filled out her sparse frame with 20 pounds of rippling muscle. Mixed with illegal hormones, her new look brought diverse reactions from men. She had been involved in the Indian Wars of the Amazon basin, a minor insurgence in Central Canada, and fighting on the Pacific floor.

Wendell Wilkie's dream of 'One World' had finally been kicked into reality. It had been a long time in coming and a world had nearly been destroyed. Although some traced InterPol's sudden link with the UN to the dramatic expansion of environmental politics, Ingrid knew humankind and its love for power. Only one emotion was capable of erasing it—fear. Fear of sudden death. She knew what had caused the transfer of power. The nuclear wars of the Middle East and Africa killed presidents and prime ministers along with the infantrymen. Winds swept nuclear dust into neutral nations, killing millions. It was fortunate indeed that the Soviet/American standoff had served as a model for international politics. Once two opponents on any issue gained the technology for mutual obliteration, they were left alone.

191

After all, hadn't the United States and the Soviet Union had the technology for fifty years? Had they gone to war? No. Both were still in powerful presence. Surely the knowledge that total war would destroy everything, accomplish nothing, was enough to keep such wars from occurring. So, with hopes that were to prove false, both warring nations were left alone. Their problems assumed to have been "solved."

Some felt that this was the greatest mistake that humankind had ever made. Ingrid knew differently. It had been a mistake, all right, but a fortunate mistake. If the superpowers had continued the policies that they practiced during the 1960s, '70s, and '80s, the smallest infraction could have drawn both superpowers into total war. There would have been no world society to pick up the pieces. The fact that terrorists had managed to obtain enough nuclear material to destroy three major cities proved that individual security policies were not enough—that some powerful, world organization had to be established in order to control nuclear technology.

A second mistake, in the form of a misprint, occurred on the original of the paper that the UN representatives eventually signed. Just how much power the UN had been given would not be realized until the early 21st century. The United States and the Soviet Union had reached an impasse in negotiations concerning, ridiculously, the distribution of oil products from the Persian Gulf. Both were beginning to decentralize power production and switching to hydrogen as a source of fuel. Two generals met and decided upon a totally impractical and romantic solution. Two men would fight a lonely duel.

Where was difficult. The entire planet's surface was under the watchful eyes of satellites and computers. Even local police forces had access to satellite information. By the same token, the arrivals and departures of deep space craft were rare enough to be noted. That left them with only one area away from eye and radar: the shadow of space on the far side of the moon.

There would only be a few thousand witnesses, and they could easily be eliminated. L-2. Hazera Ysroel was still an infant, a few floating factories and a lonely toroid. The single hiss of a laser could destroy that. That same hiss had succeeded in destroying the city's single communications satellite.

But the Israelis were more resourceful than either power had realized. Bulkheads automatically closed at the ends of the swath that was cut in the city's side. Power was shut down and the survivors huddled in putrefying air as the battle raged nearby. As the winner arose victorious above the lunar horizon, life-support systems were switched on. Hazera's single remaining radio sparked to life. Attitude jets transformed the city into a ship, which rose above the moon's opposite horizon and beamed the story Earthward.

The duel was a case of mutually agreed-upon murder. Had the parties involved been individuals, they would merely have been imprisoned. But the parties, it came out, had been the leaders of nations, and the attack upon Hazera had been an act of war.

War was illegal; therefore, the nations themselves had been punished. At one time, Manhattan had been an island. It was now a crater. Moscow was mostly a crater, too. The Russians were furious and the UN could see their point. However, the Machiavellian principles on which the communists operated had made them some bitter enemies. Was it the UN's fault that the seat of the Soviet economy was also the seat of their government? Interpol's expanded corps took over. The Americans blamed the blast for their falling behind the rest of the world economically. They even had it in their schoolbooks. Ingrid knew that the American economy had been stumbling for a long time. The Americans' economic and corporate records had been on computer long enough to be transmitted elsewhere before the blast.

Of course, that was a time before Ingrid had been born—a time 60 years gone. Now, the only borders that existed were those on maps, and those made by religion, language, and culture.

The present problem was something new, but something that the world had long been ready for. She looked down the list before her. The first thing that she had done was to invalidate those on the panel who were Jewish—Aaron, Abrams, and Gold.

She leaned against the podium. "Gentlefolk," she said, "for decades the UN has been worried about attack from space. It wouldn't take much for one of the cities, as a political entity, to destroy us. For this reason, we have placed 2,400 ships into orbit. Of course, we hope that we will never have to use them.

"For a long time, it has been thought that should an attack occur, it would be from one of those cities at L4 or L5. These, of course, have no lunar mining rights and must rely on material from the asteroid belts or asteroids that happen to drift by in Apollo orbits. The laws that have been passed in the 20 years since the Texan Incident have gotten the space cities upset with us. These are the laws that limit the amount of material which can be brought from the asteroid belt and into the Earth-Moon system. Their industries have reached the upper limit in terms of the material that they can legally process. While other cities are being built, the companies have expanded faster than thought. It will be another five years before they can further expand.

"The courts are clogged with suits against the UN. However, the UN still provides more than it takes. Apparently, the cities still regard the Texan ruling as little more than an irritation. While their economic growth has been slowed, it has not been threatened.

"The first city to take the law into its own hands is quite unexpected. The long-ignored by us Israeli city—

Hazera Ysroel. They still hold exclusive mining rights to a large portion of the lunar nearside. However, the coming of a plague in 2079 effectively sealed them off from commerce with Terra. What the various Israeli industries are concerned with is research craft. Automated and permanently outward bound, there is no danger of them contaminating Earth.

"So we were somewhat surprised when a large, unlisted object was shown under construction by radar scan. An inquiry brought a response that this was a solar mirror—busywork for their unemployed. Since the object was the proper shape, if not the average size, of a solar mirror, we shrugged our shoulders and went about our business.

"However, one of our agents sent us a disturbing diagram." She reached for the podium's console and darkened the room.

Behind her, a screen illuminated a head-on view of what appeared to be a solar furnace. The image slowly rotated to reveal a string of beadlike structures around the back side.

"What the devil are those things?" said a voice behind her. Ingrid smiled to herself.

"Those," she announced, "are Mitsu Mark 18 fusion generators."

"*Project de Sauvon!*" exclaimed a voice behind her.

"Ah!" she cried. "I see that someone has already recognized our problem!"

There was an outburst of conversation, and she again had to use her gavel.

"Order!" she commanded. "Order! Yes, we have quite a problem. The problem is that the Mark 18's true power is unknown. It is registered as having the kind of power that one would expect from a generator of that size; however, there are some suspicious rumors that it is capable of a lot more! So far, it's only been sold to belters and Hazera, so the UN itself has not had the opportunity to test it. Don't take those rumors too seriously, however. Our physicists say that this much power is impossible! However, on the solar furnace, there *are* 12 of them!"

"But that's what they're using on *Svenglid*!" came a voice.

"And the Mark 18 is what we'll be using against Hazera!" she said. "The plan has already been made with the heads of Interpol.

"We made a big mistake. After *Project de Sauvon*, we never guessed that energy weapons would again be used. *Project de Sauvon* was not designed as a weapon. It was supposed to be a radar telescope for mapping distant moons and the cometary orbits. But though it wasn't designed as a weapon, it could still be used as one. After the project was vetoed, the idea of the use of energy weapons against Earth was forgotten—it was too easy just to drop a rock on us, and it was against such projectiles that we prepared ourselves. When *Project Ra* is completed . . ."

"But this thing is . . ."

"*Robert's Rules of Order*?"

"May the Swiss representative address the chair?" General Magnusson nodded her head.

"If this thing is as big as it looks, and it has that many Mark 18s strapped to it, it could wipe out an entire hemisphere!"

Ingrid smiled. "That has yet to be proven, but I can see your point. It's too big to be a weapon that one plans to use. Once brought from behind the moon, it will probably be used to threaten us. If we do not meet their demands, it will probably be used."

"Wouldn't it be cheaper to threaten with that plague that they have in their city?"

"Yes, but this is more blatant and impressive."

"Is it worth the cost?"

"Our agent has reported the belief that Professor Cohen is deranged. If this is the case, then the cost is not an object. You may think that it would be difficult to find collaborators in such a scheme. However, it must be remembered that paranoia is a very subtle form of madness. If people are locked from communication with other sources, then that paranoia becomes contagious."

"May the Brazilian representative address the chair?"

She nodded.

"How do we know that this is a microwave dish? Can we be certain that this will be used in the manner that you describe?"

Ingrid folded her arms and leaned against the podium behind her. Son of a bitch! The Brazilians had always been pacifists, and as chief manufacturers of fuel alcohol and carbohydrate compounds, they had an extremely powerful voice. She pressed her lips together. History was filled with losers who had waited too long.

"Shouldn't we question the Hazerim as to its use?" the Brazilian asked.

"What it is and what its use will be are beside the point," she answered. "It is illegal to build anything that even vaguely resembles Sauvon. And the fact remains that they did not report its real purpose. They in fact, concealed its real purpose from us!

"What do you propose we do about it?" The question almost carried a note of sarcasm. They all knew her to be a military woman.

"It's true that we propose an attack, but not against any but military targets on Hazera itself. Our scans of the structure inform us that she's well armored. Few if any civilian lives will be lost, since our proposed attack will concentrate almost exclusively on the mirror itself. It is our *only* answer—and I must stress this, gentlemen, because time is of the essence. Can I have your vote, please?" The rapid explosion of words and her final emphasis on the word "please" were psychological tricks that she sometimes regretted. It brought about a rapid, almost panic response. A way of forcing a vote to your side, by giving your view and not letting the voter think. She looked down at her console and hissed to herself. Thirty-nine green lights and one red. She was certain that the red light was the Brazilian. Few pacifists had the emotional fortitude to resist subtle coercion.

"The vote has been carried," she announced. "The decision has been to attack!"

"What is the plan?"

"The Japanese space capital was contacted on the inward swing of its orbit. They refused to cooperate, but with some persuading, we managed to confiscate 287 Mark 18s. These will be the engines of our primary attack fleet. We are choosing our healthiest corps members to withstand the G forces involved in our first attack wave. Of course, our first thought should concern the mining colonies on the lunar nearside. Through communications satellites, these are constantly chattering to Hazera itself.

"Now, let me demonstrate one of the UN's own secret weapons." She walked to the end of the room and pressed a door switch. The door slid open. "Gentlemen?" she said. Two men entered with microwave dishes mounted atop tripods. In the center of these were microwave transceivers. The two men set up the dishes at opposite ends of the room. Both then walked out. One of them returned bearing a small black box with two antennae. A smile played about Ingrid's lips as the black box was set, forming with the dishes an equilateral triangle. She picked up a microphone and reached down, handing it to the Swiss representative.

"Would you do the honors?" she asked.

The representative held the microphone to his lips. "What do you want me to say?" he asked.

His voice came out in a duplicate so tinny that its sound was greeted with laughter. This came not from the dish into which the microphone was tied, but from the back of the room. It was a standard, microwave hookup.

"You'll have to excuse the reproduction," Ingrid

laughed. "But if it were better, we might not be able to distinguish it from the original."

She nodded to the man with the black box. He flipped a switch.

"Now try it."

"Hello?"

This time, the reproduction was not heard. The room was, once again, filled with conversation.

She banged her gavel. "The machine works," she said, "from the slight leakage of radiation that falls off to the side of a laser or maser. It's sort of a white-noise producer, but it's infinitely more complex. Basically, what it does is fill in the spaces between the wavelengths of transmission. Being placed at a little distance from the transmitter itself, it cannot do this precisely. However, all that remains of the original message will be interpreted as static by the standard eliminators. Overlaying this will be computer simulations of standard transmissions from the moon to Hazera.

"Three ships of the sort that usually carry water to the lunar cities are being fitted out to carry troops and equipment. These will be landing in the Japanese sector. You know the size of a water tanker.

"No one would attempt a full-out battle on the lunar nearside except the UN. Therefore, we expect that the Israelis are unprepared for any more than the standard, occasional attempt at industrial sabotage—certainly not 1,200 ground troops with better than a hundred pressurized combat vehicles." A lunar map of the Israeli sector appeared on the screen. "We'll be attacking from the east," she said. "Here, you can see that the line of defense is only 20 kilometers wide. Once beyond it, there should be no trouble. There are occasional patrols that run up and down the launch ramp's length, and there are additional defenses about the cities. However, the defenses about the ramp are all outwardly directed. If we slip through the defense's narrow end and follow along within the guns, we should be able to capture the ramp's entire length at about the running speed of the combat vehicles. Once the radios are turned off at Dos Telerl and Akkiba, one of the dishes will be rotated toward Earth. The white-noise machines will be turned off and the computer simulations will keep going. The dish pointed at Terra will generate a single pulse on the emergency band.

"We will be using the moon as a radar shadow. The other cities are being contacted and silenced by us. The Earth is visible from Hazera, but always in partial eclipse with the moon. Radar reflective balloons will be blown up in near Earth orbit to simulate that part of the fleet which is on its way to Hazera. Chaff will also be used to confuse sensors. A ship explosion will be used as a cover story. The attack fleet's path will have to twist, corkscrew fashion, to avoid being seen. They will have to stay in line with the moon as Hazera moves in its halo orbit around the LaGrange point.

"We have yet to check out the Mitsu Mark 18's power, but we can guess that such a rocket engine should make the moon in under a day. They will still be flying pretty fast when they level off over the lunar surface. They'll be doing so a hundred kilometers above it. Flying low, the ships will again fire their engines for acceleration to Hazera.

"While over the moon, they will be flying in 'v' formation. Once clear of the lunar horizon, they will regroup into an open cone formation, about 15 kilometers in diameter. This will, in turn, swing into a hollow cylinder of ships 100 kilometers from *Ra*. *Ra* will remain our main target. Thirty-seven, however, will peel off from the back end of the formation. These will be used to attack the city itself. We will place most of the attack in two principal areas. We will attack Knesset at the hub—this is the seat of government and we hold these persons responsible. And we will also attack those areas in which military installations are held. It was hoped that we could avoid attacking the Byuttim. However, our agent has reported that there are silos of attack fighters attached to the sides of these living quarters. We will concentrate our attacks on these silos. Additional military installations include those banks of lasers near structures of economic and survival importance. These we will have to ignore. We want as few innocent people as possible killed.

"*Ra* is going to be a tough nut to crack. This is the reason we'll be using the Sanyo Mark 18s as engines. While it would be unreasonable to believe certain rumors, it is natural to assume that they are in some way superior. *Ra* is protected by one laser per degree of circumference—"

There were gasps about the room. "And six particle beam accelerators," General Magnusson continued. Again there were gasps. "How can we possibly—"

"Assuming a number of things, we could not," said Ingrid.

"First of all, you're assuming that these weapons are hooked up—that *Ra* is finished. While the weapons may be hooked up, it is doubtful that they would be viewed as necessary until *Ra*'s real purpose was revealed."

"Isn't it possible that they are in place and operational in the event that *Ra*'s real purpose is discovered?"

Ingrid sighed and nodded. "That's a chance that we're going to have to take. However, they were probably designed to lock on and destroy our ships as they were built. It is doubtful that they were designed to destroy ships with the supposed added speed of the Mark 18. We'll be relying on three factors: surprise, speed, and number."

Paul stood uncertainly in the toy store.

"*Ha'im ani yakhol la'sar?*" asked the man behind the counter.

"Does anybody here speak English?" Paul asked.

"*Attah et ha-*UN-*i?*" asked the fellow excitedly. The excitement faded from his face. "*Tsarli,*" he finally answered. "*Ani lo medaber Angli.*"

"*HaRochel?*" asked Paul uncertainly. "The flying model? *HaRochel?*"

"*HaRochel!*" exclaimed the shopkeeper, coming out from behind the counter. Paul was shown three different kinds of models. The third was about a meter in length, and the box included a control box. Paul guessed that it was the one that he had seen on Tri-D. The man lugged the box back to the counter and Paul handed him his UN credit card.

A woman walked in the door.

Predictably, the card was rejected when the man punched in an answer to an inquiry. He handed back the card and shrugged warily.

Paul turned to the woman. "Do you speak English?" he asked.

"Little," she answered.

Paul could feel himself blushing. "Could you tell him to charge it to 'Public Relations'?"

"What?"

"Uh . . . Good will between the UN and others?"

"Oh!" She translated.

This time the charge was accepted and Paul left with the box under his arm.

Abraham's mind was not on the game. He was too happy for Shoshanna. An advance of half a million pounds! It had to be the largest advance an Israeli writer had ever received. Perhaps her father would now allow her to marry. Perhaps her father could see that she was capable of supporting the entire family, and him, until the depression was over.

He slammed his fist into the table and switched off the screen. No. Her father was just too narrow-minded!

A chime sounded.

"Uh-oh," Abe muttered to himself. "Trouble!" He spun around in his chair and answered the intercom.

"What is it, Gollum?" he asked.

"I've got a problem in the lock of Ball Mill Number 17."

"Lawrencite?"

"No. We're processing partially purified ingots from the moon in that mill."

"Take me to it," Abe said. He felt his weightless body move against the straps of the seat. The little car began heading toward the factory.

"What seems to be the trouble?" Abe continued.

"I don't know. One of the ingots isn't acting right. I'm afraid that I caused a jam."

Abe turned on the screen, which was now lit with the exterior view. The factory was blazing so brightly that he could hardly look at it. "Could you fix the wavelength, Gollum? I can't see any detail."

The factory darkened.

"Give me a look at the problem."

The exterior shot faded into one inside. A group of slice-of-pie ingots had wedged themselves into a wall that extended across the entire cylinder. A fine mist of rock and powder floated before the lens. Magen used friction to move the crushed ore from the ball mills into the furnaces. It wasn't a perfect means of moving the ore, and a small amount always drifted back into the reception lock.

"I thought you were programmed to keep this sort of thing from happening," Abe remarked.

"Under normal conditions I am," came the response. "However, this is something unusual."

"In what way?"

"One of the ingots isn't acting right. When ingots settle on the moon, the most massive material will sink to the bottom. I assumed that this ingot, like any other, would tend to drift in a certain direction when pushed at a certain point."

"And it didn't? Give me the waldos, Gollum."

"Here you are," responded the machine. "No, it drifted straight, and all the other ingots piled into place on top of it."

Abe chuckled and slid his hands into the controls. The waldos—the artificial hands inside the reception lock—responded to his own. He pressed them against the ingots' flat faces and tried to maneuver them into the cracks between. After several minutes passed, he leaned back. The ingots were weightless and, as a result, the robot hands were weak. They had just enough power to start the ingots in a slow drift. Abe was finding that they hadn't the strength to move the firmly wedged masses of oxide. He cursed under his breath. "Well, it looks like you've created quite a problem. I've often wondered what the jackhammer on the bottlesuit was for."

"Do you want me to detach the reception lock from the factory?"

"*Ken.*"

As he watched, a small cylinder moved away from the complex. Disposal of heat was a problem in a vacuum. Waste heat was carried away through irradiation from enormous fins, each several kilometers across. Still, in order for certain structures to maintain the high temperatures necessary for materials processing, the entire factory glowed with an orange heat. In order to free the jam, he would have to enter the reception lock.

New materials had been developed to withstand the high temperatures, and since most lunar ores were oxides, the entire factory fairly reeked of oxygen. The factory had to be fireproof as well. The necessity of maintaining a delicate orbit limited the amount of gas that could be vented in any direction. As a result, the interior pressure was often nearly twice as much as on Earth, and composed of pure oxygen. The cylinder still remained attached to the factory via cables.

"Abe?"

"Yes, Gollum."

"I think it would be wise to keep the lock pressurized. It might help dislodge the jam if we were to evacuate the ball mill and use the vacuum to dislodge the ingots."

"How long will it take to chill the lock, in that case?"

"About an hour."

"Have you run cost-effectiveness measures?"

"I have. It will prove cost-effective."

Although the bottle suit was heavily insulated, it was not provided with false color imaging. If the interior were the same temperature, all glowing with the same heat, he wouldn't be able to see anything if he entered it now. All that would have been visible was a brilliant orange glow. In most cases—repair of the waldos, for instance—evacuating the lock would carry most of the heat away. As it was evacuated, the lock would have been cooled by chillers, tiny tubes of which the lock was constructed. Each was filled with liquid waste oxygen. What kept the oxygen liquid was certainly not temperature! It was pressure. The lock was composed of high-temperature silicate oxides. If it were to cool unevenly, it would crack. As Abe watched, the reception lock slid past him, making room for the ball mill, which would also be moved away from the factory. This would allow the temperature change to pass through three, not two objects.

As Gollum opened the chillers, Abe went back to his game. By the time he climbed into his bottle suit and entered the lock, it would be glowing a dull brick red, easily banished with the suit's lights.

"*Erev tov*, Poppa," said Shoshanna, emerging from her office. Yonah sat reading a novel on his dator.

"*Erev tov*," he answered.

"Where is Paul?"

Yonah shrugged. "He went out about an hour ago. Claimed he had some shopping to do. I can't really blame him. If we started with the next set of diagrams, we'd still be working at one tomorrow morning. We're finally getting somewhere. I was getting worried with the High Holidays coming up. Launch time is right after that."

"I know," Shoshanna answered. "How many more *Yas'arotim* have to come in?"

"Just one more," responded Yonah. "The next to the last linked up and began transferring fuel today. The last passed the Martian orbit about four months ago. I don't know exactly when it's due to arrive. That's not my end of it."

Shoshanna nodded. So, the last of the robot bucket brigade from Jupiter was nearly home. How much longer would her father be needed by the company? Well, they had enough money for several years.

"Where's Asher?" Shoshanna asked.

"He's up in his treehouse," Yonah answered.

She smiled. "He's usually at school by the time I'm up. And I plan to be a little late getting home again. I'll give him his lunch tokens before he gets involved in his studies."

"Solomon's again?" Yonah asked.

"Yes. I think Solomon is giving me a party. He won't say so, of course." She had been suspicious all along, but when Abe called her from work, telling her he'd be late but that she should arrive early anyway, her suspicions were confirmed. She threw her arms around her father. "Oh, Poppa!" she exclaimed. "I'm so happy!"

"Congratulations, sweetheart," her father said. "I hope it makes the best-seller list."

"No," she merrily contradicted. "It's too good!" She gave him a kiss and wandered out onto the patio.

"Asher!" she called up into the tree. "Asher, are you up there?"

"Yeah, Sis. Come on up."

She mounted the metal straps of the ladder. Asher was lucky. Not many fathers would be willing to put together a treehouse for their sons.

Asher put down his dator as his sister's head poked through the hatch. "Hi, Sis!" he said.

"Hi, Asher! I knew your Poppa should have had this enamel baked on! It's peeling! And rusting! Look at your pants!"

Asher shrugged. "I haven't been up here in a while," he confessed. "What's up?"

"They're giving me a party at Solomon's tonight. I brought up your lunch tokens."

Asher clicked them together in his hands. "I *hate* tokens!" he said. "How come kids can't have credit cards like everybody else?"

"What do you want with a credit card?"

"Well, if anybody steals it, you can just report it. Then, the first time they use it—"

"Asher, has somebody been stealing your lunch money?"

Asher thought for a moment. Izzy would kill him if he ever told. He shook his head.

"Are you sure?"

Asher began to shake his head and then nodded.

"I see. Well, it would be impossible for you to have a credit card. First of all, it's illegal. Second of all, children have to learn that money is a thing. It has a beginning and an end just like any other thing."

"I'm not a child! And I wouldn't overcharge!" Asher interrupted.

"I know you wouldn't. But a lot of kids would. That's why it's against the law. And while the law doesn't apply to all cases, it applies to most. That's why we have to live with it.

"It's getting dark. I would imagine that Gollum's just about got our supper ready." She looked through the dimming glare of Hazera's chevron shielding. The level's outer shutters were closing. "Let's get inside."

"I wonder where Paul is," said Yonah, punching for the time on his wrist dator. Asher was setting the table.

Shoshanna folded her arms. "He'd better hurry," she said. "That food sure smells good!"

The front door slid open. "*Shalom*, everybody!" exclaimed Paul from under a mound of packages.

"Paul!" declared Yonah. "Where have you been?"

"Back home, it's the custom to buy gifts for people when we stay in their homes," Paul said, somewhat bashfully. "Of course, it's the custom to give them when one leaves, but I feel that I was so rude my first night here— Well, Christmas comes but once a year!"

The family looked at one another.

"For the past week I've been trying to take the family out to dinner, a show, an amusement—something! At least to salve my conscience for the way I behaved the first few nights I was here."

Yonah waved his hands in mock disgust. "We've been through all that! You've apologized and it's over. We've been trying to take you out, and you refused unless you paid! You bought drinks for everyone, or so Shoshanna told me. We'll have none of that!"

"Here," Paul said.

Yonah opened the small wrapped box. "Micro-laser cutting tools!" he exclaimed. "Paul, you shouldn't have! I can't—".

"Take 'em," Paul commanded. "Shoshanna?"

She opened the box and blushed deeply.

"Oh, no!" said Paul. "Another *faux pas*?"

She chuckled in embarrassment. "Well, things may have changed on Earth, but here—" She paused again to blush. "We consider perfume a little personal for just friendship."

Paul smiled weakly. "I hope that you'll manage to explain things to A—any large friends you may have."

She smiled. "I'll do that," she said.

Yonah looked over her shoulder. "The more expensive the perfume," he said, "the deeper the feeling."

Paul again felt himself blushing.

"We really can't accept these," Yonah said. "They're much too expensive."

Shoshanna raised a brow. "Probably bought on his UN credit card," she said.

"Money out of pocket," Paul lied heatedly.

"Shoshanna!" barked Yonah.

"What did you bring me?" asked Asher excitedly.

"Asher!" parent and sister choroused.

"It's okay." Paul handed him the largest package of all.

Asher tore off the wrapping. "*HaRochel*!"

A chime sounded. "Abe?" said a voice.

Abe looked up from his game. "Has it cooled?" he asked.

"Enough," came the answer.

The domed hatch of the bottle suit swung open. Abe pushed himself, feet first, inside it. As he fastened the straps and checked out the control panel, he said, "You know, I wish that you'd evacuated that reception lock. It gets hot enough in those suits. Besides—"

"Besides what?"

The bottle suit dropped away from the car as Abe extended the six arms and flexed them. "Oh, nothing," he answered. "I've just got a bad feeling about this." He tried the jackhammer, watching the bit vibrate silently in the vacuum.

"What do you mean by 'bad feeling,' Abe?"

"I don't know," he responded. "There's just something about this that stinks, that's all."

The computer paused. "Abe," it said. "You don't have to enter the lock if you don't want to."

"Why?" asked Abe. "Is something wrong?"

"I have learned to trust human intuition. I have learned that it is correct 37.382—"

"Okay! Okay!"

"I was just trying to give you an exact figure, Abe."

"It's as exasperating to listen to as it must be for you to say."

"It's not exas— I'm sorry, Abe."

The car moved between the bottle suit and the sun. Some of the suit's chillers opened with a hiss, propelling Abe toward the reception lock. The doorway rotated toward him. The cables, which still connected the reception lock to the ball mill, twisted. It was as though Gollum were playing a gigantic game of cat's cradle.

"How long have I got?" Abe asked.

"The suit is well insulated," Gollum returned. "Having air to transmit heat will only cut its efficiency by half."

"About 90 minutes, then?"

"Yes. Tell me when you become uncomfortable."

The small outer door to the reception lock slid open. Inside was a brick-red glow. "An airlock to an airlock," thought Abe for the thousandth time. If pressure weren't so important in moving material sometimes, the whole idea would have been ludicrous. The bottle suit drifted into the stove-pipe opening. As the little lock cycled, Gollum said, "We seem to have a pretty good seal between those pieces. I'm going to pump most of the oxygen over to our side. The additional pressure could break that jam. However, if the jam does break, your reaction time would be too slow to avoid being sucked in along with the ingots." The inner door opened on a ruddier glow. "I want you to turn over control of the bottle suit to me," Gollum said.

Abe flicked the single switch that provided the suit with shared attitude control. He flicked another switch and the monotonous red was broken up into color and image by the suit's lights. He trained the lights on the jam. Small bits of broken rock ticked against the suit as Gollum brought him closer. Gollum finally stopped the suit and rotated the jackhammer arm toward the wall of stone and ingots. "Try here," said Gollum, pointing with the lights. "It seems to be the thinnest." The jackhammer went into motion.

*　　*　　*

"So," said Yonah from the head of the table. "It was very nice of you to buy Asher that toy. But I think it would be best if he were to return it tomorrow morning."

Paul looked over at Asher, playing with his food. The boy looked ill.

"I think," Paul said, "that with your permission, I might have a better idea."

"Suppose," he said, "that Asher were to tell us at whom the stone was thrown. And why. He could then keep the toy as a reward for telling the truth. I can't encourage throwing stones, however. He'll still have to pay for the CRT in that column."

"I don't know," answered Yonah. "By breaking that projector, he's broken two of our commandments. He's done more than just destroy another's property. People may need to use that map. Asher has '*placed a stumbling block before the blind*'."

Paul could tell by the twinkle in Yonah's eyes that he was merely hedging, making Paul's offer all the more enticing.

"Sounds like a pretty good idea to me," interjected Shoshanna. "What do you think, Asher?"

"I can't tell you!" pleaded the boy. "He'd beat me up!"

"Who's been stealing your lunch money, Asher?" Shoshanna asked. "Yes. I know."

Asher looked over at the model. "He'd beat me up," the boy pleaded. "I'm so small!"

Shoshanna leaned back, crossing her arms. "Asher," she said. "There was a time when all the mountains of the Middle East got into an argument. They were trying to decide on whom the Ten Commandments would be given.

" 'It is on me that they shall be given,' said Mount Carmel. 'Because I am the biggest.'

" 'No!' said Ararat. 'It is on me that the Commandments will be given. For it was on me that the Ark landed. For I am the tallest!'

"Just then, God heard the mountains arguing. 'Stop!' he commanded. 'The Commandments shall be given on Mount Sinai. Mount Sinai is the smallest, and your God loves those who are most humble.'"

Asher blushed.

"God is a pretty good role model, Asher. We Jews won't let him beat you up."

"Well," Asher answered. "Maybe while you've got your eye on him. What's going to keep him from beating me up if he catches me alone?"

A look of anger began to cross Shoshanna's face, then stopped. Asher had a relevant point. She thought for a moment. Her face brightened and her eyes narrowed. "I'll talk it over with your school counselor. And the boy's parents, if need be. Suppose—just suppose that he was appointed your personal bodyguard. Anything that happens to you, he is responsible for. He'll have to answer to us!"

"Iz—"

She silenced him with a wave of her hand. "Before you tell us, Asher, I want your promise that you won't badger him. Placing a stumbling block before the blind twice in one month is too much!"

"I won't! Izzy did it! He stole my lunch money! He's been stealing it for weeks! He pushed me into a maintenance shaft!"

Both Yonah and Shoshanna straightened. "Maintenance shaft!" they both chorused.

"We wondered what you were doing in there!" said Yonah.

"That's why I threw the rock at him!" He began to wrestle his way out of his seat and toward the toy spacecraft. "Let's fly it!" he exclaimed.

"Tomorrow!" said Shoshanna firmly.

"Aw, Sis!"

"You've got your supper to finish," she answered, "and your school work to do."

"Aw, Sis!"

Paul and the rest of the family laughed.

" 'Placing a stumbling block' seems to cover a lot of territory," Paul observed.

"Most of our commandments do," answered Yonah.

The jam seemed to be giving way. Gollum confirmed this by the thin hiss of oxygen rushing from one side of the jam to the other. It was rising to a roar. Abe himself couldn't hear it through the thick insulation of the bottle suit.

"Abe," said the computer. "I think that you'd better leave now."

"Just a moment. Let me—"

"Now! Abe!" The bottle suit began to move away from the jam. "I was thinking," said the computer, "about your premonition. However, until recently, I was too busy to run any checks on that ingot. I had to open circuits that are usually closed in this area of my operation."

The pumping of oxygen from one side of the jam to the other had ceased. Gollum hoped that it could get Abe out in time, so it kept Abe occupied with its explanation. It would have been so much easier had Abe been a machine. It could then have hurled Abe right out the lock without having to worry about his being crushed by acceleration or impact. And should he collide with a bit of floating debris, repair might have been easy. But Abe wasn't a machine. And being an organism, it was best not to alarm him under the present circumstances. The wait had not occurred because Gollum was busy, although it was—the wires and optical circuits involved could have shifted their functions in microseconds. The real trouble came from the fact that on entering the lock, the ingots were stone cold, and the lock was a vacuum. The nearest spectroscopic scanners were on the far side of the ball mill, and there were no absorption scanners available. By the time the ore had passed through the ball mill, it would be emitting visible light. In that condition, the ingots could be spectroscopically checked for content.

The computer didn't curse the harsh conditions under which it was now forced to operate. Under life-and-death situations, Gollum lacked emotional programming. Gollum hadn't flooded the lock with oxygen until it was sufficiently chilled for Abe to enter. That also had robbed the structure of heat. Now, it was barely glowing. Gollum waited as the glow gradually spread to the outer ingots of the jam. Fibers of superglass and metal twisted themselves into a new component. There, the radiations were sorted. While Gollum balanced mass, raised sheep, and fed families, it sorted this and other data. As soon as Abe mentioned his apprehension, Gollum found some spare cells and calculated the probability of an ingot having a perfectly balanced mass. It was one in better than 278 million. Since Gollum had processed more than 150 million, there was the chance that this was the ingot. On the off chance, it checked all of the ingots in the other mills and every ingot that had passed through them since it had begun operation. While some ingots had approached perfectly balanced mass, none had attained it.

The heat passed slowly inward, the wavelengths getting longer. The outer group of ingots showed the usual—titanium, aluminum, silicates—in the usual amounts.

The heat passed slowly inward.

The computer, meanwhile, checked the jammed wall of stone for the places where it was thinnest, as Abe worked with the jackhammer and the bottlesuit's claws.

One of the ingots was beginning to glow strangely. Gollum checked it. Silicates, oxygen—that was correct. But the darkening agents weren't metal oxides or the usual impurities—the principal one was carbon! For all intents and purposes, carbon didn't exist in the lunar surface at all! Fortunately, the ingot had been disguised in a manner that would fool only human eyes. Gollum couldn't have told either until the temperatures exceeded those under which a man could survive.

Gollum made a note to request reflection spectrometers as he explained the situation to Abe. He fired the explosive bolts on the cables that connected the lock with the rest of the factory. They snapped. Due to misinformation, the stress points of the jam had been improperly calculated. The shock of the explosive bolts broke the jam. One of the ingots near the center cracked. Pure oxygen at a brick red heat rushed in to meet nearly a ton of magnesium wool. The bomb went off, exploding into blue-white flame. The reception lock blew apart. Equipment fused. Gollum's senses were blinded. Poor Abe hadn't had time to scream. He was now a part of that vapor. Gollum mourned.

"Surprise!" exclaimed Shoshanna. "I made it myself!"

"Strawberry cheesecake!" exclaimed Asher. "My favorite!"

"Since you won't be able to come to the party tonight," explained Shoshanna, "I thought that you ought to have some pleasure at my success!" She picked up a knife and began to slice.

A chime sounded. "Pardon me for interrupting," said Gollum's voice. "I have an important call waiting for you in your office."

Shoshanna handed Paul the knife. "Would you do the honors? Gollum says that he's got an important call," she translated.

Paul accepted the knife and continued cutting the cake.

"Not such big pieces!" exclaimed Yonah. "It's pretty rich, knowing Shoshanna!"

Shoshanna pressed the mezuzah at the door to her office. The ceramic panel slid open, and she entered. The wall screen was illuminated with a picture of Abe's supervisor. He looked uncomfortable.

Immediately, the pleasure vanished from her face. "What's the matter?" she asked. "Won't Abe be able to make it to the party tonight?" She paused. "There's been an accident, hasn't there? Abe's been hurt."

The expression on the supervisor's face hadn't changed. "Shoshanna," he said, "I think that you'd better sit down."

Her face had paled to the color of cotton when she emerged from her office. Her jaw was pinched with strain, the skin of her face drawn to parchment thinness.

Her father rose, kicking back his chair. "Shoshanna," he exclaimed. "What's wrong?"

She ran toward him. Yonah threw out his arms to embrace her. The cry that escaped from her lips was half sob, half moan.

"Shoshanna! Shoshanna!" her father cried. "What is it?"

But she had already stepped past him and was on her way toward the front door. By the time Paul, Yonah, and Asher arrived at the door, she was rushing toward the elevator terminal.

Yonah turned and rushed toward the door to her office. It slid open. Although open only a few seconds, Paul could see that the screen was illuminated with the face of a stranger.

"What is it?" Asher asked. "What's the matter with Shoshanna?"

Paul reached down to place a hand on Asher's shoulder. "I don't know, Asher," he said. He looked over at the closed door of Shoshanna's office. "I think that we'll know in a minute."

Asher turned and walked toward the couch. He fondled the box containing the spacecraft model. "Is it something big?" he asked. "Like when Momma died? Will we still be able to fly it tomorrow? Can I still have fun? Or will I cry again?"

Paul didn't know how to answer.

Yonah burst out of Shoshanna's office. "Asher!" he said. "You've got studying to do!"

"But Poppa!"

"Go!" Yonah turned toward Paul. "Did my daughter tell you anything about her involvement with a young man named Abraham?"

Paul sucked in a breath. "Yes," he answered quietly.

"Why didn't you tell me?"

"My purpose here was business, Dr. Goldstein," Paul answered firmly. "I felt that it was in my best interests not to involve myself in family matters."

Yonah collapsed on the couch. "You were right, of course. I told her! I told her not to involve herself with him. It's dangerous work! She could only come to grief."

"What—"

"Abe was killed," Yonah answered. "Just a few moments ago. A French bomb disguised as an ingot."

"Oh!" Paul responded. "Are you sure it was French?"

Goldstein clasped his hands. "No one else could do such a thing. May their souls rot in hell!

"Go to her, Paul. I know where she is. She has called it 'the only shul in Hazera that God himself built'. It's a park, under a glass dome at the top of the Byutt. It's the last stop on the smaller elevators. She'll be there somewhere. The sky's black, but it's the only patch of wilderness that we have.

"Go to her, Paul. I forbade her involvement. She won't be looking to me for comfort."

Paul nodded quietly. "Okay," he said. Obediently, he traced her path across the park to the elevator terminal.

"Dr. Greenberg! Dr. Greenberg!" A hand waved to him from the crowd. It was Professor Weinberg from the bar. "What's the matter with Shoshanna?" he said. "I tried to catch her, but—"

"You'd better cancel that party tonight," said Paul before racing on. "Abe's dead."

He caught the elevator and rode it to the top of the Byutt. "Shoshanna! Shoshanna!" he called.

She finally emerged from a stand of bamboo. Her face was white and drawn, but unstreaked by tears. "Paul," she said with a ragged voice. Her arms opened, but she stood still. Paul had been waiting, hoping for such a moment ... and what he felt now surprised him. It was as though his entire being was being drawn toward her. He felt like spinning water rushing toward release from—years—how many years? Without thinking, without calculating, without planning, Paul found himself rushing toward her. He felt her hair against his cheek. The welcome weight of her head on his shoulder. He waited for her sobs, which he oddly wanted to come. It would mean release for her. Her fists clenched into the back of his neck, but the sobs wouldn't come. For a blinding moment of rationality, Paul wondered how best to behave in the pseudo-prudish society. Would he, by attempting to catch her in her weakness, by making love to her, be considered to have "taken advantage"? He let his new feeling, his new emotions carry him. It was only a moment before he placed his hand beneath her chin and raised her lips to his. . . .

Chapter XI

September 5, 2086   NEO UN Battle Station:
                                        Armageddon
Elul 26, 5846   Thursday
9:00 a..m., Greenwhich Meridian

Cynthia Gomez stood on the huge port and looked downward. She was proud of herself. Although the station was huge, 1800 meters in diameter, it still took only a little more than a minute to rotate. Every 30 seconds the cloud-dotted Pacific spun beneath her. In another 30 seconds, she was looking "downward" at the ship-studded sky. It was as though she weren't looking at something real but a film, its screen between her feet. She wasn't a bit dizzy.

Just out of boot camp, she had been trained as a ground troop. What she was doing in space, she didn't know. Something about "vacuum assault training." She heard footsteps coming up behind her. In the deserted hallway, she turned, and then vaulted over the railing, back onto the walkway. What she had been doing, she knew, was childish and probably dangerous. If it weren't, why had they put a railing around the huge glass port in the floor?

Suited in UN blue, the African broke into laughter. "You did pretty well," he said. "Dizzy?"

She answered his laugh with more embarrassment than humor. "Not a bit. It's like watching a disc."

"I wish I felt that way. I got so dizzy that I couldn't stand up."

"It's a shame about the explosion," she said, "but the debris is pretty." She indicated the bright sparks that had spun beneath her among the ships.

"There wasn't an explosion," he said. "At least not one that wasn't planned. That's not debris, it's chaff."

"Chaff?"

"Yeah. You know. The stuff they use to confuse radar. From every city in space, we're no longer a fleet. Just one immense blip."

"Couldn't telescopes—"

"Certainly. If they care to look. But you'll notice how the ships are grouped together. You see that large ship over there?"

"You mean the Japanese tanker," she said, noticing the red disk painted on the side.

"Yes. Well, our ships are beneath it, above it, around it. From every possible angle, it can't be seen. We—our ships—are blocking the view. Something big is going on. Something *very* big."

"You're one of the ground troops, aren't you?"

"Yes."

"Have you tried calling home?"

A wave of fear passed through her.

"That's enough!" The voice of command snapped them both to attention.

A third figure casually walked around to the other side of the viewport. Cynthia felt her stomach lurch; the floor nearly fell out from under her. It was General Magnusson herself! She looked at the young African.

"What is your business here, Private?"

"I just wanted to see out the port, General Magnusson."

The general's Nordic gray eyes fell on Cynthia. "Did you start this speculation?"

Cynthia's eyes wandered in the direction of the young spacer.

"I asked if you were the one to start speculating!"

"No, ma'am."

General Ingrid Magnusson's hard gray eyes turned to the young African. "You are confined to quarters," she snapped, "until such time as you can learn that you are not up here to speculate. You're here to do a job! Is that understood?"

"Yes, ma'am!"

"You're here to obey orders! Is that understood?"

"Yes, ma'am."

"Dismissed!"

Cynthia felt the young officer's presence disappear. The iceberg eyes returned to her.

"Well?" the general asked. "What do *you* think?"

"I—I'm not paid to think, ma'am," returned Cynthia. "I'm paid to do a job!"

A smile played about the general's lips. "Are you afraid?"

"No, ma'am!"

The general's eyes took in the taut figure. She sighed. "At ease.

"Then you're a fool, Private. I saw you shudder when the ensign suggested that there might be something more to this. What are you afraid of?"

The private didn't know what to say.

"Are you afraid to die?"

"No," the girl answered truthfully.

"Why not?"

"Because you're—I mean—you're dead. And that's it. Isn't it, ma'am?"

For a moment, a look of greater age crossed the older woman's face. "If you're lucky," she finally answered. "If you're not afraid to die, then what are you afraid of?"

"Of running, ma'am. Of freezing up. I'm afraid of being a coward, ma'am."

Ingrid Magnusson's fist slammed the railing. "Is that what they sent me?" she demanded. "A bunch of green recruits!" Her eyes stared downward at the port for a moment, before rising to meet Cynthia's gaze. "So!" she said. "You haven't seen battle, eh?"

Cynthia shuddered. "No, ma'am," she finally answered. There was a pause. "Is there any way to know if you're a coward before—"

The general studied her for a moment before shaking her head. "No. There isn't. You won't know until you panic. If you're crazy enough to run toward the enemy, you're a hero. If you've got the good sense to run away, you're a coward."

"What do you do about them? The cowards, I mean."

"We shoot them. Otherwise, everyone else would run as well."

"Yes, ma'am."

They heard the door hiss open. Ingrid's liaison officer stepped briskly toward her.

"Dismissed," the general snapped. She returned Cynthia's salute while noting her name tag. They waited until the young woman had stepped through the door and it had closed behind her. General Magnusson turned toward the liaison officer. "What's up?"

"It's about those engines that you got us."

"Yes?"

He held up a disc. As she accepted it, her eyes caught the curving, bejeweled knife strapped smartly to the side of his uniform. He was a Gurkha. Quietly, she prayed that she'd never be fighting against them. She'd seen what that knife could do.

She snapped the disc into place and punched for 'load.' "Jesus!" she gasped as the numbers appeared on the tiny screen. "This is impossible!" she exclaimed.

"I'll tell you what our physicists say in a minute. We've run it through computers. With standard tanks and the limits of human endurance, it will be most efficient to get the attack force to the moon at two Gs. Any larger number isn't worth it. At that acceleration, they'll be there in an hour and a half."

"But there isn't an engine in the world that can do that!"

"There is now. Our physicists say that the Sanyo engine somehow creates antimatter in its combustion chamber. And you were wondering why the Tokamak Projectors were so huge!"

"How does it work?" General Magnusson was familiar with antimatter. It had been produced in small quantities for decades, but it was as expensive as hell. She knew that if you could produce large enough quantities, planets as distant as Mars were only days away. Anything that could create power and, at the same time, produce those tiny packets of still more power was worth investigating.

"I wish we could tell you how it works," answered the liaison officer. "But the Japanese have a notice on all hatchcovers. 'These hatches are only for use by qualified personnel.' Preceding this is the notice 'Danger of Death.' They mean just what they say. They're all rigged to explosive charges. We've checked the patent office and they've patented nothing unusual. They've taken more precautions for secrecy than would be imagined."

"Jesus Christ! The Jews could destroy an entire hemisphere with that thing that they've got! They could wipe out our entire planet! Leave nothing but a cinder! Can't we ask the Japanese how this thing works?!"

The Gurkha shook his head. "Not a chance. All we know is that there are five people in all the Japanese cities that know how the machine works. We've tried truth drugs—everything! Nobody seems to know who they are. I mean that they *really* don't know. Repairmen seem to know bits and pieces, but nothing that we can tie into a unified whole. Apparently, their finding of it was a serendipity—a new branch of physics, of which we have, as yet, no inkling."

"What's the ration of antimatter that it produces?"

"We don't know. We turned it up to the point where the physicists were so terrified that we had to turn it down. Oh, it doesn't violate the laws of thermodynamics. Let's just say that it operates at 20 percent efficiency. We've got something pretty powerful!"

"I'll say! Jesus! Can we use it?"

The Gurkha smiled. "Prime Minister Tetsu stated that he feared this would be your response."

"What about the pokers?" The word 'pokers' referred to the first assault team. The term came from the phrase 'slow poke.' Not wishing to draw undue attention to themselves, the tanks and other equipment were strapped inside immense Japanese water tankers. Water was a valuable resource for the moon. The immense cities lost several thousands of gallons a day to outgassing. The arrival of three ships to a field on the Israeli perimeter would draw no attention. The trouble was that the large ships were slow freighters. They followed the old Apollo route to the moon, with a minimum usage of fuel. The trip would be taking them three days. It might not be necessary to send the Hazera attack fleet until the lunar cities were secure. She planned on having the fleet do any fast mopping up that might be done, hence the circuitous route of having the ships level out above Dos Telerl. At least the path to Luna would not be the corkscrew which otherwise would have to be accomplished in order to keep the fleet out of view of Hazera. To the moon in an hour and a half!

"The last two tanks are being loaded," answered the liaison officer, pointing downward through the port.

General Magnusson looked to see two nondescript metallic balloons in the tow of a space tractor. A winged shuttle, its hatches open, floated nearby. Almost instantly, the scene spun out of view, to be replaced by the Pacific. She looked back up again and into the real world. Her head used to spin at such sights, but now she was a veteran spacer.

"Did the recruits see any of this?"

"No. That freighter drifted from in front just a few moments ago."

"These viewports are to be off-limits! And I want the bastard who let those two in here."

Those Gurkhas! Not a shudder, but a smile!

"Yes, ma'am!"

"When will the troops be ready for boarding?"

"We've scheduled them to start in about four hours."

General Magnusson leaned back, placing her hands in her hip pockets. "Okay. Give them ... oh ... ten minutes' notice."

Again the Gurkha smiled. "Yes, ma'am."

Paul placed the binoculars against the face plate of his helmet. Looking downward, he could just make out " ... oston, Mass." The device was in sunshine, but upward-thrusting attachments cast bothersome shadows.

"Can you see what it is?"

"It's a fuel pump. Old. Seems to be reasonable on a hydraulic system, however. I can just make out the date that they've got stamped on the metal—2018. Hmmm."

"That is old!" observed K'khol.

"That might be the date the mold was made, but whatever it is, it's probably been out of production for 30 years. Let's see. You say that it's used to rotate this building for displacement of G forces?"

"Yes."

Paul took his face plate away from the padded double-view screens of the binoculars. "It's apparently an old fuel pump for a chemical rocket engine."

K'khol cursed in Hebrew as Paul nodded. Such pumps were once used to inject fuel into the reaction chambers of hydrogen-oxygen engines—the most powerful chemical reaction possible, even in theory. The fuel was virtually forced into the pressure of a powerful explosion. Paul raised a hand. "We might have to deal with that kind of pressure if we're rotating a structure of this size," he said. "But such pressure would only be needed if we were rotating it at a higher speed than makes sense. Also, I don't like the looks of those bellcranks."

"Why?"

Paul handed him the binoculars. "Look," he answered. "See for yourself."

K'khol accepted the instrument and held it against his face plate. "How much rotation do you think they could make?" Paul asked.

"I'd say 90 degrees!" K'khol answered.

"Can you imagine this city reaching any emergency that would necessitate a thrust of one G along its axis?"

"I'm not certain. I would imagine that one G of thrust would break this city apart!"

"You're assuming that the thrusters would be at the center. You've already stated that there are packages of attitude jets all over this city, evenly distributed among the Byuttim.

"Hand me the binocs. Unless the Knesset is equipped with thrusters at the hub, it's going to fall apart." Paul accepted the instrument and looked upward, toward the administration center.

"See any?"

"No. Jesus! I didn't know that the Byutt supports and elevator tubes could slide around like that! Looks like pneumatically controlled shock absorption and that's all. Can't see any thrust. What's that?"

"What?"

"A line of light. There! It was just visible for a second. There's another one!"

"Probably a meteor."

"Industrial sabotage?"

"*Ken*—I mean, yes. Happens quite a bit."

"I know," Paul answered, remembering Abe.

Another streak of light. "I take it that we're seeing some sort of defense mechanism?"

"Yes. There was some talk about putting a charge on Hazera. The passage of meteors through a magnetic field would generate electricity. The electricity would have no place to go and the stone would vaporize."

"Probably just a rumor," Paul answered. He looked again at the flashes. "Putting a charge on this city would suck in every electron or proton within a hundred thousand kilometers. I can't see how such a charge could be economically maintained. Besides, that doesn't explain all the shielding you people have against solar storms. Your field should take that shielding's place."

"*Ken.*"

"Some sort of laser defense? I'll have to ask Gollum about this. Somebody's really pitching stones at you people.

"Let's go inside. I'll meet you in the amusement section—the same airlock—around two this afternoon."

The outer door to the upper level airlock opened, and they stepped through. "How is it that you've got so much time on your hands?" K'khol asked.

"I don't know. Yonah's attending some high-level conference in another Byutt. Shoshanna's been spending so much time in the *Mik*— What is it?"

He heard K'khol chuckle through his suit phones. "*Mik'veh*," he said.

"—So much time in the *Mik'veh* that she's getting waterlogged."

"The Days of Awe don't explain that fully. Did you screw her?"

Paul twisted off his helmet and glared.

"You don't have to be angry about it, Dr. Greenberg. Some friends of mine know Shoshanna. She's been acting strangely lately. We placed a little bet. Okay?"

"It's none of your business! If you want to gamble, there are some things better left alone!"

Paul didn't know why the question angered him so. He had been treating women as objects of conquest, then sources of information, for so long that the emotion confused him. It was true that Shoshanna's seduction had different results than those he had expected.

*   *   *

Afterwards, in the park, she had begun to cry. She struggled away from him and turned to run. Paul sat on a bench and stared into space, wondering. He'd stared thus, between the trees, for a long time. He didn't try running after her or calling. He knew that it wouldn't help—he'd never find her.

He didn't see her at all for two days. Yonah thought that she was only suffering from grief. Paul didn't understand it exactly, but he knew that he had made it far worse. Her refusal to dine with them confused Yonah, but food was vanishing from the refrigerator in increasing amounts. Paul knew that she was recovering.

He woke in the middle of the night, thirsty. The Goldsteins had given him the run of the house, so he felt comfortable in helping himself to a bottle of *Kha'im Ma'im,* the local soda pop.

Putting on his bathrobe, he wandered downstairs. Paul saw her from the balcony, sitting alone in the darkness. She looked up but didn't move. He passed her silently, going into the kitchen. Opening a bottle, he sat on the couch across from her and switched on the lamp on the end table. She looked down, slender fingers covering her eyes.

"Hello," Paul said softly.

Silence.

"Would you like something to drink?"

She shook her head. "I'm sorry, Paul," she said, her voice husky with weeping.

"It is I who should be sorry," he said.

"I didn't stop you," she answered. "And in not doing so, I've sinned against God, against you, and against Abe's memory."

"I forgive you. Can you forgive me?"

A smile crossed what he could see of her mouth. "One out of three isn't that good," she answered. "I don't know too much about your culture in such things: but I believe that you were trying to help." The pitch of her voice rose with her emotion. "If only I could have cried," she said. "If only I could have, then that feeling would have gone."

Paul rose from his seat.

She quickly motioned with her hand and turned away. "No, Paul! Please! Don't touch me!"

Paul relaxed back onto the sofa.

"Thank you, Paul. It's just that I've never felt so unclean!"

"You aren't."

"It's nothing personal. You understand."

"Yes."

"It is the month of Elul," she said. "The time when our ancestors trembled. The Days of Awe are approaching."

"I've heard that phrase before," answered Paul. "What does it mean?"

Shoshanna snickered through her tears. "Do you really understand me?" she asked. "You've just proved yourself a *terrible* Jew."

"I was raised in San Diego," Paul explained. "Everyone's a Roman Catholic there. Ours was the only Jewish family that I knew of."

Again the smile. "And you weren't very Jewish?"

"No."

"The Days of Awe," she explained, "mark the end of the Jewish year. They begin with Rosh Hashana and extend through Yom Kippur. Traditionally, these are the days when God judges us. It is a time of fasting and reflection on the sins that we've committed during the year. And I feel that I have sinned more deeply than I have ever sinned before! I am a harlot!"

"Why?"

She was silent. Long moments passed. "Because I used you without loving you," she finally answered. "Because Abe was gone, I—" She broke into sobs.

Paul kept his seat.

"When I thought of Abe," she said. "When I thought

that I would never see him smile again, or hear him laugh, or feel his arms around me, it was like broken glass inside me, twisting, turning, cutting. And I couldn't cry, Paul. I wanted to scream, but even that died in my throat!" She lapsed into silence, gathering the strength to continue. "I was so strong," she said. "I had to be, fighting for so long, for such an unpopular cause. Nobody knew that when life handed me its little shocks, I had Abe to run to. Now I had to deal with the greatest shock that I'd experienced since Momma died. And the one person that I had to run to was gone. He was the source of that shock. I guess that's what you electronics people call a short circuit—a closed loop. The emotion kept rebounding from one fact to the other. Abe was dead and there was no Abe to run to." She paused again.

Paul held his silence, walking into the dimness beyond the reading lamp. He rummaged through the liquor cabinet. Since the bottles were labeled in Hebrew, he had some trouble finding what he assumed to be brandy. He tried it. Brandy with the distinct taste of plums. He poured her a glass and returned with it.

"Thank you," she whispered, taking a sip.

"No, I ran to you. In the back of my mind, I knew that it was simply that your arms— Your body was different. But some demon in my mind told me that your arms weren't enough." Again, she lapsed into sobbing.

"The mistake was mine as well," Paul answered. "You must realize that on Earth, we're much more casual about such things. Often, when a woman loses a lover, she doubts her ability to attract another—" He trailed off, knowing that he was lying. "Finish your brandy and try to get some sleep." He rose from the couch.

The next day, Paul returned early to the house. All was quiet. "Shoshanna! Shoshanna!" he called. He breathed a sigh of relief. She would be gone until just before Asher came home. Quickly and quietly, he entered the bedroom and looked beneath the bed. The dator was still there, and the disc in it was still turning. The work that he was supposedly doing while out with K'khol was being done via *Oomi Mi* on the moon. He walked to the computer console and flicked a switch.

"Hello, Paul," said the computer's voice.

Paul leaned back in his chair, crossing his legs and placing his hands behind his head.

"What's up?" the computer finally asked.

"I've been thinking. Since Abe's death, I mean—"

"Yes?"

"How many sabotage attempts of that kind are there?"

"If, by 'that kind', you mean elaborate and fanciful, possibly two or three a month, for the time being."

"For the time being?"

"Yes, I believe that Prime Minister Cohen discussed this with you. Since 2056, the number of attempts has been increasing by 20 percent per year. It's a matter of geometric progression. We get a total of nearly 10,000 a year now."

Paul sat bolt upright. "Ten thousand a year! How many is that per day?"

"About 27," the computer answered.

Paul leaned back. So, the situation was bad, but not as bad as those linear flashes of light would have him believe. What he had seen accounted for a far greater number than 27 per day. But if they weren't stones being pitched at the city, what *were* they?

"I do hope that you will reconsider speaking to the UN Security Council on this, Paul. You can see how such things affect the people here. Both the Goldsteins and I hope that you have come to regard us as more than numbers in a printout, or charges in a memory bank. We hope that you have come to regard us as friends."

Paul breathed a sigh. "I have," he said. "And I promise that I will speak to them. I'm not sure that I can make that great a difference—"

"Every little bit helps," the computer answered.

"Yes. I just wanted to satisfy my curiosity. Thank you, Gollum."

"You're welcome, Paul."

By now, Paul was used to following K'khol through the maze of corridors and rooms that made up Byutt Sebulon's airlock sections.

Paul got his first look at the probe he had ordered the moment the door opened. The machine, about the size of a basketball, rested on a workbench—a simple black sphere.

"Easiest to make," explained K'khol. "Just blow up a balloon and spray it with molten metal."

"Have you taken regular radar scans of the area?"

"Yes. Our computer models should be fairly complete if the circuit diagrams you gave us were accurate."

Paul leaned against a workbench and folded his arms. "I'd allow for 20 percent variation. I'm giving it only a 50-50 chance of getting through."

"Couldn't we get more information by simply sending a person?"

"Possibly, but remember that we aren't certain exactly how closely those radio pulses are timed. What we'll be doing is echoing the radio pulse that the worker bus sends to *Svenglid*'s security system. Since our probe will be passing the bus at a higher speed, aberration is going to cause a slight shortening in the wavelength. Also, since it is an echo, the probe's response is going to come a few nanoseconds after that of the bus. There's a chance that the probe won't make it. Too high a chance to risk losing somebody. I suspect that the system for wavelength selection is like the coding machines that were used by the Nazis in World War II."

"May they rot in hell!"

"Uh, yeah. If what I suspect is true, the probe should make it. We can't risk any transmissions after the probe is inside *Svenglid*'s sphere of protection, so we've got three recording instruments for each sensory device—one recording instrument and two backups. I want that information analyzed separately before it's examined as a whole. That's why there are so many sensory devices. They'll give us as much information as they can possibly get. Analyzing that information in bits may give us some insights that we wouldn't get if we examined it as a whole. Each sensory device has three recording devices in case something happens to the other two.

"We may not get a second chance. I'm not about to risk losing any of that information. Remember, timing is extremely important!"

"We have the bus schedules," answered K'khol. "They're always on time."

"You'd better believe they are!" Paul answered.

"Uh, one more thing, Paul."

"Yes?"

"I can understand the magnetometer. That's for determining if *Svenglid*'s computer is active. And I can understand the reflection spectrometer. We can determine *Svenglid*'s structural material from that. But why the mass detector? Couldn't we get the thing's mass by reflections from the spectrometer?"

"A reflection spectrometer only shows us what's on the outside, K'khol. Mass detectors are still so primitive that they have a rough time telling a fly from an elephant. However, if that is a starship— Here." He pulled out his dator and inserted a disc. After punching on the keyboard, the disc spun madly, then stopped. The screen lit up with what looked like a flattened doughnut.

"*Svenglid*'s computer and probe package," Paul explained. "Okay, *Svenglid* is a combination fusion-ramjet—"

"I know that," interrupted K'Khol.

"The UV lasers can't ionize everything in *Svenglid's* path. Therefore, the forward three-quarters of the doughnut is a combination of lead and graphite shielding—several thousand tons of it. The mass detector will show us if it's there."

"If it isn't, then we can decide that *Svenglid* is to be put to some other use, or it's been abandoned and all of the shielding we've been buying is going elsewhere."

"Exactly!" answered Paul. "Another thing, K'khol." Paul turned and, together, they departed. The door slid closed. "The flashes of light that we saw outside."

"Yes?"

"They weren't meteors. I checked with Gollum. Apparently they don't even match your prime minister's paranoid fantasies. The number of sabotage attempts that she and Gollum state are some 10,000 a year. That's including meteors, K'khol. It's a big number, but it only breaks down into 27 per day. What we saw would account for a lot more than that."

"So? What do you think they are?"

"There aren't any thrusters around the hub—at least none of sufficient size to prevent Hazera from breaking up if she were moved along her axis of rotation. I think that what we saw was sunlight reflecting off guywires as Hazera turns. They've tied it together to move it somewhere."

"Where do you think that they want to move it?"

"Hazera may be well enough protected against industrial sabotage. However, it's a pretty flimsy structure if you want it to withstand an attack from the UN fleet!

"What doesn't make sense are the lasers and particle beam weapons that they've placed on *Ra* itself! Weapons to protect one of the mightiest weapons of war ever built?"

"It's probably because it's strictly a long-range weapon, not built for close-in fighting."

"True. But my guess is that they plan to move the city behind *Ra.*"

K'khol laughed. "Wouldn't it be easier just to move *Ra* in front of the city?"

"It might, *if Ra* were less massive than the city!"

"You think that there is more mass in that dish antenna than there is in Hazera Ysroel?" K'khol broke into a guffaw of laughter, then stopped himself.

"Consider," answered Paul somewhat heatedly. "You've got 12 Mark 18 fusion generators strapped to the back of it. In order to use *Ra*, you'll have to move it from the moon's back side, and probably fairly rapidly. If you're going to accelerate a structure of that size at, say, a quarter of a G— Well the mass of the generators alone is going to require additional mass in terms of structure."

"That still wouldn't—"

"Plus!" Paul interrupted. "A reflector of that size could not focus on small, nearby targets. And while it is protected by laser and particle beams, there have been none built for the protection of the city itself. If, however, Hazera is moved behind *Ra*, well, you know that the UN has particle beams of their own. If *Ra* is to be used both as a weapon *and* as a shield, you know that inadequate shielding can be worse than no shielding at all. Inadequate doesn't bar radiation, but propagates it. The only thing that could protect Hazera against our particle beams would be massive, massive quantities of—"

"Lead!" K'khol interjected. "Then you think that they expect to be attacked?"

Paul's eyes narrowed. "Probably not as soon as we're going to. Probably not until Hazera's movement is detected by *Oomi Mi*. They feel that once Hazera is seen moving toward *Ra*, the UN will put two and two together. They *want* to be attacked by the UN, probably as a show of force. But we've beaten them to the punch, K'khol. Two and two is already ours. We know that they've been mining massive quantities of heavy metals on Mercury. We know that they've bought massive quantities of lead and graphite elsewhere. If it isn't in *Svenglid*, it's probably in *Ra*. We've still got time, K'khol. We've still got time!''

There was no way that Paul could have found the *Materet's* floating workshop without K'khol's help. They met on yet another level and he was taken to *another* room filled with the same portable equipment.

"You know," said K'khol. "We've tried similar systems, but yours was the first to really work."

"Yes?"

"At least, with this speed and accuracy. Of course, the Materet can't afford molecular electronics, but your engineers seem to have overcome most of the problems that came with using old-fashioned chips."

He pointed toward a drawing board and a man nearly finished with a circuit design. It was ready to be photographed.

"We're incorporating many of your ideas into the other equipment," K'khol explained. "We think that we ought to be able to get a man out there in a few days. It seems that Doppler shift and relativity aren't the only things that can be overcome." He grinned sheepishly. "Well, not overcome. But you've eliminated the limits, the delays in our circuits, enough to get a probe past Svenglid's defense systems."

"What did we get?"

"As you know, the standard engine uses deuterium and fuses it into helium."

"Yes."

"That much has been checked out. Not too much that we could tell about the engine. Mass seems heavier than we expected. Standard metal exterior plating, and the fuel seems to be the standard tritium-deuterium mixture that was common 20 years ago, when the project began."

"How did you determine that?"

"We installed a cold strobe in the probe. It was just a flash."

"Jesus! You shouldn't have taken the chance!"

"It was too quick for the human eye to perceive."

"But there is equipment!"

K'khol shrugged. "We got an answer and nothing was harmed. We felt it was worth the chance. Those shadows are a good place to hide things. Just fuel, though. In fact, everything checked out until we got to the instrument package."

"Well?"

"Nothing."

"What?"

"Nothing. You heard me. It's a stage prop. It's foil stretched over a frame of thin wire, with some plating on the sides that would be visible from other cities or the moon—a spacer version of paper maché."

"Then *Svenglid* has been abandoned," said Paul. "All of the actual assemblies and rocket probes that I've seen have been just stage props as well."

"So, we can forget *Svenglid*." Paul's eyes narrowed. "If they are going to use *Ra* as a combination weapon and shield, I've been wondering why they chose the shape of a solar furnace. In making *Ra*, they could have chosen one of those radio shields that they use to back orbital radio telescopes. Why the cupping?"

"A solar furnace is more typical of an industrial city" K'khol answered. "If they were telling the UN that it was just busy work—"

"I'm confirming a suspicion of mine, K'khol. I was trying to think of what else *Hazera* might want to hide behind the cupping."

K'khol looked at him blankly and then shrugged.

"Your factories," Greenberg answered.

"But they're too hot! If they were attached on the back of *Ra*, their heat would spread throughout the entire structure! That's apt to get uncomfortable!"

"What about your larger, major factories? Haven't they been shut down? Since the coming of the plague, I mean. See if you can get an IR scan on them. See if they haven't been cooling more rapidly than they might through normal irradiation. If they have, they could fit behind *Ra*—between *Ra* and Hazera. That would confirm my suspicions."

"And if they haven't been cooling down as rapidly as you think? And they don't fit?"

"Then there's another answer."

"I still say that the construction of an enormous solar furnace is less likely to arouse suspicions than something like a shield for a radio telescope."

"Why?" Paul asked. "A super-maser doesn't have to be a cup until it's used. It can be made up into thousands of panels that can change shape in minutes under computer control. Why should it be connected into one solid structure? It would be cheaper and far more impressive if it weren't.

"A solid structure—a solar furnace—preassumes that you will be processing enormous quantities of metal. Besides, hasn't most of the busy work been in things like art and science? A radio telescope back here has not been financed, and it would be an ideal cover! *Oomi Mi* has been engaged for the last 20 years in looking only for intelligent signals—not radio astronomy. A better cover would have been something of more esoteric significance, but of little economic value.

"In such a case, the shield would be a logical backing for a radio telescope, and the super radio telescope would have been the weapon. Why incorporate them together under a cover that has literally no use?

"The only reason that I can see for a solid structure is shielding from attack. And the only reason that I can see for the cupping would be so that the factories could fit in behind the structure, attached to it, along with the city."

For a long time, K'khol was silent. Finally, he spoke. "If the city plans to use *Ra* to usurp the power of the UN, then the UN's resources will be under our control. Why should we want our factories in such a case?"

"I don't believe that Professor Cohen is that far-sighted. I believe that she intends to enforce her exorbitant demands on the UN. She has repeatedly stated that she desires a fleet of UN ships in permanent orbit about the moon."

"If she's going to build such a weapon, then why doesn't she use it to eliminate those cities of which she is so afraid?"

"Moral reasons," answered Paul. "When someone is mentally ill, we are wrong to judge them only as monsters. She is being moral within the precepts of her own madness. And she will continue in that morality until her concepts of reality change.

"There is a difference between building such a weapon and actually using it."

"She *won't* be using it!?"

"She will probably theaten to use it. If we don't comply, she will probably use it against small targets. She will be wanting to take as few lives as necessary to achieve her ends."

K'khol knitted his brow. He had misjudged Paul. Paul was out of his environment here, but his logic had opened up more questions than it had answered. "I'll get you those IR readings," he said. "But I want to take one more manned look at *Svenglid*. There are too many buses and workers still there to write it off completely as an abandoned project."

"I'll go with you," said Paul. "I have my suspicions, but I want to make certain myself."

Once the thrusters had cut off and General Magnusson had recovered from the initial space sickness, she entered a dreamy perception of reality. As she pulled herself down the access tube, she kept shaking her head to clear it.

The Nepalese, following behind, gave her a grin. "It's an effect that hits some people," he said. "It wears off in a few hours."

"As soon as we look at our destination," she answered. "I'm heading for the gym. I'm willing to bet that it can be *worked* off in a few minutes. How are the AFVs working?"

"The airlocks are fairly small." the Gurkha answered. "We can only test two at a time. So far, they seem to be doing okay."

General Magnusson nodded. The Armored Fighting Vehicles and Armored Personnel Carriers had been designed for use at the bottom of Earth's ocean of atmosphere. Their use on the floor of the Pacific had already replaced their alcohol engines with electrical ones. And they were already provided with life support. Still, for use in vacuum, a number of changes had to be made. Moving parts had to be polished and freed of grease. Additional structural support had to be provided so that they wouldn't blow apart, instead of collapsing as they might under water. Any number of changes had already been made, and the crews were still busy. Most of the additional changes couldn't be made within the tanks' thick armor plating. As a result, most of the changes had to be welded to the outside. There was additional armor added, mostly to the AFVs' leading edges and down one side. Once beyond the Israeli perimeter, the tanks were supposed to line up into two columns. The side with plating would be directed toward the Israeli cities and launch ramp.

Ingrid's knuckles whitened on the hand grips as she moved down the tube. "Cost effectiveness!" Those idiots back at the UN accounting office! Always assuming that everything would work out just fine! In reality, Ingrid couldn't remember a battle plan that had survived contact with the enemy. She thought of the stuff that the Israelis had placed about their perimeter. It may have been designed for repelling small groups, but some of it could do some real damage. If there were repair crews out there, there was nothing to prevent them from seeing what was going on and turning that equipment around for use against her tanks. And that equipment would be aimed right for the precious life-support equipment on an unarmored side of her tanks! More damage was going to be done to the tanks than the UN accounting office could imagine! As she moved into the gold-tinted quartz blister, she tried to hang herself in the exact center. But unconscious movements eternally started her drifting in one direction or another. They were silent. Through the yellow radiation shielding of the quartz, the moon shone with the lambent butterlight of an autumn evening. Ingrid found herself dreaming of such moons reflected in lakes and oceans. Only the absence of a chill night breeze kept its mood from overtaking her. She gripped one of the handholds in the blister's framework and pulled herself toward the transparent quartz.

"It's the sky," the Gurkha answered in a voice as dreamy as her feelings. "It's the sky. She's all around us now, and the moon has to try harder to be large."

She closed her eyes and pushed away from the quartz. Suddenly a voice broke through the silence of the tiny glass-enclosed room.

"Emergency! Paging General Magnusson! Emergency!"

Cursing under her breath, Ingrid kicked away from the many-paned window. Reaching a back wall, she flicked a switch on the intercom as she grabbed a plastic strap.

"General Magnusson," she answered. "What's up?"

There was the ring of a chime. "This is now a priority one, two-way communication," the emotionless voice of a computer announced.

"Radar blips!" a more human voice exclaimed. "Hundreds of them pouring out of the cities at L5!"

"That fat-assed, stupid son-of-a-bitch!" she cursed. She had a distinct dislike for self-appointed generals. And Villeneuve, the political dictator of Paris Nouveau, was bearing out her reasons.

"Get clarification of those blips," Ingrid commanded.

"If they're what I think they are, you can send the rest of the UN attack fleet to intercept those idiots!"

"Okay. We're getting clarification. The 'puter will put it on your screen." General Magnusson's fist pounded the intercom's frame when the image appeared. The big center engine was easily identifiable. So were the two engines strapped to either side. The screen showed four views—side, top, front, and rear. The command capsule was tear-drop shaped and it was obvious that it doubled as an escape boat. It gave the front a fine psychological effect. It took the computer three or four seconds to bounce signals that far and build up enough of an image for itself to identify. General Magnusson recognized it even before the rotary rocket launchers appeared on the screen.

"*Chats Savauge*," she cursed. The screen gave a count of 340 of the deadly machines.

"Do you want me to give them a hail?"

"Are they going anywhere?"

"No. They're still grouping."

General Magnusson's eyes narrowed into a fine squint of thought. The pylons that held the launchers were filled with 120 rockets. She wasn't sure what kind of warheads they held. Bursting from the center of each rotating, rocket-filled launcher was a proton beam weapon. Four swivel-mounted groupings of lasers studded the command module.

"I think that the bastards want to help," she said. "I'm on my way to our future GHQ. If those sons of bitches give a burn, I want you to plot their course. Is that understood?"

"Yes, ma'am!"

"C'mon," she said to the liaison officer. "Frogs are going to give the show away."

"*Erev tov*," said Yonah, walking in the door. "Did you take Asher to the theater?"

"Yes. Shoshanna had to go to another Byutt. She had to report to the studio."

"I thought you were taking her there."

Greenberg smiled. "We had a difference of opinion," he said.

Yonah sighed. "Oh," he said. "I see. I hope that it is over the grief that she is expressing over Abe's death. The *Talmud* gives limits on grief and is against mortification of the flesh. Uh, you did fight over her grief, didn't you?"

Paul lied with a silent nod.

"Good. It is a hard thing. I worry about her when I'm gone. At any rate, I'm certain that she can take care of herself on the way to the studio. Our inter-Byutt train system is quite good. Have you tried it yet?"

Paul shook his head.

"Quite good," reaffirmed Goldstein. "Very safe. I had a part in designing the circuits." He went to the liquor cabinet and poured himself his customary glass of Arak.

"Are you hungry?" Paul asked. "There's some fish in the refrigerator."

"No, thank you. I ate on the way back. Where's Asher?"

"He's up in his room, studying. It's more like play," answered Paul. "The schools have changed a great deal since I was in them."

Yonah smiled. "You can imagine how they've changed since I was a lad." He looked up at the clock. "It looks as though I just made it," he said. "Isaac ben Isaac is on in five minutes. Maybe you ought to call Asher down." He winked. "I'll look over our interpretations as soon as the show is over."

The Isaac ben Isaac show was the sort of talking program that on Earth had been popular over a century ago. Apparently it was broadcast live with special safeguards against discing. Hotel accommodations had been provided for Shoshanna by the Israeli network. Live programming must have held more appeal here than on Terra. A program, otherwise, would have been edited and stored on disc. Even with Yonah translating, Paul could sense some charm in the program's spontaneity.

He relaxed with plum brandy, while Asher had fruit juice. Both Yonah and Asher did their best at translating, often interrupting themselves to listen closely or laugh at a joke. Finally, they lapsed into silence as Paul stared politely at the incomprehensible conversation. Still, most of the show had dragged on before Shoshanna was introduced.

During a commercial, Yonah explained that ben Isaac was mortally afraid of intellectuals. While producers often arranged to have scientists, teachers, writers, and professors speak, Yonah felt that ben Isaac was afraid of asking stupid questions. Therefore, he rarely gave them more airtime than the final few minutes. Yonah shrugged. That was the way he was.

Finally, following a commercial, Shoshanna appeared in a chair, sitting next to Isaac on the simple but tasteful set.

Isaac explained Shoshanna's grief and thanked her for appearing under trying circumstances. Again, both Asher and Yonah attempted to translate, but were soon caught up in the rapid pace of the conversation.

Shoshanna explained that the book she had been working on had fallen behind. Fortunately, the publisher had given her an extension. As the conversation continued, the look on Shoshanna's face changed from sadness to steely resolve. It was evident that they were speaking of Shoshanna's favorite cause, that of sexual equality in religion.

Finally, she leaned back, casually crossed her legs, and draped an arm over the back of her chair.

Yonah leaned forward. "She says that she has an announcement to make," he explained.

She spoke. Isaac ben Isaac's face went slack in mute shock. So did Yonah Goldstein's.

"Asher," said Yonah quietly. "Go to your room."

"But Poppa!"

"Asher! Do as you're told!"

"What is it?" Paul asked after Asher had disappeared.

"Do you remember," asked Yonah. "the great *Talmudist* that we spoke of on the night of your arrival? A certain 'Karl'?"

"Yes."

"*She* is Karl!"

Chapter XII

General Magnusson stood in her vac suit, looking out over the ceramic-covered plain. Like most landing ports, the surface had been made simply by pouring molten slag over the crater floor. The surrounding vacuum assured that the material would remain liquid long enough to settle into a smooth, glossy surface, covering many square kilometers. Layering and computer control, combined with internal heating, assured that it wouldn't break up into jagged cracks.

An elevator was moving toward them on the landing field. Most of the faciities were not designed to handle the unloading of military vehicles. However, there were several old derricks that had been originally designed for the unloading of tractors and other heavy equipment. Most of the early stuff had been designed on Terra, and that under a deadline. As a result, the cheapness of metal and lack of available time had forced the engineers to ignore the low lunar gravity. The net result was that the old derricks were perfectly capable of unloading tanks and armored personnel carriers.

The general scowled. She knew that the Japanese had been unwilling, but she didn't know that they would be getting in the way at every opportunity. The shortness of equipment had been enough. She watched two figures far below. One, a UN officer, bounced comically up and down in anger. The other, a Japanese worker, politely tapped the side of his helmet and rotated his shoulders from side to side, an indication that the headphones in his suit weren't working.

"Should we delay the attack?" came a voice through her headphones.

She shook her head, and then remembered that the motion was invisible inside her suit. Following the example of the man on the ground, she experimentally rotated her shoulders. "No," she answered. "Get the people unloaded and get them some sleep."

The elevator hit the side of their vessel. She could feel the metal ringing silently through the soles of her boots. The elevator cage began to rise up the open framework of the shaft. She pointed toward the silently gesturing Japanese below them. "Take that son of a bitch inside and check out his headset. If it works, I want him brought back out here and his suit cracked. I hate to make examples, but we've also got to get some cooperation."

"Yes, ma'am."

"Also, there are going to be some changes in the battle plan." They stepped aboard the elevator.

She searched for and found the red 'down' button. The elevator began to descend. Getting down on one knee, she drew an imaginary line down the elevator floor. "Our tanks and APCs will be moving in four columns, not two," she said. "It will shorten the columns and probably slow us down. But we've got to keep a line of shielding toward the bulk of their weaponry. It's outwardly directed now, but if there are any repair crews out there, we can't count on them staying that way. Idiots at the UN had only one side of our tanks armor-plated . . ."

Midway between the immense ship's thrusters and the ground, the elevator jerked to a halt.

"Goddamnit!" she cursed. More sabotage! She couldn't very well ask the UN to set off one of the

bombs on the orbital Japanese cities based on the
actions of the civilians. But she could have those that
were caught throwing sand in the gears shot. The
elevator would be moving soon enough.

"I've got the information that you asked for," said
K'khol. "You were right about the factories. They are
far cooler than could be expected, and they couldn't
have been cooled by IR radiation alone."

"Paul nodded, satisfied. "Rosh Hashana," he said.
"A whole day with my guardians attending services.
It gave me a lot of time for poking my nose into
others' affairs."

He heard K'khol chuckle in his suit radio. The door
to the tiny airlock finally opened. Paul stepped into
the sunlight. The black suit reflected all radiation of
a wavelength lower than that of visible light. Even
then, there was a large gap that allowed it to absorb
the long wavelengths of radar. To radar and the human eye, they would be invisible against the background of space. Little could be done about the
reflections from such things as the faceplate or suit
antenna. But these were comparatively small matters. The big problem was the absorption of heat.
While the suit effectively bounced off infrared itself,
the absorption of visible light and radar waves still
created heat. This necessitated a great collapsible fin
that could expand on his back. If one faced the sun, a
good deal of that heat could be radiated away by the
fin. While chillers supplemented the effect, exertion
was not recommended.

He had been able to get some practice in at
Astropolis with similar devices, but this was the first
time he'd been able to use this particular model. It had
the advantage of being covered with a shiny wrapper,
duplicating a regular suit. The wrapper was now
folded and placed in one of the black suit's pouches.
Black suits, of course, were illegal, except for UN
operatives. Their sole purpose was to avoid detection.

K'khol clamped a small device to the top of one of the railings. With Paul, he then climbed to the railing's top. Paul averted his eyes while doing so, looking outward, rather than down into the starry blackness.

The camera eyes of the device checked the stars against a map in its tiny memory bank. It located three of them, then waited. Finally, with the spin of the great city, they appeared in their proper part of the sky. Stepping off into space would now fling them toward the immense starship. Immediately, a short-range radio signal burst forth from the tiny box. A red LED blinked on within their helmets. Although they were near the bottom of Byutt Sebulon, there was still the danger of dashing themselves against its side. K'khol gripped Paul's hand firmly and leaped far out into the vacuum. Paul felt his stomach heave, but once beyond the immense structure, he relaxed. They turned their faceplates toward the sun. Light-sensitive circuits sensed the sun's brilliance and darkened the glass over their eyes. It would be a long, long fall.

The UN computer constructs worked perfectly. They informed those at Akkiba that the flashes on the lunar horizon were the disastrous accidental explosions of fuel tanks.

The explosions could be stopped, but it was a shame to lose all those volatiles.

When asked if they needed any help, the computers checked the records of human response, found the answer, and made certain that the monorails were down within range of the white-noise generators.

"By all means!" the computer simulations responded. "Help is needed!"

Dozens of fuel experts boarded the little cars and sped down the rails. Their first response, halfway to their destination, was confusion. Their own conversations were taken up in the middle by computer simulations—of themselves!—mindfully built up from records taken only a few hours before. None of them were aware that the lunar cities were under attack as they sped by the tanks and armored personnel carriers. By that time they were already screaming in terror, as their little cars left the broken rails to be crumpled and smashed in the lunar sands. Some of the cars failed to decompress. The few space-suited figures who managed to stagger out of the wreckage were taken to the enormous mass driver's repair and maintenance sheds. Those who knew English were interrogated as to the terrain and obstacles that lay ahead.

General Magnusson followed behind the front line of tanks and APCs. Most of them had, as expected, been wiped out by automated weapons at very close range. Automated weapons had been on the edge of Israeli territory and similar weapons had guarded Dos Telerl.

Ingrid smiled grimly as she held a pair of binoculars against her face plate. Those tanks that had held the leading edge of her attack had been dummies—robot duplicates designed to draw automated fire. Three times, repair crews at the edge of Israeli territory had confirmed her fears. Having turned outward-facing weapons toward them, the total loss of manned combat vehicles was 37. The loss of automated vehicles was almost total. Three-quarters of these were gone as they approached Akkiba.

Dos Telerl had fallen without a whimper. The UN maps of armed police and military stations were totally accurate. A very few of the occupants had boiled out onto the surface like hornets, but they were quickly cut down by UN fire. The confusion caused by the cutting off of radio communication, and the simulations, was almost total. The first objective of the tanks peeling off from the main columns was the life-support computers. Since most of the city was underground, it was merely a matter of rolling across the lunar surface to their locations. Those structures outside of the ramp that stood above-ground were easily blown apart. Automatic systems effectively sealed residents below.

As expected, there had been some protection systems around the city's life-support computers. Despite being some 20 feet underground, the computers were protected against oxidation by storage in vacuum. It was a simple matter to break into the central control rooms, these being the only pressurized portions of the assembly. The technicians were disposed of by that very action. From there on, it was a simple matter to seal off air conduits to the police and military installations, then wait until those inside gave up to surrounding troops.

An armed group of 6,000 was left behind to control nearly a million Chassidim.

While the two cities were still in turmoil, while Akkiba was still fighting back, a signal was sent toward Terra.

For whatever comfort it was worth, Paul and K'khol clutched the small boxes at their waists. They were the radio reflection devices that had gotten the probe past *Svenglid*'s defense mechanisms. If their timing was correct, they would pass one of the worker buses as it, in turn, passed through *Svenglid*'s protective layer of radar. A signal would be sent out by the bus, and the boxes would reflect that signal toward *Svenglid*.

The long brilliant line that was *Svenglid* grew beneath their feet. Although Paul had never prayed in his life, he found himself closing his eyes and moving his lips as though doing so.

Then he felt K'khol's grip on his arm tighten. He looked and K'khol was pointing upward. Following the line of K'khol's finger, he saw a tiny point of light. It was growing. The grip on his arm again tightened. A brief jet of gas burst them out of the way and started a tumble that the suits' computers quickly corrected. For an instant, Paul got the impression of an elongated vitamin pill-shaped structure as it hurtled past rows of windows through which grim faces looked outward. The only thing that Paul could be sure of was the long ladder that connected the tiny craft's decks. His eyes followed the 'pilot' within the transparent dome at the rearward end.

Again K'khol's hand gripped as they scanned the sky above them. A bit of debris entered the defense shield's perimeter and flared into vapor. Both men breathed a sigh of relief. They had come through the field unharmed. As long as they were undiscovered by human eyes, they would be safe! Paul slapped K'khol on the back—another mistake, and one he immediately regretted. K'khol began to tumble, and Paul found himself in a backward roll. Bursts of gas fired from the suits by computer immediately corrected. K'khol cursed in Hebrew. "I don't want you to try such foolishness again!" he said. "We need that reaction mass to get back to the city!"

Paul was silent. If K'khol had been a member of a larger, more formal group, he wouldn't have been with Paul. Yet, at the age of 19, he was already a specialist in matters of espionage. A more solidly organized rebellion would have recognized K'khol's value and promoted him to their version of a desk job, keeping him out of the battle. And as a result, K'khol would have been miserable. Paul had seen it happen with others.

As it was, K'khol was in the thick of things and loving every minute of it, and Paul was grateful. In this environment, he was like a fish out of water. All of the habits that he had accumulated over a lifetime didn't work here. They may have worked in Australia, South America, Africa—even on the floor of the Pacific. It would not have been so bad had he come to Hazera as a tourist. As an agent, it made him a buffoon. He would have paid anything to see himself through K'khol's eyes, even though he knew he wouldn't like the view. On Terra he was a hardened, responsible agent. Here, 'muddling through' was hardly the phrase. He wasn't sure what he would have done without K'khol's help and guidance.

His thoughts were interrupted when the magnetic, rubberized soles of his shoes finally made their slow contact with *Svenglid*.

As Shoshanna stood, swaying in Synagogue, she could feel the eyes of others upon her. At least while the prayer continued, the constant pressure of anger and disapproval was quietly lessened to an occasional glance. She prayed all the harder, and now it was not just for forgiveness, but God's help and guidance. While no one would bother her during the Days of Awe, later there would come demonstrations and fury. The conflict would go on for years. She was certain to be called before the Sanhedrin, those sacred men with long grey beards and ancient wisdom. How often she had dreamed of the attachment of the title '*Rav*' to her own name.

So many things had been changed by the Second Holocaust—as many changes had been wrought as by the First. If the First Holocaust had been the true source of the Second Israel, then the Second had, for good or for ill, been the source of religious resurgence. It was true that here, women had total equality. Women were leaders in science, business, and politics—leaders in every field except religion. If she were right, if God was with her, she would lead the way.

During the sermon, the rabbi had spoken specifically against her, saying that sexism in religion was purely a matter of semantics, that the ancient laws would not have been set down if they were not meant to be followed. While the sermon was in progress, she took obvious pains to show she ignored it. She knew that there was historical precedent for her beliefs. While the Days of Awe were in progress, she knew she was safe.

This was the time when people would be settling their scores with God—and one another. They wouldn't be creating new scores to settle. Afterward would come the debates, the demonstrations, and the hatred. It was a score that she would settle at last. As she ignored the sermon, her eyes studied the wall.

It was an exact duplicate of another wall, far older, that stood in the ruins of Jerusalem. The wall still stood. There was no bombed-out rubble in Jerusalem, only radioactivity. The building had fallen because of neglect, but not the wall. Perhaps, someday, they would find some way to go back and scrub it down.

The red light on the panel came on. Simon DeVliegar turned to Jon Bleau. "We're off!" he said.

The fighter's engines flared into life. Already they were moving away from the planet. The thunder continued for long moments.

"How long is this going to go on?" DeVliegar complained.

Though the G force was slight, the other grimaced. "Whoa!" he said as the moon rose rapidly over the horizon. The engine's thunder grew. They were pressed further into their seats.

"Jesus!" exclaimed Bleau. "What have they got back there?"

DeVliegar knew what Jon was talking about. They were both aware of the odd, tulip-shaped engines that had been attached to the fighter's backside.

"Gentlemen," said a voice over the intercom. "This is your captain speaking. "How does it feel to be test pilots? I say test pilots because what we have strapped onto the back of us is none other than the Mitsu Mark 18. I'm certain that you've heard of it as a device of legendary power! Well, you can forget all the rumors you've heard because they defy the laws of physics. What is back there is even more powerful than any rumors that you've heard. In short, the

Mitsu does *more* than violate the laws of fusion physics. The way that it does this is in not being a fusion engine.

"So far, sales of the device have been restricted to miners in the asteroid belt and more sales than we thought to Hazera Ysroel. It was marketed and registered as a fusion generator. However, we now know that its power source is something far more than atomic fusion.

"How the Mark 18 works, the Japs themselves don't know. Somehow a force in nature is either intensified or accelerated. Protons vanish to become proton, antiproton pairs. Each electron brought into the action becomes an electron-positron pair. The result is matter and antimatter—and far more cheaply than it's ever been manufactured before. I'm not saying that we've got a free lunch here. But ours are the first engines to work with fully 20 percent efficiency. This is your captain signing off. This bit 'o news has been brought to you fellas by the UN, designed and tailored not to alarm you when this burn lasts 45 minutes. Relax, fellows. We'll reach our destination in a little over an hour and a half."

For long moments each of the gunners, openmouthed, stared at one another. Finally Simon asked the question that was on both of their minds— "Where?"

Jon raised his wrist dator against the Gs. At first he thought his choice was happenstance. Then he remembered how the object dominated the sky before the shielding closed around them. For what seemed like long moments, he struggled with the stylus to punch the keys. Finally, "We have three choices," he said. "L4, L5, or the moon. The Cap's mention of Hazera probably means that it's our target."

"L2!" said Simon. "I thought the trouble was in the asteroid belt!"

Jon let his hand drop back to the arm of the acceleration couch. "Maybe there's a fueling depot there. We've only got standard tanks, you know," he answered, forgetting the antimatter that was being created behind him. "But I'm sure that it's Hazera. The moon was what was directly ahead of us when the shielding closed. It's not going to be moving very far in an hour and a half."

"Why are we hurrying?"

"You heard him. We're test pilots. We'll be briefed just before deceleration, I'll betcha. I'm not going to worry about it—going to take a nap. It's too much effort to continue yelling over these engines.

"But before my nap—"

"Yes?"

"Our speed at turnover will be 187,000 meters per second."

A column of men and women moved through the underground mall of Akkiba. Behind them marched two guards in UN blue, guns at the ready.

Ingrid watched them as they passed. Her com buzzed. She unclipped it from her belt and raised it to her lips. "General Magnusson," she announced crisply. The file of prisoners continued past in the standard position, hands behind their bare heads.

"Mopping-up operations are almost complete," said a voice on the com. "There are still a few snipers. Cleaning out these corridors has been a bitch! But at least there aren't that many places to hide."

Ingrid smiled in admiration. "They're still fighters," she said. "Have you access to your dator? Mine got seared by a laser."

"I wish you'd stay out of the action. You're too valuable to us, old girl."

"If you guys did a better job of mopping up . . ." she answered. "I want you to check on a woman. A Private Cynthia Gomez."

There was a pause as the man at the other end punched at his dator. "Dead," he finally answered.

"Her APC survived the automated defense systems at the outer perimeter around Dos Telerl. She died in the first assault."

Another pause as she gathered her thoughts. "Jerry," she said. "I want you to punch in her code number and follow it with 7283. Have you got that?"

"Yes."

The code was linked to a secret experiment that was attempting to link genetics with courage. To the families at home, soldiers always died bravely. Now their last moments were coded automatically—'B' for 'brave', 'C' for 'coward'. It was strictly confidential. She would certainly be called before the board, *if* the board were to hear her request to the colonel. For the colonel, the code was meaningless, and if he were a good colonel, none of his business.

"B," came the answer.

Ingrid fell against the wall in relief and smiled. A suit punctured in the vacuum of the surface was a clean death—no time for pain or suffering. Cynthia had been rushing forward as she fell. She had made it as good a death as death could be.

"Thank you," she said to the com. "That will be all."

The Gurkha appeared at her side and smiled, clutching her arm. In some things there was understanding. She answered his smile.

There was a sharp crack as a glass bullet broke the sound barrier. It shattered against the wall near her head. She couldn't remember whether the glass shards had knocked her down or years of military training and action. The shards stung in her cheek and she could feel the wetness of her own blood. "Get that son of a bitch!" she commanded of the Gurkha.

"Glass bullets might be good for thin-skinned airlocks," she thought to herself, "but they sure are hell on people."

The Gurkha drew his weapon and rushed off.

K'khol and Paul knelt in the shadows of *Svenglid*,

'sitting' with their knees locked beneath a foam-metal girder. Paul pressed himself upward, feeling comfort from the knee's positioning. His elbows rested on another girder, a pair of binoculars raised against his face plate.

"Do you see anything?" K'khol finally asked.

Paul took the binoculars from his faceplate. "We were right, K'khol," he said. "There's a patchwork of standard metal plates on the side of the thing, probably directed toward the other cities, the moon, and the major shipping lanes. But the rest of the thing is nothing but foil!" From here, the view was close to 30 kilometers in distance. But now looking at *Svenglid* from the engine section, a view shared by nobody else, he could see it for the sham it was. He could see the underside of the 'instrument package.' The wrinkles and corrugations that identified foil were evident even from this distance. The stuff resembled sheet metal as closely as gum wrappers glued to cardboard. Paul had once read a book on robotics, on how the dream had preceded the reality. Among the fictional robots on magazine covers and in movie posters had been a child in a home-made robot costume. The foil he was looking at might have been enough to fool radar, but to the human eye, it was no more convincing than that long ago child's attempt to appear metallic—nothing but foil. "This project is *abandoned*," Paul finally said.

"Then why the robot buses?" asked K'khol hotly. "Why the workers? Why the high security?"

"The workers don't exist," answered Paul. "The security is simply to keep others from finding out.

"The sheet metal shows a nearly complete package from the moon. The foil is to prevent nearby spacecraft and people from running into it. My guess is that the project is only partially completed. Yes, they have the engines. Yes, they have collected the fuel. After that, UN funds were diverted for the building of *Ra*.

"The plan could have come with the purchase of the Mark 18. It's supposed to be a fusion drive, but the UN tells me that it's something far more. The Japanese have only been selling the device to the cities of the asteroid belt—and you. It's only been sold to those who are alone, either because of distance, or in your case, in quarantine. You're the only city in the Earth-Moon system that's been able to purchase the device. The Japanese never gave their reasons and didn't have to.

"Let us assume that you purchased the Mark 18 after a standard sales pitch. On purchasing it, however, you were sworn to secrecy as to its real power.

"I would imagine that the Mitsu is actually too simple to be protected by a patent—that's why the secrecy. If someone didn't want to buy it, and knew how it worked, they could simply build one. As soon as the secret is out, it will revolutionize power production.

"*Ra* was only conceived and built after your government's realization of what they had. The dozen additional Mitsu's were sold to Hazera without question. After all, rumors would only stimulate sales, and space cities with such a smug ace in the hole could hardly be expected to loose the secret. If the Japanese can conceive of the Sanyo's use on a weapon, they can probably use it in counteraction. The Japanese consider themselves safe."

"Then why does Hazera maintain buses? Who are they?" asked K'khol, pointing toward the workers they had seen through the binoculars.

"Robots," Paul answered. "Yonah showed me some models he built of ships with animated crewmen. It would be much easier to build them full scale—Disney was doing it more than a century ago. Your workmen from the dead Byutt, with the azure sleeves, might represent some sort of bizarre tribute. The dead coming back to insure that their lives were not lost in vain.

"By manning their synthetic work crews from the quarantined Byuttim, they are covering the fact that there are no workers at all!"

K'khol hissed and pointed. "Is that a robot?" he asked.

"I'm willing to bet it is," Paul answered.

"It could be a real security guard," K'khol said.

"With all the automatic security, I don't see why they should bother. We're the first to get this far, aren't we? My guess is that it's either a robot or dummy. If it's a robot then it's probably not very sophisticated."

"You want to tap him on the shoulder?"

Feeling more and more sure of himself, Paul rose from his hiding place. His mind still carried enough uncertainty to soften his walk on the rubberized soles. Cautiously, he approached the figure from behind. Nobody could have been more surprised than he, when on clamping a hand on the figure's shoulder, it turned.

Quickly, Paul grabbed the 'grease gun' that had been cradled across the figure's waist. A violent twist and both of them had kicked free of the ship's hull. Paul cursed to himself. The exertions were already warming his suit; exposure to sunlight didn't help. Quite suddenly, their outward drift was halted.

Paul briefly looked down to see that K'khol's hand had grabbed the figure by the ankle. He was pulling them back toward the surface of *Svenglid*. The figure was a living security guard! A human security guard! Paul had misjudged Hazera. His conversations with the Goldsteins about the awful power that Gollum held, and the automatic, potentially dangerous machines that he had seen all around him since arriving, none of it directly under human control, had caused this terrible slip. He wanted to best the machines, to show the Israelis that humans could overcome them. Had he been on Earth, there would have been no doubt in his mind that it was best to back

machines with personnel. Now, in possibly deadly
lessons, he was learning that the Israelis felt the
same way. Damn!

Paul held fast to the gun, keeping it from pointing
in either his or K'khol's direction. K'khol saw one of
the man's hands wrest itself away from the gun and
reach for the long-distance radio switch on his forearm. He deftly pulled the man's antenna near and
snapped it off. The vacuum about them was filled
with Hebrew curses. K'khol hooked both legs under a
protruding girder and continued pulling. His eyes
caught a glint of metal to the side. Tethered to the
girder and forgotten was a tiny self-contained power
tool. With one hand, he reached out and grasped it. A
pull brought the guard's waist level with K'khol's
head. He reached up, grabbing the complex of the
life-support system on the guard's back. Locking his
arm through a tank bracket, he pressed a forearm to
the back of the helmet. By this time, the guard had
been pressed flat against the girder complex in which
K'khol struggled. Paul's feet kept crying for the black-
ened magnetic surface of the catwalk. The guard, in
his struggles, kept kicking them away. Paul neither
would, nor could let go of the man's rifle.

Almost in contradiction to Paul's every instinct,
K'khol shouted out, "Let go! I've got a welding torch!"

Paul refused. The terror of having no place of footing made the gun his only anchor. Consequently, the
laser narrowly missed him when it flashed. The man's
struggles ceased. His air tube was whipping about,
severed. Paul regained his footing and pulled away
the 'grease gun.' Still struggling to capture the severed air hose, the guard was pushed, tumbling, off
into space.

"Some robot!" K'khol remarked.

Paul didn't know which shocked him more: K'khol's
offhand remark about the man that he had just murdered, or the simple fact that this offhandedness suddenly shocked him. K'khol was a fanatic. And they

were good people to have on your side. Paul found himself wondering who the murdered man had been, and wondering if K'khol had deliberately set up the situation as an excuse to murder one of those whom he considered an enemy—a guard, faceless and machine-like in his vacuum suit. "I don't know about you," *K'khol* was continuing. "But I'm burning up. We'd better get into the shadows right away!"

Paul nodded, fearing that he would faint. The battle had raised the temperature of his suit to the point of fairly searing his skin. Although Paul's struggles had begun before the Israeli's, raising the temperature of his a good 10 degrees above that of K'khol's, the Israeli dived ahead of Paul into darkness. Paul could almost hear the suit's tiny coolant pumps working overtime, the fluid thudding into the radiator fin at his back. Once in shadow, Paul felt for a girder, wisely clipping a short line to it. "We'd better hide someplace far away," K'khol remarked. He looked at his watch. "We've got a full hour before the next bus leaves. We'll have to lie low until then, but we dare not go into the sun before we cool off!"

"That was just my bad luck," Paul spat drunkenly. "Take my word for it! The bulk of those figures are robots or dum ..." But that was as far as he got before unconsciousness overcame him.

"I'd suggest," said a voice on the intercom, "that you gentlemen get into vac suits." Outside of their control, the gunner's seats retracted, pulling them out of the plastic bubble and into the safety of the ship's hull. The heavy lead shielding beneath the clear plastic rolled aside.

DeVliegar looked at Bleau.

"Proton radiation and a few flecks of grit," Jon explained. "It's scratched the bubble. Our speed."

DeVleigar again turned his attention to the bubble. The empty blackness beyond was invisible, hidden by the milky white of proton scratches. DeVliegar

had seen the plastic fur, which was pulled out of
space helmets during the early days of spaceflight.
The high mass of relativistic protons had pulled the
plastic out, dragging it behind. Now ships were usually protected by an intense magnetic field. Apparently, 187,000 meters per second adversely affected
that magnetic field's function, and the high speed
assured that they would run into far more relativistic
protons. DeVliegar found himself able to catch a small
crescent of blackness around the bubble's trailing
edge. They were at midpoint turnover. The captain's
message was clear enough. In 45 minutes, they would
be attacking someone. The explosive escape bolts that
ringed the bubble would have to be blown. In its
present state, the protective bubble had lost its
usefulness—it was no longer transparent. Although
the cannon were aimed and fired by computer, there
were certain targets for which a man's aiming and
firing were more useful. They couldn't rely entirely
on instrumentation. If the cowling that contained the
guns' automatic drive mechanisms was hit, the guns
would be given over to manual control. Not that a
man could do much at the speeds that they were
flying. However, craft in pursuit used random bursts
from attitude jets in order to avoid being hit by
automated fire. Records of man-powered guns hitting missiles and craft in pursuit were enough to
verify that intuition played a far greater part in knowing such a craft's position in advance than had previously been supposed. Thus, the very presence of a
gunner.

Fortunately for Simon and Jon, putting on a vac-
suit consisted of no more than screwing the helmet
onto the neck ring. Both of them flipped the 'all
secure' switch on their control panels. Weightless,
there was a small surge as the ship rolled over, tail
first, toward the moon.

"Gentlemen," the captain's voice said in their headphones. "Our primary objective is the space city,

Hazera Ysroel. *Dazh-bog* squadron will be attacking an object, a project of theirs, called *Ra*.

"You gunners! At *no* time will you take over manual control of your guns.

"We'll be going so fast that we'll be past what we're going for while you fogheads are still aiming. Under no circumstances does the UN want innocent people killed or massive crippling of their economy."

"I see," remarked Bleau. "We want to take over their factories when we move in."

"With the plague?" asked DeVliegar.

"We'll be going in backwards with engines thrusting. Our engineers say that our computers could handle things at the speeds we'll be traveling, but they aren't so sure about the gun mounts. Gears can strip. Mechanisms can break down. When we hit the city, we'll still be going at a pretty good clip. Once clear of the city, your lasers will be turned over to your control. You will be expected to cut off any pursuit. The range of your lasers and the magnification on your sights have both been tripled."

Jon stared blankly at the lead shielding that had long since slid back into place. Although they were both shielded by the body of the ship, they wondered what kind of 'dose' they were getting from the rebounds from plastic molecules.

"Why Hazera?" wondered DeVliegar. His theory had been right, but as far as both of them knew, the UN's opinion of the Israeli city was ambivalent, if anything. Why were they suddenly the enemy?

"You had it in bootcamp," responded Bleau to DeVliegar's question. "It's not our job to ask. Our first and most important lesson."

Then the engines fired with even more force. Both settled back. It would be a long burn.

"Cross your fingers," said K'khol. He projected an arm straight outward, then pointed his forearm down. Paul followed the 'spacer's point' and saw a white star growing bigger and brighter. The bus passed them. Their suits' boxes successfully duplicated the bus's radio pulse. The suits' computers speeded them along on their attitude jets to match the bus's velocity closely. It was as if the rush of the bus's passing had somehow sped them along. For long moments, K'khol and Paul held their breaths. Then, looking below them, they saw a bit of debris explode into vapor and they knew that they were through. They broke into laughter.

K'khol steered them to a point about a kilometer from the great city's spin. Naturally concealed in their black suits, they hung in the huge structure's shadow.

"What are you waiting for?" Paul asked.

"With all of the reaction mass that you wasted in our suits, I'm waiting for the right Byutt to turn in our direction."

Paul welcomed the shadow's pleasant chance to cool off. "But how can you tell from here? I couldn't read those signs even if they were printed in English!"

"Come up here by me," said K'khol.

Paul activated the suit's attitude jets. In a few meters he found himself looking at the sun through the Byuttim, downward across the hundred-meter stories of the great structures. What had before been only a hint—a flash of light, a color—burst forth in all its glory.

The sides of the structures were illuminated in stained glass. It was hard to keep from gasping at the beauty.

"Replicas," explained K'khol. "The Chagall windows of the old Hadassah Hospital in Jerusalem, one of the truly good things done by our artists and engineers. Each is 500 meters high, five meters in thickness."

Paul nodded within his helmet. He had read articles and seen discs of this remarkable work of artistry and engineering. He had, of course, seen the

immense panels of colored glass behind the elevators
and elevator terminals, but he hadn't realized their
significance until now.

"Every Jew on Earth or in Hazera knows each line
and color, every pattern and glow, what each symbol
implies and means.

"There we are. Grab on to me. You may not have
enough control over your suit jets to keep pace with
the Byutt. Paul grabbed hold. K'khol jetted a corkscrew path a dozen kilometers in diameter. Paul felt
his weight return and clung to K'khol's shoulders.
The twisting marked the same slow cadence of the
great spinning city. The stars spun. Centrifugal force
was fighting against the jets. The rectangular shape
of the structures seemed now to stand motionless
before them. They grew as they moved inward. The
beauty of the stained glass finally vanished as they
moved downward across the face of one of the
Byuttim.

At last, their feet touched down on one of the
outside catwalks.

"Well!" exclaimed K'khol. "That wasn't very fruitful."

"It verified our findings from the probe, and it
allowed us to formulate new theories."

"About what? Robots?"

"With *Ra*, what purpose does *Svenglid* serve?"

"With *Ra*, what purpose does a security guard
serve?"

"A security guard could prevent others from finding out that *Svenglid* had been abandoned," Paul
explained.

The 'cycle' light of the airlock changed from red to
green. K'khol twisted the helmet away from his neck
ring, and grinned above a shaggy beard. The tone of
Paul's disgust brought him his first apology.

"Israelis are fond of arguing," K'khol explained.

At least Paul took that for an apology. "That's too
bad," he finally said, absently.

"About arguments?"

"No. About the windows. It's a shame that they're only visible from that angle."

K'khol's grin widened. "It's planned that way," he said. "Beautiful things are made precious by their rarity. During lunar eclipses, we have people who sign on for rides. They take the people out and they can see the colors illuminated by the city's lights. A wonderful sight! They are quite brilliant at night, when the sun is masked, the shutters closed, and the windows themselves illuminated by the lights inside. That's the only time when you don't have to— How do you say? Look down a pipe."

He clasped Paul's hand as he peeled off the suit. "Now, if you'll excuse me, I have been a bad Jew. Today is Rosh Hashana. I must prepare for evening services. *Shalom.*

Paul spent a good while wandering about the streets. There was something in the windows that had caused a slow and subtle change—a sad stirring of forgotten things, of things he had never known. It had been so long since he felt anything, he wasn't sure. The feeling had returned as it had when he sighted the Hebrew markings on the *Parr* shuttle. Thrills like those caused by a clarinet or oboe thundered in his veins. The fact that he was one of them, part of it all, somehow made his heart quicken. His work on *Svenglid* was finished, at least for this week. Perhaps he would go with the family to shul tomorrow. It was strange to be haunted by such duplicity. Since coming, he had realized himself to be a part of a great people. As he had come to know the Goldsteins, there had grown a feeling of warmth, even affection. It was odd to be feeling affection again after all these years.

He had to hold his cause for the UN. He was pleased to find his patriotism still at work, a thing separate from friendship with the individual. He could see why the UN wanted someone who was a nonpracticing

Jew, someone who had been nonpracticing since birth. Even so, with his affection for the Goldsteins and the intellectual richness of the culture that surrounded them, it was a shame that the woman who was in charge of it all had gone mad. Mad!

"Yah hoo!"
The fleet of ships swung around the moon. The engines flared, pushing the men back into their seats still further. The weighted gimbals of their seats swung them about as centrifugal force overcame the lunar gravity, seeming to place the moon above them.
"Do you always have to yell like that?" asked Jon.
But DeVliegar was already grimacing as the burn stretched from seconds into unnatural minutes.

"Just a moment," said the rabbi.
Shoshanna looked up from her prayers and reached down to tousle the head of a bored-looking Asher. She smiled to herself. She could remember when she would have rather been out playing.
The rabbi replaced the *Torah* within the *Ark* and closed its brilliantly crafted doors. He returned to the podium. The smile vanished from Shoshanna's face. Reflecting from the rabbi's robes was a reddish light—an indicator lamp on the podium that displayed a city emergency. The rabbi reached beneath the bookstand and flicked his fingers over a tiny keyboard. The shimmer on his robes changed to green as he examined the readout. A switch was thrown and Gollum spoke:
"All people will return to their homes. Please move quickly and quietly. While this is an emergency, there is no need to panic. All precautions are being taken.
"Members of the *Pal-Halala* will report to their squadron commanders. The elevators on the left of the Knesset shaft are being reserved for your use.
"All other citizens will use the elevators to the right of the main shaft.

"This is the voice of Gollum. All people will please . . ."

Shoshanna frowned. "The *Pal-Halala*"? That meant that the city was under attack. The command "report immediately" meant that the attack was already in progress. A surprise attack? Out here? The only place of enough size for concealment was the moon!

She bit her lip. Who would possibly attack with the knowledge that the UN fleet was right behind them?

Yonah gripped her arm. He was right. This was no time for contemplation. She pressed a hand to the back of Asher's head. "C'mon, Asher," she said. "We'd better get going."

They emerged from the synagogue with a start. The sunlit shutters were already closing. The shutters on the other side, so tiny against the expanse of stained glass, were already closed. Her father gripped her hand all the tighter and hurried his step. She passed that squeeze on to the hand of Asher. All of them broke into a fast trot.

When they reached the elevator, their pace seemed to slow with the bulky machine's movement. At last, the huge door slid open. They hurried, shortcutting with everyone else through the park.

"Who are they?" Yonah asked.

Shoshanna looked to see a small huddle of grim-faced, business-suited men.

Although they wore no uniforms, Yonah recognized them by their blank sameness—the neat suits and unrumpled capes, the short, spacer hairstyles, the clean-shaven faces. But most of all, by their thin-lipped slits of mouths and the steely hardness in their gaze.

"The Hazera Internal Security Force," Yonah said, when he had placed the pieces together.

One of them turned as they approached the door.

"Dr. Goldstein?" he asked.

Goldstein stopped. "Yes?" he answered.

"Have you a UN representative in your place of residence?"

"*Ken*. Isn't he home? What's the matter?"

The man reached into a pocket and flashed a wallet with a badge. "Hazera Internal Security." A hard, synthetic smile. "No trouble. Paul Greenberg is simply wanted for questioning," he said.

Shoshanna looked open-mouthed at her father. "Isn't Paul in?" she asked.

The grim man shook his head. "Perhaps it would be best if we waited inside," he said.

"Of course," said Yonah, pressing the thumb lock. "Is there anything that I can get you, gentlemen? A glass of tea?"

Suddenly, something was wrong. It was as though a switch were suddenly pulled within Paul's mind. Almost immediately, he realized that the streets were filled with people, all heading in the direction of the elevator terminals. He joined them, heading for the place that had become, emotionally, his home.

Yonah rose to his feet. "Where have you been?" Was there a note of accusation in that voice?

Paul grinned sheepishly. "A silly thought," he explained. "Out window shopping is the best way of putting it."

"You know that it's Rosh Hashana and our shops are closed."

"It's hard working all day at a keyboard," Paul complained in what he hoped was a friendly manner. "A walk is certainly worthwhile and I thought some of the vending machines might still be functional. I thought I might find . . ." He shrugged.

A hand clutched him from behind. "Dr. Greenberg," said a voice.

Paul turned. He was shown an official-looking but unreadable badge.

"What's going on?" he asked.

"A large UN battlefleet has just cleared the lunar horizon. Since they refuse to answer any of our inquiries, we must assume that we are the target. Why? We don't know.

"Internal Security, Dr. Greenberg. Sorry to inconvenience you this way, but we've been told to round up all UN personnel for questioning."

Paul looked at four others behind the first. It would be useless to attempt a fight, at least for the time being. He looked back at the stern gazes of the family. He might have to rely on their friendship. He thought quickly. The dator that he had used to communicate with UN people on the moon was still sitting on his dresser. The black suit and most of his equipment was stored with K'khol and the Hazera underground. A few more pieces of equipment were stored in his room. If he could restore the faith of the family and prevent the dator's internal programming from being recognized, he had a chance.

Finally, he looked at Yonah. "But I haven't done anything," he insisted.

"I believe you, Paul," Yonah answered.

Paul looked at the man. "Will there be a lot of waiting involved?" he asked. He knew that in such cases, there always was.

The grim one nodded.

"Then let me take my dator and some discs," Paul said. "A few things . . ."

"Certainly." The Internal Security representative smiled his hard, cold smile.

"How long will I be?"

"Probably a couple of days."

"Then let me get some things together," Paul said. They followed him upstairs.

"The damned thing's turning!"

The battle was over before either man noticed. However, the radio messages that chattered in their earphones made both men glad that their target was the city itself.

Barely an hour after clearing the lunar horizon, the ship began a hard, sharp deceleration. Suddenly, as the first messages came from the 'destruction' of Project *Ra*, Hazera loomed upon them. More from tradition than any logical purpose, their seats swung about, facing the flare of the ship's mighty engines. Their opaque plastic bubble was blown, falling away from them into the blast. The straps that held their helmets to their seats prevented the sharp pull of deceleration from tearing their heads from their bodies, or more logically, simply breaking their necks. Still, they hung from their straps, facing into two and a half Gs of deceleration. Their tongues were pressed against the roofs of their mouths to prevent the discomfort caused by its slimy weight against their teeth. Their eyes hung like ripe fruit in their sockets. Hazera flew at them just slowly enough for the image to register on their retina.

The radios chattered from *Dazhbog* squadron. "The damned dish is turning toward us! Violet flashes! We're too late! All of the lasers! All of the accelerators are working! They're picking us off like fish in a barrel!"

Just then, the ship that carried Jon and Simon collided with an immense wheel at a thousand kilometers per hour. It swung up, ever wider, ever broader, totally enclosing their field of vision. There was a slight surge of centrifugal force as the ship's computers steered them within centimeters of a huge warehouse through a hole in the vast spokes of a bicycle wheel.

The radio messages grom *Dazh-bog* squadron continued to chatter. "Evacuate! Evacuate!"

Simon pulled his tongue away from his teeth to mutter, "I think I just did." Then he held his voice. The radio messages continued to come in.

"The damned thing's turning! They're taking the

ships from the outside of our formation and moving in! There's no place to run! Jesus! Look at those ships! They're just big, expanding balls of plasma!"

"Evacuate! Evacuate!"

"How?" came a voice that was strangely calm. "We're surrounded by lasers and particle beams, all of them constant, all of them moving. There's no place to run, nowhere to evacuate. They're . . ." There was a burst of static.

"This is *Domovoi* Leader to *Dazhbog* Leader. "Do you read me, *Dazhbog* Leader?"

More static.

"Move inward! Group at the center! Ram the damned thing if you can! *Dazhbog* Leader? Come in, *Dazhbog* Leader!"

"*Dazhbog* Leader ain't here, *Domovoi* Leader. Sorry about the delay, but being surrounded by vaporized ships don't make for good reception."

"This is *Domovoi* Leader to *Dazhbog* squadron. How many of you are left? Over."

"Three!" came the sardonic reply.

"How did you get out of it? Over."

"Grouped at the center and rammed the son-of-a-bitch. Not that it did any good. Center was practically nothing but aluminum foil, maybe three centimeters in thickness. Reflection from the jets raised our temperature enough to melt the back end of the ship. Direct heat from the engines must have melted through enough so that we didn't lose our engines and controls. Flammable materials inside destroyed the rest of the crew—that, and the impact. We were just able to spin our chairs around and pull back into the ship in time. Everything inside is gutted by fire. Vacuum now, but still glowing. We'll open some chillers. Fortunately, our computer shows that the central control room is still operative. We gunners had our suits plated with aluminum from the dish when we crashed through. It's painful just to move in the goddamned things. Are working our way, burning our way through to the control room."

"Take your time. We've got you on radar. If you keep your present burn going for another half hour, it will place you in an elliptical orbit that will take you back to the lunar near-side. We'll see that you get medical attention. Then we'll regroup for a second attack. Are your guns still operative?"

"One set. Our set and up yours, *Domovoi* Leader. The rooms around the command center evacuated before the heat could melt through. We've got the captain and first mate's bunks. Enough food and fuel to last. We'll spray on our own medicine when we get through. My buddy and I (burst of static) is over real quick. Didn't we, buddy?"

A low moan was cut off by another burst of static.

"With these engines we can make it to the asteroid belt in a day or so, and we've got a couple of dozen— several hundred—meters of fused metal to protect us from proton radiation. I think I can keep this other guy going until we reach a belter hospital.

"Is there anybody in those two other ships?"

(Static).

"Is anybody there?"

(Static).

"Well, radio's going. Should be able to sell the engine for plenty (static). Damned shame I can't (static) . . . trol those other ships remotely. Three times the pesos (static) . . . Dios . . . Or should I say, 'Shalom'?"

"*Domovoi* Leader? This is *Uhura*. Number one, two, niner. Do you want us to give pursuit?"

"Negative."

Out of the thousands of men who had attacked the main objective, two were still alive. By the sound of it, one was going AWOL and the other was badly injured—too badly injured to give a damn.

Chapter XIII

September 12, 2086   Byutt Sebulon, Level 15
Tishre 4, 5847   Thursday
7:15 a.m., Jerusalem Time

Paul awoke in the small chamber. He looked up at the single window far overhead. The door was standard, but there was no internal switch to open it. The heavy ceramic walls were coated with a special shellac that rendered graffiti impossible. The toilet was open and the smell of disinfectant was heavy. There had been little change in jail cells during the past hundred years. So, for the past two days, Paul had sat toying with his dator. His contact with the outside amounted to little or none. Three meals a day. And the walls of the little structure were not entirely soundproof. Some sort of public announcement had been made—at least, Paul had heard something lengthy. It had come through a badly muffled loudspeaker, so he wasn't sure what it had said. He doubted if he could have followed it, even if he spoke Hebrew. The announcement had been followed by cheers. He had heard snatches of argument. Something was more than reaching a head. Paul bit his lower lip, waved casually to a camera imbedded in glass, and walked into an alcove. There he pressed a switch and a panel slid open. He extracted a cup and sipped at the coffee, frowning. There were too many questions and not enough answers.

Prime Minister Cohen crossed her arms and looked at the engineer, smiling her famous smile. She looked like a benevolent grandmother—warm, reassuring.

"How much damage?" she asked.

"It's still quite serviceable," the engineer answered. He grimaced. It was as though she were talking about some minor probe, possibly ruined by its passage through a massive magnetic field. A 20th-century equivalent might have been storm damage to a barn. "Fortunately, the magnetic fields were able to divert most of the debris through the center," he continued, grinning, "along with a couple of ships. If the magnetic fields hadn't been active, there's no telling how much damage would have been caused."

"What about the UN?"

"You'll have to ask the generals about that. It's my understanding that they're still recovering from the shock of *Ra*'s potential. They've used up most of their stock of super engines. Right now, most of what's left of their fleet is moving in close orbit around the moon, watching us. At least they're giving us enough time to make repairs."

"And the damage to the city itself?"

"Very minor. Fortunately, we were able to divert most of the beams and projectiles with the backup magnetics. You'll recall that many of these were installed in the city itself. A good deal of their fire was aimed at the Knesset, which possesses the strongest magnetic projectors and shielding. Those structures of military importance were likewise protected. Fortunately, the attacks that we've had over the past 25 years have made us fortify those structures beyond what the UN expected. If few of the attacking ships were damaged, then our damage was also slight."

Rachel Cohen looked out the window. The great dish of *Ra* was now close enough to be visible as more than a star. The major projects and factories had been moved closer together after the attack. The long spear of *Svenglid* was visible, slowly turning, through another window. Her current offices were near the center so that the only gravity that existed came from the velcro-coated floors and seats. Her doctors objected, but an old woman was most comfortable here.

"Public reaction?" she asked.

"About what you would have expected," came the answer. "About half the population is Orthodox. More than we expected are going back to Dos Telerl. It's a good thing. We've still got one more load of volatiles inbound from Jupiter. Even so, it's still going to be a thin line. We'll probably have to ration toward the end."

"Is there any chance of intercepting the inbound tanker?"

The engineer shook his head. Prime Minister Cohen grimaced. Then for a moment she was thoughtful.

"It must be hard on the Chassidim," she said. "I wish that I had their kind of faith. Has there been any ruckus over the *Parrim* headed toward the moon?"

"Some have had UN escorts on the way. None of the escorts has opened fire. Apparently, they're sure that the *Parrim* are unarmed. They've been probing and checking on every wavelength. They won't find anything inside except food, water, and people. No explosives. They've jammed all of our attempts at radio communication."

Again Professor Cohen was lost in thought. "Can you imagine," she said, "having so much faith that when something you disagree with happens that you're willing to pick up everything you own and leave?"

The engineer grinned sardonically. "The Messiah *could* come," he said.

"And the children shall return to the Land of Israel," she said, not sure whether she was quoting anything. "How long will it be?"

"The half-life of some of that stuff is 20,000 years or better."

"Then he won't come in my time," she said. "Or yours."

"The only One Who can break the laws of this universe is He Who created them."

Rachel laughed. It was good to be teased. It was good to be an old woman and still be teased. "Stop playing Chassid," she answered.

The engineer blushed. She had put him too *much* at ease.

Jon Bleau sucked at his bulb of coffee. Although the ship was being rotated, creating what passed for gravity, Jon, like most spacers, clung to zero G equipment. A bulb was safer than a cup, assuming the ship decided suddenly to go somewhere.

His partner at the cannon joined him.

"Are we still going to attack?" Jon asked.

"Looks like," Simon answered.

Jon's mind drifted back to bootcamp. Their sergeant had told a story there about obedience, a story about a demonstration that had been given to a visiting dignitary. A Chinese officer had gathered up a hundred of his men and ordered them to march off the edge of a cliff and then return. One was still in enough of one piece after the jump to return. The officer turned him around once again, and marched him off that same cliff. This time, he didn't come back.

There had, at the time, been another man in bootcamp—an American of Vietnamese ancestry named Thomas Hang. He had been a great source of amusement because if he were pinched or jostled in any way, and something were on his mind, it would spill out. So, when the sergeant climaxed the story with, "And men, what do you think of that?", a startled Hang had responded, "Crock of shit!" The entire company broke into laughter.

"Who said that?" cried the sergeant, pacing back and forth. "Who said that?" The company laughed all the harder.

Jon Bleau had laughed as well. Now, he wasn't so sure.

An entire squadron of ships wiped out, and the UN

expected them to go back? To attack once again? Perhaps the defector, the traitor and coward who had seen enough of military action, knew that this would be expected of him.

At this point, Jon wished he could join that single remnant of *Dazhbog* Squadron. He could now be on his way into the safety of the asteroid belt. Maybe the tale told by the Sarge hadn't been such a crock after all. He knew he would make the attack. Like the thousands of others unscorched by *Ra*, he knew that he would be the only survivor. There was nothing else *to* do. Nowhere to go. Now he wondered about those men of so long ago. And wondered if he might not have done the same.

"Dr. Green?"

Paul looked up, startled.

"Or is it Mr. Green?"

The face of Prime Minister Cohen shone from a wall that he had assumed to be ceramic.

"I didn't think that I was important enough to be bothered with," Paul answered.

The image sighed. "Everyone is important, *Mr.* Green. I am often too busy for everyone. But for the moment, the whole *megillah* is out of my hands and in those of Gollum. So I thought I'd call and see how you were."

"Don't give me that! I have been held here for three days! No reason or charge has been given. I was told that I was being brought here for questioning. Where are the questions?"

"Please, Mr. Green!"

"*Dr.* Greenberg!" he bit back.

"Dr. Greenberg, then, although that identity was erased from the UN's central banks the moment that your ships cleared the lunar horizon. Our computers are still in touch, thank goodness! I wish that people would trust one another enough to talk. I'm afraid that you've been abandoned here, Mr. Green. The UN attack has failed. I was hoping to invite you up for lunch, but unless you keep a civil tongue ..."

"Okay, okay," Paul answered, perplexed.

"Very well. Excellent. You do not need to be questioned. As I've already stated, we know who you are and why you are here.

"Oh, by the way. You didn't kill that poor guard on *Svenglid*, did you?"

Paul shook his head.

Ms. Cohen seemed to sigh in relief. "Then your only crime is espionage and misinformation. Of course, we'll have to have the identity of the man who did kill the guard. I can get you a pardon, but I'm not quite so sure about how his family will react."

"I don't ..."

The prime minister silenced him with a wave of her hand. "I'll leave you to clean up, Mr. Green. You did bring a clean suit to jail with you, did you not?"

Paul nodded, still perplexed.

"Good! I hate to sit across a lunch table from a scruffy man. I'll speak to you again on the elevator. *Shalom*, Mr. Green."

"*Shalom*," Paul answered as the wall went blank.

The last of the Paris Nouveau ships were arriving, their engines bright stars as they approached the fleet, tail first. One by one, the stars went out.

"What's the matter?" asked Bleau.

"You said not to trust them."

"The lion and the deer have a common enemy in the forest fire. But when it's over ..." Bleau shrugged.

"So, as soon as they refuel, we start our attack run. What's the target this time?"

"The city. I've already fed the ID for targets into the computers."

"You ready?"

Paul looked up from fastening the clasp of his dress tunic and nodded. He attached, with much difficulty, the formal cape to the buttons at his shoulders. Dressing was difficult without the use of his prosthetic arm.

"Please," he said once again. "Can't my arm be reactivated?"

The man spoke into a wrist com, listened for an answer, and shook his head. "Sorry, but there's no way we can put your arm back on with partial power. Otherwise, we'd say go ahead. But you're much too dangerous with it in action and we still don't trust you enough to have it activated around our prime minister. This way, please."

Paul followed. He felt the presence of two security guards behind him, but didn't give them the satisfaction of looking back.

The security room had been a temporary holding cell on the amusement deck. Now, in the middle of what should have been day, it was empty.

"Where is everybody?" Paul asked.

He felt the man ahead smiling grimly. "Most of the people are in their homes. The Chassidim have returned to the moon. They've each been given 10,000 Israeli pounds. They'll probably be going to Earth."

"But why?"

"I hope your people will treat them well," the officer continued. "Dos Telerl and Akkiba are now under UN control. I suppose that you know that."

Paul grimaced. The officer had evaded his question, and not too skillfully. Apparently there were still some things that they thought he was not yet ready to know. "No," Paul finally answered. "I don't know anything. Did the UN take over?"

"I would imagine that to be the case. Your people apparently cut out our communications systems and replaced what they were broadcasting with computer simulation. By the way, I must compliment the UN on them. They were extraordinarily realistic. It took a great deal of energy and a great deal of time to program for them. Thousands of our people must have talked to friends and relatives on the moon. They didn't know that they were talking to charges in a memory bank.

"Apparently, the UN had a cover story concerning the taking of recordings for the crime computers on Terra. They said that they were worried about something that was happening out in the asteroid belt. That's a neat way of getting everyone's voiceprints, images ... We only had a few hints at what was really happening, when the UN's ships cleared the lunar horizon. It seems that no one took into account the few things that could happen between the time that the recordings were made and the attack actually took place. Or the UN chose to ignore these differences. It was a short enough span of time.

"Our first real hint appeared when one of the people reported talking with a friend from one of the *Parrim*. It seems that this friend spent several weeks' savings for an expensive cape made of Japanese silk. Akkiba isn't large enough to have its own recording station, so they had to take a train to Dos Telerl. After the legal recordings were made, one of the gaskets on his suitcase blew, ruining the cape. You can imagine how surprised his friend was when he called him and found him still wearing it. He asked the simulation about it, but the only story the computer could produce from its memory banks sounded phony. Other items popped up that couldn't be explained away.

"A moustache mysteriously reappeared ..."

Paul chuckled and looked over the empty, cobblestoned street.

The man caught his glance. "You'll forgive my avoidance of your questions, *Mar* Green. I've been asked to save that privilege for Professor Cohen. I think you'll find that she's a most reasonable woman, and she took a liking to you when you met. She's not as crazy as our underground seemed to think. You'll be the first UN representative to hear what's really been going on. Seeing it, hopefully. Most of our attempts to communicate with the UN have been jammed. It appears that they aren't even interested in hearing our part of the story. We're going to have to put some of the machines that we've built into action sooner than we expected. And I'm afraid that you're stuck here, well, for the rest of your life."

"I'm to be executed," Paul said.

"No. In fact, Ms. Cohen says that she's willing to give you a full pardon, providing that you help us."

"Help you! Help you what? Wipe out the UN fleet? Take over the Earth-Moon system? The UN?"

"Nonsense!" the man barked back. "*Ra* is not a weapon, Mr. Green!" He paused. "Ms. Cohen will tell you. Then you can make your own decision—the only decision that you can make, under the circumstances."

Paul was silent. If the only alternative to such madness was death, then death he would take.

The officer looked at his dator. "We've got to hurry," he said. "I didn't know that putting on your clothes would take so long. Run, Mr. Green! To the elevator terminal!"

He barked orders to the other two men in Hebrew. The two on either side of Paul turned off, cutting with him through a diagonal alleyway—a shortcut to the elevator terminal. Paul saw his chance. With the arm disconnected, it would be difficult. He picked up the prosthetic arm and pulled it across his body. Suddenly, he spun about in a half twist. The hard steel frame of the arm's inner workings swung outward. The man who was running to his left ran directly into the backward snap of the arm. His face bloodied, he crashed to the cobble. Paul tried to dive through an open window and into a basement, but the arm was dead weight, throwing him off balance. Someone tackled Paul about the waist, bringing him face-down into a ceramic wall. He might have known that the contents of the basement would have been an amusement park hologram. He was pulled back to his feet by the collar and a handcuff went around his good hand. He heard a snap as it was connected to the useless prosthetic.

"That was very foolish, *Mar* Green," said the leader. "Our time is already running short. We must hurry."

"Before what?" Paul asked.

Rough hands gripped him in the other's silence. They hurried him into a trot.

"Hurry!" the officer commanded of Paul. "If we can make it to the elevator, we've got a chance. Otherwise, we'll all be killed!"

Paul knew the sincerity of fear. His step obediently hurried. It was evident that they were now more concerned for themselves than for him. If he broke now, he could probably get away. But he wasn't foolish enough to try it without knowing the danger that they faced. Paul could see the sweat stains growing beneath their arms. He could do nothing as long as he was bound, and he could do nothing if he were dead. He increased his pace.

The elevator door was directly ahead. They plunged through it. Paul was mildly surprised to find it as empty as the shtetl outside, and he was further surprised to see a long net, cylindrical in shape, stretched from the floor to the ceiling. One of the men, forgetting his charge, raced toward it.

"*Lo, et!*" announced the officer, pressing Paul against the near wall. Rapidly, he fed the destination into the elevator's computer.

The rotation of the great city began to slow.

The floor suddenly tilted, sending them rolling down the side of the huge cylinder. The young man who had been hurrying toward the crash webbing fell on top of them. It had been a fall of five meters, but with whatever force the city was slowing, it was less than a terrestrial G. The force was increasing. By the time the man had reached the end of his fall, though unhurt, he struck Paul with breath-stealing force. Still it increased. Paul found himself pressed into the heavy glass of the elevator's wall. The two at his side were pressing into him. The man atop's weight grew. Something flashed toward Paul's face. It was a pocket pen that somebody must have left in one of the seats. He turned his head to one side and it bounced, stinging against his cheek.

"What's . . ." Paul began, but was interrupted by the squeal of straining girders, the snapping of . . . Paul was silent. The elevator was moving in a direction that *had been* up. The tiles outside were moving unheedingly by.

There was a light . . . a change of illumination. Paul looked in the direction that had been up. The prime minister's familiar face lighted the ceiling. Her brows shot up in surprise.

"Our charge tried to escape," explained the officer.

Rachel closed her eyes and nodded in understanding. "I might have known," she said, peering out of the same sort of webbing that now hung in the elevator. She smiled at a secret joke. "I should have known that my flair for the dramatic would get me in trouble."

The ships had long since blasted out of lunar orbit. Svenglid, *Ra*, and Hazera were clearly visible as bright stars. Jon looked at them on the screen and wrinkled his brow. If he had a ruler to lay down, he might have drawn a straight line between them. It was probably an optical illusion caused by the reddish fireflies of the factories that swarmed close in to the three mighty structures. He stepped up magnification and broke into a howl.

"Look at it through magnification!" cried Bleau. "Look at *Ra*! It's three-quarters turned away from us! If they try to turn it toward us, it will break apart. They could never turn it in time!" He laughed. "Hazera is helpless against us. They're out-armed and out-armored. They haven't got a chance!"

Simon returned his laughter. Then their whoops

were cut off by a burn from the ship's superengines. They felt the Gs press them back into their seats. They were slowing for the attack run.

"Is everybody all right?" asked Prime Minister Cohen.

"*Ze tov*," returned the officer.

"I don't want anybody hurt, but that may be unavoidable."

Paul looked up with eyes bright in fear and confusion. "What are you doing?" he demanded. "What's going on?"

"We wouldn't have told you until this time. The city is losing its gravity, ceasing its rotation, slowing to a stop." She smiled. "I was hoping that you'd get a better view of the situation from the crash webbing that's hanging in there. It would be far safer for you. But I can't take responsibility for your own foolishness."

The elevator burst through the roof of the Byutt. Paul got a glimpse of the rooftop garden. He saw that the lakes and streams had been drained. Some of the plants were tilted disconcertingly toward him. Paul wondered how the plants would do without the centrifugal spin. The soil, he realized, would be temporarily held by the plants' root structure. They couldn't possibly hope to detain Hazera's spin for long. If they were intent on moving Hazera behind *Ra*, then stopping its spin shouldn't be necessary. Any slight lateral acceleration could easily be taken care of by the city's pneumatic shock absorbers. What were they up to?

"Look to your left, *Mar* Green."

Paul looked. He saw the slowly turning needle of Svenglid moving to a stop with the city's motion. He turned his attention back to Professor Cohen.

"You can't get away with it," Paul stated.

"Away with what, *Mar* Green?"

"An attack on Terra," Paul finally said. "We know

about *Ra* and we know that it isn't a solar furnace. Moving the city behind it isn't going to stop us. Moving the city isn't going to help."

"We think it will, *Mar* Green."

Paul saw that the ancient woman's eyes were twinkling.

"What is *Ra* if it isn't a solar furnace?" she asked.

"I've been told that it isn't a weapon. I can't believe that."

She looked at him in game-playing amusement. "It wasn't designed as a weapon, but I'm afraid that we had to use it as such," she said. "We destroyed the fleet that the UN sent to attack us. They felt that the speed the Mitsu engines gave them would surprise us—surprise *Ra*. Had they know that *Ra* was designed to deal with articles going near the speed of light, they wouldn't have attacked. Its purpose isn't that of a weapon, but it worked as such.

"I hate to talk of such things, *Mar* Green. The UN's noble blue, going foolishly to their deaths. It's a shame we didn't think in the direction that your thoughts would naturally lead. I mean, really think it through. Quite frankly, we didn't believe that anybody would succeed in inspecting things so closely that such a conclusion could be reached. Although I suppose that for one such as yourself, such a conclusion was logical. You are a UN agent, *Mar* Green. A spy. As such, you've had to deal with the lowest in humanity, the incredibly wealthy, and the incredibly powerful. Those who have been spoiled by that wealth and power. Those who wanted—and tried to get—everything. But there were others, weren't there, *Mar* Green? Those who worked against the UN for a cause that they truly believed to be noble? Those who fought against the UN in an attempt to make things the way they were before the UN came—before the technology that made the UN indispensable came? I'm not talking about the wealthy of the Pacific floor. I'm talking about the Indians of South America, the Laplanders, the Nepalese.

"Wasn't there some sense of sorrow when it came to fighting these?

"There are two kinds of men who take your occupation, *Mar* Green. Both of them are emotionally ill. One of these is emotionally destitute, biochemically different from the rest of us. They seek thrills, danger. That thrill overcomes any sense of morality. The money is secondary to this sort. They seek their thrills as daredevils, professional soldiers, spies. Criminals. You aren't that sort. I know because I use both.

"You were stunted in your emotional growth. You had some shock—some terror. And you failed to grow after that. You withdrew, pulling yourself into a shell of your own building."

Paul blushed. He choked. Memories flooded back. He squeezed his eyes shut. "How do you know this?" he asked. "How could you possibly know?"

"We made some body scans as you entered, Paul." The use of his first name brought a sense of trust, of comfort. She knew how to handle people well. "More than a hundred years of practice," Paul told himself. Still, he felt the pain ebb and flow away.

"You told Yonah that your duodenitis was new. The doctors told me that there was a great deal of old scar tissue there. The ulcers have been with you a long time."

Paul turned his head, looking away. Was it his imagination or was the needle of *Svenglid* shortening, turning?

"I'm doing more than offering you a new job, Paul. I'm offering you a rebirth. I use men like you until their illness is over. The UN perpetuates that illness artificially. I can see their reasons for doing so, but I can't accept the morality. It's not a policy that we Jews follow. I won't hold you responsible for anything that you've done in the past. I can't, because without feelings of one's own, how can we be expected to feel for others. We aren't the wealthy of the Pacific floor, *Mar* Green. We are the Laplanders, the Indians of South America, and the Nepalese. We are fighting for the right to be different as we've fought all through history."

Paul looked up at her with new understanding. "The right to be different," he repeated, whispering it after her. The right to deliberate nonconformity. The right to believe and live differently. "But the price!" he cried aloud. "At what price to the rest of humanity?"

Rachel Cohen shook her ancient head. "No price, Paul," she whispered. "No price. And more in return that anyone on Terra currently dreams. We only wish to fulfill our contract with the UN."

Commander Louis Renoir looked through his sights and grinned. At last, space would be free of the Jewish scum! Money-grubbing insects whose only reason for living was to make a franc at another's expense. He, like everyone on Paris Nouveau, had been taught to regret the failure of the Nazis in the last century. Even the Arabs had failed to destroy them with the atom bomb! They clung to their existence like the cockroaches that infested his own ship!

There was a time when all the world had thought the French were finished. Louis looked back over his shoulder and chuckled at an unseen Terra. The world, and that was all there had been. France had been a place of moral depravity, sinking lower and lower since its own revolution, barely following in the footsteps of America, Britain, and the Soviet Union. France had taught them. A France in space might never have existed had not a resource-rich Canada broken in two. A cultural tie—that's what the newspapers of the time had called it.

Louis? He was aboard a ship that he would have called lucky. He was one of the few who would destroy *Svenglid*, the space project itself! Not that they were supposed to. Not under UN regulations or orders. Theirs was a secret mission. A few hits in the right places would assure that the contract for a deep-space probe would go to Paris Nouveau. He would make certain that the contract was secured for the great leader of the French space cities. A mighty French alliance in space! What did it matter if the nation of France itself had disowned them for 'moral reasons'? All pride and the judgment of morality itself belonged to the pioneers! The strong Frenchmen had left the weak and useless where they belonged. On Terra!

Louis didn't know that his mind and emotions had been twisted, raped, pulled, folded over, and snapped shut. He didn't know that he had been molded by propaganda techniques so subtle that a psychologist of the 20th century wouldn't have immediately recognized them as such.

He took a preprogramed look at the nearness of Svenglid to Hazera and smiled. It made it easier, to hit Svenglid and make that hit look like an accident.

"What was the main problem in building Svenglid?" Rachel asked.

"I suppose building engines that would take it to relativistic velocity," Paul answered.

"Very well. What is the second problem?"

"Interstellar debris in Svenglid's path," Paul answered.

"How does Svenglid overcome this?"

"By cycling that interstellar matter down into its engines and using it as fuel. There isn't enough stuff spread across this part of the galaxy for a real ram-jet. We're the old sailing ship with the new steam engine. We run on steam, but if the wind is there, why not?"

"How is the debris sucked in? How do we use interstellar dust and gas as fuel?"

"Why, magnetic fields, of course! Any ionized material that lies in front of the ship is sucked down its center for use as additional fuel."

* * *

"The factories are moving together. Hazera is moving toward *Ra*. When the three are linked, they'll try to turn the whole thing around. The factories will go behind the cupping of the weapon. Hazera is going to use *Ra* as a shield. It's just as our captain told us," laughed Simon. "But like you said, it can't work. They'll never turn it around in time!"

Jon looked through his screens uncertainly. He looked off to the side through the naked vacuum and the vanished plastic bubble. It was no longer an optical illusion. *Ra*, Hazera, and Svenglid were in a straight line! He looked questioningly at the target and then away again. "What's that?" he asked.

Simon looked. The thin delicate hemispheres of distant flame were drifting away from their vessel. Rockets were moving away from the wide, conical formation.

"I don't know," he answered. "Somebody's breaking up our formation, leaving our flank wide open."

Rachel Cohen smiled. "You have explained how the Bussard Ramjet would use the interstellar matter as fuel," she said. "But only ionized matter can be manipulated by magnetic fields. What about the stuff in *Svenglid*'s path that isn't ionized? That stuff which would be hitting the front of our ship as proton radiation, were it going fast enough. Even the tremendous amount of shielding that *Svenglid* carries—"

"Is supposed to carry," interrupted Paul.

Again the smile. "Very well, then. Is supposed to carry," she said. "Even this shielding cannot protect the delicate molecular electronics inside from damage. How is this stuff taken care of?"

"Lasers," Paul answered. "A ring of ultraviolet lasers placed around the shielding and computer targeted to material lying ahead of the craft. This would ionize that material so that it can be sucked down into the engines."

The *Chat Savauge* was not a large ship. With a crew of four, it contained a control room, from which the targeting programs were punched in, and bunks, a kitchen, and a small recreation center in the long narrow confines of its fuselage.

Louis Renoir looked out of the teardrop swelling of the control cabin. He never knew why they even bothered installing windshields in spacecraft. One could fly by instrumentation alone. One didn't need to fly at all with computers. Cameras were much harder to hit and less dangerous than windshields. He looked at the quiet blackness and the silent stars. Radar showed that Svenglid was slowly moving. Perhaps the Jews intended to place the great, worthless hunk of spacecraft between themselves and the attack fleet, or at least the fuel and dummy probe. It was his job to see that those engines were destroyed, giving the stricken Hazera no chance of rebuilding its shattered economy. If all went well, the city would go into bankruptcy. It would be abandoned, perhaps even blasted out of existence as a threat to the health of the solar system. Once gone, the filthy Jewish virus would never infect the nobler blood, the races of the solar system who prided themselves on their cleanliness. He thought of the documentaries that he had seen of the squalid city and felt the bile rise from his stomach. They had brought the disease on themselves! The Jews were no more than cockroaches, rats, lice, or any of the thousand vermin that had followed man into space. He would die, never knowing that the pictures he had seen were computer simulations, and that the documentaries had been founded on 20 years of accumulated propaganda.

"Wildcat!" said a voice, in English, over his radio. "Where are you going?"

Renoir shrugged and smiled. "I am sorry, *Mon-*

sieur," he said. "There seems to be something wrong with our central navigation computers. Perhaps it is Jewish sabotage, *non?"*

He looked down at the navigator, who returned his smile. The navigator sat at a 90-degree angle, head away from him, a silhouette against the bright sunlight shining through his tiny office's double porthole.

"Get it fixed and head back as soon as you can! You're along to help us, goddamnit!"

"Oui, Monsieur. We will do what we can." He switched off his throat mike and turned to the gunner, hard at work on the keyboard of the targeting computers. "Try to hit the engine bell on the outside," he said in French. "Liquid deuterium is pumped through the bell as a coolant. If we can break through the shell's outer jacket, it will be useless to them.

Professor Cohen's image folded its arms. "And just suppose that there were larger chunks of matter in *Svenglid*'s path," she said. "Chunks of matter too big for the UV lasers to deal with?"

Paul looked puzzled for a moment. "Such a thing is so unlikely that we never considered it. You may have a point. That could well be why the other two probes failed. Why, even a chunk of iron the size of a pea could— I suppose particle beam accelerators could blast and ionize an object the size of Ceres if they were powerful enough."

"Good God!" came DeVliegar's awed voice.

"What is it?" asked Bleau.

"Switch your screen up to maximum magnification!" Simon exclaimed. "See for yourself! The head of Svenglid!"

Jon did as he was told. The dummy probe attached to Svenglid's nose was gone, blasted into slice-of-pie pieces that were drifting away and back. No, Svenglid itself was moving. John thought he caught the spark of an attitude jet. In the probe's place was a long hollow pipe composed of metal, electronics, photonics, and magnetics. Jon found that he had to keep changing the position of the camera to observe it. It was swimming on its attitude jets, accelerating at only a tenth of a G. It was definitely moving.

Where? He followed the arrow point of the enormous spacecraft. The assembly of factories, city, and weapon were almost complete. "Why, it's a vast probe!" exclaimed Jon. "They're stealing a starship! They're hijacking Svenglid! They're riding the goddamned thing all the way to Centauri!"

DeVliegar found himself laughing. For the first time in his life, he found himself laughing from— What? Irony? Hysteria? A defense mechanism from the sheer dimensions of what he was seeing? He didn't know.

He felt himself swell with pride at just being a human being. Six million people! Six million people who had the guts and brains to do what they were doing. For decades, Hazera had begged for protection that the UN couldn't provide! Now they were providing their own protection. A wall of vacuum 4.2 *lightyears* thick!!! And at the same time, they were fulfilling their contract. DeVliegar laughed, his eyes filling with tears. He was thankful for the decelerating Gs that were pulling the tears away. "Tell the captain," he said. "Tell anyone! The attack has got to be stopped!"

But there are no Earthlike planets in the Centauri system," Paul protested. "How do you hope to survive?"

Paul looked above him. The huge shield of Svenglid was closer, much closer. He looked back at the image of Rachel Cohen.

"Our studies of the tri-star system of Alpha Centauri have made it plain that it contains at least three planets with large rings," she answered. "If that system is anything like our own, we can expect to find comets, asteroids— There are an infinite number of possibilities in those rings alone!

"In short, *Mar* Greenberg—" She grinned as Paul watched the spearhead of Svenglid push into Hazera. There was a heavy ringing of metal. "—we don't *need* Earthlike planets."

Paul looked in the direction that might have been above—the great shield of *Ra-Svenglid*, the machine that would transform interstellar dust and gas into fuel. It was growing closer. When contact was complete, the ship would be ready.

"Naturally," explained Rachel, "the ship won't be going quite as fast as promised. But three-quarters lightspeed is better than nothing. Our original plan was to launch Svenglid out of the asteroid belt. However, one of the advantages of the Sanyo engines is that, as well as accelerating random vacuum decay, it accelerates the decay of the neutron. A proton and an electron, easily controllable with Svenglid's magnetic fields. Unless someone is directly in the craft's blast, they will be unharmed by gamma radiation. There is only alpha and beta, which can be sent in no direction of habitation. It is quite easy to launch Svenglid from here."

Commander Louis Renoir again looked through the sights. The great spacecraft's engines were drawing within striking distance of the *Chat Sauvage*'s tiny missiles. The great craft was trying to move away from his on its attitude jets. The Jewish computer must know his purpose by this time. However, it couldn't fire its engines this close to the moon without raising the wrath of the many UN followers. Too many people would be killed by its radiation. The engines would have to be fired a good deal away from the Earth-Moon system. Logic told him, as he pursued the craft, that even from this angle, he was safe. He grinned as the great round blackness of the exit nozzle came within the display's sights. The

crosshairs moved to one side. A bomb exploded in
the combustion chamber might be contained by the
machine's huge Tokamac—it would only accelerate
the great mass ever so slightly. But a hit on the
exterior of the exhaust bell would release the cooling,
pulsing liquid deuterium. If he could catch the nozzle,
all the better. In any case, that particular, very expensive exhaust bell and Tokamac would be useless.
To his side, below him, he could see the flare of the
rockets through the darkened double portholes. The
computer had launched. The tiny, deadly missiles
were on their way.

Suddenly a flare was all that he could see—for as
long as his retina lasted. He, the missiles, and his
ship were now an expanding cloud of plasma—fuel
for Svenglid.

When the three combined, the main engines would
fire. Panic overtook Paul. In a smooth motion, Paul
kicked away from the wall. The deceleration of
Hazera's centrifugal spin was complete. Once again
he was in microgravity. It was an opportunity that
would last only for a moment. It was a chance, the
barest possibility, that he might somehow start the
elevator again toward Hazera's core. He thought of
the ships that nestled in their hangars on the edges of
Hazera. He thought of the landing shelves and docking collars. He found the switch and the elevator
started. Hands tried to grasp him. He kicked them
away. His pursuers gave up, nestling near the wall
and watching him curiously. Rachel watched too,
just as silently, as the elevator's weightless car entered the great hotel-government complex of Hazera's
core. The desperate chance that Paul might get away
overcame for him all logic. He might make it to a
place where he could steal a ship, take it back with
him to Terra. If he could make a ship soon enough
after the engines fired, there was the barest chance
that the stolen ship's engines would overcome Sven-

glid's inertia, that he would find himself hurtling back to that mottled sphere of blue, brown, and green. Earth! How sweet its name seemed to him in that last desperate gamble for freedom. He pushed himself from the wall and toward the elevator's door. The kick gave him more speed than he thought. The gleaming tiles and patterns were sliding past the elevator's glass walls. Here he could steal a ship.

The spacers were dumfounded. It was a desperate gamble. The spacers had been taught through a lifetime to avoid movement during the ofttimes cataclysmic disorientations of dockings and shifts in the direction of motion. They were familiar with the disorientations and stomach-heaving movements. To them, Paul's gamble wasn't a gamble at all. It was doomed before it had begun. It was something that they knew so totally, so completely, that at first they didn't understand his actions at all.

At last, recognition gleamed in the prime minister's eyes. Paul could be seriously hurt. She looked past nearly 80 years of her life in the Second Israel, remembered her leaving and how it had felt. Paul could be hurt.

"Stop him!" she shouted.

"We dare not!" barked back the answer. The entire structure shook with the impact, and then, with Svenglid's magnificent fire! Paul's mind skimmed back as he fell. It was amazing how long a fall could be. Without his artificial arm to balance him, he had kicked his way near to what had once been the ceiling. At one G of acceleration, he fell toward the far wall, dragging his skinning hand against the rough stucco of the ceiling. Thirty-two feet per second, 98 meters. The physics of falling raced through his brain.

An old conversation came back to him. "Have you seen the ocean?" asked Dr. Goldstein.

"Of course," his now-absent personality had replied. He closed his eyes at his own foolishness. The feel of bare sand beneath his feet, the call of a seagull,

the roar of the blue green waves—all came back to
him. As a child of ten, he had stood giggling on the
beach, up to his waist in seawater. The bright sun
burned its way into his salt-coated skin. The warmth
was wonderful and the sea so cold. He giggled as
wave after wave raised the level of the water into a
surging rush over his head. He squinted in horror at
the wave that now came. It was fully five meters
high. It would sweep him off his feet and carry him
away. As he turned to run back to the safety of the
beach, the wave and the far wall struck him down.
As blackness closed over his mind, Dr. Goldstein's
question came back. "Have you seen the ocean?"

"Of course." Ocean . . . Home . . . Two things that
he would never know again.

"We're going home!" exclaimed a voice on the ship's
intercom.

A man came by the small rec room. DeVliegar and
Bleau were drinking coffee from squeeze bulbs. They
watched on the monitors.

"What about you boys?" The question was directed
at DeVliegar and Bleau. One of the gunners was silent; the other grinned. "No way!" came Simon's
answer. "Have you ever seen such a sight?"

"What's up?" Bleau asked.

"The fleet's gone democratic. The admiral's taking
votes on whether we should even try. Whoa!"

The man in the hallway grabbed a strap and hung
on for dear life. "Deciding vote," he grinned.

The rec room spun in its weighted socket. Both
men grabbed the table. Centrifugal force drained the
blood from their faces as the ship peeled away from
its original course. They were going home. Theirs
were the only ships that could have now been used to
attack the behemoth, could hope to accelerate with it
long enough to attack. Their awe of the people of
Hazera was too great—a manned ship to Centauri,
when every unmanned attempt at interstellar travel

had failed. A manned expedition to Centauri that numbered six million!

"How fast do you think they can take that thing?" DeVliegar asked.

"With the power of the engines, probably three quarters of the speed of light. Apparently they won't be using Jupiter or the sun as gravitational whips. Even then . . ."

"You seem distracted," observed DeVliegar, "as though something were bothering you."

"I've been thinking," answered Bleau. "Freud, Marx, Einstein. I wonder how many are remaining with us? How many are going away?"

Paul lay in his hospital bed. His neck was in a cast and the stump of his arm hurt terribly. The prosthetic had been removed, and now, an odd tangle of wires and tubes enclosed the stump. Before this luncheon with the prime minister, he had been unconscious, drugged, or in pain. There was no escaping now. He had been in the hospital for 12 days, according to Professor Cohen. They would be accelerating for nearly a year. Paul had been right. The buildings had pivoted at 90 degrees, pointing their basements away from their direction of motion. Hazera had folded like some gigantic flower as it raced into the long darkness. When the acceleration was completed, Hazera would reopen, and the ship would start its long coast to the sun's nearest neighbor. It would spin again and, for three years, life would go on as always, except that there would be no metals to process—at least, not for a while. They had enough to keep everyone alive for a long time. In fact, the living standard of those on welfare would rise during the journey. Cutbacks had had to be made before they took off, and some had been below the belt. But supplies would be plentiful for the next five years. A good deal of the expected passenger list had returned to the moon, and thence probably to Terra. But using historical models, they had to watch their rationing carefully. Revolution onboard a space city was bad enough. The Israelis had seen what could happen with Paris Nouveau. Mutiny on board an interstellar spacecraft could be far worse. Everyone's needs, for now, would be provided for. And once in orbit around Centauri's three stars, the economy would boom as Hazera was rebuilt and expanded.

"But what are you going to do with me?" Paul asked, forgetting his previous conversations.

The prime minister leaned back and wiped her mouth with a napkin. She picked up a glass of wine and raised it to her lips. "What do you think?" she asked before drinking.

Paul sighed. "I suppose I'll *have* to be put on trial for espionage, one way or another."

Ms. Cohen gave him a smile that tightened for a moment into a tired grimace. "Must you always be so suspicious?" she asked.

"I deserve it," he answered. "I could have killed a lot of people."

"You did," Professor Cohen reminded him. "But it was through misinformation, not malice. You were ill at the time, *Mar* Green. Mentally ill. The right kind of ill for an agent, but while here, our psychological profiles have shown you to be gaining your feelings. You wouldn't feel guilt, if that weren't so. What happens to you now depends on you. I do have an alternative, if you're interested."

"Very much."

"Excuse me," said a nurse. "But Mr. Green has to rest now."

"Hold on just a minute!" exclaimed Rachel. "There's someone I want him to see. She's right out in the hall!" A security guard raised her to her feet, and Rachel Cohen toddled to the door.

Paul looked up in time to see the nurse, with the usual disregard for social graces, place a hypodermic against his shoulder. There was the pressurized kiss of an injection.

The guest was Shoshanna. Dressed for the occasion of meeting the prime minister, she took his breath away. The nurse, the security guards, and the prime minister left. Paul felt himself going dizzy, and lay back on the pillows. "There isn't much time," he explained.

Shoshanna knelt at the bedside, reaching across to take his remaining hand. "Paul," she said quietly. "You know there is no choice. You are a Jew. As a Jew you will come with us. As a Jew, you will help us build again. Are you with us, Paul?"

Paul tried to answer, but his mouth was too dry. His vision was a blur. Shoshanna licked her lips apprehensively, though, and reached into her purse. She brought out a symbol of her nonconformity, but it was a symbol of Judaism as well. Before she was called before the Orthodox Rabbinical Courts, she had to make her statement clear. *"Thou shalt wear frontlets between thine eyes."* The sacred *teffilin*. Until the last Shabbot, it had only been worn by men. It was a tiny box bearing the scripture. One was wrapped about the arm, the other tied to the forehead. She held it out to him. It dangled enticingly by its leather cord. His hand reached out.

"Did he accept?"

Shoshanna smiled, blushed, then nodded. "He didn't have much choice." Her smile broadened.

"He will make someone a fine husband," answered Professor Cohen.

Shoshanna's blush deepened. She then paled, biting a lip. "How long?" she asked.

"The technique is still highly experimental. The doctors are just rushing the paper into print. Paul is their first human subject. They've been trying similar techniques to regenerate human limbs for over a hundred years. I wouldn't expect too much."

"I won't. How did you get Paul to sign the papers?"

"He was still under anesthesia."

Shoshanna frowned.

"A dirty trick, I know," explained Rachel. "But he had to pay somehow for the trouble he caused us. With the help of God and modern medicine, the arm will be regenerated."

Shoshanna walked to the window. This had once been a micro-G hospital. It wouldn't be again for close to a year. Near the city's core, the tiny structure had windows that looked directly out on the stars. Shoshanna gripped a railing there, staring into the blackness. She heard the low whine of the prime minister's prosthetic legs as they approached.

"A *pruta* for your thoughts," the prime minister said.

"I was thinking of the *Talmud*," Shoshanna said. "Something that was written nearly a thousand years ago."

"What was it about?"

"Ourselves. It's in the *Megillah*."

"You're the great Rabbah," said Rachel. "What does it say?"

"They were mystics," Shoshanna answered. "It is said by the the Chassidim that they could see into the future. The Rabbi said, *'When they go down, it shall be to the dust of the earth.'* " At this, Shoshanna raised her head, peering into the void.

" 'When they rise, it shall be to the stars.' I wonder if they *could* see into the future. I wonder if they could . . ."

GLOSSARY

(Please note: In Hebrew, the definitive or English "the" exists as the prefix "ha." Plurals are set according to the sex of the object and, as in many languages, most objects have sex. The suffix "im" denotes the plural of a male noun, while the suffix "ot" denotes the plural of a female noun.

Transliterations from the proper Hebrew and Arabic, as well as any responsibilities for omissions, are those of the author.

Ad mahar   (Hebrew) Until tomorrow

Ad haerev   (Hebrew) until the evening.

Adonai   (Hebrew) acknowledgment of right or power. And English equivalent might be "sir." Also commonly used in prayers when addressing God.

Allon   (Hebrew) Oak.

Apikorsim   (Hebrew) Root word, "epicurean," often used among orthodox jews to denote goyim or outsiders.

Attah medaberit 'Ivri?   (Hebrew) Do you speak Hebrew?

Attah talmid tov   (Hebrew) You are a good student.

Ave   (hebrew) Father.

Barukh adonai eloheinu   (Hebrew) Opening words of

the Sabbath prayers: "Blessed art thou, Oh, Lord God . . ."

B'Vakhasha (Hebrew) Please.

Boker tov (Hebrew) Good morning.

Byutt (Hebrew) house.

B'Angli (Hebrew) "in English"

Chats sauvage (French) Wildcats.

Cho (Japanese) stomach, bowels.

Dazhbog (Slavic Folklore) God of the sun.

Dinar A fictional futuristic Israeli currency

Do itashimashite (Japanese) "You are welcome."

Domovoi (Slavic Folklore) Familiar or genie of a house or home.

Downstairsnikim (Yid-English) People who live downstairs.

Dozo arrigato (Japanese) Thank you very much.

Dybbuk (Yiddish folklore) A spirit which possesses the body of a human or animal.

Erev (Hebrew) Evening

G'henna (Yiddish) Hell.

Golem (Yiddish Folklore) A mystical creature made of clay and brought to life by the insertion of a tablet into its mouth, on which is written the true name of God. It is thought that on this legend Mary Wollstonecraft Shelley based her novel, **Frankenstein.**

Goy(im) (Yiddish) Outsider, NonJew.

Goyische (Yiddish) Goy-like, outsiderish.

Gozaimasu (Japanese) "You are welcome"

Ha'im ani Yakhol l'sar (Hebrew) "May I help you?"

Haddasah   Jewish women's service organization.

Hai   (Japanese) Yes

Hatzav, or Tzav   (Hebrew) Turtle

Hakeseph   (Hebrew) the money

Haver shelli   (Hebrew) My friend

Hazera Ysroel   (Hebrew) The Seed of Israel

Kakhol   (Hebrew) Blue

Kaleb   (Biblical) A spy who went forth into the land of Canaan.

Kappa   (Japanese Folklore) A water demon who challenges his victims to finger wrestle and then devours them when they lose. Can be weakened and thus beaten by tipping water out of a depression in its bowl shaped head.

Ken   (Hebrew) Yes

Kha'im Ma'im   (Hebrew) Water of Life

Knesset   (Hebrew) The Israeli parliament

Kurds · A member of a pastoral and warlike people now living in what was once Kurdistan and is now part of Iran. Currently politically and militarily active.

L'chaim   (Yiddish toast) To life!

L'hitriot   (Hebrew) See you later.

Lo   (Hebrew) No

Ma Hadash?   (Hebrew) What's new?

Mah   (Hebrew) what.

Materet   (Hebrew) underground.

Mikveh   (Judaic) Ritual bath.

Moshav   (Hebrew) Communal farm where the families are allowed separate dwellings, as opposed to a Kibbutz where dormitory style sleeping arrangements are the rule.

Narkoman (Hebrew) Drug addict

Nachon (Hebrew) Right? True?

Naim meod (Hebrew) It's a pleasure.

Nu (Yiddish) Exclamation of insight, surprise or puzzlement.

Nursaria (Spanish) Pre-school

Oomi Mi (Japanese) To listen in.

P'Nina (Hebrew) Mother-of-Pearl.

Palavir (Hebrew) Air Force

Palhalala (Hebrew) Space Force.

Parr (Hebrew singular) Ox or cow.

Parrim (Hebrew plural) Oxen.

Parrot (Hebrew plural) Cows.

Project de Sauvan (French) Project Bounce.

Putz (Yiddish) Prick.

Rav-Tura'i (Hebrew) Sergeant Major

Rochel (Hebrew) Hawk.

Sabal (Hebrew) Stomach.

Salaam (Arabic) Greeting, peace.

Sanhadrin (Hebrew) Council for the interpretation of religious law.

Sephardic Jews of North Africa and Southern Spain.

Seren (Hebrew) Captain.

Shabbot (Hebrew) Sabbath.

Shahar L'phi Ha'Zmun (Hebrew) A matter of time.

Sharm El Sheik (Arabic) Town on southern tip of

Shotair   (Hebrew) Police.

Sinai Peninsula. Very close to equator and therefore perfect for launches into orbit.

Slikkim   (Hebrew plural) Originally a secret cache of weapons during Israeli War of Independence. Here a hidden missile base.

Sunni   (Arabic) Largest sect of Islam.

Svenglid   (Norse myth) Magical spear hurled by Thor.

Talmud   Codification of the Old Testament.

Technion   (Hebrew) Technical School.

Ten li hakeseph   (Hebrew) Give me the money.

Tenach   The Old Testament not including the books of the Aprocrypha.

Torah   The five books written by Moses, those being Genesis, Exodus, Leviticus, Numbers, and Dueteronomy.

Tov   (Hebrew) good.

Treyf   (Hebrew) Food which is unsuitable, not Kosher.

Tsar li   (Heb-English) "Sorry."

Tsiporah Katanah   (Hebrew) Little Bird.

Tsli kah   (Hebrew) Excuse me.

Uhura   (Swahili) Peace.

Upstairsnik   (Yid-English) One who lives upstairs.

Yarmulke   (Hebrew) Ritual cap worn by Jewish men during the execution of religious duties.

Yesh l'kah keseph?   (Hebrew) Have you any money?

Yoshua   (Hebrew) Joshua.

Yonah   (Hebrew) Jonah.

Yesh L'Kha   (Hebrew) Do you have?

Yas'Or   (Hebrew) A sea bird.

Zonah   (Hebrew) prostitute.

Zaddick   (Hebrew) A great or wise man. A religious leader.

Ze   (Hebrew) This is.

PATRICK TILLEY
CLOUD WARRIOR

"Reminiscent of Stephen King's *The Stand*." — *Fantasy Review*

"Technology, magic, sex and excitement. . .when the annual rite of selection for the Hugos and Nebulas comes around, CLOUD WARRIOR is a good bet to be among the top choices." — *San Diego Union*

"A real page-turner!" — *Publishers Weekly*

Two centuries after the holocaust, the survivors are ready to leave their underground fortress and repossess the Blue Sky World. Its inhabitants have other ideas....

352 pp. • $3.50

BAEN BOOKS

"You wanted an hour," Gallen reminded him. "You've got fifty-three minutes left." She reached up and fitted the tab of the door's chain bolt into its slot. The snick of metal on metal was no harder than her blue eyes.

"Check. I interviewed a Soviet defector who appeared to be ... *could be*—" Fox said bluntly as he eased to the foot of the bed and sat facing the side wall rather than the woman by the door—"Abdulhamid Kunayev." The bolt above her head wouldn't hold a solid kick: it provided a symbol of the bargain Gallen had accepted; lighting a long fuze would have done the same. "In the course of the interview, the defector stated that President Crossfield is a Soviet penetration." Listening to himself, Fox realized how crazy he sounded and began quickly to explain: "He—"

She cut him off: "What evidence did this . . . defector . . . cite to support those statements?" Her voice was emotionless but it seemed to have risen an octave.

"Captain, I didn't *believe* them," Fox said despairingly in a low voice that trembled. There was a mirror over the long desk built into the wall opposite the bed; he closed his eyes rather than stare at his own face, battered by weakness and failure. The implications of the Kunayev contact were too important for validation to depend solely on him; but nobody was going to make decisions based on the information he'd collected until and unless he could convince Shai Gallen that there was some decision to make concerning Larry Fox, GS-11, Field Collector of moderate experience, beyond how deep under Langley to bury him.

He didn't know how in hell to begin doing that, but he realized as he monitored his thoughts that at least he was worried about it—human again, with human feelings, not just a computing gunsight—though somewhere in him that gunsight was locked onto his memories like a targeting array, waiting for someone to squeeze the red switch.

"Sir," Fox said a little too loudly as he attempted to override the quaver in his voice, "the defector broke contact almost at once." Gallen wasn't a girl he'd known in the Lebanon; she was his DDO—operations director for CIA; he *had* to handle this like the professional he ought to be. "He said he was afraid of the U.S. because the President was a mole, then he took off as if he saw something in the street below. I was prevented from following him by my Turkish contact. So I didn't see what happened—I lost contact with the defector."

Gallen got up from the armchair with a look of cold fury on her face. Her glasses didn't distort the glaring eyes behind them: the lenses were clear, an excuse for the heavy frames. Fox was willing to bet that the attache case beside the DDO held at least a recorder and a voice-stress analyzer. Gallen's glasses would house either an actual intercom connecting her to a crew outside the room, or an audio monitor giving her a readout from the stress analyzer. The tone in Gallen's ear would change as the level of stress in Fox's voice went up and down. There were more reasons for stress than the subject choosing to lie, however; he hoped she'd remember that.

Abruptly Gallen slammed the wall behind her with the side of her fist: "Give me some *reason* that a man with Kunayev's resources would pick a low-level line operative to tell his story to ... some reason not to think you're feeding me crap which, based on the increased message traffic and troop movements on the Sino-Soviet and NATO borders, the Soviets know damn well that Blaustein's Assessment boys would love to believe. Come *on*, Larry—*find* something. Even you've got to realize that you're dead in the water if I can't help you and that I *won't* help you if it puts my credibility, and therefore hundreds of my field operators, in jeopardy. If anybody's going to get fucked here tonight, it's you, not me. We're not talking about flow-charts now, we're talking about extended chemical debriefing." Her fist uncurled and her hand cut a tight, angry circle in the air.

Fox looked at her and took a deep breath. . . .

Contest void in Vermont, Florida, Quebec (Canada) and wherever prohibited or restricted by law. Entries must be received by September 30, 1985.

ROGER MACBRIDE ALLEN

A vanished ship...
a sudden siege...
and the only way
out was to fight!

THE TORCH OF HONOR

"Move over, Anderson! Shift chairs, Dickson! This guy is on your wave length!" — Sterling E. Lanier, author of THE UNFORSAKEN HIERO

"The technological innovations come hurtling at the reader one after another, borne on a stream of narrative action that's fast enough in itself to take you off your feet."
— Fred Saberhagen, author of BERSERKER! and EMPIRE OF THE EAST

WITH AN AFTERWORD ON SPACE FIGHTERS BY G. HARRY STINE

352 pp. · $2.95

Also from Baen Books:

WITH MERCY TOWARD NONE by Glen Cook
The sequel to THE FIRE IN HIS HANDS
352 pp. · $2.95

OCTOBER THE FIRST IS TOO LATE by Sir Fred Hoyle
Author of A FOR ANDROMEDA
288 pp. · $2.95

Distributed by Simon & Schuster Mass Merchandise Sales Company
1230 Avenue of the Americas · New York, N.Y. 10020

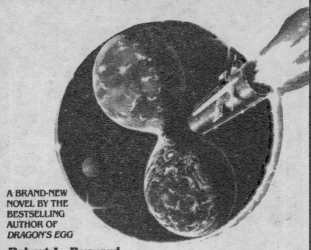

A BRAND-NEW
NOVEL BY THE
BESTSELLING
AUTHOR OF
DRAGON'S EGG

Robert L. Forward

THE FLIGHT OF THE DRAGONFLY

"His SF-scientific imagination is unsurpassed...this is a must!"
— *PUBLISHERS WEEKLY*

"Outshines *Dragon's Egg*...rates a solid ten on my mind-boggle
scale. If there were a Hugo for the most enjoyable alien creation,
the flouwen would be frontrunners."
— *LOCUS*

"I much enjoyed *The Flight of the Dragonfly*. Part of my
enjoyment came from knowing that the man damned well
knows what he's talking about...."
— *LARRY NIVEN*